Maya B   author
whose chart toppers   omantic
suspense, contempora   ... Scottish historical
romance. She lives in the South with her husband and three
children and other assorted babies, such as her two Bengal
kitties and a calico who's been with her as long as her youngest
child. She's an avid reader of romance and loves to dish
books with her fans and anyone else who'll listen!

She   ry much enjoys interacting with her readers on
Twitte   maya_banks and facebook.com/AuthorMayaBanks.
For m   bout Maya's books visit www.mayabanks.com.

Praise   he sensational novels of Maya Banks:

'T   awesome . . . I love Maya Banks and I love her
                Burton, *New York Times* bestselling author

'Ma   nks writes the kind of books I love to read!' Lora
Leigh   *v York Times* bestselling author

'Qu   ced . . . plenty of smoldering explicit sex, delivers a
satis   one-two punch of entertainment that will leave
read   ger for the next book' *Publishers Weekly*

'Ma   ks . . . really dragged me through the gamut of
emo   From . . . "is it hot in here?" to "oh my god" . . . I'm
read   e next ride now!' *USA Today*

'A d   motional, highly satisfying, edge-of-your-seat read
. . .   ing and cutting-edge romance' *Joyfully Reviewed*

'A cro   een the *Bared to You* or Fifty Shades series and the
Wicked Lovers series by Shayla Black' *Book Savvy Babe*

'A must-read author . . . her [stories] are always full of
emotional situations, loveable characters, and kick-butt story
lines' *Romance Junkies*

By Maya Banks

The Surrender Trilogy
Letting Go
Giving In
Taking It All

Maya Banks

Letting Go

headline
ETERNAL

First published in the United States of America in 2014
by Berkley,
a member of Penguin Group (USA) LLC.
A Penguin Random House Company.

First published in Great Britain in 2014
by HEADLINE ETERNAL
An imprint of HEADLINE PUBLISHING GROUP

1

Cataloguing in Publication Data is available from the British Library

ISBN 978 1 4722 2110 0

Offset in Palatino by Avon DataSet Ltd, Bidford-on-Avon, Warwickshire

Printed and bound by CPI Group (UK) Ltd, Croydon, CR0 4YY

Headline's policy is to use papers that are natural, renewable and
recyclable products and made from wood grown in sustainable forests.
The logging and manufacturing processes are expected to conform to the
environmental regulations of the country of origin.

HEADLINE PUBLISHING GROUP
An Hachette UK Company
338 Euston Road
London NW1 3BH

www.headlineeternal.com
www.headline.co.uk
www.hachette.co.uk

For Lillie and Katie
for keeping me on track!

ONE

JOSSLYN Breckenridge surveyed her appearance in the mirror, nervous even though no one would see her. Except Dash. She knew without confirming that he'd be here, just as he'd been here on this day for the previous two years, waiting to take her to the cemetery to visit and put fresh flowers on her husband's grave.

The flowers were on the counter beside her, just waiting for her to pick up and carry out of the house. But she hesitated, because this year . . . This year was different. She was apprehensive and yet resolved.

She had to move on with her life. She had to let *go*. It hurt, and yet at the same time, it brought her a measure of relief, as if a great weight had been lifted from her shoulders. It was time. All she had left to do was visit Carson's grave and make peace with her decision.

She smoothed her shirt and ran her hands down the legs of her jeans. Not what she normally wore to the cemetery on the anniversary of her husband's burial. In the last two years, she'd worn black. It hadn't seemed respectful to go casual, as if the visit wasn't that important.

But she also knew that Carson wouldn't want her to live like this. He'd want her to be happy. And it wouldn't have made him happy to know she still mourned him so deeply.

With a sigh, she applied a light gloss to her lips and quickly fastened her long hair into a ponytail, leaving part of it loose in a messy bun.

This was the real Joss. Not fussy. More comfortable in jeans and a casual shirt than the expensive dresses and jewelry her husband had loved to spoil her with. Only underneath her clothing did she wear the sexy lingerie her husband had so loved to see her in.

She closed her eyes, refusing to look back, to remember how it felt when he touched her. How his hands moved over her body, knowing it better than she knew it herself. He knew exactly how to please her, how to touch her, kiss her, make love to her.

He'd given her everything she could have ever wanted. His love. His respect. Everything but the one thing she needed most, and it was something she could have never asked him for. She'd loved him too much to ever demand of him something he *couldn't* give her.

She shook away the heavy veil of sadness, determined to get through the day and on with her life. Her *new* life.

She picked up the flowers, her favorite, and brought them to her nose, closing her eyes as she inhaled. They were what Carson always gave her. Every birthday. Every anniversary. Or any time just because. Today she'd place them on his grave and walk away. This time for good.

She didn't need to see the cold slab of marble that marked his life and death to remind her of her husband. That wasn't the way she wanted to remember him. She was through torturing herself by standing over his grave, missing him with her every breath.

He'd live in her heart and soul always. *That* was where she'd visit him in the future. Not on the grassy knoll that covered the casket underneath.

She walked briskly to the front door, letting herself out and blinking against the sudden wash of sun. Though it was spring, the Houston weather was already warm and she was glad she'd worn the short-sleeved T-shirt instead of the black dress she always wore.

And there was Dash, leaning against his car, waiting for her as she knew he would be. He straightened when he saw her, and she saw a brief flicker of surprise before he schooled his features and extended a hand to her.

She slid her fingers over his and he gave her hand a light squeeze. No words were necessary. They both grieved the loss of her husband and his best friend.

"You look lovely, Joss," Dash said as he walked her around to the passenger side.

She smiled, knowing she didn't look particularly lovely today. And he was likely surprised by her casual appearance, but he didn't remark on it. He took the flowers and carefully positioned them in the back so they wouldn't fall over, and then closed her door after ensuring she was fully inside.

She watched him stride around the front of the car, his long legs eating up the distance in a matter of seconds. Then he slid into the driver's seat and his scent wafted through her nostrils.

Dash always smelled the same. Utterly masculine, though she knew he never wore cologne or aftershave. He was a no-frills kind of guy, much like Carson had been, though her husband had worn expensive clothing and even his casual wear was tailored to fit his personality.

Even Dash's car fit his personality. A sleek black Jaguar. How appropriate he drove a vehicle named for a predator. He fit the part well.

They'd been partners in business, but Carson had always been the front man. The one who wined and dined clients, the polished spokesman, the one who sealed the deals, attended all the social events while Dash worked behind the scenes. The closer. The one who always did most of the legwork and fixed the problems.

Carson had often laughed and said he was the looks and charm and Dash was the brains of the operation. But Dash was certainly not lacking in looks or charm. They were the complete antithesis of one another. Carson was fair-haired to Dash's dark brown, and while Carson's eyes were blue, Dash's were a deep brown, enhanced by his darker coloring. He wasn't any less attractive than Carson. His was just a quieter attractiveness. Silent. Brooding almost. He had made Joss nervous back when she'd first met him when she and Carson had dated. Theirs had been a whirlwind courtship. Carson had swept her off her feet, and Joss had known that Dash was concerned that his friend was getting in way over his head. Moving too fast. The fact Joss knew that had made her wary of Dash, but over time, he'd become her rock. Especially after Carson had died.

As they drove out of Joss's exclusive subdivision, Dash reached over for her hand, lacing his fingers through hers, and as he'd done before, he squeezed lightly, a gesture of reassurance.

Joss turned and smiled at him, telling him without words that she was okay. As they stopped at a red light, Dash studied her intently, almost as if he were trying to decipher what was different about her.

Evidently satisfied with whatever he'd seen in her eyes or expression, he smiled back, but he kept hold of her hand as he navigated through traffic on the way to the cemetery, just a few miles from where Joss and Carson had lived.

They drove in comfortable silence, but then they'd never conversed much on the day Dash drove her to the cemetery every year. Oh, Joss visited at other times, but Dash always accompanied her on the anniversary.

But that wasn't the only time she saw Dash. He'd stepped in from the moment Carson had passed away and he'd been her rock ever since. That first year especially, she'd needed him desperately and he never hesitated, no matter what she needed, whether it was help deciphering the paperwork and red tape after her husband's death or simply coming over to keep her company on the days she felt herself falling apart.

She would be forever grateful for Dash and his unwavering support over the last three years, but it was time to move on. It was time for her to stand on her own two feet and it was time for Dash to stop having to babysit her.

Today was not only about her letting go of Carson, but of Dash as well. He deserved more than to be saddled with the responsibility of his best friend's widow. He had a life of his own. She had no idea of his relationships or if he was even *in* a steady relationship. She realized with sudden clarity just how selfish and self-absorbed she'd been since her husband's death. Dash had been a steady fixture, one she'd taken for granted, but she would do it no longer. It would be a miracle if Dash were in a steady relationship because not many women would be tolerant of Dash dropping everything to rush to the aid of his best friend's widow.

When they arrived at the cemetery, Dash parked and Joss immediately got out, not waiting for him to come around for her. She opened the door to the backseat and leaned in to retrieve the flowers.

"I'll get them, Joss."

Dash's low voice brushed over her ears, causing a prickle at her nape. She picked up the vase and turned with a reassuring smile.

"I've got it, Dash. I'm okay."

He gave her an inscrutable stare and she got the impression he was studying her again, trying to peel back the layers and get into her head. It was as if he knew something was different but couldn't put his finger on it. Which was just as well, because Joss would die if Dash could read her thoughts. If he knew just what it was she'd planned and how she intended to move on with her life.

He'd be horrified, no doubt. He'd wonder if she'd finally snapped and he'd probably haul her into a shrink's office so fast it would make her head spin. Which was why she had no intention of letting him know.

Her girlfriends were another matter. Chessy would understand absolutely. She'd even be encouraging. Kylie . . . not so much.

Kylie was Joss's sister-in-law, Carson's only sibling. They'd both grown up in horrific circumstances, and just as Carson could never provide what Joss craved—needed—neither would Kylie ever understand what drove Joss.

She might even be angry with Joss's choices. Might think it was a betrayal of her brother. Joss could only hope she'd support Joss even if she didn't fully understand.

But she was getting ahead of herself. First the cemetery and talking to Carson one last time. Then she'd tackle her best friends over lunch. She needed as much as possible to keep busy today, because tonight?

Tonight was when it all began.

Joss waited for the betraying sting of tears as they neared Carson's grave. But oddly, she felt at peace for the first time in three long years. Yes, it was time.

She knelt and gently brushed away the leaves and dust at the base of the headstone before setting the vase of flowers in the middle. Her gaze drifted upward to the inscription. The reminder of Carson's birth and death.

Her finger slowly traced the words. *Beloved husband, brother and best friend*. Those words said it all. A reminder of those left behind who mourned him still. She'd insisted that Dash be honored on the headstone, as he was every bit as much family as herself and Kylie. She only wished they'd had children so his legacy and memory would live on through them.

But as with any young couple, they'd thought they had all the time in the world. Carson was apprehensive about having children. He feared that he shared the same genetic traits that his father had possessed. No matter how many times Joss had gently reminded him that he was nothing like his father, Carson still lived in fear of hurting those he loved the most.

She understood his fear. She knew how much he loved her. She also knew he'd die before ever hurting her or any children they had. But the darkness of his past still overshadowed his present. The past still haunted his dreams at night. Though Kylie, his sister, hadn't spoken of it often, Joss knew that Kylie had the same nightmares that Carson had. That she shared many of the same sleepless nights Carson experienced.

A wave of sadness overtook Joss. Such a waste. Carson's father had destroyed the lives of two innocent children. Worse, he lived on well into their adulthood, influencing their choices, always living in their fears even though he was dead. He still held them in his grasp from the grave, his memory and the memories of all he did torturing them still.

"Joss?"

Dash softly called her name, breaking through her thoughts, and she realized just how long she'd knelt there at the base of the monument, tracing the inscription with her fingers.

He sounded worried and a little uncertain, and Dash was never nothing if not sure of himself.

She turned, tilting her head up so her gaze connected with Dash's.

"Give me a moment, please. Wait for me at the car if you don't mind. I'll only take a few minutes and then I'll be ready to go."

Again, surprise flickered in Dash's eyes. Never before had she asked to be left alone at Carson's grave. It had been too difficult, too emotional. Dash had always remained at her side, steady and strong, her rock to lean on. He'd stayed with her as long as she wanted to remain and then he'd take her back to the car and back home, where he'd spend the rest of the afternoon sitting with her as she cried on his shoulder.

Not today. Not anymore.

"If you're sure," he said hesitantly.

She nodded firmly, making sure no tears threatened. She wasn't going to unravel in front of him. She'd been doing that far too long.

"All right," he conceded. "Take your time, honey. I've arranged to take the entire day off."

She smiled. Of course he would have. But she didn't intend for him to spend it with her as he'd done in the past. There was too much to get done before tonight. And she didn't want to chance breaking her resolve and confiding in Dash. Not only was it not appropriate, but he would most certainly not approve. He'd think she'd lost her damn mind.

And maybe she had. Or perhaps she was just getting it back.

She turned back as Dash headed toward the car and then pushed herself upward to stand over the grave. She stared down, her jaw tight, locking down her emotions for the conversation she intended to have with her husband.

"I love you, you know," she said, almost as if he were standing there in front of her. "I'll always love you, Carson. But I want you to know I'm going to move on. Try to move on," she amended. "Starting tonight. I know there were . . . things . . . you couldn't give me. And I want you to know I never resented you for that.

God, I loved you far too much to ever expect you to give me something it was impossible for you to give.

"But you're gone now."

Her voice cracked as she said the last, and she swallowed back the surge of tears.

"I'm lonely, Carson. I miss you so much. Not a day goes by that I don't miss you. You were so good to me. The love of my life. I know I'll never find that again. Finding perfection once in a lifetime is incredible. But twice? No, I know there'll never be another for me like you. But there are things I . . . need," she whispered. "Things you couldn't give me. Things I'd never ask you for. And I wanted to come here today to tell you. To say that I wouldn't be back. Not because I don't love you or that I'm going to forget you. But this isn't what I want my memory of you to be. I want to remember you in life. And us in love. And it's too painful for me to come here and talk to you, knowing that I'll never get you back."

She took a deep breath and forged ahead.

"I've found a place that specializes in . . . dominance. I need to know if it's what I'm missing. If it's always been what I'm missing. Maybe I'll find the answer. Maybe I won't. But I have to try. I have to know. And I couldn't go without telling you. Without explaining that I never lacked for anything when we were married. I never doubted even for a moment that you loved me, and you would have given me the moon if I asked. But this . . . This I couldn't ask you for. And right now I need something to fill the void. There's a hole in my soul, Carson. One that I may never fill again. But right now I'd take even a bandage. Temporary solace, if you will. I just wanted you to know. I'll be okay. I'm not going into a dangerous situation. I've made certain that I'll be safe. And as painful as it is for me to say this, I'm finally letting you go. I've held on to you for too long now. I can't do it anymore. Life is happening around me. Life goes on. That sounds so trite, doesn't it? But it's true. Chessy and Tate worry for me. Kylie worries. And Dash. God, I'm surprised he hasn't washed his hands of me yet. I've been such a burden to him—to them all—these last three years and I don't want to be that woman any longer.

"You gave me the confidence and independence to fly. I want that back again, Carson. You taught me so much. You gave me the world. The problem is when you left, you took my world with you. And I want it back again. I want to live and not be this hollow shell of myself that I've been since you died."

She sucked in a steadying breath, knowing what she said next was dumb. But she had to get it off her chest. Say it and then let go of the nagging emotion.

"I also want to tell you that I forgive you. I know that sounds so stupid. You don't need my forgiveness. But I was so angry with you for so long for leaving me. I was so selfish. I've spent three years being angry and resentful, and starting today, I'm not going to be that person anymore."

She let her hand drift down to glide across the sun-warmed marble of the headstone.

"I love you. I miss you. I'll always love you. But good-bye, Carson. Wherever you are, I hope you're at peace and I hope you know how very much I loved you. Thank you for loving *me*."

She closed her eyes as tears gathered and she didn't reopen them until she was certain she could return to the car where Dash waited without looking like she'd fallen apart.

With one last glance at the grave and the flowers that had already lost a few petals to the wind, she turned, squared her shoulders and walked away. The wind picked up and the sun broke further through the clouds, shining down on her face. She turned her face upward, soaking in the warmth as peace enveloped her in its gentle embrace. It was as if Carson were sending her a message, or perhaps she only imagined him blessing her decision.

Dash held the door open for her, his gaze fixed on her face as if he were trying to ascertain her mood. She was careful to keep herself from showing any outward emotion. Because what she would say next she was certain he would object to, and if he thought she was upset, he'd never leave her alone the rest of the day.

She waited until he was behind the wheel and they were driving away before she turned to him.

"I have lunch plans today, so you don't have to stay with me. And I have plans for tonight as well," she murmured, letting him make of that what he would.

Dash's brow furrowed, and he made no effort to hide his concern. He reached for her hand as they stopped at a light.

"What's going on with you, honey?"

His tone was worried and his eyes were boring intently into hers.

She gave him a half smile. "I'm having lunch with Kylie and Chessy. It's time I stop with the grieving widow act every year on the same day. It's been three years, Dash. He's gone and he's not coming back."

She halted a moment, the pain of her statement momentarily stealing her breath. But it had to be said. To be acknowledged. And perhaps saying it aloud made it that much more real.

She could swear she saw relief flash in his deep brown eyes, but it was gone so quickly she was sure she imagined it.

"Are you sure you don't want me to come over after you have lunch with the girls?"

She shook her head. "No. It's not necessary, Dash. You've babysat me for long enough. It's time for me to stand on my own two feet. I'm sure it has to come as a relief to you that you don't have to hover over me for fear I'll lose it. I'm just sorry I've been such a burden to you for so long."

This time a glint of anger flashed in those dark eyes. "You're not a burden, damn it. Carson was my best friend, Joss. He—and you—mean a hell of a lot to me."

She squeezed his hand as he accelerated after a car behind them honked angrily when Dash didn't immediately go when the light turned green.

"And I appreciate that. I appreciate all you've done for me. But it's time, Dash. I have to do this. He's gone. I have to accept that."

Dash didn't respond. He directed his gaze forward, tension thick in the interior of the car. Had she angered him? She'd only been honest, and she'd sincerely thought he would be glad that he no longer had to treat her like a fragile piece of glass. That he could resume his own life without making her a priority in his.

When they arrived back at her house, she got out, as did Dash. He walked her to the door and she went in, turning back to tell him thank you and good-bye.

"This isn't good-bye," he said tightly. "Just because you think you no longer need me doesn't mean I'm going to just disappear. Prepare yourself for that, Joss."

With that, he spun on his heel and strode back down the sidewalk, leaving her staring open-mouthed as he drove away.

TWO

JOSS zipped into the parking lot of the Lux Café on Westheimer and parked her BMW roadster next to Kylie's silver Mercedes coupe. The car had been a gift to Kylie from Carson on her twenty-first birthday, just one year before he'd been in the fatal car accident that had taken him from both his wife and his sister.

Carson and Joss had gone to Las Vegas frequently. Carson loved to gamble and he'd taught Joss how to play all manner of casino games. He'd even sharpened her poker skills enough that she'd become a formidable opponent at the tables. Carson had always chuckled when her winnings topped his own, though she refused to play at the same table as him because his competitive streak was such that he didn't like to lose. Even to his wife.

Their favorite place to stay was the Venetian, where Joss had discovered the Lux Café and all the wonderful food on the menu. She'd been delighted when one had opened in Houston, and it had quickly become a favorite place for them and their friends to eat.

She hurried to the entrance, checking her watch with a grimace. Carson had always teased her about her lack of punctuality, and she was fifteen minutes late for her lunch date with Kylie and Chessy.

The two women were waiting inside when Joss rushed in.

Joss's gaze immediately settled on her sister-in-law. The anniversary of Carson's death was as hard for her as it was for Joss because Carson was her only family. Joss had made the effort to make sure she and Kylie remained close after his passing. They'd clung to one another, both grief stricken over their loss.

Shadows were evident in Kylie's eyes, but they brightened when she saw Joss and immediately went to hug her.

"How are you?" Kylie whispered.

Joss squeezed her and pulled away with a smile. "I'm okay." And she meant it.

Then she turned to Chessy and pulled her into a hug.

"You doing okay today?" Chessy asked quietly.

"Let's sit and then we'll talk. I'm starving," Joss said with a grin.

The other two women looked delighted over Joss's mood. It shamed Joss that she'd been a burden not only to Dash over the last three years but to her closest friends as well. But no more. Today . . . Well, today was the first day in reestablishing her life. Of getting back on track and filling the void left by the death of her husband.

They were seated in a spacious booth—Joss hated the long rows of tables that were practically on top of one another. Even if her conversation was casual, she hated to be overheard by others. And today of all days, she wanted to be afforded complete privacy.

"You look . . . different," Chessy mused, as they opened their menus.

Joss left hers closed because she knew what she wanted. The others made fun of her because with all the wonderful selections on the huge menu, she usually got the same exact thing and today was no different. Shaking Beef. Her absolute favorite thing the Lux Café served.

"I am different," Joss said in a low tone.

Kylie's eyes widened. "What's happened?"

"It's not what has happened. It's what's going to happen," Joss said firmly.

"Uh-oh. Do we even want to hear this?" Chessy asked.

Silence fell over the table when the waiter appeared to take their orders. Only after he'd departed did Kylie prompt Joss to explain what she'd meant.

Joss sighed and then glanced up at Chessy. "I wanted to ask you . . . I mean I know this is a personal question, but you've talked about it before and if it's too personal, feel free to tell me to mind my own business, but I'd really like to ask you some questions about you and Tate."

A dark shadow crossed over Chessy's face and sadness entered her eyes for a brief moment before she shook it away. But the look hadn't gone unnoticed by either Joss or Kylie, who exchanged quick puzzled looks.

"You know you can ask me anything," Chessy said lightly, though the lightness of her tone seemed forced to Joss.

Deciding to try to figure out later what was behind that, Joss plunged ahead.

"You've said that you and Tate have a dominant, submissive relationship. That he calls the shots in and out of bed. I just wanted to know . . . I mean this sounds stupid because of course you're happy. Anyone who sees the two of you can see how in love you are, but I wanted to know more about how it works."

Kylie paled and Joss hated bringing up the subject in front of her, but she didn't want to hide something this important from her sister-in-law. Not just a sister-in-law but her best friend. Kylie and Chessy were her two best friends in the world. She couldn't *not* share this with them because it was huge. A monumental *leap* forward from the life she'd led the last three years.

"Joss? Why are you asking?" Chessy asked in a puzzled voice. One laced with concern.

Joss took another deep breath and closed her eyes. She reached for Kylie's hand because she knew this would be hard for her sister-in-law.

"You both know I loved Carson with all my heart. He gave me everything. But I've always had this . . . need. Craving. Desire. I don't know what to call it. But I've always craved . . . dominance. And everything that goes with it. And it's the one thing I knew Carson couldn't, wouldn't give me. I loved him too much to ever demand it of him. We spoke of it once. Early in our relationship. Before I knew about his childhood. He was always so afraid he'd turn out like his father. The idea of doing anything that might hurt me or that may be construed as abuse appalled him. And I think in the beginning he feared losing me because he couldn't provide me with that kind of relationship."

Kylie's gaze had dropped, but Joss could see the tears gathering at the corners of her eyes. Joss tightened her hold on Kylie's hand, lending her strength that she hadn't had until now.

"And you want it *now*?" Chessy asked, her brow furrowed.

Slowly Joss nodded.

Kylie's head came up, a protest already forming on her lips, but Joss silenced her with another squeeze to her hand.

"I don't want a relationship. I mean not a permanent one. I found perfection once. I know I'll never find that kind of love again. But I need something to fill the void. A void that's always existed, but while I was with Carson it wasn't so aching. I wasn't lonely. He provided me what I needed, even if a tiny part of me always wanted and needed more. I know that sounds terrible. I loved Carson with all my heart and soul, and I would have never done anything to hurt him. But he's gone. I've had to come to grips with the fact that no matter how hard I wish it, he's not coming back."

Emotion knotted her throat and she blinked as hot moisture clouded her eyes. She wiped hastily at her cheeks, not wanting to make a scene in public. Kylie's head lowered again, a tear sliding down her pale cheek.

"I'm lonely," Joss whispered. "And I need something, someone to fill that void that Carson left behind. It's time for me to let go and try to move on. I've found a place . . ."

"What kind of place?" Chessy asked bluntly.

"It's called The House."

Chessy's expression eased. "Yes, I know it. Tate and I have a membership there. Tate is friends with the owner, Damon Roche. Damon is married and has a child now, so he isn't quite as active as he was before, but he still runs it."

"He's who I talked to," Joss admitted. "He vetted my membership. He was very kind to me. He wanted to make sure I knew what I was getting into."

"And do you?" Kylie blurted, lifting her head again. "Joss, this is serious. What if you get hurt? What if you hook up with the wrong man? You know what kind of monsters exist out there. God knows, my father was one of them. How can you even think about going blindly into a situation like this?"

"I'm not going blindly," Joss said gently. "It's something I've given a lot of thought to. I've researched endlessly, which was what brought me to The House. I've toured the premises. I've been there during its busiest times. I know what to expect. And Damon has assured me that, especially for my first visit, I will be very carefully monitored."

They were interrupted when the waiter brought their entrées, but food was the last thing on the women's minds now. Their plates sat in front of them untouched as their conversation continued.

"I just wanted to know what it was like for you and Tate," Joss said softly.

Again, pain glittered in Chessy's green eyes. She pushed her dark hair behind her ear in an effort to disguise her hesitation, but Joss didn't miss it and she wondered what the hell was going on with her friend. She seemed . . . unhappy. And maybe it had been there for a while now, but Joss had been so self-absorbed that she hadn't paid attention to the people around her.

"Is there something you aren't telling us, Chessy?" Joss demanded.

Chessy looked at once guilty and then surprised. "No, of course not. And to answer your question, when it's right, it's the most wonderful thing in the world. I never regretted giving Tate my complete submission. He always took such wonderful care of me. Cherished me. Protected me with his every breath. I was always his priority. And he was so demanding."

Joss frowned because every example had been said in the past tense.

"Is that not the case now?" Joss asked.

Chessy smiled brightly. Too brightly. "Of course it is. I was just saying. And well, perhaps it's not as perfect as it used to be, but that's to be expected. Tate has been so busy making his business a success, and when the newness wears off any relationship, it's easy to fall into a routine. Don't worry. We're not divorcing or anything," she said with a laugh.

But the forced gaiety bothered Joss. She shoved aside her sense of foreboding to focus on the matter at hand.

"Again, if this is too personal a matter to discuss," Joss said. But Chessy waved her off and motioned for her to continue. "What kinds of things do you and Tate do? I mean are you into bondage? Pain? Floggings? Or is it a simple matter of you obeying his commands and him calling the shots?"

Kylie looked as though she'd be ill, and she fiddled with her food as if she were trying to block out the conversation. Her face had grown pale, and Joss began to have second thoughts about bringing this up in front of her. But she hadn't wanted Kylie not to know. She owed her sister-in-law that much. To let her know she was going to at least *try* to move on and perhaps become involved, even if temporarily, with another man. It certainly wasn't something she wanted Kylie to find out by chance. She wanted Kylie to hear it from her.

"I think it's a matter of what you want," Chessy said quietly. "Yes, we practice all of those things and much more. I am his to do with as he wishes. He knows how far he can go. We've been together long enough that he well knows my boundaries. Perhaps better than I know myself. But it's important in the beginning that you're very honest with your partner and that you set boundaries. He needs to know exactly what you are and aren't comfortable with. And you'll need a safe word until your relationship evolves enough that he knows just how far he can push."

"I feel like a kid in a toy store," Joss said ruefully. "I want to try everything. At least once. I don't *know* my boundaries. I won't know until they're crossed."

"Then it's even more important that you pick the right guy. One who understands that you're new to the scene. That you want to experiment but that you reserve the right to pull the plug at any moment. And for God's sake, Joss, don't agree to go home with a guy until you know him very well. Stay at the club. Do all your experimenting there in a public facility where there's plenty of security."

Joss nodded. She'd already considered that, and no way was she bringing a guy home. To the place she and Carson had lived and loved. It would be the height of disrespect to practice what would have appalled her husband under his own roof. And neither would she agree to go off with some stranger where God only knew what could happen once he had her alone and at his mercy.

It wasn't that she hadn't considered all the risks. She had! She'd visited The House more than once. She'd questioned Damon Roche endlessly, and the man had exhibited a huge amount of patience and understanding. But now she was having second thoughts listening to Chessy's warnings.

But no. She'd thought this through. It was all she'd thought about over the last months. And while moving forward with her new life on the three-year anniversary of her husband's death may seem tacky, for her it was symbolic. She wasn't backing out now.

She'd positively shivered when Chessy had stated that she was her husband's. That she belonged to him and he could do as he wished. Joss wanted that. She craved it with a dark need she didn't even fully understand. It wasn't that she hadn't belonged heart and soul to Carson. She had. She'd held no part of herself back from him.

But this need for dominance went deeper than just belonging. She wanted to be . . . owned. Cherished. Utterly adored. All the things her husband had given her but . . . *more*. She wanted to cross that gray line. Wanted to shatter her boundaries. She wanted to discover what they were and just how far she was willing and wanted to go. How would she know if she never tried?

"You're going to do it, aren't you?" Kylie asked quietly. "I can see it in your eyes, Joss. I know that look. You're actually going to do this."

Joss nodded, feeling a sense of relief at affirming it.

Chessy reached across the table to catch Joss's other hand and squeezed it until Joss was holding on to both her friends' hands.

"Then I wish you luck," Chessy said.

"Hey, don't you have to go?" Joss asked, suddenly remembering that Chessy had mentioned several days earlier that she and Tate were spending the afternoon together. "Isn't Tate expecting you? I don't want to keep you. I just wanted to ask you those questions."

Again that barely discernible flicker in Chessy's eyes before she dropped her gaze and her hold on Joss's hand.

"No," Chessy said lightly. "He had to cancel. An important matter came up at work."

Joss grimaced. "Sorry. I know you were looking forward to it. Unfortunately, I do have to run. I need time to prepare for tonight. Though I've made up my mind about it, I'm still nervous enough to need time to get ready and talk myself into going through with it."

Chessy smiled. "I'll expect a report first thing tomorrow, and if I don't get it, I'm coming over. And if you aren't home, I'm calling the police!"

Joss smiled. "Of course I will."

She rose after placing several bills on the table to cover lunch. Kylie stood too.

"I'll walk you out," Kylie said.

Chessy shot Joss a raised brow look and then glanced pointedly at Kylie. Joss sighed. She knew what was coming. With a wave to Chessy, Joss walked out of the restaurant, Kylie at her side.

When they got to the cars, Kylie put a hand out to Joss's arm.

"Joss, have you really thought this through?" she asked in a pleading tone. "I'm really worried about you. This isn't like you at all. What would Carson think? Joss, he'd die if he knew!"

"Kylie, Carson *is* dead," Joss said gently. "We can't bring him back. God, if I could, I'd do it in a heartbeat. I'd forget everything about my wants or needs if I could have him back. But he's *gone*."

Tears clogged her throat. Tears she'd refused to allow herself to shed today. She'd been determined that this year would be different. That she wouldn't spend the anniversary of her husband's death listless and grieving.

Kylie's eyes were grief stricken. Tears welled up and slid soundlessly down her cheeks. "I miss him so much, Joss. He was my only family. I still can't believe he's *gone*."

Joss enfolded her in a hug, holding her tightly as Kylie's shoulders shook. "You're wrong. You have family. You have *me*. I'm not going anywhere. This doesn't change things between us. I swear it. But Kylie, I have to pick up and move on with my life. This is killing me. My grief has been slowly killing me, and Carson would *hate* that. He'd never want me to spend the rest of my life mourning him. He'd be the first person to want me to be happy even if it wasn't with him."

Kylie pulled away, wiping hastily at her tears. "I know that. I do. And *I* want you to be happy, Joss. But does it have to be this way? You don't understand what it's like to be at the mercy of a monster. You can't possibly want to put yourself in a position where you're helpless under a man's power. He could hurt you. Abuse you. *Believe* me, you don't want that. You could never understand how degrading and powerless that feeling is and I *do*. And I don't want that for *you*. Carson would never want that for you."

Joss gently wiped away the rest of Kylie's tears. "Not all men are like that, Kylie. I know your concerns. I'm not negating what you and Carson went through. I'd never allow that for myself. And look at Chessy and Tate. You know what kind of relationship they have. Do you honestly believe Tate would ever harm a hair on her head? He loves her. He adores her. He absolutely respects the gift of her submission. And *that's* what I want."

"But he *is* hurting her," Kylie said fiercely. "You had to have seen what I saw today. What we've seen for the last while. She's not happy, Joss, and I'm worried about her. What if he's abusing her?"

Joss blinked, utterly shocked by Kylie's assertion. Yes, she'd noticed that Chessy wasn't her usual cheerful, sunny self. She'd sensed that something was off about her best friend, but never had she entertained, even for a moment, that Tate was hurting her physically.

"I don't know exactly what's going on with Chessy and Tate," Joss said carefully. "But I do know that there is no way he's abusing her. Chessy would never stand for it. She's too strong and independent, despite the fact that she gave Tate her submission. Not to mention she'd tell us if he was hurting her. We're too close of friends. We'd know, Kylie. We'd *know*."

"No one ever knew the hell that Carson and I endured," Kylie said painfully. "We hid it from the world. Our father appeared to others as a doting parent incapable of ever doing us harm. But behind closed doors he was a *monster*."

"Please don't worry about me," Joss said. "And don't worry about Chessy. I'll talk to her if it makes you feel better. I know Tate. We all know Tate. We've all been friends for years. There is no way he is abusing Chessy. And sweetie, I know you're not happy with my choice. I don't expect you to accept it, but I'd like for you to respect it at least."

"I love you," Kylie said brokenly. "And I'd never forgive myself if I didn't at least try to steer you away from the path you seem so determined to take. But if this is really what you want, if it's what you need and it will make you happy, then I'll try to respect your choices. I just don't want to lose you too."

Joss hugged her again. "You're not going to lose me. You're my sister and my best friend. Carson was not my only tie to you and now that he's gone it doesn't mean that our tie is severed. You're my family, Kylie. I love you."

Kylie pulled away, a watery smile quivering on her lips. "I'll expect a report tomorrow just like Chessy. I won't sleep tonight for worrying about you. I just hope you know what it is you're getting into."

"So do I," Joss murmured. "So do I."

THREE

DASH Corbin parked his car outside The House and sat for a moment, wondering again why he was here tonight. Normally on the anniversary of Carson's death, Dash would spend the day—and evening—with Joss. Not that he didn't spend plenty of other days with her, but for the first two anniversaries of Carson's passing, he'd spent the entire day with Joss. Holding her. Comforting her. Supporting her.

And it was his own personal hell.

It sucked to be in love with his best friend's wife. He'd lived with guilt for the entirety of Carson's marriage to Joss. Carson had known. He'd guessed, though Dash had done his best never to allow his feelings to show. But his best friend was perceptive. He knew him better than anyone else ever had. They weren't just business partners. They were as close as brothers, though Dash hadn't existed in the hell that Carson and Kylie had endured growing up.

No, Dash's family was the complete antithesis of Carson's. If you could call the piece-of-shit bastard who'd fathered Carson *family*. Dash's parents were still as solidly in love now as they were forty years ago when they'd married. Dash was one of five siblings, the middle child. Two older brothers. Two younger sisters who were spoiled and protected by their older brothers.

Carson had been befuddled by Dash's close-knit family from the moment he'd first met them. He hadn't known how to react to a normal, well-adjusted family setting. But Dash's family had embraced Carson—and Joss, when Carson had married her. And even Kylie, though she was more reserved and more wary of his large family than Carson was.

Dash sighed again and got out, walking to the entrance of The House. He wasn't even interested in any action tonight, but he was restless and on edge. Joss had occupied his thoughts the entire day. Ever since he'd taken her to the cemetery and had seen the difference in her.

He didn't know what to make of the abrupt change. She'd walked out of her house in jeans and a T-shirt, looking so young and beautiful that it still made his chest ache to remember the image of her.

And then she'd asked to be left alone at the grave and she'd stayed there, her lips moving as she'd spoken to Carson for a long while. When she'd returned, there was a marked difference in her demeanor. And then that spiel about not needing him. *Apologizing* to him, for fuck's sake. Apologizing for being a goddamn burden. For taking up too much of his life and time. Hell, she didn't even realize she *was* his life. Or at least he hoped she would be.

He checked in with the man working the door and wandered through the lower levels. The social rooms. The places where people met up, drank good wine, mingled before moving upstairs to the common room or one of the private suites.

There were plenty of beautiful women and no shortage of interested looks thrown his way. It had been a while since he'd come here to work off some steam. Usually after he'd spent time with Joss, pretending the woman he was with was her. It made him a bastard, but he made certain the woman he was with was taken care of. She had no way of knowing that she was a poor substitute for the one woman he couldn't have.

Was she finally moving on? She'd talked the talk during the car ride home. She'd been blunt, painfully so, and it had cost her. He'd seen the naked emotion in her eyes when she'd said that Carson was gone and he wasn't coming back and she had to move on and accept that. But did she mean it?

He was afraid to hope. And he was afraid of making the wrong move. He couldn't afford to fuck it all up by pushing her too soon. She viewed him as a friend. She viewed herself as a burden to him. Someone he'd babysat through her grief. Never even realizing that he lived for the moments when he was with her.

Carson had known that his best friend was in love with his wife. He'd known and accepted it. Dash had been afraid that it would ruin not only their friendship, but their business partnership as well. But Carson had understood. He trusted Dash never to act on that attraction. And he'd also exacted a promise from Dash that were anything ever to happen to Carson, Dash would be there for Joss.

Hell of a note when his best friend entrusted his wife to his care if something happened to him.

Worse was the fact that Carson had exacted that promise mere weeks before he'd been killed in an accident. Almost as if he knew. Had he sensed that something would happen and that Joss would be left a young widow?

At the time, Dash had brushed off the very serious pledge that Carson had confronted him with.

If anything ever happens to me, man, I want you to promise me. Promise me that you'll be there for Joss. I know you love her. If there ever comes a day that I can't be there for her, I want you to promise me that you'll take care of her and love her like I do.

The words echoed through his mind. Prophetic? Or just coincidence?

At the time, the promise had just been a painful reminder of all that Carson had and all that Dash didn't. Joss was . . . She was *beautiful*. Not just physically. She could light up a room by simply walking in. She had a gentle smile that could charm even the hardest heart. And she'd never so much as looked in the direction of another man after she'd met Carson. God knows, there'd been no shortage of men only too willing to seduce another man's wife. But Joss acted as though she had no clue of her effect on men. And that made her all the more desirable to Dash.

After making a quick round of the social rooms, he picked up a glass of wine—Damon Roche served only the best—and headed up the stairs to the common room.

There was the usual eclectic mix of sexcapades occurring in the large, open room. Though there were no actual partitions, the room was sectioned off simply by the participants taking their own spaces for their activities.

A mixture of sounds and smells greeted him as he walked farther into the room. The slap of flesh on flesh. The smack of a whip or a flogger. The sighs, moans and cries of ecstasy. Some of pain. Some of pleasure. The air was thick with the scent of sex.

He crossed the room, taking in the occupants, wanting to ensure that Tate and Chessy weren't present tonight. Not that he was a prude by any stretch, but seeing his other best friends having sex wasn't high on his list of priorities. Though he shouldn't have worried because he hadn't seen them at The House in months. The few times in the past he had seen them, he'd cut short his own visit, because he would never do anything to make Chessy uncomfortable.

She was a very special woman, and Tate was a lucky son of a bitch to have such perfection. Submissive. Beautiful. Gifting Tate with her absolute trust. There was not a more precious gift than a woman who gave her submission to a man.

It was what he wanted for himself, what he'd always sought out in any relationship he'd formed. But for Joss, he'd deny that part of himself if it was the only way he had a chance at having her. Knowing Carson's background, Dash knew with certainty that Carson and Joss had never delved into that lifestyle.

But then he'd never gone beyond casual sex after Joss. Once she'd come into Carson's life, a whirlwind, there hadn't been another woman for Dash. He sated his needs, made certain his partner's were met as well and then he moved on, never willing to commit, even though he'd known that Joss was unattainable. Only now that wasn't true. She was free. But could she ever love another man as she'd loved Carson?

That was the question of the day. And could Dash be content with only a part of her heart?

He nodded before he could stop himself. Hell yes, he'd take any part of her he could get. The question was, when did he make his move?

Today had given him the first ray of hope in three years that Joss was ready to move past her grief and live her life again. He'd been patient. He'd been whatever she needed him to be. But he wanted to be so much more.

He retreated to the corner of the room, politely declining with a gentle smile a woman who offered to service him. Another night he may have let her, close his eyes and imagine Joss under his firm but tender grasp. But tonight his thoughts were consumed with Joss, and he couldn't muster the heart to pretend as he'd done so many other times.

His family thought him a fool for not moving beyond his feelings for Joss a long time ago. They'd eyed him with sympathy for the last three years. His brothers had even asked him when he was going to act. But he'd known it wasn't time. Not then. But now?

He couldn't help the petal of hope that unfurled when he'd been with Joss earlier today. He'd seen the difference in her eyes and in her demeanor. But then that bullshit apology for being a burden, and she'd acted as though she were finished being that burden to him.

To hell with that. If she thought he was just going to step aside, she was very wrong.

He stood watching with waning enthusiasm, not even sure what had driven him here tonight. What he wanted was to be with Joss. Watching a movie and trying to get her mind off her grief, which is what he'd done the last two anniversaries—and plenty of times in between. The day hadn't gone at all as he'd expected. He'd cleared his calendar, made certain his clients were covered so that he could spend the day with Joss.

He hadn't expected her to all but dismiss him after their trip to the cemetery.

His gaze was drawn to the entryway where a couple entered, and he did an immediate double take.

What the ever-loving *fuck*?

He stared, unable to believe what he was seeing. Joss had just walked through the doorway, a man Dash knew from The House at her side, his arm wrapped intimately around her waist, his hand splayed very possessively over her hip, leaving no question of his . . . ownership. Or *impending* ownership.

She was dressed in a killer black sheath that hugged and outlined every single one of her perfect curves. And she wore a pair of fuck-me shoes that just begged for a man to do just that. Fuck her in those heels until she screamed his name over and over.

Her hair was upswept, a few tendrils floating lazily down her slender neck, drawing attention to the delicateness of her features.

And she looked scared to death.

Dash was striding across the room before he even realized what he was doing. For that matter, what the fuck was *she* doing? Here! In a goddamn establishment devoted to all manner of sexuality.

And the man she was with was a regular at The House. He had a string of submissives, and rarely was he with the same woman twice in a row. And yet here he was with his arm wrapped very possessively around Joss, lust evident in his eyes.

What the hell did she think she was doing?

He was just a few feet away when Joss lifted her shocked gaze to his, her mouth falling open in surprise just as mortification seized her features. Panic flickered in her eyes and she took a step away from the man at her side.

The man, Craig, was quick to pull her back, and that infuriated Dash all the more. Dash reached for Joss's arm, swiftly pulling her into the safety of his side.

"What the hell, Corbin?" Craig demanded, reaching for Joss's other hand.

Dash immediately inserted himself between Joss and Craig, shielding Joss with his body.

"Get the fuck away from her," Dash barked. "*Now.*"

Craig's eyebrows shot up and he stared for a moment before finally putting his hands up in a gesture of surrender. Not typical for a man like Craig. A Dominant who didn't yield to anyone. But then Dash was convinced he likely looked like a crazy person about to explode, judging by the wariness in Craig's gaze. And Craig wouldn't be wrong about that assumption. Dash was precariously close to losing his tenuous hold on his control.

"I'll just go find other company for the evening," Craig murmured.

"You do that," Dash said behind clenched teeth. "And don't ever make the mistake of coming near her again or I'll take you apart. We clear?"

"Yeah, man, I got it."

Craig gave Dash—and Joss—a wide berth before continuing into the room.

Dash turned to see Joss's pale, shocked face and swore under his breath. He grabbed her hand and hauled her into the hallway. She still hadn't uttered a word. Her face was stricken, and she looked so humiliated that Dash wanted to put his fist through the wall. The last thing he wanted was to embarrass her, but fuck it all. What was he supposed to do when she showed up looking like a woman a man would die to possess? A woman *he* was dying to possess.

He ushered her down the stairs and down the hallway to the exit as fast as he could without making her trip in those spikes disguised as shoes. He was tempted to throw her over his shoulder and barrel out like a caveman. He managed to temper that particular urge. Barely.

As soon as he had her outside, he turned to her, trying to curb the anger that coiled through his veins.

"Where's your car?" he clipped out.

"I d-didn't drive," she stammered out. "I took a cab."

Jesus. That was worse. Had she not expected to go home alone tonight? Was she planning to sleep over with whatever guy she hooked up with here? But then how the hell did he know if this was even her first time? For all he knew she could be a regular and maybe she and Craig had hooked up before. Dash certainly hadn't been in enough recently to be caught up on the goings-on at the club.

He herded her over to his car and opened the passenger door, ushering her inside.

"Dash?"

The one word, laced with fear and uncertainty, cut him to the core. Damn it, the last thing he wanted was for her to be afraid of him. He had to calm the fuck down before he lost his damn mind. And destroyed any chance he had with her.

"I'm taking you home," he said in a more gentle tone.

He walked around to the driver's side and slid in, starting the engine and backing out almost before he had his door closed. He roared down the winding drive that led up to the house and waited impatiently for the gate to open to allow him to exit.

As he accelerated down the highway, he felt Joss's nervous gaze flicker toward him. Saw her bite the bottom of her lip as she obviously struggled with what she wanted to say.

He reached for her hand, squeezing it in a reassuring manner.

"We'll talk when we get home," he said, his voice a command, one that he hadn't used with Joss before.

But it worked. She immediately closed her mouth, though her bottom lip was still sucked between her teeth as she nibbled nervously. Mortification still gripped her features, and it made Dash ache to know she was suffering. Embarrassed. Likely thinking he was going to tear a strip off her hide. And maybe he was. He wasn't at all sure what the fuck he was going to say to her yet.

They drove the rest of the way in tense silence, her hand firmly trapped in his. He could feel her trembling and it slayed him that she feared him. He'd nip that in the bud just as soon as he got to the bottom of this.

She looked surprised when he pulled into his neighborhood, which was just a few miles from her own subdivision. She turned to look at him, a clear question in her eyes.

"We'll talk here," he said shortly as he pulled into his drive.

She went silent again, her head bowed as she stared at her lap. Undone by her defeated demeanor, he reached over and gently cupped her chin, nudging until she was forced to look up at him.

"It'll be okay, honey. Now come inside so we can talk."

She nodded and he got out quickly, walking around to collect her from the car. He led her inside his house, satisfaction gripping him that she was in his space. Finally.

Though they'd spent plenty of time together over the last years, it had always been in a neutral location. Or her own home, the one she'd shared with Carson. The last time she'd been in his house was when Carson was still alive, and the couple had been frequent visitors back then.

He curled his arm around Joss's waist as he ushered her through the foyer and into the living room. She stiffened but made no move to distance herself from him. She was too busy looking like she was waiting for the anvil to drop from the sky on her head.

When they entered the living room, he loosened his hold and took a step away, dragging a hand raggedly through his hair. Then he turned, not sure how exactly to pose the questions burning his tongue. Fuck it. He only knew one way. Blunt.

"What the hell were you doing in The House tonight, Joss?" he demanded.

She flinched at the fury in his tone and her eyes became shadowed.

"You have no idea what you're getting into by being there," he continued. "No idea at all. Do you have any clue what could happen to you? What Craig would have done to you? Let me tell you. He would have had you bent over while he flogged your pretty ass and then he would have fucked you without mercy, uncaring of your pleasure. It would have been all about his own. He would have taken you and used you and wouldn't have given a damn about you or your pleasure. What the hell were you thinking?"

She wet her lips, her eyes going glossy with tears. Ah hell. The last thing he wanted was to make her cry when she'd made it the entire day, or at least the time she'd spent with him, without shedding a single tear.

"I do understand, Dash," she said quietly. "I understand far more than you think."

His brow furrowed. "Have you been going to The House before tonight?"

She shook her head. "No. This was my first night."

"Jesus Christ, Joss. What the hell? Do you have any idea what might have happened to you if I hadn't been there? There is no way in hell I'm allowing you to go back to that place. You don't belong there."

Her lips quivered and then she seemed to mentally shake herself. She steeled her features and leveled a firm stare at him.

"I know exactly what I was doing. You don't understand, Dash. You'd never understand."

"Try me," he challenged.

She stared at him a long moment, her eyes uncertain, almost as if she were trying to decide whether to trust him. He was on edge, because damn it, he wanted her to be able to come to him for anything. Anything at all. And he wanted her trust.

Then she closed her eyes and sank onto the couch, sitting forward, her face buried in her hands. Her shoulders shook and it was all he could do not to go to her. Not to comfort and hold her and tell her everything would be all right. But he waited. Because whatever she had to tell him he sensed was huge. And that it would forever change the way he looked at her. At any possibility of them being together.

She lifted her head, her eyes swimming in tears. "I loved Carson with all my heart and soul. He was my soul mate. I know that. And I know I'll never find that kind of love again."

Dash's breath caught and held because that wasn't something he wanted to hear. That she'd resigned herself to a loveless existence because she didn't think another man would ever love her as Carson had. When in fact, Dash was that man. He *already* loved her—*had* loved her forever—and given the opportunity, he'd show her that she damn well *could* find another man who'd give her his everything.

"Carson gave me everything I could ever possibly want or ask for. Except . . ."

She broke off and looked down again, her shoulders sagging in defeat.

"Except what, Joss?" Dash asked softly, puzzled by her statement. He knew damn well Carson would have given her the moon. Anything that was in his power to provide Joss, he would have done absolutely.

"Dominance," Joss whispered.

Dash's nape prickled and a curl of . . . hope? quivered through his veins. His pulse raced and he had to calm himself and clarify that he'd heard her correctly. Because there was a whole lot he didn't understand.

"Dominance?"

She nodded. Then she looked up at him, misery clouding her beautiful eyes. "You know how he grew up. What he endured. How he and Kylie were horribly abused. In the beginning, when we first met, we talked about my . . . need. What I thought I needed and wanted. And he wouldn't—couldn't—bring himself to do anything that could possibly be construed as abuse. He worried constantly that somehow he would inherit his father's abusive nature, that it was somehow genetic, and he'd die before ever doing anything to hurt me. As if he would! It was why he was reluctant to have children. He wanted them. God, he wanted them and so did I. It's my biggest regret that I didn't have his child, a part of him to live on now that I've lost him. But he was so terrified that he'd abuse his own children."

The last part came out in a sob and Dash could no longer keep his distance. He crossed the room, sat on the couch next to her and pulled her into his arms. She buried her face in his chest as he ran his hands through her hair.

"Carson would never hurt you or his children," Dash said with absolute confidence.

Joss pulled away, her tear-filled eyes gutting Dash. "I know that. You know that. But *he* didn't. And I couldn't convince him of that. His father messed him up, Dash. Him and Kylie both. They never recovered from all he had done to them and it affected them well into their adult life. It still affects Kylie. When I told her what I planned to do, she freaked."

"I'd like to hear what it was you planned as well, Joss," Dash prompted gently. "What was tonight all about?"

Joss turned away, clenching her fingers into tight fists. "I know you think I don't have a clue what I was getting into, Dash, but I'm not stupid. I didn't just up and decide to go to The House. It's something I've thought about and researched for months. I talked with Damon Roche a lot. He wanted to make sure I knew what I was getting into and that I wasn't making a hasty, emotional decision."

Well, thank God for that. Damon was a solid guy. He may run an establishment that catered to every conceivable kink or fetish, but he took it very seriously and he vetted his members very carefully.

"But it's like I told you today, Dash. Carson is *gone*. He's not coming back. And I have to pick up and move on. I can't mourn him the rest of my life. I need . . . I want . . ."

She faltered and Dash simply waited for her to collect her thoughts because this was huge. He was learning a side to Joss he never suspected existed. How could he have?

"I have to know if what I think I want and need is true. I have this need inside me, Dash. It's an ache, a hole in my soul that's even larger now that Carson is gone. I loved him too much to ever ask or demand that he give me something he wasn't capable of. And it sounds like I was unhappy. God, I wasn't! I loved him, Dash. I loved him with all my heart and I don't regret a single thing about our marriage."

"I know, honey. I know," Dash murmured.

"But that need has *always* been inside me and I can't even explain it to myself, so how can I make you understand that this isn't a game? It isn't me being irrational and looking to fill a void left by Carson's death. It's always been there. *Always*."

"Try me," Dash said simply. "Tell me what it is you want. What you need. I'll listen, Joss. And I won't judge you. I'll just listen and we can talk about it."

Relief shone in her eyes. Had she expected condemnation? Had she expected him to accuse her of being disloyal to Carson or his memory?

"I want to be . . . owned." A shiver stole over her body, one he could feel even with the short space that separated them now. "I want what Tate and Chessy have. I want a man to possess me, to own me. I want to submit to him and I want him to take care of me. Protect me. God, it makes me sound like some helpless, dependent twit. But that's not it. Carson taught me to stand on my own two feet. To be independent. It's not that I have to have this in order to survive. It's what I want. My *choice*."

Dash put his finger over her lips to silence her. "Shhh, honey. You don't have to defend your choices to me. I'm here to listen. Don't defend. Just tell me what's going on in that pretty head of yours."

His heart was about to beat out of his chest. Had fate been kind to him after all? Had a gift he'd never dreamed of receiving suddenly dropped into his lap? Had Carson known—of course he'd known. He knew of Dash's sexual preferences. That he was dominant and that he desired submissiveness in a woman. Now the promise that Carson had exacted from him made so much more sense. Carson had known his wife wanted something he himself could never provide her, and he wanted to make sure that if something happened to him that Dash would step in and give her what Carson had never been able to. God, the sheer selflessness that such a gesture entailed was mind-boggling. He'd been granting his blessing. *Jesus.*

"This isn't a decision I made lightly, Dash. I was okay with it. Until I saw you tonight. I was so mortified. And I felt guilty, because seeing you there made me feel as though I were betraying Carson. I didn't want you to know. Chessy and Kylie knew. I told them. They're worried about me, but they also know I took all the necessary precautions before just showing up at The House tonight. And I was ready. Or at least I thought I was. But then you were there."

Her brow suddenly furrowed as if it had just occurred to her that Dash had been there. He could see the question in her eyes before she ever voiced it.

"What were *you* doing there, Dash?"

For a moment he brushed aside her question because there were so many other more important things to discuss. It was all he could do to hold himself back. To temper the urge to brand her. To move in, take her and give her everything she said she wanted—needed.

"I need to know something from you first, Joss. I need to know how serious you are about this. I need to know if this is truly what you want and what you need and that it's not just an experiment or you looking to fill a void."

"I can't be any more serious," she said in a resolved tone that convinced him she was indeed that.

He leaned forward, his breath mingling with hers, their lips so close he could feel the warmth from the inviting bow. Just a fraction of an inch and he would be kissing her.

"I was there because that's who and what I am, Joss," he said, taking in her response, watching every flicker that crossed her eyes. "It's always been what I am. And let me tell you this right now. If this is what you want. If this is what you need. Then I'm going to be the only damn man you offer your submission to."

FOUR

JOSS sucked in her breath and held it until she was light-headed and precariously close to toppling over. Dash's lips were so close that she could feel the harsh exhalation of his breath. She could see the determined glitter in his eyes. And for the first time, she became aware of him as something more than a friend. Her *husband's* friend. Someone she'd turned to for support many times over the years.

She couldn't even process his heated declaration, but she knew he was utterly serious. There was a glint in his eyes, a firm set to his jaw. She could see the pulse thudding at his neck and she could smell every part of him, his scent wafting tantalizingly through her nostrils.

Dash dominant? Not that she had any difficulty in believing that of him. He was a man well accustomed to getting his way. He had a quiet authority about him. He didn't need to be loud to get his point across. She'd been present too many times when he'd spoken and everyone had immediately quieted, listening to what he had to say.

He wasn't someone who shouted orders. He didn't need to. There was an intensity to him that made people aware of the power emanating from him. She hadn't been blind to it, nor was she immune. As she'd pondered just earlier that day, in the beginning he'd intimidated her. She'd felt his concern and disapproval over how fast her relationship had progressed with Carson. But once he'd become convinced that she was the right woman for his best friend, his loyalty to her was sealed.

But his words still rang in her ears. That brusque vow. She shivered under the intensity of his gaze, those dark eyes eating her up, exposing her, making her feel vulnerable.

"I d-don't understand," she said helplessly, her hand lifting and then fluttering downward again as she tried to make sense of the entire evening.

And then his next words tilted her universe even further off its axis.

"I've waited a long damn time for you, Joss. I thought I'd never have you, and I was okay with that because you made Carson happy and I know Carson made you happy. But as you said, he's gone now, and I've waited. For what seems like an eternity I've waited for the right moment. For when you were ready. Maybe I waited too long, or perhaps now is the perfect time. But if you think I'm going to stand by and allow another man to touch what I consider mine, you're very mistaken."

She shook her head, overwhelmed by it all. Dash spoke as if he wanted her. Had wanted her for a long time. But no. That wasn't possible. He'd never betray his best friend. Had Dash developed feelings for her after Carson's death? Was he simply stepping in for his best friend, wanting to take care of Carson's widow?

She didn't want to be an *obligation* to Dash. She'd been one for far too long. Today had been about letting go. Not only of Carson but of her dependence on Dash.

And what flabbergasted her more was that Dash was everything she'd said she wanted, if she was to believe his impassioned statement. Dominant. He liked submissive women. And he wanted to introduce her to the lifestyle. He wanted to possess—to own—*her*.

"I don't know what to say," she said honestly. "I never imagined. I didn't realize . . ."

"No, I suppose you didn't," Dash murmured. "It's not something I could just come out and say. But Joss, *you've* made the first move. Now it's my turn to make all the others. You've laid out what you want. What you need. What you desire. And I'm going to be the man who gives you those things."

She stared back at him, still utterly overwhelmed by the day, the moment, *this*. How had so much changed so quickly? Then she shook her head in automatic denial even though a part of her, the part that had gone for so long unfulfilled, screamed at her that this was it. This was what she'd been looking for. But Dash?

No, they were just *friends*. He had been her *husband's* best friend. How would it look to others? How would her friends, his family, *Kylie* take the shift from them being friends to becoming lovers? More than lovers. Much more. She couldn't even fathom just how much more this kind of relationship he proposed entailed. It wouldn't be a one-night stand. Two people hooking up in the heat of the moment. What Dash proposed was . . . permanent?

"Stop overanalyzing this, Joss," Dash said in a patient tone. But his jaw was still tight. His eyes still glittered with unshakable resolve. God, was he serious? How could she even question that when every single part of him screamed of his absolute certainty?

And Dash was not impulsive or remotely flighty. That wasn't who or what he was. She'd known him long enough to know that his every movement, whether in business or in his personal life, was carefully thought out. But the idea that he'd obviously given *them* such careful consideration blew her mind.

"But Dash. We *can't*."

She said it emphatically even as she questioned why they couldn't. But of course they couldn't, could they? There was more than just him and her to consider. There were their friends. Kylie. His family. It was all making her head ache with the speed at which her world had been irrevocably altered. She hadn't experienced such a tailspin since the day she'd learned her husband was gone.

"Why not?" he asked simply, calmly. As if he hadn't just upended her carefully ordered existence.

Well, but that would be a lie. Her world had been upended on the day Carson had died, and it had never been set to rights. Until now? Was this what she needed to get her life back? To reclaim herself? Was Dash what she needed or would any man do? Even as she thought it, she knew it wasn't so. She wouldn't feel this way—this uncertain—with another man because it wouldn't be personal. She wouldn't have feelings she couldn't sort out for another man.

"What does this mean, Dash? I don't understand any of it. You said you've waited. What are we talking here? How long have you waited? You act as though you want me—have wanted me. But I had *no* idea. How could I have? You are—were—my husband's best *friend*."

"Be careful of what you ask, Joss," Dash warned. "You may not be prepared for the answer."

She blinked, not knowing what to make of that particular statement. Was she blind? Was she a complete idiot for not seeing this before? She mentally went back over all the times Dash had been with her over the last years. But all she saw was unwavering support. Emotional support. All the times he'd picked up the pieces when she was certain that she'd fallen apart.

But he'd kept her strong. Pushed her when she hadn't always wanted to be pushed, but he'd never taken her anger or rage personally. It was a wonder he hadn't walked away from her a long time ago. But if what he suggested was true . . .

Oh dear God. What was she supposed to do? What she wanted was being placed squarely in her lap. But Dash?

She looked up at him again, this time without the blinders. Without the knowledge that he was untouchable, a friend. Her husband's best friend. Someone she could never even look at with anything more than the bonds of friendship.

And what she saw took her breath away.

This was a living, breathing, gorgeous specimen of alpha male. The promise of dominance and a whole lot more shone in his dark eyes. She shivered as she took in the way he looked at *her*. Had he always looked at her as he was looking now? Had she been completely oblivious to the strong current of attraction that arced between them as strongly as any electrical surge?

Her gaze wandered over his face, down his body, took in the broad set of his shoulders, his muscled chest, even the thickness of his muscular thighs. Not an inch of spare flesh to be found on his body.

Then heat consumed her cheeks and she looked away, embarrassed to be caught checking him out in such an obvious matter.

But he wasn't bothered. Indeed, he looked . . . pleased.

"That's it, Joss. See me," he breathed out. *"Finally.* See me. Who I am. What I am. And that I want you with my every breath."

"How long?" she whispered, remembering his admonishment that perhaps she wouldn't want the answer to her question. But now she had to know. She had to know how long he'd gone unnoticed by her.

"Forever?" he said with a casual shrug. He tried to play it off lightly, but she could see the shadows that suddenly entered his eyes. The . . . pain. And the longing. Oh dear God. It couldn't be true. It simply couldn't.

"Forever?" she croaked out. "You mean before . . . When Carson and I were *together*?"

He gave a clipped nod and all the wind left Joss in a sudden whoosh, leaving her sagging on the couch. He made a sudden grab for her, steadying her before she could topple sideways.

"I didn't know," she murmured faintly.

"Of course not. I didn't *want* you to know," Dash bit out. "I wouldn't have laid that on you, Joss. What could you have done? You were in love with another man. Married to another man. My best friend. You knowing would have solved nothing and would have put a strain on our relationship. On the three of us."

She raised her gaze to him, haunted, she was sure, because what she had to ask next . . .

"And Carson?" she whispered. "Did he know?"

Dash hesitated only a moment, as if he were deciding just how blunt to be with her. Then he gave a quick shake of his head, almost as if he were deciding that she should have it all. That maybe he thought she was finally ready to hear what she'd been ignorant of for so long.

"He knew," Dash said grimly.

"Oh my God," Joss said shakily. "He knew? And you were friends? Dash, I don't understand any of this!"

Dash sighed and then gently pulled her forward until she was nestled into his chest. He laid her head against his shoulder and kissed the top of her hair as one hand glided downward, separating and stroking the tresses that had now tumbled down from the clip that had secured them earlier.

There was so much more in his embrace than the comfort he'd offered for the last three years. She knew it now, but hadn't known it then. Her entire body was on high alert. Her pulse raced and thudded in her veins. Her breasts tingled and her nipples beaded and tightened against the dress. She hadn't worn a bra and she knew that Dash could feel the imprint of her nipples through their clothing.

"Carson understood," Dash said in a low voice. "And yes, we were friends and we *remained* friends because he knew I would never betray him and he knew you would never betray him. He knew that I would never act on my attraction. But yes, he knew. And I think it gave him a measure of comfort to know that if anything ever happened to him I'd step in. That I'd be here and that I'd give you everything you could possibly want or need."

She pushed off his chest to look him in the eye. "But Dash, that had to have been . . ."

She trailed off, seeing the fire in his eyes. As if he'd suppressed his need and want for so long and now it was unleashed, vibrant and blazing in his eyes.

"It was hell," Dash quietly confirmed. "It was heaven and it was hell. Heaven when I got to spend time with you. When I simply got to look at you or see you smile. It was hell going home at night knowing you were in Carson's arms and not my own."

"I didn't know," she choked out. "I didn't know, Dash!"

His expression gentled and he put his hand up to stroke her cheek, rubbing downward in a tender caress.

"I didn't want you to know, Joss. I was in an impossible position and I never wanted that for you. For Carson. I loved you both and I would have never done anything to destroy your marriage or cause trouble. So I waited. But I'm done waiting and you need to know that."

Her breath caught again at the sincerity emblazoned on his features.

His hand trailed downward until his fingers brushed ever so lightly across her lips. She was tempted to lick them, wanting to taste him on her mouth.

"But now I feel as though I've been handed a gift I never dreamed of receiving. I was prepared to deny everything about myself. For you. I never imagined you'd want what it is I can give you. So I would have suppressed that need to dominate. I would have never demanded anything of you that you weren't prepared to offer freely. But now that I know what you want? Brace yourself, Joss, because now that I know, I'm not going to hold back any longer. I can give you all that you want and need and so much more. So very much more. You just have to decide whether you trust me to give that to you. And whether you think you can possibly come to care for me as much as I care for you."

She did lick her lips then. Nervous. Anticipation tingling up her spine. And hope. Slowly unfurling like the petals of a flower at the first brush of spring. Warming in the sunshine after a long winter, waiting to bloom and burst free of constraints.

"I don't know where to start," she said honestly. "Tonight . . . It went nothing as I had planned."

"Thank fuck for that," Dash muttered. "God, when I think of what could have happened had I not been there. It's fate, Joss. She's a fickle bitch and at long last she's smiled on me."

"What happens now?" she asked quietly, her gaze never leaving his.

He leaned in, cupping her face with exquisite tenderness and reverence. His lips hovered precariously close to hers, his breath warming her skin. And then he kissed her.

Heat exploded through her veins, rushing until she could hear the roar in her ears. It was like an electric shock, something so unexpected and yet wonderful. Desire, long dormant, rose like a fury, curling through her womb and spreading outward like a wildfire.

Her skin prickled, chill bumps rising and dancing across her skin until she shivered uncontrollably against him.

He deepened the kiss, swiping his tongue warmly over the seam of her lips until she parted them breathlessly and he swept in, colliding with her tongue. He moaned softly against her mouth. She swallowed up the sound, suddenly hungry, so very hungry for more.

Never had she imagined feeling this way again. Of experiencing the intense craving, of having desire grab hold and completely overtake her. She'd been cold, so very cold, for so very long, and now she was warm. Bathed in fire. His heat consumed her. His smell, his taste, the very essence of him. How could she have never known? How could she have never imagined? How could she have never seen him as the desirable, alpha male who was currently kissing her senseless?

When he pulled away, his eyes were hooded and flush with answering desire.

"What happens now, Joss, is that you are mine. At long last, you are mine. And if all you said is true, if what you want and need is my dominance, then be assured. I *will* possess you. I *will* own you. And you will never know another man than me."

FIVE

DASH watched the myriad of emotions washing through her eyes. She was so expressive. She'd always been so. It was one of the things he'd enjoyed most about her. One only had to look into her eyes to know her mood. Happiness, sadness, excitement.

Arousal.

The last, he found, was extremely satisfying. Never had she looked at him as she did right at this moment. Triumph surged, even as he tempered his reaction. This wasn't in the bag. Not by a long shot. Her next words confirmed that for him.

"I need time to think . . . About this—us," she said in a shaky voice. "This was so unexpected, Dash. I don't want to make a hasty decision that I—we—will later regret."

Her honesty was another thing he'd always admired about her.

"Of course," he murmured. "There's no rush." Even as his mind screamed that there was every need to rush. He didn't *want* her to think about it. Didn't want her talking herself out of it. But he couldn't blow this. Not when he was so close to getting what he'd wanted for so very long.

"I don't know how long . . ."

She trailed off, lifting her hand to her temple as if it ached before letting it flutter back down to her lap. He took her hand, rubbing the pad of his thumb over her silky skin. Such slender, delicate fingers. Like the rest of her. He couldn't get enough of touching her. He'd certainly touched her in the past, but always in the capacity of a friend. Affectionate. Nothing even resembling intimacy. They both knew his touch was intimate now, and it was a thrill he wouldn't soon get over.

"Take your time, honey. But I want you to promise me something, okay?"

When she didn't immediately look up, he lifted his free hand and cupped her chin, his touch as delicate as her skin.

"Look at me, Joss. This is important."

She lifted her gaze to his, all the turmoil boiling in her gorgeous blue eyes.

"I want you to take as long as you need to think about it—us. But I want you to promise me that you won't go back to The House. Not without me. Not for any reason. Not until this is decided between you and me, and I hope to hell that, even if you don't choose me, that you won't go there on your own. I don't want to imagine you under another man's hands. Him touching you everywhere I want to be touching you. Do this for me at least."

"You're issuing me an ultimatum," she said in a low voice. "You want me to promise that if I don't choose you, I'll deny what my heart wants. What I need. How is that fair?"

"Love isn't fair," he said bluntly, watching the flash of surprise in her eyes, how they widened at his statement.

He didn't follow up on it. It was certainly too soon to lay that on her, on top of everything else the evening had wrought. She needed time to ponder other matters without him spouting declarations of love that she wouldn't believe were sincere.

"What I'm asking you for is a chance, Joss. Choose *me*. Let me initiate you into the world you want so badly. Give me that at least. If it's not what you want, if it turns out this isn't what you need, then we'll step back and reevaluate. What I want is the opportunity—the exclusive opportunity, if you will. Because I've already said that I would have suppressed my need to dominate if that's the only way I could have you. You knocked me for six when I saw you walk through the door into the common room and my world has been spinning ever since. All I want is a chance, honey. A chance. And I don't want you going back there. Not without me. Not with anyone else until I've had the chance to prove to you that I'm all you need. Is that so wrong of me to ask?"

She stared at him for a long moment before finally and slowly shaking her head.

He leaned forward, brushing a kiss across her furrowed brow, trying to relax the lines that had formed under the force of her concentration.

"I'll give you time, Joss. All the time you need. But don't wait too long. You've waited this long to act. There's no need to waste further time when this is something you've obviously given a lot of thought to. You know you can trust me. I hope to hell you already do. And that's a huge step over any other man you would have chosen and a hell of a step up from the guy you came into the common room with. Because, honey? I care about you and your pleasure. Craig doesn't and he wouldn't. Given the opportunity, I'll lay the fucking world at your feet. There isn't anything I wouldn't do to have you, to possess you. I just need the chance to prove it to you."

The longing in her eyes was nearly his undoing. His impassioned speech had spoken to the heart of her. Of that he was certain.

"I won't take long," she said huskily. "I just need time to think. This is a lot. I mean I had no idea, Dash. Today was going to be me letting go. Not only of Carson, but of you as well. I felt like I'd been a burden to you for far too long and that it was time for me to stop leaning on you. Time to let you get on with your life. I can't imagine you've had any long-term relationships. Most women wouldn't appreciate you dropping everything to comfort your best friend's widow. I thought I was doing you—and myself—a favor by picking up the pieces and standing on my own two feet. And now you want that even more. I can't wrap my head around it, and as I said, I don't want to make a snap decision that we'll both regret. I care about you, Dash. Very much so. I don't think I've ever properly thanked you for all you've done for me."

"I don't want your thanks, Joss. I want you. Simple. Just you. And your submission. But as I said, if it turns out that this isn't what you want, then it doesn't have to be that way between us. I'd sacrifice a hell of a lot to have you any way I can have you."

Sorrow filled her eyes. "I don't want that for you, Dash. I don't want you to change for me. I don't want you to be someone you aren't. That's as bad as if I'd expected—demanded—something from Carson I knew he wasn't willing or able to give. I would have never asked him for that. So I can't ask you to deny who you are for me."

He pulled her forward into his arms, his lips finding hers, silencing her. She melted so sweetly into his body that it was all he could do not to sweep her into his arms and carry her to his bed. But he'd waited this long. He'd wait for as long as it took for her to be ready.

"How about you let me decide the sacrifices I make. Didn't you make sacrifices for Carson? That's what love is, honey. You wanted and needed something he couldn't give you, but it didn't make you love him any less."

She went still against him and then nestled even farther into his embrace, tucking her head underneath his chin. God, they fit. Like two puzzle pieces. He wrapped both arms around her, anchoring her there, simply enjoying the feel of her in his arms in a way he'd never been able to enjoy before. Because now she knew where he stood, and she was allowing it. She damn well knew he was holding and touching her not out of friendship, but as a man who very much wanted her heart and soul.

"Now about that promise?"

She slowly drew away and looked him in the eye. "I promise, Dash. Just give me a little time to sort through all of this. It's been a difficult day for me, and everything I thought was going to be, didn't turn out the way I expected at all. I need to process this."

He nodded and started to speak, but she continued on in a rush.

"I don't want to use you, Dash. And maybe I was okay with using a stranger. Someone who didn't mean anything to me. But I won't use you. Not you. I won't use you as a crutch or some experiment. You mean too much to me. Your friendship means too much to me."

He smiled and tenderly stroked a piece of hair from her cheek to behind her ear. "But honey, I don't mind if you use me. As long as the end result is having you. I've used all manner of women over the past few years. I'm not proud of that fact, but it is what it is. They were all a poor substitute for what I couldn't have at the time. You."

"You pretended they were me?" she whispered in an astonished tone.

He nodded. "Again, I'm not proud of it. But there it is. I couldn't have you, so I slaked my hunger and desire for you with other women. And maybe it changes the way you'll look at me. It's a chance I have to take. But I won't lie to you. There have certainly been other women. I thought I was in a position to never have what I most wanted, so I dealt with it."

"I don't fault you for being with other women, Dash. God,

how could I? I was *married*. I would have never expected you to be faithful to a woman who wasn't even yours!"

"I'm glad," he said simply. "Because, honey? Once I have you, there'll never be another woman. And you can take that to the bank."

Her eyes widened in surprise again. It was as if it had all just sunk in at once. Her eyes dulled and went hazy with shock. Her body trembled and she balled her fingers together to try to hide the fact that they were shaking.

"I want you to stay here tonight, Joss."

He held up his hand when the protest formed on her lips. And then he cupped her chin, stroking his thumb down her jawline.

"You've been thrown one hell of a curveball. I get that. And I'm not asking you to go to bed with me. Not yet. Not tonight. But stay here in the guest room. I'd feel better if you weren't alone. I'll make us breakfast in the morning and then I'll take you home. And then I'll give you time. In the morning we'll set a date. Dinner. Dancing. Whatever pleases you. Then you can give me your answer, and depending on the answer, we'll go from there."

She swallowed visibly and he could see the indecision in her eyes. Her weighing her options and trying to absorb the events of the day.

"Stay," he whispered, angling his head to kiss her again.

She emitted a sweet sigh as his tongue pushed in to taste her all over again. Kissing her was addictive. Now that he'd kissed her for the first time, he knew it would never be enough. He wanted to taste her everywhere. Her breasts. He wanted to get between her legs and savor every inch of her feminine flesh. And then he wanted to brand her. Possess her in every conceivable fashion there was to possess a woman. Until she had no doubt as to his ownership. No doubt that he was the last man who'd ever make love to her.

"Stay," he said again, as he reluctantly ended the kiss and drew away.

She sucked in a breath and then exhaled it in a long wave, her shoulders slumping downward with the action.

"All right," she conceded. "I'll stay."

SIX

WHEN Joss walked into Dash's kitchen the next morning, he knew she hadn't slept well, if at all. But then neither had he. How could he when he was imagining her in the next bedroom? So fucking close and yet a world away. Out of reach. He'd lain in his bed, staring up at the ceiling, alternately thanking and cursing fate.

He was so close. *This* close to having his heart's desire, and he kept wondering if this was all some sick joke fate was playing on him. Dangling the proverbial carrot in front of his nose only to cruelly yank it away. What if Joss backed out? What if she'd acted on impulse and after careful consideration chose to change her mind?

He couldn't handle it. It had been bad enough before when he'd *known* he had no chance with her. But now? Now that he'd kissed her, had tasted her, had held her in his arms? He couldn't bear it if he lost her now. Before he even had her once.

Not that once would ever be enough. Not with her. Other women? Once had been all he'd ever wanted. He hadn't *wanted* to form relationships even though not doing so was torture in itself. He saw Joss and Carson. Was tortured by what they had and by knowing he'd never have the same.

Most of the time he sucked it up and dealt. But the nights

when he couldn't, when he was lonely and aching for what could never be, he'd gone to The House. Sated his needs and then went back to his self-induced purgatory.

He hoped to fuck that was over. For good. He could only hope. If willing it made it happen, then she'd have already been in his bed. Tied to it so she'd never leave.

Desperate? That didn't even cover it. Not by a long shot.

He had no pride when it came to Joss. And he didn't give one damn.

He poured a cup of her favorite coffee and slid it along the bar as she sat down. She was wearing one of his T-shirts, a fact that made him absurdly happy, and a pair of pajama bottoms she'd had to cinch tight to keep from falling down her hips. Not that he would have minded . . .

"You didn't sleep, baby," he said in a gentle tone.

She flinched and closed her eyes, but not before he saw a surge of grief swamp them.

"Please don't call me that," she whispered.

"Of course. I didn't think. I'm sorry," he said softly.

It was what Carson had always called her.

"There are plenty of other endearments I'll use for you, honey."

She opened her eyes and a smile flirted with the corners of her mouth.

"Now, that's better. Surely it wasn't that bad of a night?"

But even as he said it, he knew it likely had been. It had been hell for him, and he wasn't the one who'd been handed a huge shock. And on the anniversary of Carson's death. He inwardly winced, but then timing wasn't always his friend. He wasn't going to not act just because it was the date of his best friend's death. Fate—and Joss—had forced his hand.

"It was a lot to take in," she admitted, bringing the cup to her lips.

She took a sip and then closed her eyes as pleasure washed away the lines of fatigue on her face.

"You spoil me," she said, lowering the cup.

"No, but I intend to."

"So last night wasn't a dream then."

He leaned over the counter so they were face-to-face, their gazes locked. "It was a dream. *My* dream. Now all we have to do is make it reality."

"You make it sound so simple," she murmured.

"It is. Or it isn't. It's what we choose to make it. Me? I'm a straightforward guy, but then you know that already. I've waited long enough, so you'll have to excuse my impatience now that what I want is within reach."

"How is this supposed to work, Dash? I spent all night thinking—wondering—what this all means. Before it was surreal. It was in the abstract. Not real and in my face. I fantasized. I wondered. I even conjured up various scenarios. But now that it's here, right in front of me, I don't know what to do. What to expect."

"Why don't we both eat. We'll talk over breakfast and I'll answer any question you want the answer to. But as I warned you last night, if you're unprepared for the answer, it's best you don't ask."

She nodded. "No, I want the truth. I want the reality. I need to know what this means. What me *being* with you means."

He reached over to squeeze her hand. "Head over to the breakfast nook. I'll grab our plates and meet you there."

He watched as she shuffled the short distance, holding the mug of coffee between her palms as if trying to infuse her entire body with its warmth. He'd much rather wrap himself around her. He'd give her all the warmth she needed and so much more.

Patience, Dash. Don't blow this, man. Not when you're so fucking close. You've waited too long for this.

He tempered his eagerness and took his time gathering the plates and bringing them to the table where Joss sat. She just looked . . . right. In his house, wearing his clothes, still slightly rumpled from just coming from bed, even with her hair blow-dried from her shower. The only thing that would make it better is if she'd just come from *his* bed.

Soon enough.

He slid the plate in front of her, watching her eyes widen, a broad smile curving her lips.

"My favorite," she said huskily.

He smiled back at her. "Of course. Did you think I'd serve you anything else? Waffles with lots of butter and even more syrup. Dig in and enjoy. I'll bring back milk and the bacon."

She sighed. "I do love them but I can't indulge often. Too many calories!"

He shook his head as he returned again with their drinks and the plate of bacon. "There isn't a thing wrong with the way you look, Joss. Utter perfection from the top of your pretty head to the tip of those pretty pink toes you sport."

She flushed, her cheeks going a shade of pink that nearly matched those toes.

"I don't know how to take this . . . this change in our relationship. I'm off balance. Just yesterday I was planning to let go of you much the way I had to let go of Carson. And now . . ."

She lifted her hand in bewilderment and let it fall back to her lap.

"That wasn't happening," he said mildly. "You may have

thought you were getting rid of me, honey, but I'm not going anywhere. I would have waited for as long as it took, but there was never a question of me making a move. You just happened to make it first."

He watched her process his declaration, the brief furrow of her brows as they knitted in consternation. As though she was still trying to understand everything he'd dumped on her in the last twenty-four hours. And then she lowered her gaze, effectively putting an end to her silent contemplation.

She dug into her waffles and he watched, savoring her enjoyment over the breakfast he'd prepared for her. She ate as she did everything else. Artlessly. No self-consciousness. She was a woman unafraid to show her pleasure over even the simplest things. And he intended to bring her a hell of a lot more pleasure than waffles for breakfast. He had in mind a hundred ways he wanted to spoil her.

"Now, you wanted to know how this works. What exactly do you mean?" he asked.

Her fork stilled in midair on its way to her mouth. Then she lowered it, licking her lips in agitation.

"You have to know, I mean you *do* know now, that I'm completely new to this. I told you the things I wanted, but you haven't told me what *you* want. How you expect this to work. What you'll want of me. What you'll *do* to me."

She shivered as she said the last, and he hoped she was imagining all those things he'd do to her. And that those images intrigued and aroused her as much as they did him.

"I think the question is, what do you *want* me to do to—with—you."

Impatience flared in her eyes, an emotion he was well acquainted with.

"Dash, please. Don't play games with me. This is important."

At that his expression became utterly serious. He leaned forward, his gaze boring into her.

"This is no *game*, Joss. Don't think that even for a minute. What I feel for you, what I want to do to you, is no game. Not by a long shot."

"Then help me out here," she said in a pleading tone. "I'm lost without a road map. I need your honesty. I need to know what you're thinking. I need to know how you see this playing out."

"I think," he said carefully, "that if we are to get into the particulars of our relationship, I'd prefer to do it in the living room where I can at least be touching you when I tell you my expectations and you outline your own."

"And what if I don't *know* what it is I want?"

He could sense her frayed nerves. He knew she was precariously close to cracking. No matter his impatience, no matter his urgency to claim what he wanted and had wanted for a damn long time, she needed delicate handling and all the reassurance he could grant her while still remaining firm. He couldn't—wouldn't—allow her to slip through his fingers when he finally had her exactly where he wanted her.

"You know, honey," he said gently. "You were clear enough last night. Just because you're no longer dealing with a stranger doesn't mean that things change. If anything, you should be much freer and without inhibitions with me. I want to know every single thing that's going on in that pretty head of yours. And you'll get everything in mine as well. That I can guarantee."

She rose, simmering with impatience—and nervousness. "Then let's do it. I want to know. I *need* to know before I make any decisions."

He caught her hand, pulling her into his side, wanting simply to touch her as he'd wanted to from the moment she'd entered his kitchen. He caressed her cheek and watched her eyes go warm with pleasure. It was a look he'd savor the rest of his life. Because she saw him. Finally, she saw him.

He guided her into the living room and sat down first on the leather couch before pulling her down and into his arms. She stiffened for a moment and he simply waited. Then she relaxed and melted into his arms, laying her head on his shoulder.

He could smell the scent of his shampoo, could feel a slight dampness that hadn't been removed when she'd blow-dried her hair after her shower. He liked his scent on her. If he had his way, she'd smell like him all the time. His. He closed his eyes, savoring the moment—and the thought—that finally, she would be his. No, she hadn't yet voiced her decision but he wondered if she knew he could see acceptance in her eyes already.

She was nervous, yes, but he also saw the agreement simmering in those gorgeous blue eyes. Anticipation licked up his spine. Spread out from his groin until his balls ached with it.

She tilted her head up so she could see him and then to his surprise, she touched him. Grazed her fingertip over his jaw. It was as soft as a butterfly's wing and yet he felt it all the way to his soul. It scorched a path over his skin, his entire body alive with pleasure at her touch.

"Tell me, Dash. Be honest with me. What will it mean to belong to you? What do you expect of me? I need to know these things. I need to know what I'm supposed to *do*. What you *want* me to do."

"It will mean . . . everything," he breathed out. "To me and I hope to hell to you as well. You'll be mine, Joss. In every sense of the word. Mine and no other's. I will take care of your every need. Provide whatever you could possibly want. In return for your submissiveness, I'll give you the fucking world on a platter. I'll cherish you, protect you, spoil and pamper you endlessly."

"That sounds like a pretty awesome deal for me. But what about you, Dash? What do you get?"

"You," he said simply. "Just you, Joss. And believe me when I say that's enough. It's all I want. It's all I need. Just you."

The yearning in her eyes took his breath away. She hadn't exaggerated. She'd been as lonely and as aching as he had been the last three years.

"And what will you do to me?" she whispered. "How will you exert your dominance? And do you want my submissiveness only in bed or will it extend out of the bedroom as well?"

"What would you prefer?" he asked, turning the question back on her.

She shook her head, her lips forming a tight, determined line. "I already told you what I wanted. It's time for you to give me an idea of what you have in mind. I want it all, Dash. No sugarcoating. I want to know exactly what *you* want."

"I want *everything*, Joss. And by that I mean I want your complete obedience in and out of the bedroom. I'll call the shots. You might think I'm caging you, but honey, it will be the most gilded cage in the world and there won't be a woman on earth who is more cherished or spoiled than you."

She sucked in her breath, her eyes widening.

"Now, I think what you're asking and what you want to know relates to the more physical aspects of our relationship. Am I right?"

She nodded, her cheeks turning that delightful shade of pink again.

"I like complete submission, but surrender is more than just physical surrender. It's complete *emotional* surrender as well. And in some ways, emotional surrender is much more powerful and a much more precious thing to be given. It's an *honor*, and I don't say that lightly. A woman can give her body and never share her heart, her mind, her very soul. But a woman who gives freely of both body and mind is the most precious of gifts to receive. I don't fool myself into thinking that at any time the women I've been with— have dominated—have given me anything but their body. And I was okay with that, because they didn't have my heart either. We shared our bodies and nothing more."

He paused a moment, allowing her to absorb his heartfelt words. Watched as she processed them, her eyes reflecting a myriad of emotions. Then he touched her, much like she'd touched him, running his fingertip lovingly down the line of her jaw and finally to brush across the softness of her lips.

"With *you*, Joss, it will be so much different. So much better. So much *more*. Physically? I'll want complete and unfettered access to your body. It will be mine to do with as I please. Bondage, spankings, there are no limits. I like to inflict pain, pleasurable pain. Pain can be the sweetest of pleasures if given in the right manner. There is nothing more that I wish than to see my marks on you. The blush of red after I've flogged your sweet ass. I want to tie you up so that you are completely helpless and at my mercy, but honey, I'll have the most tender of mercies with you."

Her eyes had glazed, going dark and swirling with desire. He knew he was speaking to the heart of her. Every single thing she'd fantasized about, she'd dreamed about and ached for, he was *going* to give her. And he'd enjoy every damn minute of making all her fantasies reality.

He dropped his hand down the curve of her neck until it rested just over the beat of her heart.

"Emotionally? I want your heart. Your soul. Your complete and absolute trust and your surrender. I want your *gift* of submission and I'll cherish it as I cherish you. I'll respect it and never give you cause to regret your decision. *That's* the promise I make you."

She stared at him in bewilderment, her eyes flashing, shadows lurking in the hollows. "How did you *know*? How *could* you know, Dash? How can you see what I've only been able to see myself lately? How could you possibly reach into my head and *know*?"

He smiled and kissed her brow, running his hand around and then up and down her back, reveling in the feel of her in his arms. Finally in his arms.

"Because it's what I want most too, honey. It's what I've wanted for so very long. And I'll make you another promise. I won't rush you. I won't overwhelm you. We have all the time in the world. Yours will be a gentle initiation into my world. Now that I know you can finally be mine, I intend to savor every moment."

"You act as though I've already made my decision," she murmured.

"Haven't you? Perhaps you need time to justify it, but you've already made your choice, Joss. I saw it in your eyes when you walked into my kitchen this morning, and it was all I could do not to do a fist pump or something equally adolescent. You make me that way. Like a kid just gifted with his fondest desire. Birthday and Christmas all rolled into one."

"I want—I need—to talk with Chessy and Kylie. Especially Kylie. She'll be hurt by this. She won't understand."

Then her eyes widened in alarm and she glanced frantically at the clock above the fireplace.

"Oh my God, Dash! I have to call them! I completely *forgot*. I promised I'd call them. They were worried. Chessy said if she didn't hear from me she was calling the police. I hope she hasn't already!"

Dash chuckled. "Go call the girls. Tell them you're in good hands. There's plenty of time to explain to them later. But for now put them at ease. I'm glad you have such loyal, devoted friends.

Our friends," he amended. "And Joss, they *will* understand. If they love you—and they do—they'll only want you to be happy."

She surprised him again, this time framing his face in her hands and kissing him full on the mouth. Liquid pleasure rushed through his veins unlike anything he'd ever known. He allowed her free rein, held himself back and let her do the kissing, the exploring. And when she pulled away, her eyes were glazed with passion, surely a mirror of his own.

Oh yes, she saw him. He was filled with triumph and intense satisfaction. The blinders had come off, and she saw him, not as a friend, not as support, but as a man who wanted her with everything he had.

And she wanted him.

There would be many wonderful days ahead, but he'd always remember this one. Not that he harbored any idea that it would be easy and that they wouldn't have obstacles to face and overcome. But they would get there. He'd make damn sure of it.

"I'll be right back," she said in a husky voice. "I just need to tell them I'm okay. And yes, I'll explain everything to them later. They'll want to know. For now I'll just tell them that I backed out of The House. Kylie will be glad. She didn't want me to go."

"She worries about you," he said.

"Yes, and she has good reason to fear the monsters of the world," Joss said painfully. "She didn't want for me what she had to endure for all those years. She fears dominance, control, abuse and being powerless."

"Yes, that's understandable," Dash said quietly. "But you don't fear that from me, do you, Joss?"

The shock in her eyes filled him with fierce satisfaction.

"No, Dash! Never!"

He kissed her again before pushing her upward from the

couch. "Go and make your calls before the police get involved. If I know Chessy, she was absolutely serious about calling the police. It wouldn't surprise me if she hasn't hauled Tate over to your house already. You call the girls. I'll call Tate and let him know you're okay."

SEVEN

JOSS leaned back on her couch with a deep sigh and flopped her head backward to stare up at the ceiling. She felt emotionally wrung out, and for the first time she couldn't blame it on Carson's death or the anniversary of it.

It was a different kind of turmoil, one she'd never imagined when she'd bravely—or rather thought she was bravely—taking control of her future. Now that future was one huge question mark.

She sighed again and closed her eyes, weariness assailing her. She would have drifted off, despite the chaos her mind was in, if the doorbell hadn't rung. And rung again. Insistently.

She knew without confirming that it was likely Chessy or Kylie or even both. They wouldn't have been put off by Joss's phone call simply telling them she'd backed out. They'd want to hear the entire story themselves.

With a resigned groan, she pushed herself up from the couch and shuffled toward the door.

Dash had dropped her off barely half an hour earlier after all the necessary phone calls had been made. He'd kissed her. She shivered as she remembered the raw desire she'd seen in his eyes. Felt the heat of his kiss. Remembered his fingertips sliding down her face to her neck as he'd said good-bye and that he'd see her soon.

The promise in his voice had given her much to think about. Now that she was back on her own turf, so to speak, she had a lot to contemplate and process.

As soon as she opened the door she wanted to groan again. Chessy and Kylie *both* stood staring back at her. Chessy's gaze was sharp and discerning, looking over Joss as if she could peel back the layers of Joss's thoughts. Kylie looked more uncertain—and worried.

Chessy pushed by her, Kylie following behind in her wake.

"Okay, spill it, girlfriend. We don't buy that bullshit you said about simply deciding to opt out of The House and spending the evening with Dash instead."

Joss followed Chessy and Kylie into her living room and flopped back on the couch she'd just vacated.

"And don't think you're going to leave a single detail out," Chessy continued. "I'll sic Tate on Dash if I have to. One way or another, I'll get the dirt, so you may as well cough it up now."

"Are you all right?" Kylie asked anxiously. "Did something happen last night, Joss? Did someone hurt you or frighten you?"

Joss smiled ruefully. What to say to those questions? Yes, no and yes?

"I'm fine," she reassured. "Honestly. It's complicated."

Chessy's lips tightened and she got that "aha" look on her face that suggested she'd known something was up.

"What happened then?" Kylie asked.

"What *really* happened, Joss?" Chessy pushed. "I saw you yesterday. I heard you. And whether you had any apprehensiveness, I know you, and you were bound and determined to go to The House and see it through. And then I get a phone call saying oh never mind, I didn't go and I'm at home?"

She snorted in disbelief.

"I went," Joss hedged.

Kylie's forehead furrowed. "But you said you didn't."

"I didn't say I didn't go," Joss corrected. "I merely said I changed my mind."

"And?" Chessy asked quietly. "What happened, Joss?"

Joss sighed. "Dash happened."

Chessy's mouth rounded into an O about the time realization sparked in her eyes. "Oh shit. Dash was there, wasn't he? Oh my God, did he freak?"

Kylie looked absolutely confused as she jerked her head back and forth between Joss and Chessy, trying to keep up with what was going on.

Before Joss could answer, Chessy pushed forward.

"I'm so sorry, Joss. I should have warned you, but shit. Dash is hardly in there. I mean I know he's a member, but it didn't even occur to me to tell you that, because what were the odds that he'd show up on the night you went?"

Kylie shook her head in bewilderment. "Dash—*our* Dash—goes to The House? *Why?*"

Joss's cheeks warmed and she and Chessy exchanged looks of understanding.

"He's a Dominant," Chessy said gently. "Like Tate."

Kylie went silent, processing the revelation. Tension vibrated from her, and it made Joss uneasy for what she'd have to tell both her friends. But especially Kylie.

Kylie was . . . Well, she was very black-and-white. Her world-view was very narrow and she didn't often venture outside the parameters she'd set. She had good reason to be as she was, but it didn't always make things easy. Kylie was rigid, and this would likely throw her for a loop.

"He was there when I walked in with another man," Joss said in a low voice. "It didn't go well."

Chessy winced. "I don't imagine it did."

"He hauled me out and took me back to his house intending to lecture me after he scraped an inch of skin off my hide. He didn't think I had any clue what I was getting into."

"And did you inform him differently?" Chessy asked.

Joss nodded. "That's when it got . . . interesting."

Kylie's perplexed look deepened and Chessy's eyes widened. Both of her friends sat forward, picking up on Joss's tone.

Joss sucked in her breath, knowing her friends would know sooner or later and she'd rather it come from her.

"Dash said . . ."

She struggled with just how to put it. This was much harder than she imagined because she still hadn't come to terms with it herself!

"What did he say?" Chessy prompted.

"He said that if that was what I wanted—what I needed—then he was going to be the only man who gave those things to me."

"Whoa," Chessy breathed.

Kylie's reaction was a bit more explosive. "*What?* I don't understand. He what?"

"He wants me," Joss said in a low voice. "Has wanted me a long time. I didn't know. I feel so stupid, but I had no idea!"

"Wow," Chessy said. "I mean I used to think, a long time ago, the way he looked at you sometimes . . . I thought there was something there. But then you and Carson were so happy and Dash remained friends with you both, and Dash never made a move after Carson died, so I thought I imagined it."

Kylie's face flushed with anger. "He had a thing for you when you were married to my brother?"

"It's not like he ever acted on it," Chessy gently chided. "You can't control who you're attracted to."

"Carson knew," Joss murmured. "Dash told me that Carson knew and that it didn't affect their friendship."

"I would certainly prefer him to some stranger you pick up at The House," Kylie said, an edge still to her voice. "But I'm worried about this. You and him. I never imagined Dash to be that kind of person. I worry that he could hurt you physically and emotionally, and I worry about the strain it might put on all our friendships."

Chessy's features tightened. "That kind of person? What's that supposed to mean? Tate's that *kind* of person, Kylie, and he'd never hurt me."

"You know I didn't mean it like that," Kylie said wearily. "I'm worried about Joss, okay? It seems like lately she's making a lot of impulsive decisions, and I don't want her to get hurt. And I worry about this thing with Dash. I'm not sure how I feel about the fact he was attracted to his best friend's wife."

Impatience and frustration warred with Joss. "I've considered all of those things," she snapped out. "I've taken into account how it would affect our circle of friends, especially if it didn't work out."

She sucked in a breath before continuing.

"I've never looked at Dash as anything but a friend until now, and I'm not sure how I feel about that. I hate feeling like I'm betraying my dead husband for even considering this. I would have never been unfaithful to Carson, even if I'd known that Dash had feelings for me. And I don't like you questioning his integrity because he had feelings for me that he never acted on until now."

Kylie grimaced and looked away. Chessy leaned farther forward, taking Joss's hand in hers.

"Yes, it could change things," Chessy said in a calm voice. "But you can't live your life without taking risks. If this is something you want to go for, you at least need to try. It's worse to live with the what-ifs than it is to take the plunge and fail. You have nothing to lose and everything to gain."

"I have *everything* to lose," Joss said in a raw voice. "I lost Carson and it would devastate me to ever lose Dash's friendship. It would devastate me to lose yours or Kylie's. I don't want to lose anyone else I love."

Chessy's face filled with love and understanding. It made Joss's eyes go watery, and damn it, enough with the tears. It was time to move beyond all that. To stop being such an emotionally fragile person.

"Sweetie, life is all about risk and there are no guarantees, as you well know," Chessy said gently. "Let me ask you something. If you knew back when you and Carson got married that you'd only have a few short years with him, if you knew he'd die, would you have done anything differently? Would you have walked away from him then to spare yourself the pain of losing him later?"

The question shook Joss to her core. Without even thinking about it, her response was immediate.

"No, of course I wouldn't have walked away! I'd do it all over again, and I wouldn't change a thing, even knowing I'd lose him. Because what time we did have together was wonderful. I wouldn't trade it for anything in the world," she said painfully.

"Then why aren't you willing to take a chance with Dash?" Chessy asked. "What if it works out? What if he makes you happy? What if he gives you what you want and need? What if you find love again? What if you have one wonderful year with him, and he gives you what you need and then you split up? Wouldn't you rather have that year and not live with regret over not ever giving it a chance? You can't stop taking risks just because you lost someone already. It's no way to live, in fear of living in case of pain."

"She has a point," Kylie said grudgingly. "And I do want you to be happy, Joss. Even if it's not with Carson. I'll support you no matter what happens with Dash. As you told me, we're sisters, and we're best friends."

"Thank you," Joss said sincerely. "Thank you both. I don't know what I'd do without such wonderful friends—sisters. You've both given me a lot to think about. And I do have to give this careful consideration."

Chessy squeezed her hand. "We'll leave you to it then. Just know that I'm only a phone call away. And I also want you to know, that no matter what, I love you. Tate and I both love you. And he'll personally kick Dash's ass if he ever hurts you."

Joss smiled, but sadness tugged at her heart. She didn't want to cause a rift between her friends. She didn't want Tate to ever become angry with Dash over her.

Kylie rose and then leaned down to hug Joss fiercely. Joss returned the hug and then pushed herself up to go walk her friends out.

"Keep in touch, hon, okay?" Chessy said. "And if you ever need to talk, just pick up the phone. Night or day. It doesn't matter."

"I will," Joss said truthfully. "And thank you both again for caring about me. I'm not going to do anything to cause anyone hurt. I hope you both know that."

"We do," Kylie assured. "And I'm sorry if I hurt you with the things I said. I do love you, Joss. And I do want you to be happy. I know that Carson would want you to be happy. It takes a pretty special guy to remain friends with a man who had feelings for his wife. If Carson could and did live with that, then so can I."

Joss hugged them both and then watched as they walked down the paved sidewalk to where they were parked out front. She stood there as they drove away and then she went back inside to get her purse and her keys.

It was automatic to get in her car and drive toward the cemetery. She wasn't even aware of what she was doing until she neared the gates leading inside. She braked and came to a stop at the entryway, staring ahead at all the headstones that dotted the landscape.

She'd been coming to talk to Carson. To explain about Dash and ask Carson's blessing. When she'd sworn she was moving on, letting go, and wouldn't return here. Not again.

With a shake of her head, she backed up enough to execute a U-turn and then drove away, aiming her car in the direction of Dash's subdivision.

EIGHT

HE shouldn't have brought her home. He shouldn't have left her alone after dropping such a bomb on her. He should have kept her here with him, within touching distance. Not given her time and space for her to change her mind or talk herself out of what he knew she was agreeing to.

Dash gripped the back of his neck as he poured another cup of coffee and glanced at the remnants of his and Joss's earlier breakfast. In a kitchen that had never entertained another woman. Certainly not breakfast after a sleepover.

He liked her stamp in his home and in his space. Liked the remembrance of her walking into his kitchen wearing his shirt, and those sleepy, beautiful eyes.

He hadn't wanted to let her go. Not after finally making a move to make her his. But it was the right thing to do.

You had to let her go to see if she'd come back to you.

He shook his head at the absurdity of his thoughts. It wasn't like him to spout hokey psychological shit, and he wasn't one of those who indulged in philosophical crap "like if you love someone, set them free."

He was more of a "if you love them, then never let them go" person. And yet he hadn't kept Joss. He'd driven her home and had very civilly informed her that they'd be seeing one another soon. And then he'd kissed her. Not as he'd wanted to. She'd looked too fragile, too close to unraveling at the seams, and so his kiss had been one of comfort and reassurance. Not a kiss of a man consumed with passion for the woman he was holding.

He looked up when his cell rang, and he remembered he had an important call today. He cursed, because his mind was not on business. Bringing in a new partner, while necessary, wasn't ideal at the moment. He'd wanted to ease Joss into it, and then everything had changed. Would this put a barrier between them at a time when she was finally seeing him as more than a friend?

He picked up the phone and strode into his office, his mind quickly shifting gears to the task ahead. He had to put Joss out of his mind, at least until he squared away this particular matter. And then? He was pulling a full-court press. He missed Carson too, but his best friend was gone. His business partner was gone. It was time to start thinking about his own best interests instead of pushing them down, as he'd done for the last six years.

He and Carson had founded a successful consulting business. Corporations called on them when they needed or wanted to downsize and cut costs. Most of their contracts came from the many oil companies in the Houston area, but they also did consulting work for other large corporations and even a few smaller ones.

Carson's natural affinity for people and Dash's analytical mind had been a very successful combination. The two had worked in tandem, Carson on the front lines, wining and dining potential customers, Dash on the back end, doing the analysis, drawing up the proposals that Carson would later present.

Only now Dash had been forced to be both the front line and the back end. By bringing Jensen on, Dash would effectively take over Carson's responsibilities and push himself to the forefront while Jensen would handle the behind-the-scenes details.

"Dash Corbin," he said, when he entered the confines of his home office.

He closed the door behind him and then went to his desk to open his laptop as Jensen Tucker gave his greeting.

"I'm glad you called," Dash said. "We have a lot to discuss. Did you have time to look over the documents I couriered over?"

Jensen Tucker was someone Dash had met through business a few years earlier. He and Carson had dealings with him, and Dash respected the other man. Thought he'd be perfect as a partner when he and Carson looked to expand. That was all before Carson's death.

Dash had set aside their plans and focused on keeping the business afloat because he'd wanted to make damn sure Joss and Kylie were both provided for. Kylie was a damn good office manager, but losing Carson had put a strain on her. Dash had wanted Kylie to take a break from work. Take a few weeks off to deal with the grief and shock over her brother's death, but she'd insisted on coming in to work. She'd needed the outlet, something to occupy her time, but Dash knew it was a temporary bandage. He wasn't sure if Kylie had ever truly dealt with that grief or accepted Carson's death.

Neither Joss nor Kylie would likely take well to Dash replacing Carson, but perhaps Joss would be more accepting than Kylie since Kylie was the one who would have to work with someone other than Dash and her brother.

The two men spoke of their ideas, Jensen adding several of his own that Dash found appealing. They'd met several times already but all that was left was for Jensen to formally accept and the two businesses to merge.

What was once Breckenridge and Corbin would now become Corbin and Associates. Leaving room for further expansion down the road if he and Jensen so chose that route.

Jensen wasn't an arrogant ass who insisted his name be plastered or that he receive credit. Dash wouldn't have minded giving the man his due, but he was content to leave Dash's name at the forefront and work more behind the scenes.

Where before Carson had been the front man and Dash had worked out the kinks, troubleshot and worked the back end, now Dash would take his place, leaving Jensen to do more of the legwork.

He hadn't planned it as a way to be able to give Joss more of his time and not be so wrapped up in his work. After all he hadn't had any clue that he would be making a move this quickly. But the timing was perfect, because if he had his way, work would take more of a backseat to his relationship with Joss now that he finally had her precisely where he wanted her.

The men spoke several more minutes, confirming what Dash already knew. That Jensen would be joining him. All that was left was for him to come on board and for Dash to announce it.

"There's one thing, Jensen," Dash said at the end of their conversation.

"I'm listening."

"I need time—a few days—before we make this public. I want to tell Joss and Kylie myself."

There was a pause. "Are they resistant to my presence?"

Dash could hear the wariness in the other man's voice. The hint of irritation that Dash would approach a business decision allowing emotion to rule. But Dash wasn't heartless.

"They don't know about your presence," Dash said. "And I want it to come from me. No one else."

"And will they be trouble?"

"No," Dash said shortly.

"I can give you a few days. Nothing more."

"That's all I need. We'll meet on Monday. My office."

Jensen agreed and then rung off, leaving Dash sitting at his desk in brooding silence.

He'd told Jensen the women wouldn't be trouble. And they wouldn't, simply because they had no choice in the matter. Carson had left Joss enough to keep her financially protected her entire life, but the business had been left in Dash's hands. Joss had no power, no decisions. She'd have to accept whatever Dash decided. As would Kylie. But neither had to like it, and Dash didn't want this to drive a wedge between them. Any of them.

When he finally made his way from his office back toward the kitchen, he heard the sound of a vehicle outside his house. Frowning, because he wasn't expecting company, he walked toward the window that looked out to his drive.

To his surprise, he saw Joss's car parked there. But she hadn't gotten out. She was still sitting in the driver's seat, her hands curled tightly around the wheel.

A curl of apprehension snaked down his spine as he stepped out the front door. When she saw him, the car door opened and she stepped out.

It was obvious even from a distance that she was upset. She was pale, her eyes large and wounded. And when she lifted her gaze to meet his, fear gripped him.

He was ten kinds of a fool for pushing her so hard, so soon. This was it. She was here to tell him . . . no. And this time, she'd run, and she'd keep running. He may never see her again, and that simply wasn't an option.

He'd lost her before he'd ever had a chance to win her.

She looked desperately unhappy. Sadness shadowed her eyes and that was the very last thing he wanted for her. It hurt him to see her like this. It hurt him to know that he was the reason for her sadness.

"Joss," he began.

To his surprise, the moment he said her name, she hurried toward him and threw herself into his arms. He caught her against him, holding her so she didn't fall. So they both didn't fall. And he savored the warmth of her body, her softness tucked so sweetly against him.

For a moment he closed his eyes and inhaled the scent of her hair, wondering if this was good-bye.

"Oh Dash," she said, his name catching on a sob.

"What is it, honey? Why are you so unhappy?"

He stroked a hand down her hair, pushing it behind her ear as he gently pulled her away so he could look into her eyes.

"I was on my way to the cemetery," she blurted. "I was going to explain to Carson. To ask for his blessing or perhaps make him understand. It sounds so stupid, I know."

Dash slowly shook his head. "It's not stupid, honey. He was your husband. You loved him very much. It's only natural that you'd want to share this kind of thing with him."

She closed her eyes as a tear slid down one cheek. That single tear nearly ripped him in two. He didn't want Joss sad any longer. He wanted her happy. Even if it was *without him*.

"I didn't go," she said. "I couldn't. I promised him—myself— that I wouldn't go there anymore. It's not how I want to remember him. I can't go there anymore. It hurts too much."

"You came here instead. Why?" he asked, dreading her response.

She lifted her gaze back to his, emotion smoldering in those beautiful eyes. Eyes that were drenched with moisture. Misery clouded the depths, and he swore viciously to himself, because this wasn't what he wanted at all.

"Because I have to try," she whispered. "I won't know unless I—*we*—try."

His insides caved in, relief overwhelming him. His knees wobbled and he had to steady himself so they didn't both end up on the ground.

Then he hugged her to him, holding her, savoring her touch and smell. He pressed his lips to the top of her head and closed his eyes, giving silent thanks that she hadn't bolted. That she had enough guts to give them a chance.

It was all he'd ever ask. If he could have this, he'd never ask for another single thing in his life.

"Joss, look at me, honey," he said gently, putting enough distance between them so he could angle her head upward. So she met his gaze.

"If it makes you this unhappy, then you have to know I won't ask it of you. I only want you to be happy. For us both to be happy. Preferably with one another."

"I won't know if you—this—will make me happy unless we try," she said softly. She licked her lips, nervousness evident in her features. "I *do* want to try, Dash. But you have to promise to be patient with me. I don't know what to do here. I don't know how to act or react. I'm without a guidebook. This isn't something I ever imagined happening."

He caressed her cheek, wiping away the last traces of tears.

"We have all the time in the world, Joss. No rush. No impatience. Give me your trust. And your submission. I'll do my very best to ensure you never regret it."

Her expressive eyes gleamed with sudden light. Her pupils flared and he saw the stirrings of desire in the deep pools. Asking for her submission had fired her imagination. Had reminded her of all she wanted.

"What do we do now?" she whispered.

"For now, come inside. Let me make you a cup of coffee.

There's nothing more I'd love than to just sit with you awhile. We can talk. Just be. We'll talk about us. Make a date. I want to take my time with this, Joss. It's too important to rush. I've waited this long. I'll wait a hell of a lot longer if I have to."

"I'd like that," she murmured, her eyes warming.

He saw her acceptance. Not only of what he proposed, but of the inevitability of them. As a couple. He watched closely for any signs of hesitation. Of fear or uncertainty. But her gaze remained steady until he was satisfied that this was truly what she wanted. A chance. His chance to have her.

He was nearly undone by the implications. Joss in his arms. In his bed. *His.*

"There are other things I need to discuss with you," he said, reminded of his conversation just moments ago with Jensen.

She cocked her head to the side, evidently picking up on the change in his mood.

"What is it, Dash? Is something wrong?"

He tucked her hand into his and then guided her into his house.

"No, nothing's wrong. Just something I want you to hear from me."

She tensed but remained silent as he took her into the kitchen where the half pot of coffee remained from earlier.

He poured two cups and warmed them in the microwave before returning to her, handing her one of the mugs.

"Let's go into the living room where we'll be comfortable," he urged.

When he had her settled on the couch, he took the armchair that was diagonal to the sofa, even though what he wanted most was her in his arms. Against him. Her body warming his.

He sipped idly at the coffee, wondering which of the two tasks he should tackle first. Cement their relationship? Or possibly crush her with the news that he was replacing Carson?

He winced, deciding to postpone the latter until after they'd discussed their relationship.

"I know this was a lot for you to take in, especially on the day of Carson's death," he began. "I need you to understand that I didn't plan it that way, Joss. You forced my hand when I saw you at The House. Yes, I absolutely intended to make my move. Soon. But the anniversary of your husband's death wasn't when I wanted to begin this with you."

"I understand," she said quietly. "And I'm sorry, Dash. I don't remember if I told you that or not. But I am. Sorry for the way it happened. For it even happening at all. You have to know that wasn't one of my prouder moments when you saw me at The House. I was . . . embarrassed. That certainly wasn't the way I would have wanted to tell you."

"You didn't intend to tell me at all," he said dryly.

She grimaced and then slowly shook her head. "No. How could I? You were Carson's best friend. I thought your loyalties would be with him. I imagined if you knew, you wouldn't approve. And I couldn't bear your disapproval, Dash. I couldn't lose you. Not over something so . . ."

She trailed off, obviously unsure of the word to describe her wants and needs. He leaned forward, catching her gaze and holding it.

"First of all, I hope we've gotten past your fear of my disapproval. Secondly, your desires aren't meaningless, Joss. They're who you are. They make you who you are, and you can't change that. Not for me. Not for anyone. You shouldn't have to. I understand why you suppressed that part of yourself while you were married to Carson. I get that. But honey, he's gone. You said it best. He's not coming back, and there's no reason for you to continue denying your wants and needs, who you are and what you are. Even if I weren't who I am, I would never expect you to be anything but who and what you want to be. But as we share the same needs and desires, it's my hope that we can forge ahead and discover a new world . . . together."

She swallowed visibly and then leaned back, running a hand through her silky hair. "So what happens next, Dash? I was being honest when I said I'm without a map. Now that I've gotten to this point, admitted to myself and to you what I want and need, what do we do?"

He smiled and then because he could no longer stand the distance between them, he got up and slid onto the couch next to her. It was a compulsion to touch her now that he could. After so long of keeping neutrality between them, the door was finally open. They were embarking down a path there was no returning from.

Regardless of whether things worked out long term for them, there was never any going back to the easygoing friendship they'd maintained for so many years. Part of Dash embraced it wholeheartedly while another part of him feared irreparable damage between them. Of opening a rift that could never be mended.

It was a risk he was willing to take, even if it required the utmost caution. By nature he was cautious. All the risk he incurred was in his business life. His personal life had always been carefully ordered, strictly maintained. His dominance exerted itself, and he always kept his emotions and actions in check. Except when it came to Joss. She brought out another side to him, one never seen or experienced by others.

She made him want to throw caution to the wind and revel in the storm.

Never had he imagined that the part of him he feared she couldn't accept was the one thing she wanted the most. He'd always assumed that he'd have to suppress his natural tendencies if he wanted any chance with her. Never would he have dreamed that she'd not only accept it—and him—but that she would overtly seek it out.

He didn't know whether it made him the luckiest bastard alive, or perhaps the most stupid. Only time—and Joss—would tell.

If only he had a window into the future. Just a glimpse down the road to see if this thing between them flourished and thrived. Then he'd know if he was making the right choice for them both.

But no, there was no looking into the future. Nothing but here and now and his instincts and heart's desire to guide him. He just prayed for the wisdom to differentiate between what he craved most and what *she* actually wanted and needed.

Desire and frustration could color a man's perception for sure. They were two emotions he was well acquainted with since meeting Joss the first time. Wanting, needing her with his every breath. Knowing she would never be his. That she belonged to another man. His best friend.

Fate, the fickle bitch, was finally smiling on him. He just hoped to hell she didn't get the last laugh.

He pulled Joss into his arms and reclined against the back of the couch, bearing her so she cuddled against his chest, molded into his side, her hair teasing his chin. And her scent. God, she smelled so damn good. He was torturing himself needlessly. She was here in his living room, in his arms, asking him what was next. All he had to do was take the leap. Close his eyes and jump.

"As I said, I don't want to overwhelm you, honey," he murmured, trying to collect his scattered thoughts. "So it's important that we take things nice and slow. The last thing I want is to scare or hurt you. But I'm tired of waiting, Joss. I've wanted you so damn long and now that you're here and the gloves are off, I'm ready to move forward."

She slid her open hand over his chest, stopping right over his heart. He picked up her fingers and kissed the tips of each, enjoying the way she shivered in reaction.

So responsive. So expressive. God, what she'd be like in bed. His bed.

His dick roared to life and swelled against the confines of his jeans. What had been a comfortable position was now torture as his body screamed for release.

"You won't hurt or frighten me," she said quietly. "You don't have to worry, Dash. I know you. I trust you."

His breath caught because he sensed there was more to her statement than just those simple words. A request?

"What are you saying, honey? Be honest with me. What are you trying to tell me?"

She pushed upward, levering herself so she stared down into his eyes. Her dark hair, such a startling contrast to her sapphire-colored eyes, tumbled downward, spilling onto his chest until he ached to bury his fingers in it and kiss her until neither of them could breathe.

She licked her lips and then nibbled delicately at her bottom lip, a sign of her nervousness. But her eyes were earnest as she stared down at him.

"I know you want to take things slow. I know you don't want to rush or make a mistake. But I don't want to wait. I want to *feel*, Dash. I want to live again. I want to feel like a woman again. I've been so alone and . . . cold," she whispered. "So very cold for so very long. I want to remember how passion feels. How it feels when a man makes love to me, when he touches me. And I don't want you to ask. Does that sound stupid? I want you to take . . . control. I just want you to do whatever it is you want to do. I want you to make the decisions for both of us."

He stopped breathing. His heart was pounding so hard that he was surprised it wasn't making an audible sound. His blood pumped through his veins with such force that he felt light-headed.

She was handing him everything he'd ever dreamed of on a silver platter. Her trust. Her submission. Her. Just her.

He cupped her cheek, caressing the baby-soft skin with his thumb. "Be very sure of what you're asking, Joss. Very sure. Because I want it. I want it all. And I'll take it. You have to be damn sure you're prepared for the reality, though."

She shivered, chill bumps racing across her arms and shoulders.

"I'm sure," she whispered.

NINE

JOSS'S heart was racing, her pulse thundering in her veins as she took in Dash's dead serious expression. There was something incredibly sexy about the way he looked at her right now. So intense. So determined. But it was the edge in his expression, the tightness of his jaw and features, that gave her a giddy thrill.

Like she'd just unleashed the lion. A very hungry lion. And she was about to be devoured whole.

She shivered uncontrollably at the image of him biting her, sinking those perfectly straight white teeth into her tender flesh. Of him marking her, possessing her, branding her.

All the things she'd fantasized about with a dominant male. Only she'd never imagined Dash in the role of the man dominating her, and now? It was all she could think of. Dream of. Fantasize about.

He'd made her see him for the virile, mouthwateringly gorgeous, alpha male he was. He'd forced her to see beyond the veil of friendship and she *liked* what she saw. Anticipated what she saw and now knew to be true.

Now that she'd thrown down the gauntlet, would he react to the challenge? Would he take her at her word or would he be cautious and take it slow?

It was the last thing she wanted. She didn't want caution or reserve. She wanted it *all*. Everything he had to give her and more. She could see the hunger in his eyes, could see the lust and desire as if it were written in ink on his forehead. He made her feel alive for the first time in three long years. He made her feel feminine and desirable. Beautiful. He made her feel *beautiful*.

And she'd been honest. She didn't want to think. Didn't want to have to make decisions. Maybe that made her a coward, but she wanted to relinquish absolute control. She wanted to . . . surrender.

"God, Joss."

Her name came out a harsh whisper, rushing out in a forceful exhalation of his breath. His eyes burned, a quick and sudden fire that turned her insides to water.

"*Know* what you're saying, honey. Understand what you're asking. Because I'll only ask this once. If you agree, if this is what you want, then there's no going back. You'll be mine and only mine."

She nodded, her throat too tight to give voice to her assent.

"The words, honey. Give me the words so there's no misunderstanding."

"Yes," she croaked. "God, Dash, what do I have to do? Beat you over the head with it? Don't make me beg. I want this. I want *you*."

Regret shimmered in his rich brown eyes, and he put a finger to her mouth. She wanted to lick it, to see if he tasted as good as he looked, as she imagined.

"You'll never have to beg. Not for me you won't. I'll give you whatever you want. Unconditionally and without reserve. And I'll never question you again. But there are a few things we need to get out of the way—important things—before we get swept away in everything else."

"All right," she quietly agreed.

His voice had dropped, the tone serious, his gaze brooding and yet . . . hopeful. Almost as if he was afraid she would change her mind and cut and run. Maybe she couldn't blame him. If it was true that he'd waited all this time, had wanted her all this time, he likely felt like the rug could be pulled out from underneath him at any moment. Or perhaps he thought this was all a dream, one he'd wake from and it would all be gone.

It was a feeling she was well acquainted with. Ever since she'd seen him in The House, her world had been irrevocably altered. It would never be the same no matter what happened between them.

She feared that. Her biggest fear was that this wouldn't work out, that it would end badly and she would have lost not only Carson, but also a man she considered her friend. Perhaps not her best friend. Her friendship with Chessy and Kylie was steadfast, but it was a different kind of friendship than the one she had—or rather used to have—with Dash.

When she'd decided to let him go on the same day she relinquished her hold on Carson's memory, she hadn't been happy. Far from it. She'd felt as though she were losing someone important to her all over again. Only now she stood to gain far more.

Or she could lose it all.

Maybe she was crazy for even entertaining this. She and Dash may well be better off shutting the door that had been opened. But could they ever return to a normal friendship now?

No. Not after all of this. Not after he'd laid it all on the line. Even if she ended the relationship before it ever began, there was no going back to the way it was. Ever.

Her only option was to pursue this. Lay it out just as he'd laid it out so bluntly. And hope like hell that she didn't lose more than she gained.

"You've explained what it is you want and need," Dash said,

his voice now controlled as he stared intently at her. "But we haven't discussed my needs. My expectations. Nor have we discussed your boundaries and what happens if I ever cross them."

Her brow furrowed. They were fast venturing into unknown territory. Of course she had no idea of Dash's expectations. How could she when she'd never dreamed he was the kind of man she craved? A dominant, alpha male unafraid to take what he wanted. Not ask. *Take*.

She didn't want a man who asked permission. She didn't want a man who treated her like a fragile piece of glass. Carson cherished her. No doubt about it. And she loved him for it. Loved him for always treating her so precious. But now? She wanted a man not afraid to cross the line. Because she had no idea what the boundaries were that Dash spoke of. Hers. And she wouldn't until he *crossed* them.

She wanted to see just how far she could be pushed. She was seized by a decadent thrill at the thought of exploring the darker edges of desire. Sex. Power. Dominance. She wanted it all. Wanted to revel in a strong man's authority and control. Oh how she craved it with every fiber of her being.

"We'll start with yours," Dash said, closely examining her as if he could read her thoughts.

Maybe he could. He and Carson had both mercilessly teased her about being an open book. They'd told her she'd never make it as a business partner, not that she had any desire to join their company. She didn't know how Kylie stood working for the two intensely driven men! They'd both told her on more than one occasion that one only had to look at her to have a direct window to her soul.

It could be construed as criticism, but both men had made their statements with great affection. As though it was a compliment instead of a fault.

"But I don't *know* my boundaries," she said in frustration. "How could I? Dash, you know this is new for me. That my only experience comes from my fantasies."

"I know, honey, but we have to establish what you would do if I do cross a boundary of yours. I understand you won't know until it happens. What I want is to implement safeguards for that eventuality. Because I will push you, Joss. I know you think I'm being gentle with you and maybe I am. For now. But once you're under my control, I'll push your limits."

She nodded her understanding.

"Now, many people in these kinds of relationships use safe words. I'm not a fan of them myself, but I understand the necessity of them. Especially for a woman being introduced to this world for the first time. After a while you won't need a safe word because it's my job to find out your boundaries and push you to the very edge without crossing that line. Does that make sense?"

"Chessy told me it was important to communicate with the man I . . . experimented . . . with that I was new to the scene and to make it clear I reserved the right to pull the plug at any time."

"Chessy is a very smart woman. She's knowledgeable about the lifestyle," Dash said.

"She should be," Joss muttered. "She and Tate . . . Well, you know since you both have memberships at The House."

Dash smiled. "I can see the question in your eyes. I could swear I also see a hint of jealousy. Or maybe that's wishful thinking on my part. You want to know if I've ever seen Chessy and Tate, and specifically Chessy . . . naked. Am I right?"

"I'm more interested in whether or not you've ever been with her," Joss said quietly.

Dash's expression softened. "Did Chessy tell you Tate shared her with other men?"

Joss's eyes widened. "Does he?"

Dash chuckled. "Guess you aren't as knowledgeable as perhaps I thought."

"That's not an answer!"

"Does the idea of me being with Chessy bother you?" he asked curiously.

Joss flushed. "Yes. No! Yes, damn it, it does. Sorry. I know I can't judge your past. But yeah, it bothers me a lot. I mean I know you've had other women. I would certainly have never expected you to wait for me forever. How could you have known Carson would die and leave that opportunity for you? But the idea of you being with my friend . . . Yes, it bothers me. I won't lie."

Dash slid his hand over hers, squeezing warmly. "Sorry, honey. I was teasing you and I shouldn't have. To answer your multitude of questions, yes, Tate does, upon occasion, share Chessy with other men. No, I've never participated. Yes, I've seen her naked, though I've tried to be careful and avoid The House when I know they're going to be there."

Joss latched onto the part about Tate sharing Chessy with other men. It boggled her mind because Tate was forbiddingly possessive of Chessy. When they were together, Tate was always in touching distance. When Joss had been married, it hadn't bothered her. She hadn't been envious. She'd been thrilled that her friend was married to a man who so obviously adored her. Jealous of the kind of relationship they had? Yes, a tiny part of her had been very envious.

After Carson had died, it had been painful to watch Tate with Chessy because it reminded her of all she'd had and lost. That close connection to another man. The knowledge that he loved her absolutely and without measure.

"He shares her?" Joss asked again, incredulity seeping into her voice.

Dash gave her a gentle smile. "It's who and what they are,

honey. It's a kink they both enjoy. Tate likes to watch while another man dominates his wife—under his direction. So technically the Dominant acting out a scene with Chessy is in fact submissive because he takes orders from Tate."

Joss shivered at the mental image and wondered what that was like. Could she have sex with a man while Dash watched and directed? Her nipples tightened and came to erect points. Her respirations sped up as pictures flashed through her mind. It was too much to take in. Yes, she'd known of Chessy and Tate's relationship. She knew Chessy gave one hundred percent of her submission to Tate, in and out of the bedroom as she'd discovered recently.

What was it Chessy had said? That she was Tate's to do with as he chose. She hadn't considered to what extent that held true, but wow. As shocking as it was, it was also extremely . . . arousing.

"Is that something that turns you on?" he asked silkily.

She caught his gaze and saw his eyes glittering and she wondered if it turned *him* on. Would he want to do that with her? Give her to another man while he stood on the sidelines? She hadn't imagined Dash to be the sort who would share anything, especially a woman he was in a relationship with.

"I don't know," she said honestly. "In theory it sounds . . . hot. But the reality? I'm not sure how I'd feel about that. It's definitely not something I'd want to do right away. I would think that takes a certain level of comfort. And trust."

Dash nodded. "Very true. The man and the woman have to be in complete accord. Their relationship has to be cemented before introducing elements like that. For the woman, she has to have complete trust in her Dominant in order to allow him to give her to another man. That kind of trust is priceless."

"And for the man?" Joss asked, her curiosity only growing. She felt horribly naïve and ignorant of such things. But now that she'd begun her journey into that very world, she was starved for knowledge. It all fascinated her. "What does he get out of it? Wouldn't he have to have absolute faith in the woman he gives to another man?"

Dash nodded again. "Absolutely. The man has to trust that he is able to provide everything his woman needs, and that her experience with another man is not only pleasurable for both himself and her, but he also has to trust that when it's all said and done, he is the one she goes home with, is committed to, and that the experience doesn't give her a taste of the forbidden that she indulges in when he's not a participant."

"Permission to cheat," Joss murmured. "It blows my mind."

"No, not cheating," Dash corrected. "Not at all. Cheating is emotional betrayal. When consent is given by both parties, there is no betrayal. It's why a relationship has to be absolutely solid before ever venturing into that territory. There can be no doubts, no misgivings, and trust has to be well established between the couple. Otherwise it's a doomed exercise."

Joss cocked her head to the side. "Does it not work out sometimes? I mean do you know of situations where jealousy became involved? Or the woman ends up cheating or is no longer satisfied with what her Dominant is giving her?"

Dash shrugged. "Of course. It happens. I've witnessed couples still in the beginning stages of their relationship rush into situations they have no business being in. It usually doesn't end well. I've found what most often happens is that the man becomes jealous over another man pleasuring his woman and then he starts to doubt his own abilities. He mentally compares himself with the other man in question. Wonders if the guy pleases her more than he can. If she prefers the other guy to her Dominant. As I said, it takes a special level of commitment and trust for such an arrangement to work."

"And it works for Tate and Chessy," she said.

It wasn't voiced as a question, but the inflection at the end of her words made it such.

"Yes, it does apparently," Dash replied. "They're happy. Tate is happy. Chessy is happy."

Joss frowned. "I'm not so sure anymore, Dash. I'm worried about Chessy."

Dash's brow furrowed. "What makes you say that?"

Joss shook her head. "I shouldn't have said anything. I don't want it to get back to Tate. It could be nothing. Just a feeling I have."

Dash frowned. "I'd never betray your confidence, Joss. Nor do I indulge in gossip. And I damn sure wouldn't tell Tate anything that made him doubt his wife. But I'd like to know why you have your 'feeling.'"

Joss sighed. "I don't know really. She just seems . . . unhappy . . . lately. She hasn't said anything. I know that Tate has been very busy at work. But I don't think I'm imagining it. Kylie has noticed too. She actually worried that . . ."

She broke off, ashamed to voice what Kylie had suggested. She genuinely liked Tate, and she didn't believe for a minute that he would abuse Chessy in any way. Things may not be perfect between them but there was no way Tate would ever hurt Chessy. Not physically.

"She worried what?" Dash demanded, concern replacing his frown.

"I shouldn't say anything," Joss said.

"It's too late for that. Now what did Kylie say?"

Joss grimaced. "She worried that Tate was abusing Chessy. We had lunch together. You know that. And I don't know, Dash. She just seems so unhappy lately. And if you bring Tate up, she clams up and gets this look on her face."

Dash looked incredulous. "Kylie actually thinks Tate *abuses* her?"

"I don't know," Joss said honestly. "Kylie is . . . Well, you know how she is. You know what she and Carson both suffered. So it's natural that she would jump to conclusions others wouldn't."

Dash shook his head. "No fucking way. The sun rises and sets at Chessy's feet. Tate is crazy about her. If she's not happy, there has to be another reason. Maybe they argued. Who knows?"

"Maybe," Joss said. "I don't think he abuses her either. Not for a minute. I like him. I like him a lot. And he's so good to Chessy. I look at them and I feel so . . . envious. It shames me to admit that, but it's true. I look at them and I want—crave—what they have."

Dash reached out to stroke her cheek, feathering his thumb over her skin. "You'll have it, Joss. All you have to do is reach out and take it. It's yours. I'm yours. For as long as you'll have me."

She sucked in her breath. Yes, she knew he wanted her. He'd certainly been blunt enough about that. But he made it sound so . . . permanent. And she had no idea what to think about that.

She wasn't looking for permanent. She didn't want permanent. She'd found the love of a lifetime and lost it. She knew she'd never get that back. People just didn't find perfection twice in a lifetime. Once was hard enough, but twice? Impossible.

She licked her lips, suddenly uncomfortable with the direction of her thoughts.

"What about you?" she asked huskily, returning the topic to them. "Have you ever shared the woman you're with? Is that something you enjoy?"

"With the right woman, yes. I can't say I'm lining up to do that with you, though. I've spent too long fantasizing about what it would be like to have you in my bed, under my control. There's no way in hell I want to immediately jump into sharing you with anyone. I'm not saying never. If it's something that turns you on and it's something you want to explore at a later date, then we can cross that bridge when we get to it. For now? I'm more focused on you and me, specifically you. I'm a selfish bastard and I'm very possessive of what I consider mine. And Joss, you *are* mine."

Her cheeks warmed again, but she couldn't suppress the surge of pleasure that winged its way through her veins.

"I'm very okay with that," she whispered.

He smiled. "That's good. Now, let's get back to your boundaries and my expectations."

She immediately tuned in, anxious to hear what all this . . . arrangement . . . entailed.

"To start with, we'll establish a safe word for you. It's important that you only use it when you're genuinely frightened, uncertain or if something hurts you. If anything I do ever hurts you I want to know about it immediately because it will never happen again. We clear?"

She nodded.

"In time I'll know your limits even better than you," he said in a confident tone that caused her heartbeat to speed up.

"And your expectations, Dash?" she prompted.

"It's really simple," he said. "By offering me the gift of your submission, you're placing your care and well-being in my hands. I expect your obedience and your respect. Now, respect has to be earned. I get that. And I'll earn it. Obedience, however, is taught, and I'll teach you well. You'll obey my instructions without question or hesitation. If you truly don't understand a command, you've only to ask and I'll explain. But don't question just because you're nervous or hesitant about complying with my wishes, because that will not please me."

Her eyes widened. It surprised her how horrified she was over the idea of not pleasing him. She wanted to make him happy.

She wanted him to be proud of her, to take pride in her. And she never wanted to do anything to shame him or make him regret their relationship.

Was it her natural submissiveness guiding the ship here? Had she always been this way and suppressed it because she didn't understand it or realize what it was she wanted? Or perhaps she'd only recognized it when she'd come into contact with others in the lifestyle. They'd made her see what it was she was missing.

She licked her suddenly dry lips again. "Are there punishments involved? I know some Dominants . . . Well, I've heard that they punish their women if they disobey or displease them. Is that something you do?"

He smiled. "Many find punishments to be pleasurable. In many cases, punishment is in fact a reward. It sounds twisted and contradictory, but pain can be very erotic, as can control and authority. As to whether I enjoy punishments, the answer is yes. In certain situations."

"Which situations?" she pressed.

"Does the idea of my hand on your pretty ass arouse you, Joss? Does the idea of me tying you up so you're utterly helpless and then flogging you make you hot?"

Her entire body was one giant flush of heat.

"Is it wrong of me to say yes?" she whispered.

His entire expression softened, his eyes glowing with tenderness.

"Honey, nothing about your desires and needs is wrong. Nothing. Do you understand that? I need to know what pleases you, what turns you on, your deepest, darkest fantasies. If I don't know what they are, how can I give you what you need?"

She didn't respond.

He brushed the back of his knuckle down her cheekbone, stroking and then sliding back up to stroke downward again. His touch was infinitely soothing. It also aroused her. Almost violently. Never had she craved something so much as his touch right now. His hands on her body. Mouth on her skin.

"In time you'll hide nothing from me," he continued. "There is nothing you can't share with me. Nor will there ever be. You can be yourself with me, Joss. I'll protect and cherish your heart and soul. You don't need defenses around me. They wouldn't do you a damn bit of good anyway because I intend to strip you of them. Bare. Until there's nothing between us but your delectable skin."

"Your expectations seem simple enough," she murmured. "You want my trust and my obedience."

He smiled. "In theory, yes, quite simple. But obedience entails quite a lot. You'll never know from one day to the next what it is I'll demand of you. The not knowing is a powerful enough aphrodisiac. Anticipation makes it much sweeter."

"And punishments, Dash? We spoke of what turns me on, but what about you? Do you enjoy meting out punishment on your submissive?"

"If you ask if I'm a sadist and enjoy inflicting pain for the sake of inflicting pain, no. I won't set you up to fail just so I can punish you, honey. That's not the way I work. Because I find much more satisfaction in your obedience. That's what will make me happy. Not you failing a task so that punishment ensues. However, yes, there are some certain aspects of punishment that I enjoy, though I'd argue they aren't true punishments because both me and my submissive enjoy them. I prefer to think of them as sexual pleasure. That's what it's all about. My pleasure. And yours."

"You like the control," she mused. "Not necessarily inflicting pain, but inflicting your will on the woman."

"Now you're gaining a greater understanding."

She smiled. "I'll get there, Dash. Just please be patient with me. I want to learn, to explore. But I'm a little wary and uncertain. I'm so afraid of making a mistake. Of disappointing you and myself."

His expression became utterly serious. He framed her face in his palms, forcing her to look directly into his eyes.

"You will never disappoint me, Joss. I need you to know that. We'll find our way together."

She drew in a deep breath and then smiled. "I believe you. Now that we've gotten all of the talk out of the way, when do we start? And how do we start?"

TEN

"I want you to move in with me," Dash said bluntly.

Joss's eyes widened in surprise and her lips parted, a rush of air escaping the perfectly formed bow.

"But Dash . . ."

"No buts," he said firmly. "This won't be a part-time relationship, Joss. Nor will it be a secret."

Her brow furrowed with consternation and she shook her head. "But I don't want anyone to know! Not that I'm ashamed of you. That isn't it. But this is *private*. I don't want our relationship, what our relationship is, to be public knowledge!"

He leaned forward and pressed his lips to her forehead. "It won't be public, honey. Not certain aspects of our relationship. I'm not going to flaunt it. But I'll want you here with me, twenty-four hours a day, seven days a week. I don't think it would be a good idea for me to move in with you."

He let his words, their meaning settle over Joss and he saw the instant she realized his purpose.

"Of course," she said in a low voice. "I wasn't thinking. Of course you wouldn't want to be in the house I shared with Carson. It wouldn't be fair to you."

"Or to you," Dash said gently. "This is a fresh start for you,

Joss. It needs to be. And in order to do that, you have to break free from the past so you can move ahead with your future."

"It's just so sudden," she murmured. "So much has happened and it's happened so quickly. I've barely had time to process it all."

"The only thing me giving you more time would accomplish would be giving you more of a chance to back out. I'm not going to allow that. I've waited too long. I won't let you go now. Not when I'm so close to having everything I ever wanted. Maybe that's selfish of me. But I can live with it if you can."

She smiled ruefully, her eyes lightening as she glanced up at him. "I can live with that. What else then? I just move here with you?"

"That's a start," he said. "Once you're here, we'll move further into the physical—and emotional—aspects of our relationship. You'll find I'm a very demanding man, Joss. I hope to hell you're prepared for that. I won't be easy. I won't have mercy."

Her pulse leapt, jumping at the pulse point of her neck. "I don't want you to," she said huskily.

"Good. Now why don't we go over to your house so you can pack a few things. You don't have to get everything today. Just what you need for the next few days. We can always go back for more later."

Left unsaid was his concern that once she was here, once they embarked on their sexual odyssey, she would run and run hard. Go back to her home and shut him out forever. He hoped to hell she was as strong as she put off and that she truly did want all she'd said.

He had no doubt he could give her everything she could possibly want or need and so much more. The question was whether she knew exactly what it was she truly wanted.

"I'll need to let Chessy and Kylie know," she said. "They'll worry. They know about you. I mean they know about us. But still, it'll shock them that we're moving so quickly. I'll endure a lecture from Kylie."

"And not Chessy?" he asked in amusement.

Joss smiled and shook her head. "No, Chessy was supportive of my decision to go after what I wanted. She was concerned, don't get me wrong. But she understood it and encouraged me to go through with it. Kylie? Well, she thought I'd lost my damn mind, and she's scared to death of what I'm getting into."

"Then it should make her feel better to know you aren't hooking up with some random stranger who doesn't give a fuck about you."

"It upset her that you had feelings for me while I was married to Carson," Joss said quietly. "I think she felt like you betrayed Carson."

Dash scowled. "I never betrayed him. He knew. He damn well knew and we were still friends. He trusted me. He knew I'd never act on that attraction. He was my friend."

"I know that," Joss said gently. "Kylie is just very black-and-white. She has a narrow view of the world. It surprised her and she doesn't deal with surprise very well."

Dash grimaced, knowing that Jensen replacing Carson would come as another big surprise to Kylie. An unwelcome one at that.

"Why are you frowning?" Joss asked. "Are you angry that Kylie was upset?"

Dash shook his head. "No. I was just thinking about what else I wanted to discuss with you. And with Kylie."

She looked worried and he hastened to soothe her, not wanting anything to disrupt the mood between them. Not when things were so . . . good.

"You may or may not know that before Carson died, we had talked about taking on another partner. I wasn't sure how much Carson shared with you regarding business. I know he was determined that you never have to work or worry about money coming in."

Joss's expression immediately became worried. "Is it money, Dash? Is the business not doing as well? I can go back to work, you know. Even though I quit a year after Carson and I married—at his insistence—I've kept up my certifications and I've taken the necessary classes so I could keep my nursing license. I can go back to work. I don't want to be a financial burden on you. Do what you must to keep the business going. It's what Carson would have wanted."

He put his finger to her lips, loving her more than ever. She was so selfless and generous. Most women would be horrified at the mere thought of their financial security diminishing. But not her. She was prepared to go back to work. In fact, he remembered it had taken Carson an entire year to talk her into quitting. No, they hadn't needed her salary, not by a long shot, but Joss hadn't wanted to quit. She hadn't wanted to be dependent on Carson. He admired her for that.

"There's nothing wrong with the business, honey, and the truth is, what Carson would have wanted is not for you to go back to work. You have to know that. Carson only wanted you safe and happy and provided for. And he ensured that by leaving you a percentage of the business. You don't have to worry. I plan for the business to expand and become more profitable than even before. It's a fact that things faltered a bit after Carson died. My head and heart weren't in it and it suffered the first year. But I pulled it together. What I wanted to tell you and Kylie both is that I'm taking on a partner. Carson and I had planned to expand before he died. Those plans got put on hold as I focused on making sure the business remained solvent. But now is the perfect time to take on someone else. I can't do it all myself. I don't have the desire to. There are other things that I'd rather focus on now. You. And I can't do that if I'm tied to the desk and traveling all the time."

Joss blinked in surprise. "You're replacing Carson?"

He winced because while he knew Kylie would draw that same conclusion, he'd hoped that Joss wouldn't see it that way.

As if reading his mind, Joss leaned forward, her expression earnest, her eyes soft with understanding. "I don't mean it that way, Dash. I'm not upset that you're 'replacing' Carson. I suppose I just didn't realize how demanding the business was. Oh, I know how much time Carson put into it. But what I didn't know at the time was that you stepped up and shouldered far more responsibility so that Carson would be free to spend more time with me. Thank you for that, Dash. I know you made a lot of sacrifices, but I'll forever be grateful that you gave that to him. To us. That I got to spend as much time with him as I did before he died. I'll always treasure those memories. The trips. The days at home just spending time together."

Moisture rimmed her eyes, but she didn't allow herself to cry. It looked as though she exerted great restraint not to break down even though her lips trembled with that effort.

"And if by taking on another partner, it enables you to step back and have a life that doesn't revolve around the business, then you have my full support. You've given so much to me and to Carson. It's only fair that you have a turn at reaping the rewards of your success."

Damn but this woman just made him happy. He was so damn proud of her. Now if only Kylie would take the news as graciously as Joss had. But then he'd expected no less from Joss. He hadn't entertained even for a moment that she would be resentful or that she'd object. He'd definitely considered that it might be upsetting for her. That was only normal. She was a woman who'd loved her husband, a love most men would kill for, and if they could have that kind of love and devotion from a woman like Joss, they'd never want for more in their life.

He wanted it now. Craved it. Was obsessed with it and her. He'd do whatever it took to make her happy again. He'd prove to her that lightning could strike twice in the same lifetime. She'd mentioned on more than one occasion, in passing, that she didn't expect to ever find love again. Not like she had with Carson. Hell, she'd resigned herself to that fact, accepting it.

Fuck that. If she only gave him the chance, he'd prove to her that she *could* be that happy again. That not only would another man give her the world, but that he'd love her and cherish her. He'd wrap her in cotton and protect her from everything that could ever hurt her.

"Have you decided on his replacement?" she asked quietly.

He covered her hand with his and squeezed. "Honey, I'm not replacing him. No one could ever replace Carson. He built this business. He made it what it is today. I helped, yes, but this was his vision. His brainchild. He was a brilliant, business-minded man."

She smiled. "Have you decided on the new partner yet then? Or have you only just recently made the decision?"

"Yes and no," he said. "I met Jensen some years ago when Carson was still alive. Carson and I had actually discussed bringing him in as a third partner when we decided to expand. And we'd planned to in the next year. But that was before he died so unexpectedly."

"Is that his name? Jensen? Have I met him?"

She frowned, her brow wrinkling in concentration. She was

evidently trying to place the name. He almost laughed. As if she'd ever notice another man with Carson in the same room. It had been one of the things he most envied about Carson. Joss's absolute devotion and fidelity when it came to her husband.

When he was with her, she had eyes for no one else. Her focus was on him, her love for him evident in the warmth of her gaze. More than one man had looked at Carson with envy in his eyes. And the hell of it was she was oblivious to her allure. She had no idea that in a room full of business associates every male's eyes were on her. Lusting after her. Eaten alive with jealousy over Carson's good fortune.

"He was likely at one or more functions that you and Carson attended. But I don't think you were ever formally introduced. He knows who you are, what you look like, but I doubt you'd know him. He's not a loud person or someone who gains attention. He's quieter, stands back and observes. That's what makes him a solid option for the business. He has a good eye for people. Uncanny instincts."

"When will you tell Kylie?" she asked.

He grimaced again. "Soon. I spoke with him today to finalize things. And then I asked him for a few days before we went public and proceeded with bringing him on board. I wanted to tell Kylie—and you—the news myself. I didn't want to just spring it on her at work."

"You don't think she's going to take it well," Joss murmured.

Dash shook his head. "Certainly not as well as you took it."

Joss sighed. "Kylie is very loyal. She's also, as I've said, very black-and-white. No middle ground. She and Carson were very close. Carson was all she had for so long. He was all she had when they both lived in hell with their father's abuse. And yes, I agree. I don't think she'll take it well at first. After she's had time to think about it and time for it to sink in, she'll come around."

"I hope you're right," Dash said. "Because it's a done deal. No backing out now. And it's what's best for the company. In time she'll realize that."

This time Joss reached out to squeeze his hand. "Yes, she will. She's very intelligent and Carson said she was a dream as an office manager. He used to say that she kept you both organized and well-oiled."

Dash laughed. "Yes, she certainly does that. I hope you're right. I'd hate to lose her over this. It was important to Carson that you both be provided for. He wouldn't want Kylie working somewhere else."

"Just don't let her make any rash, impulsive decisions," she said. "If she does something hasty like quit, don't accept her resignation. Give her time to consider. I'm sure she'll come around."

Dash nodded. "Don't worry. I have no desire to train a new office manager."

"You know if you need help, all you ever have to do is ask. I don't know much about your business but I'm a quick study."

He kissed her again, letting his lips linger against her temple, inhaling the sweetness of her scent.

"I know, honey, but I like the idea of you not working. I like the idea of having all your time. I'm a selfish bastard. I don't want to share you with anyone and certainly not a job."

She smiled and then sighed, her expression becoming troubled as he brought the topic back to their relationship.

"You really think it's a good idea for me to move in? You don't think it's too sudden? I'd hate to sabotage us before we ever get off the ground."

"Let me worry about that," he said gently. "I want you here,

Joss. In my space. My life. My bed. There are certain aspects I won't rush you into and I'll be infinitely patient. But others? Like you moving in with me and you being with me all the time? Yeah, I'm going to press because it's what I want and I always go after what I want. I don't lose, Joss. And I'm damn sure not going to lose you."

ELEVEN

JOSS finished packing her bag and then surveyed the three stuffed suitcases with a rueful smile. It looked as though she were moving out, and she supposed, in fact, she was. Dash wanted her with him. All the time. She still wasn't sure exactly how she felt about that.

She'd enjoyed every moment of her marriage to Carson. She'd liked not being alone, and in the months following his death, she hadn't wanted to be alone even for a moment. God, when she looked back at who and what she was, she wanted to cringe.

A trip to the grocery store was enough to put her in tears. Dash had come, had taken her to the grocery store so she could at least keep her kitchen stocked. She didn't eat out. Hadn't eaten out in a year after his funeral.

Only after a year had she begun to venture out, at Chessy and Kylie's urging, for regular lunches with them. But dinner? She hadn't been out to dinner since Carson died. It had been too painful. She hadn't wanted to socialize. To get caught up in meaningless chitchat when all she could remember was the way she and Carson laughed and loved.

Carson loved eating out. Loved good food and fine dining. He'd taken her to some of the best restaurants in the country—and Europe. It was through him that she developed the taste for good wine. She didn't know the difference between a red and a white much less the nuances of the different labels and brands.

Her wine cabinet here was still fully stocked, not a single bottle opened, except for Carson's favorite. A wine she made sure she kept on hand. On the anniversary of his death, she'd open that bottle and drink with him. With his memory. She savored every sip, wishing with her every breath that he were there to share it with her.

She sighed. No more of that. She was turning a new page in her life. Maybe it was a mistake. Maybe she was making the worst decision—an emotional decision. But she was an emotionally driven person. She wore her feelings on her sleeve, and as Carson and Dash had both commented on, one only had to look into her eyes to know exactly her mood.

She didn't have the artifice or the energy to project what she didn't feel. She didn't even know how to mask her emotions. It wasn't something she was adept at. As a result, Carson had always known when she was unhappy or worried. And he'd moved heaven and earth to rectify whatever had gone wrong.

Dash would be like that. She knew. He was warm and kind. Gentle and understanding. He'd be patient with her and he wouldn't fault her for any mistakes she made. But she didn't want to make mistakes. She wanted to meet him as an equal, not some weak woman who needed him to fix her.

Only she could fix herself. Her shattered heart. That was on her and no one could do it for her. Perhaps this was just the first step in reclaiming her independence, which sounded stupid when she wanted a dominant man. When she didn't want to make decisions or be forced to make difficult choices.

She didn't want to think. She just wanted to . . . *be*. That was all. Happy. Whole again, or at least as whole as she could ever be when she was missing half of herself.

Maybe Dash could do that for her. Maybe he would give her

that missing piece of her soul. And maybe she'd made a huge mistake. How would she know unless she tried?

Taking a deep breath, she lugged her suitcases into the living room and checked her watch. Dash had said he'd give her two hours before he returned to get her. It was agreed she'd take her car to his house and park it in case she needed to go somewhere when he wasn't available. But he'd made it abundantly clear that for the most part, she would be with him. He would take care of her, of her every need, and he didn't plan for them to spend much time apart.

She wasn't sure how she felt about that either, but the lonely part of her heart swelled in relief that she wouldn't be alone any longer. The rest? She'd take it as it came. One day at a time. It did her no good to focus on the future when she needed to live for today. The present. Because as she'd well learned, the future was not guaranteed. It was what you made it.

She had fifteen minutes before Dash would arrive. Plenty of time to call Chessy and Kylie and let them know of her decision. But she'd have to endure the conversation twice and that wasn't what she wanted. She'd have to endure questions, disbelief, surprise and doubt.

It would be far easier just to e-mail them both and explain her plans.

Satisfied with that decision, she walked over to where her laptop lay on the coffee table and sat on the couch, opening it up to her e-mail program.

After pondering the best way to tell her friends what was going on she finally decided to just take the plunge. State it matter-of-factly. Not get into details. Just a basic explanation and how to reach her if they needed her. She fully expected her cell phone to start ringing the moment they got the e-mail so she typed a request that they not do so.

She informed them that she needed a few days with Dash to get her bearings. She promised to update them and that they'd get together for lunch at the end of the week. Although she didn't look forward to that lunch because it would end up an inquisition.

She'd just hit Send on the e-mail when her doorbell rang. Her pulse accelerated and she rose, smoothing her palms down her worn jeans.

This was it. Dash was here to pick her up.

She glanced around her house, her and Carson's house, sadness tugging at her heart. Maybe she should have moved right after he died. It likely wasn't healthy to maintain the house as it had been when he was alive. Pictures of them and him still dotted the living room and other rooms of the house.

Joss and Carson happy. Smiling. In love.

She had finally cleaned out his closet and put away his clothing. But all his knickknacks? Trophies, plaques, pictures? They were still where they'd been hung or positioned on the shelves. No wonder Dash didn't want to move in here. It was hard to compete with a dead man, and with all the reminders of him displayed around the house, how could Dash hope for Joss to focus on him?

As she opened the door, she muttered a silent vow that she was going to go hard at this. That she'd give Dash one hundred percent of herself. No holding back. No reservations. And she darn sure wasn't going to be doing a mental comparison between Dash and Carson when it came to sex. It wasn't fair to either man and it wasn't fair to her.

Dash stood there, sunglasses covering his eyes, but when she looked up at him, he shoved them up over his head so he could look back at her. There was something in his gaze that made her quiver on the inside. Intense. Brooding almost. And there was marked triumph reflected there.

"You ready?" he asked in a low tone.

She smiled, determined not to show any hesitancy. She was fully committed. On board. She wouldn't waffle now and she'd give Dash no reason to question her commitment.

"I have several suitcases," she said hesitantly. "I wasn't sure what to bring so I brought a little of everything. One of the suitcases has all my girly stuff. I was certain you wouldn't have all that."

He smiled back. "Not to worry, and honey, now that you're mine, it's my duty and honor to provide for you. So if there's something you need later, I'll make certain you get it."

Her brow wrinkled. "But I don't want you to buy me things, Dash. I can afford it."

His eyes narrowed and glinted fire. She had the sudden impression she'd taken a wrong turn and she'd been determined to get off on the right foot with him.

"You are mine," he said in a firm tone. "And I provide for what is mine. You've gifted me with your trust and your submission. My duty as the one who takes care of you is to provide for your every need and desire. So get used to it, Joss. I have every intention of spoiling you shamelessly. I won't be pleased if you question every gift I bestow on you."

"Oh," she breathed. She hadn't looked at it like that, but she still had a lot to learn about this kind of relationship.

So far it seemed she got far more out of the bargain than he did. Pampered? Spoiled? Cherished? What did he get in return? He'd said that she was enough. That her trust and her submission were enough. But surely there had to be more in it for him.

"Now, if we've got that out of the way, point me to your luggage and I'll get it out to the car for you."

She started to tell him that she could get it or at least help, but as if anticipating just such a statement, he silenced her with a quick, stern look. Her hand fluttering upward, she motioned toward the living room where her suitcases were.

It took him two trips to get all of her things in the trunk of his car, but he ushered her into the passenger seat and then slid in on the driver's side. To her surprise, before he even started the engine, he leaned over and kissed her. Hard. Hungry. None of the tender reserve he'd shown before.

He devoured her mouth until her lips tingled and swelled. When he pulled away, his lids were heavy with desire and his eyes blazed fire.

"Hope to hell you know what you're getting into," he murmured as he cranked the ignition. "You said you didn't want to wait, so it begins now, Joss. Right now. As soon as we step into my house, you belong to me. You're mine to do with as I please."

The words slid over her, warm and arousing. Her pulse beat hard at her pulse points, and her mouth went dry. Not even licking her lips alleviated the sudden dryness.

"I'm ready," she said quietly. "I know what I'm getting into, or at least I have a good idea. And I want it, Dash. I want . . . you."

There was savagery in his expression. She shivered uncontrollably. Arousal. But mostly anticipation. She was on the brink of something new and possibly wonderful. Maybe it wasn't. But she'd never know unless she took that leap.

When they arrived at Dash's house, Joss opened the door and started to get out, but Dash reached over the center console and took her hand, pulling her back.

Without a word, he got out and walked around to her door. He reached in for her hand and she slipped her palm over his until their fingers were twined.

She was moving into Dash Corbin's house. She was going to have sex with Dash Corbin. God, Dash was going to *own* her. She started to shake as soon as she got her legs underneath her. Reaction was quickly setting in.

It had all seemed so surreal and now it was here. She was about to embark on a sexual journey and she was scared to death. What could Dash possibly want with her? He was experienced in this lifestyle. He had certain expectations. Expectations she couldn't hope to meet.

"Joss, honey, you're shaking like a leaf."

She glanced up guiltily. She hadn't wanted him to see her nerves. But as he said, she was trembling head to toe. How could he not see it? Or feel it, for that matter. Her hand was solidly twined with his, and her skin felt cold and clammy despite the warmth of the day.

He squeezed and offered her a reassuring smile. "It's going to be okay. I know you're nervous, but there's no reason."

"It just occurred to me that you have a lot of experience in this lifestyle while I have none," she muttered. "What do I possibly have to offer you? I'm sure a novice isn't high on your list of wants."

He stopped just in front of the door and fixed her with his steely gaze.

"What you have to offer me is something no one else can ever hope to offer me. You, Joss. You're giving me you and that's all I want and need. I swear it. You have no idea how long I've dreamed of this. Of us. Together. Yes, I want to have sex with you, but it's so much more than that. You may not believe it yet, but you will. I guarantee it."

His quiet vow comforted her. She squeezed his hand back and then smiled.

"You're certainly good for my ego, Dash. I haven't felt beautiful in so very long. I haven't felt desirable. I haven't felt desire, for that matter."

"And now?" he prompted. "Do you feel it now? For me?"

"Oh yes," she breathed. "It shocked the hell out of me. I never expected to feel this way about you. Never imagined wanting you so badly. But there it is."

"Thank fuck," he muttered. "Glad to know I'm not the only one suffering here."

She grinned. "Then how about we do something about that suffering?"

He looked shocked. So much so that she regretted her forwardness. Embarrassment crept up her neck, a wave of heat that flooded her cheeks.

Then he let out a low growl, leaning down to claim her mouth.

"I think that's a damn good idea. Let's go inside. I'll get your things later. I want to get you settled in. I want you to be comfortable here, Joss. I want you to consider this . . . home."

He tugged her inside, a wave of cooler air washing over her, removing the heat from her cheeks.

She'd been to Dash's many times, but she'd never ventured beyond the living room, the kitchen or the guest bathroom. He led her through the living room and up the stairs to the master bedroom.

A prickle of awareness tingled up her spine as she took in the masculine feel to his bedroom. The bed was huge with a multitude of pillows. It was a four-poster, and she hadn't imagined him to like that kind of furniture. It almost seemed feminine, something a woman would have in her bedroom.

"What are you thinking?" he queried.

She glanced up and then smiled. "Silly thoughts. I was looking at your bed and thinking that it seemed incongruous with what I know about you. I would have never imagined you having a four-poster."

A gleam entered his eyes and amusement quirked his lips. "I

need something to tie my woman to. It's only natural that I'd have the proper equipment for the job."

Heat flooded her cheeks once more. She had to be bright red. Then came the realization that she wouldn't be the only woman in this bed. It shouldn't bother her, but it did. Dash owed her no explanations for his past sex life. She'd been married, for God's sake. She certainly couldn't have expected him to remain celibate when he didn't think he'd ever have a chance with her.

"What the hell are you thinking now?" he demanded.

"More silliness," she murmured.

"And?"

He wasn't going to let it go, and hell, she was honest to a fault, much to her detriment.

She sighed. "I was thinking about the other women who've been in your bed—this bed," she said unhappily. "Stupid, I know. But it bothers me."

Dash turned her so she faced him and he gripped her shoulders, holding her directly in his line of vision.

"There haven't been any women here, Joss. Not here. I won't say there haven't been other women, but I didn't bring them here. I couldn't. Maybe before Carson died, I may have gotten to that point, but after? I couldn't bring myself to even form a relationship. Not when I was so set on you."

"I don't even know what to say," she whispered. "It shouldn't mean so much, but it does, Dash. It means a lot that there hasn't been anyone for a while."

He leaned toward her and kissed her forehead. "It means a lot that there hasn't been anyone for you since Carson. I was afraid that by waiting so long, by waiting to declare my intentions as long as I did, that I would lose you to another man."

She wrinkled her nose. "How do you know there haven't been other men?"

He grinned. "I would have known, Joss. You may not have seen me every day, but I checked up on you. I was watching. And waiting."

She harrumphed but smiled, touched by the fact he'd been there. Waiting. For her.

He walked her backward until the backs of her legs bumped the edge of the bed. Then he lowered her down until she was perched on the edge. Once she was sitting, he gathered her hands in his and knelt in front of her.

Now, granted she didn't know everything about dominance and submission, but didn't he have all this backward? Shouldn't she be in the position of subservience to him? Not the other way around!

"What are you doing, Dash?" she asked quietly. "Shouldn't I be the one kneeling for you?"

He smiled, squeezing her hands in his. "Darling Joss. I'm at your feet, literally. I admit it's not a position I normally find myself in. But with you all the rules change. I wanted to put us on more equal footing for the discussion to come. And perhaps I wanted to humble myself to you to make a point."

"What point?" she asked curiously.

"That for all the power you cede to me, in fact, it's you who holds all the power in this relationship we're embarking on. That may sound contradictory, but it's absolutely true. You hold all the cards. You're in the driver's seat. Because it's you who decides whether to give me your submission. It takes a strong, confident woman to hand over control to her partner. And the thing is, yes, you are submitting to me, but my desire to please you far outweighs my desire to dominate and control you. Does that make sense?"

She nodded. "I suppose. I just never thought of it in that light."

"Consider it now," he directed. "And listen to everything I'm about to tell you. I'm going to lay out the rules, though I hate that word. There are no rules between us, honey. No hard-and-fast guidelines. What we do, I want us to enjoy. I want to bring you pleasure and I want you to please me. It's a mutually beneficial arrangement. One I hope we both find happiness in."

"Fair enough."

"Now, to get to my expectations. Or rules if you want to call them that. I prefer to consider them requests. Requests that you will choose whether to agree to or not. But I want you to have a very clear picture of what will go on between us because I want you to have the opportunity to back away. It's not what *I* want. I hope to fuck you want the same things I do. But there's only one way to find out. Lay out the ground rules and we'll go from there."

"Okay. I'm ready, Dash. Don't hold back any longer. I'm dying over here because I don't know what it is I'm supposed to do. I'm so afraid of making a mistake. Of disappointing not only you but myself."

His smile was exquisitely tender. It made her feel so very warm on the inside where she'd been cold for so very long.

"You won't disappoint me. I don't believe it's possible. The only way you'll disappoint me is if you walk away without giving us a fair chance. I'm not saying it's going to be all roses and sunshine in the beginning. There will be adjustments we both have to make. Compromises. But together I think we can overcome any obstacle to our relationship."

"You say the most wonderful things," she said in an aching voice. "I don't know how you're able to see to the heart of me, how you can know so much about me when I know so little myself."

He stroked his hand over her cheek and then through her hair to twist the loose strands.

"Rule number one, and these are in no particular order. So bear with me while I get to them all. And be patient. I know you'll have questions, but try to save them until the end when I'm finished outlining the guidelines. Then, once I've covered all the bases, you can ask any questions you want. Anything you don't understand we'll talk about. I'll be as honest as I can possibly be with you, Joss. Even if I worry the truth will frighten or intimidate you."

"Then tell me," she said simply. "I'm listening, Dash. I won't interrupt or question you until you're finished. No matter how hard that may be," she added ruefully.

"Okay then, the first is that when you are here with me, in this house and we're alone, I want you naked unless I tell you otherwise. Starting now, or rather when we're finished going over my expectations."

Her eyes widened but she kept her promise and bit her lip to prevent her immediate objection.

"Second, when I tell you to do something, I expect instant, unconditional obedience. You may not understand why I ask you to do what I ask, but I expect you to trust me and at least be willing to try."

She nodded. That didn't sound too hard, although she had no idea what those requests would be. Part of her anticipated the unknown. The other part of her was terrified. She hated not knowing exactly what she was walking into or agreeing to.

"I don't expect you to kneel in my presence unless I request it. The only time I want you to kneel is if I summon you. Then I'd like you to kneel, with your arms resting on your thighs, palms splayed upward. This is a standard position of submissiveness. Thighs open so that no part of you isn't accessible to me or my gaze. The only other time is when I return from work or if I'm away for any reason, when I return, I'd like for you to be in the living room, on your knees, waiting for me. I want you to be the very first thing I see when I walk through my door. I want a reason to want to come home, and if you're here, waiting for me, believe me, sweetheart, it's what I'll want more than anything. You, waiting, my reward after a long day."

She got the impression this was important to Dash. Something he enjoyed and craved. And if that was the case, she wanted to do it for him. She wanted to please him and bring him happiness. She never wanted to disappoint him. She had too much pride for that. No, she may not have the experience other women he'd been with had, but that wasn't going to prevent her from doing her damn best to be the most desirable submissive he'd ever had a relationship with.

There were no half measures for her. From the moment she'd decided to embark on this new lifestyle and explore her sexuality and her needs, she'd known that she'd throw herself completely into it. No holding back of anything. She'd give wholly and unreservedly of herself and hope that the man she was with would appreciate the gift she gave. And nothing in Dash's words had given her any reason to doubt that he would most certainly cherish and protect her gift of submission.

"When I issue a command, I expect instant obedience. No hesitation. No questions. I want you to trust me to take you to a place you'll enjoy and feel safe in. I'll never ask you to do something that I think you'd object to. That doesn't mean I won't push you out of your comfort zone. But as I mentioned earlier, the further we get into this, the faster I'll learn what your boundaries are and I'll never purposely cross them unless it's something we discuss and agree to try."

Again she nodded, because as with his other expectations, they didn't seem unreasonable.

"Now, we briefly touched on punishments and pain. Pain can be very erotic if administered correctly. Both for the man and the woman. Many women enjoy a man exerting his dominance with crops, belts, his hand or any number of other methods, all of which I'll introduce you to over time.

"But I'm not into punishment for the sake of punishments. I prefer to think of them as rewards. Which sounds stupid, but after you've experienced the various levels of pain, spanking and other things as well, I think you'll understand what it is I'm trying to explain to you.

"I will absolutely push the line. I'll bring you damn close without crossing those lines. I'll pay attention and in time I'll be as in tune with your body as even you are. It's my job as your Dominant to know exactly what you want and need, sometimes even better than you will."

"I want that," she said quietly. "I want a man who will take. A man who won't ask. Who won't force me to make decisions. I *want* those choices taken from me. It excites me. I can't explain the need or the craving I have for that, but it's there. Maybe it's always been there. And I want that from you, Dash. I'm prepared to go a lot further with you because I *trust* you and I *know* you'd never willingly hurt me."

"I appreciate that trust, Joss. It humbles me," he said gently. "You can't know how precious it is to receive that kind of gift from you."

"Is there anything else or have we covered it all?"

He smiled. "Impatient little submissive, aren't you? I love your enthusiasm, Joss. Your willingness to put so much faith in me to know what you'll enjoy. Yes, there will be other things, but I don't want to overwhelm you on the very first day you've moved into my house.

"You'll sleep in my bed every night. There are times when I'll want to bind you in the bed so that you're helpless and dependent on me for everything. I'll make love to you while you're spread out and tied to my bedposts. Where your body will be available to me whenever I choose to take it. And I'll take you often, Joss. Before we go to bed at night. During the night. And first thing in the morning before you're fully awake. I'll slide into your beautiful body and I'll be the first thing you feel each morning. I'll be the last thing you know when you go to sleep at night. And you'll go to bed knowing you are mine and that you belong, heart and soul, to me. You'll never have cause to doubt it because not a day will go by that I won't prove that to you."

"I've not heard a single downside to this," she said ruefully. "Quite frankly it all sounds too good to be true."

His expression grew more serious. "It won't all be perfect, Joss. You need to know that going in. You need to prepare yourself for the fact you may not enjoy everything I have planned. The very last thing I want is to frighten or repulse you. Or make you do something you aren't comfortable with. It's why it's so important for us to communicate. I want you to be brutally honest with me even if it's not something you think I want to hear or know. I want your promise that you'll tell me what's going on in your head when we do these things. I'll want to know how you feel, how what we do makes you feel. I don't want this to be you sacrificing your pleasure and enjoyment because you're worried about disappointing me. Believe me when I say that if I'm unable to bring you ultimate pleasure, then I don't want to be doing this.

"It may sound on paper like it's all about me. And for some Dominants it is. It isn't about their submissive's pleasure or her desires or even her happiness. I'm not that selfish, however. I hope to fuck I never become that self-centered. Pleasing you makes me happy. It's all I want. It's what I demand. So yes, while it is somewhat about my pleasure and you pleasing me, know this: making you happy is what will make *me* happy and content. I need that, Joss. I need *you*."

She wrapped her arms around his neck and held on tight, burying her face in his neck.

"What I think you are is perfect. So perfect that I wonder if *you* aren't too good to be true. Not just this situation but *you*."

"I think we're on the same page here," Dash said with a smile. "We seem to be saying the same things but perhaps in a slightly different way. But we both want the same things. You want to be happy and you want me to be happy in our relationship. And conversely, I want you to be happy, first and foremost, because trust me, honey. You being happy will make me extremely happy."

She let out the air from her lungs in a long exhale.

"I want this, Dash. I'm ready to dive in and take the plunge. I'll be honest. I don't know if I can stand a few days with you walking on eggshells and me never knowing when it all begins. I'm ready *now*."

"Then what I want you to do while I'm getting your suitcases from the car is to undress. Take your time and use the bathroom. Whatever makes you feel more comfortable and at ease. I want you naked the entire evening. I want to cook you a special meal and feed you by my own hand. And I want to enjoy the sight of your gorgeous body while I'm doing this for you. And then, when we're done eating and ready to think about bed? Then we'll go to bed together and see if you're every bit as sweet and fucking sexy as you are in my dreams. It's time to make my dreams come true. Mine and yours."

TWELVE

JOSS surveyed her reflection in the mirror and winced at the stark fear in her eyes. They were wide and it was obvious that she was jittery as hell.

Naked. He wanted her naked, and God, but that made her utterly self-conscious. He expected her to parade around with no clothing. To eat a meal with him. Naked. No barriers, no shield, no protective measures.

It was the height of vulnerability and yet it was also a signal of her trust and her willingness to do as he'd asked, or rather demanded, no matter how gently the demand had been voiced.

She sucked in a deep breath and then ran a brush through her hair, debating whether to leave it down or clip it up. Deciding that leaving it down offered at least a small measure of protection, she set aside the brush and arranged her hair so it fell over her shoulders in the front and covered at least part of her breasts.

Her nipples peeked through the strands of her hair though and she wondered if it was in fact a more erotic sight than if she'd pulled her hair up and left her breasts completely bare.

There was only one way to find out. Leave the refuge of the bathroom, quit hiding like a coward and gauge Dash's reaction to her nudity.

He'd certainly been blunt about his desire for her. She'd seen the evidence of his arousal in his eyes, in the way he spoke. But then he hadn't seen her naked. Hadn't touched her any more intimately than a few caresses to her face and her arms.

Now he would have unfettered access to any part of her body. Her breasts. Her pussy. She flinched at the crude term, but there were certainly more vulgar terms for the female anatomy than *pussy*. Words she hated. *Cunt*. That was the worst and she hoped it was a word Dash would never use.

It was silly to be such a prude about her body or how it was referred to. But she couldn't control her reaction to the harsher words. They brought to mind unpleasant images. Reduced sex to mindless fucking. No intimacy or tenderness. She wanted those things. *Needed* them.

No matter that she was turning over her body, her soul, to another man. That she wanted to submit and craved a man's dominance. She still wanted to be treated respectfully, and it was important to her that she wasn't just a sexual conquest. A woman to be used and then discarded as though she meant nothing.

She wanted to matter. She wanted to feel again as she'd felt when she was married to Carson. Wanted that connection to another man. Maybe she was a fool for even starting down this path. But she'd never know unless she tried, and Dash was a man she did trust. As determined as she'd been to move forward with her decision, the moment the man from The House had approached her, dread had filled her. She'd been uncertain and afraid even as she sought to go through with it.

She now knew that regardless of whether or not Dash had been there and called a halt to the whole mess, she wouldn't have gone through with it. She would have chickened out and ran, and she would have never gone back.

In a way she was grateful that Dash had been there and that he'd intervened, even as humiliating as she'd found the entire experience. Because it forced his hand. It made him act on long-held desires. And now she could see if this was truly what she wanted, and she could do it with a man she knew would never hurt her.

But there were different kinds of hurt. Not just physical ones. It was the emotional pain she feared the worst. Of somehow messing up a friendship she valued, a friendship she'd desperately clung to after Carson had died.

If she lost Dash too, what would she do?

She shook her head, refusing to go there. She'd procrastinated long enough. If she didn't get moving, Dash would know she was standing in there wavering. He deserved better than a woman who was having second and third thoughts. She'd agreed to this. She'd been firm in her commitment. She wasn't backing out now. Or ever.

Gathering her courage, she opened the bathroom door and stepped into the bedroom. Her suitcases were empty and stacked against the far wall. Her eyes widened when she realized he'd unpacked all her belongings and put them away already.

She walked to the closet, curious, and when she opened the door, she saw all her things she'd packed hanging on hangers. She took up the right side while Dash had moved his things to occupy the left.

Her shoes were neatly lined up on the floor beneath the hanging clothes.

She glanced at the dresser and knew without looking that he'd put away her panties and bras and pajamas. Her cheeks flushed hot when she imagined him sorting through her intimate wear and putting them away.

He'd said he would be in the kitchen, but the thought of walking in there, naked, sent terror through her veins. It made her achingly vulnerable. Powerless. But wasn't that the point? She was ceding all power to him. She'd made a point of saying she didn't want to make choices, that she wanted them made for her. It still discomfited her, that it made her appear weak and spineless. But what was it Dash had said? That it took a strong woman to submit to a man?

She held on to the assurance. Tucked it away so she could remind herself of those words every time she felt she was weak.

"Okay, this is it, Joss," she murmured to herself as she stood at the door of the bedroom. "No going back now. Once you walk out of here your decision is made."

She stood a moment, battling herself, trying to summon the courage necessary to take that final step. Her hand curled around the knob and she yanked the door open, striding through the doorway before she could talk herself out of this insanity.

She walked to the head of the stairs and looked down, seeking any sign that Dash was close or that he'd see her descend the stairs. But no, he'd said he'd be in the kitchen and that he'd give her all the time she needed to prepare.

How the hell could she ever be prepared to walk naked into the kitchen where a man waited who had been very blunt about his intentions?

"Stop being such a coward," she admonished herself fiercely as she forced her way down those steps.

At the bottom, she didn't hesitate. *Take the plunge.* She headed for the kitchen, determined to get that first moment of awkwardness away. The sooner she got it over with, the sooner her nerves would settle and maybe the fear would melt away.

Dash had his back turned to her, tending to something on the stove when she entered the kitchen. She did so quietly and yet he still knew the instant she came in. He turned, his eyes flaring with appreciation as he took in her appearance.

They burned brightly, smoldering as his gaze raked up and down her body. But it was the approval that put her at ease.

"You look just as beautiful as I imagined," he said hoarsely. "Even more so than I dreamed. You've occupied plenty of my fantasies, honey, but the reality has nothing on those dreams."

She smiled, bolstered by his praise. Maybe this wouldn't be so bad after all. Her shoulders slumped as she relaxed and some of the awful tension that had her in knots loosened and she could breathe normally again.

He set a pot off the stove and then hurried toward her. To her surprise, he slid his hand around her neck and pulled her to him, his lips finding hers in a heated rush.

"You have no idea how long I've dreamed of this moment," he murmured against her lips. "You. Naked. In my home. Here in my kitchen while I prepare a meal I intend to feed you by my hand. It's more than I ever dared hope for, Joss. I hope to hell you know that."

"I do now," she said with a smile as he drew away, his eyes glittering with desire.

"Go into the living room and get comfortable," he directed. "I'll bring in a tray momentarily."

His gaze lingered a moment longer before he reluctantly turned away and went back to the stove.

As he'd directed, she went into the living room and sank into the sumptuous leather. She wasn't cold, but the urge to pull one of the throws around her was strong. But that wasn't what he wanted. It wasn't what he'd commanded of her, and she wouldn't start their relationship off on a bad foot by disobeying his very first directive.

A few minutes later Dash entered the living room carrying a tray with one plate. Evidently he'd been serious about feeding her, because there was no extra serving. He stopped at the coffee table and slid it onto the glass top before settling onto the couch next to her.

To her surprise he reached for one of the pillows and placed it on the floor next to his feet. Puzzled by his action, she sent him an inquisitive look.

In response he simply held out his hand to hers, his gaze steady and . . . challenging? Was this a test? And if it was, what was she supposed to do?

When he continued holding out his hand, but not reaching to take hers, she slid hers into his and his fingers curled around hers.

"I want you to kneel on the pillow so that I can feed you," he said in a low, husky voice.

She held back the questions that burned her lips. Instead she simply nodded and rose, with his assistance. She sank onto the pillow as gracefully as she was able, and remembering his instructions for when she knelt, she spread her thighs and rested her hands, palms up on the tops of her legs.

"Very good," he murmured. "You're a natural at this, Joss. Make sure you're comfortable and we'll begin our meal."

It was a little mortifying to be sitting, thighs splayed where he could easily see her most intimate parts. And yet her clit tingled, swelling with her arousal. Her nipples hardened and her breathing shallowed, little puffs of air escaping her parted lips.

He forked a bite of the pasta and sautéed shrimp, gently blew on it before pressing it lightly to his lips to test the temperature. Then he held the fork to her mouth, prompting her to open.

As he held the fork for her to eat, his other hand delved into her hair, stroking and twisting the strands around his fingers. He kept up his gentle assault on her senses and he fed her more, each time bringing it to his lips first.

There was something decidedly intimate about him feeding her. How he ensured that it wouldn't burn her by testing it first. The idea that the food had been to his mouth first and then to hers was as jolting as if he'd kissed her.

Gradually she relaxed, the tension that coiled in her muscles loosening as they continued their intimate dinner in silence.

What would happen after? He'd said they'd go to bed. He'd hinted that they would have sex. But her mind was overwhelmed with the possibilities. Would he tie her up this first night? Would he exert his dominance immediately, as she'd asked him to, or would he go slower? Ease her into his world?

She couldn't decide which option held more appeal. She wanted to experience the full measure of his dominance but she didn't want to be overwhelmed from the very start. She wanted this to work.

Trust.

He'd asked for her trust. Had told her to put her faith in him. That he'd come to know her boundaries, her needs and her desires better than herself. If this was going to work, she had to do just that. Put herself into his care. Fully in his care. And trust that he'd never take things too far.

He held a glass of wine to her mouth, gently tipping it so she could take a small sip. Emotion knotted her throat when the flavor hit her tongue, making it hard to swallow. She held it in her mouth a long moment before she composed herself enough to swallow without choking on it.

It was her favorite. How had he known? It was a wine Carson bought for every birthday and anniversary. And though she'd drank Carson's favorite every year on the anniversary of his death, she hadn't tasted *her* favorite wine since the last time she drank it with Carson.

"Good?" Dash murmured.

"Yes," she said huskily. "My favorite. But then you knew, didn't you?"

He smiled. "Of course. There isn't much I don't know when it comes to what pleases you. I told you I was prepared to spoil you shamelessly. This is only the beginning."

A drop of wine slipped from the corner of her mouth and when she would have lifted her hand to wipe it away, he stopped her and then leaned forward.

"Let me," he murmured.

Instead of wiping it with his fingers, he swept in and lapped at the corner of her mouth with his tongue.

A burst of heat singed her skin. He didn't just lick it away quickly. He tongued the sensitive area and then nibbled at her lips before swiping one last time with his tongue.

"Delicious," he said, and she knew he wasn't talking about the wine.

Intimacy surrounded them, cloaking them and enclosing them in a tight circle of desire and heat. Nothing else existed. The rest of the room faded away. There was just him and her and the delicious meal he'd prepared and served her in such an intimate fashion.

She'd imagined many things when she'd considered the pathway she was taking. But nothing had prepared her for the reality. Would it have been this way with another man? She knew it wouldn't. No one but Dash could ever provide her with this experience. The depth of this experience.

"Do you have any idea how beautiful you look?" Dash said in a voice edged with desire and arousal. "Do you have any idea how long I've dreamed of this? Of you at my feet, eating by my hand, naked. So damn beautiful that it's a physical ache inside me."

She cocked her head to the side, curious as to the effect. She

could see the intense satisfaction in his eyes and it made her wonder why. What was it about a woman at his feet that gave him
such pleasure?

"Can I ask you something, Dash?"

"Of course."

He sat back so he could see her fully. She was careful to maintain her position because she wanted him looking at her just as
he was right now. With so much approval and . . . contentment.

"What is it about a submissive woman that appeals to you so
much? I've often wondered about Chessy and Tate. It's obvious he
loves her so much. He practically worships her. He's so . . . possessive of her. It's why I can't wrap my head around the fact that
he shares her with other men. But I'm straying from the point,"
she added with a light laugh. "I want to know why it appeals to
you so much." She swept her hand down her body, indicating her
position. "You like this—me—in a submissive position."

He touched her hair, stroking his hand down the long tresses,
pulling them briefly away from her breasts so he could see her
fully. There was definite male satisfaction in his gaze. That
approval removed her hesitance. Gave her confidence where
before she'd been so vulnerable.

"How to explain how I feel?" he mused. "I don't know that
there's a cut-and-dried explanation for why it pleases me. It's not
a power trip. In some cases, yes, it's about power. But for me, it
brings me great pleasure, and yes, satisfaction. It's a heady sensation for a woman to put her absolute faith and trust in me. That she
trusts me to provide for her. That she gives up control because
she trusts that I'll give her what she needs. That I'll take care of
her. That I'll absolutely protect her with my life."

"You like to be needed then."

He paused a moment, weighing her words. "I suppose that's
one way to put it. But it goes much deeper. My instinct is to pro-

vide. To protect. To absolutely cherish, spoil and pamper my woman. In this case, you. But it's a drive strictly personal to you. With other women, yes, I've enjoyed all those things. It brings me pleasure to be able to give those things to another woman. But with you it's very different. I don't just want your trust and submission. I *need* them. I need to do these things for you, Joss. Never think even for a moment that another woman is interchangeable with you. That it would be this way with another woman. Because that simply isn't true."

"I hate that you've suffered so long," she said painfully. "I never knew, Dash. I don't know what I would have done if I had known. You mean a lot to me. Even when Carson was alive, you meant a lot. It would have hurt me to know you were hurting. I couldn't have stood it."

He smiled tenderly at her, his eyes glowing with warmth and affection.

"It's why I was determined that you not know, honey. You have such a huge, soft heart. You would have been in an untenable position. You loved Carson and were absolutely faithful. He knew it and I knew it. It's why he never worried that I had feelings for you. One, he knew that I would never act on them. You both meant too much to me for me to ever drive a wedge between us. But he also had absolute faith in you. He knew you would never be unfaithful to him. That you'd never even entertain the idea. I knew that as well. It wouldn't have been fair for me to have revealed what I felt for you. It would have only hurt you and that's the last thing I ever wanted. Carson made you happy. You were happy and you damn sure made him happy. What else could I ask for? It seemed selfish to insert myself because the end result would have only been pain for us all. You. Me. Carson. I loved you both. And you would have never strayed, so what was the point? I wouldn't have wanted you at Carson's expense. It would have devastated him and I would have lost a friend. You would have lost friends, your life, everything. All for me. That wasn't what I wanted for you. It was never what I wanted for you. I only want you to be happy. And so I waited. I waited for you to be ready. But there was never a question of me stepping in. Once Carson died, I knew without a doubt that I would be the only man in your life."

"That's a heavy answer for such a simple question," she said in amusement. "Certainly gives me a lot to think about."

He cupped her chin and rubbed tenderly over her skin, his thumb feathering over her lip.

"I don't want to weigh you down or burden you unnecessarily. I don't want you to think at all. I only want you to feel. I want you to feel what I feel. I want you to burn with the same need that I burn with—that I ache with. And then I'll ease it, Joss. I don't want you hurting. Ever. I'll give you everything you could possibly ever need."

"I need . . . you," she whispered, finally giving voice to her most pressing need.

The evening—entire day—had been an exercise in frustration. She was restless and edgy, wondering, constantly battling with herself over whether she was making the right decision.

How could she know until he made love to her?

He hauled her up and into his lap before she could even blink. His hand pressed possessively against her thigh as he anchored her to his body. Her legs were draped over his lap toward the end of the couch and she was nestled into his body just as though she'd been made for him. They fit perfectly. His hard, muscled body was the perfect complement to her much softer one.

His hand moved up her body to cup one breast. For a moment

he simply held it, feeling the weight of it in his palm. Then he brushed his thumb over the straining peak and she sucked in her breath.

It was a bolt of electricity, shocking in its intensity. If she had any doubts about their chemistry and whether they were compatible in bed, those doubts fled in an instant.

She ached for him. Her body was aware, painfully so. Every nerve ending was on alert. She was wet already and he hadn't even ventured close to her most intimate flesh.

"Do you want me, Joss? Right now? Are you ready for me?"

"Yes," she whispered. "Tell me what to do, Dash. I don't want to mess up. I want our first time to be . . . perfect."

He smiled, kissing her nose and then her closed eyes and then her mouth, pulling gently at her bottom lip with his teeth.

"I guarantee that it will be perfect for me. You in my bed? There's no way to mess that up. But I'll do everything in my power to make it perfect for you, honey."

She framed his face in her hands, forcing his gaze to hers. "Don't hold back with me, Dash. Don't treat me like I'm breakable. I want . . . everything. I don't want you to hesitate or fear overwhelming me. I want to be overwhelmed. I want *you*."

He emitted a low growl, one that sent a cascade of chill bumps over her skin. Her nipples puckered into rock-hard points, aching for his touch. His mouth.

Then he simply stood, carrying her with him. She gasped at his strength, how effortlessly he picked her up.

His gaze was fierce, his eyes burning with fire as he stared down at her.

"Your safe word, honey. What is it?"

She blinked, her mind going blank at his demand.

"Think of one and hurry," he urged. "And use it if I go too far. But be sure, Joss. Don't use it unless you are absolutely at your breaking point. Trust me to take you there. I won't be easy, but the minute you say your safe word, it ends."

She frantically searched her mind, frustrated by how frighteningly blank it was. Damn it! How hard could a safe word be to think of? *No*? *Stop*? Those wouldn't do. They were words she might cry out in the heat of the moment and not mean them. It had to be unmistakable. Something that would stop him in his tracks, though she couldn't imagine ever wanting him to stop.

"*Ghost*," she finally croaked out.

If it surprised him, he didn't show it. No emotion flickered in his eyes. Would he object to her using a mention of her husband when they were in bed making love together?

"*Ghost* it is," he said in a strained voice. "You say that word and I stop no matter how far into it we are. Trust me, Joss. I'll stop no matter how hard it may be. I'll protect you. I swear it."

She reached up to caress the hard line of his jaw. "I trust you, Dash."

He kissed her hard, breathless, every bit of his pent-up desire unleashed in that single moment. It was like a violent thunderstorm, one that excited her. There was no fear. No hesitation. She wanted this. Wanted it so much she ached, she hurt.

"I hurt, Dash," she whispered, voicing the fleeting thought in her mind. "Make it stop. Make love to me. Make it all stop."

His gaze grew tender once more, his breaths ragged and filled with the same edgy pain she herself was experiencing. He was as desperate for this as she was.

"I'll make you feel good, honey. I'll make it good for both of us."

THIRTEEN

DASH carried Joss up the stairs, impatience simmering in his veins. He kept telling himself to take things slow. No matter what Joss said—demanded—no matter how much she said she wanted him not to hold back, he tempered his urges, not wanting to fuck this up. Not when he finally held all he desired in his arms.

He gently deposited her onto the bed and stood back, staring down at her gorgeous body. Her eyes were drugged and heavy with desire. Yearning. Her hair was splayed out over his pillow and her body. God, she was beautiful. She'd said she hurt, that she ached, but God, so did he.

His dick was about to come out of his pants. He wouldn't be surprised if his erection tore right through his jeans.

He had to be patient because if he wasn't careful, the minute he touched her, the moment he finally got inside her, he'd come violently and it would all be over within thirty seconds.

He wanted this to be fucking perfect. He wanted to tease and torment Joss until she was desperate for release. Though she'd said she wanted him not to hold back, she wanted his dominance, wanted him to exert his control and authority over her from the start, he knew he couldn't do it. Not yet.

This first time had to be perfect. He wanted to lavish his love on her. He wanted to make love to her. There would be plenty of time for sweaty, mindless fucking, but no, even when he allowed himself to lose his tightly leashed control, it wouldn't be fucking. It would never be something so crude with Joss.

When they made love, no matter the circumstances, whether she was bound and helpless or if he flogged her pretty ass until it was rosy with his marks, it would be something beautiful. Just as beautiful as she was.

"I don't even know where to start," he breathed.

Always he was in control. His restraint was something that never failed him. He was confident in his abilities to please the woman he was with. He never faltered. Never hesitated. But now? He felt like he was making love for the first time in his life. That he was an untried virgin with no idea what to do with the veritable feast of womanhood that lay before him.

As he pondered those thoughts, the realization came that this was, in fact, the first time for him. His first time to make love. His first time to have sex when his emotions, his heart, were involved. He'd never been in love with the women he'd been with.

Desired them? Yes. Aroused? Absolutely. But his heart had never been involved to the extent it was with Joss. He was terrified of doing the wrong thing. Of touching her wrong. The pressure he put on himself was overwhelming. The fear of failure. Of not making this as perfect as he wanted.

It was a hell of a position to be in. His heart's desire within touching distance and he was too afraid to take the plunge.

Joss, sweet, loving Joss seemed to know exactly what he was thinking—feeling. She smiled and extended her hand, an invitation for him to come to her.

"It's all right, Dash," she said, her smile as soft as her silky skin. "I'm nervous too. But we'll get through this together. I trust you to make it beautiful—perfect. How could it be anything else between us?"

He let out a groan, pissed at himself for allowing his uncertainty to show. Some Dominant he was when he was paralyzed with fear over touching her.

Then he lowered his body to hers, allowing his weight to press down on her, but he propped himself up on his forearms so he wouldn't crush her. She was tiny and delicate, so much so that she looked as though she could be broken if handled too roughly. But it wasn't her body he was most concerned about. It was her heart. Her emotions. He didn't want to overwhelm her. He didn't want her to fear him. Never that. Anything but that. He couldn't bear it if she ever looked at him with fear in her beautiful eyes.

Holding himself up on one arm, he traced the lines of her face with his free hand, committing to memory every second of this first time. He could scarcely comprehend that she was finally his. That she was in his bed, naked, and that he'd be making love to her in just moments.

He hadn't wanted her to be overwhelmed, but in fact, he was utterly overwhelmed himself.

"I've waited so long for this," he said, his voice cracking with emotion. "For you."

She smiled and turned her cheek into his palm, nuzzling farther into his touch. Then she pressed a kiss against his hand, just a simple, sweet gesture that turned his heart over in his chest.

"Make love to me, Dash," she whispered, her eyes burning brightly. They glowed in the soft light of the bedroom, alive with answering desire.

He lowered his mouth to hers, inhaling her scent as he tasted her lips. He pushed in with his tongue, licking over hers, exploring her mouth.

He was so hard that it was painful. He had to get rid of the barrier between them. He wanted his flesh against hers. Wanted to feel her softness and her warmth.

"Give me a minute to get out of these clothes," he murmured against her lips. "Don't move."

She smiled again and stretched, lifting her arms above her head. It was a gesture of surrender. Was it intentional? A signal of her submission?

He removed his clothes, nearly tearing them in his haste. Her eyes widened when his erection sprang free from constraint. He glanced down and winced, understanding her surprise. He was harder than he'd ever been in his life. His dick strained upward, so swollen and tight that the veins were clearly outlined. The head was nearly purple and already liquid leaked from the tip.

He didn't dare touch himself. He didn't trust himself not to spend himself right then and there.

"You have a beautiful body, Dash," she said shyly, color blooming in her cheeks.

He felt heat stain his own cheeks, embarrassed by her scrutiny. Never had he felt self-conscious about his body before. He kept in shape. Took care of himself. He wasn't normally modest, but it was important to him that Joss appreciated his physique. Maybe that made him vain, but he wanted her approval. He wanted her to want him every bit as much as he wanted her.

"You're who's beautiful," he said sincerely. "So damn beautiful you make me ache, Joss."

She arched her body in silent invitation. He needed no urging. He moved swiftly to the bed, no thoughts of dominance. Of commanding or arranging her in a submissive position. Tonight all he wanted was to have her. To seal the relationship beginning between them. Dominance—her submission—could come later.

"Spread your legs, honey," he said huskily. "Let me see that pretty pussy. I want to taste you. I've been dying to taste you. I want you to come in my mouth. All over my tongue."

She trembled and chill bumps danced across her skin. Her nipples beaded and puckered, an invitation for him to taste.

He wanted it all. And before the night was over, he'd taste every inch of that delectable skin. No part of her would go unexplored. He'd know what pleased her, where her pleasure points were.

He was dying for her to taste him as well. To have her mouth wrapped around his dick, her tongue lapping at his balls. But there was plenty of time for that. They had all the time in the world. Soon. Soon, he'd have complete mastery of her body. He'd have her complete obedience and submission. But tonight was all about her. Sating her desires, showing her how good they could be together.

When she hesitantly parted her thighs, giving him a clear look at her feminine flesh, he saw moisture gleaming on the delicate folds. Satisfaction gripped him. She wanted him. Was highly aroused. He desperately wanted to push into that sweet pussy, to feel her heat consume him, grip him like a fist. But he forced himself to exercise restraint.

Instead he closed the distance between them, crawling onto the bed between her splayed thighs. Unable to resist, he ran a finger through her folds, lightly grazing her clit before circling her tiny opening.

She arched upward like a shot, her reaction intense and immediate. She gasped when he continued his careful exploration. He dipped one finger inside, barely rimming her entrance. She was dripping with desire. So wet and moist. He could take her now. She was certainly ready. But he wanted her mindless. Completely out of her head before he took them both over the edge.

Savoring the thought of ultimate satisfaction, he continued touching her, petting her, bringing her closer to orgasm. When she began trembling, her entire body tightening, he drew away, giving her a moment to come down.

"Dash . . ."

His name came out needy, desperate. He chuckled and kissed the inside of her thigh, lightly grazing the skin with his teeth. She shivered again, already working back up to release. He planned to take his time, savoring every second of this experience.

Using his fingers to gently part her folds, further exposing her to him, he leaned down, inhaling deep, absorbing her scent. A low growl worked from his throat. He was desperate for her. He wanted to dive in, devour her with his mouth and then later his cock.

His balls ached with the need to possess her. And then an unwelcome thought intruded, ripping him from the fantasy of fucking her long and hard. Another groan, this time of dismay, ripped from his mouth.

"What's wrong, Dash?"

Her worried question had him raising his head. He sighed, disgusted with himself for not addressing this sooner. For not even thinking about it. He'd been so wrapped up in securing Joss's consent, so focused on the act itself that he hadn't given any consideration to protecting her.

"I'm so sorry, honey. God, I could kick myself in the balls for this. I can't believe this didn't come up before now. I gave no thought to protecting you."

Her brow furrowed in puzzlement. She didn't understand what he was getting at.

"Birth control," he said gently. "I have no doubt that you're safe. I'm not worried about getting anything from you and you have nothing to fear from me. It's not that I want to use condoms. Hell, I'd give anything not to have to use them. But we have to consider pregnancy, Joss. And if you prefer me to use condoms, I will, absolutely. Whatever you want."

Her cheeks bloomed with color and she averted her gaze a moment. He hated that the moment was spoiled. They were both so into it that this unwelcome intrusion was like a slap in the face, effectively stifling the mood.

"I don't want to use them either," she said softly. "I don't like them. Carson . . . We used them at first, when we were first together, but I'm sensitive and they made me . . . dry."

It was obvious she was embarrassed by the intimacy of their conversation. Her cheeks flamed with color and she wouldn't meet his gaze.

"I don't want to do anything to hurt you," he said. "I want you to be comfortable. If we have to wait, we will. I won't use something that you won't enjoy."

"I'm safe," she said. "I was on birth control when Carson was alive. He didn't want children. At least not right away, and as I said, condoms weren't an option. I never went off them, even after he died. I probably should have. It's not as though I anticipated having a sexual relationship with anyone. I couldn't. But it was habit and it never occurred to me to go off them. They regulated my periods and made them more bearable for me. Before I went on them, my periods were difficult. They were irregular and for the weeks I was on them, it was awful. I was moody, I hurt and the cramps and headaches were unbearable. For a time, I had to take pain medication just to make it through my period. My doctor advised that I go on birth control even before Carson and I were married, but I hesitated because I feared not being able to get pregnant when I went off them. I've read a lot that it takes some women a long time to get pregnant after going off birth control and I wanted children very much. I was disappointed that Carson was so resistant, but when it was evident that he wouldn't bend, I really had no choice, no reason, not to go on birth control, especially since condoms weren't an option."

"I understand," Dash said, relief gripping him. "And are you okay with being with me without condoms? I'm safe, honey. I can provide you my medical history. I've never been with any woman without condoms. Not even once. And I have regular checkups. But there hasn't been another woman in a long time."

Her eyes softened. "You don't have to justify your sexual history to me, Dash. And yes, I'm okay with you not using condoms. I trust you. And you already know there's been no man for me since Carson."

Her face flushed again and she ducked her head.

"He was my first. My only. I was a virgin when we met. And when he found out, he insisted we wait until we were married. And since our courtship was such a whirlwind, it wasn't as though we had to wait long. He wanted to marry me much sooner than he did. If he'd had his way, we would have been married within weeks of meeting. It was me who insisted we wait. I wanted him to be sure."

"And not yourself?" Dash asked.

"I was sure of him," she said softly. "I knew he was the one. I loved him—fell in love with him from the start. But I wanted him to be certain. I didn't want us to rush into a marriage if he wasn't absolutely certain that I was whom he would be happy with. And I wanted him to be happy. He had such a hard childhood. He deserved to be happy."

Dash's heart turned over all over again. He was seized by his own love for this special, generous woman. Most women would have jumped at the chance to marry Carson Breckenridge. Wealthy. Handsome. Successful. And he loved to spoil Joss. He did so shamelessly. From the very start. Yes, Dash had his own set of reservations over the speed of Carson's relationship with

Joss. Carson was his best friend and he hadn't wanted him to get hurt. He, like Joss, well knew of his past. His horrific upbringing.

But all reservations had fled when he'd seen firsthand how fiercely loyal and devoted Joss was to Carson. She didn't have a mercenary bone in her body. She'd insisted on continuing her job as a nurse even though Carson had pressed her to quit from the moment they started dating.

She'd persisted, however, because she hadn't wanted it to be perceived she was with Carson for his money. It was only after a year into their marriage that Carson had been able to persuade Joss to quit. And he'd done so by telling her of his desire to have her all to himself. So she could travel with him on the many business trips he took. When Joss was working, she'd been tied to her schedule and she couldn't up and leave on a moment's notice.

It had frustrated Carson, because he'd wanted Joss with him at all times. And so he'd pressured her into quitting so her time would be his.

Dash had worried that Joss wouldn't be happy once she quit her job. She was a natural in the medical field. Her specialty had been pediatrics, and before she'd married Carson, she'd planned to go back to school to become a nurse practitioner.

All of that had changed the moment Carson entered her life. Did she have regrets? Did she have the desire to complete her training and go back to work? It was something he'd discuss with Joss later. Right now he wanted to reestablish the mood that had been broken by his boneheaded move.

"You deserve to be happy again," Dash said tenderly. "And I'd very much like a part in making that happen for you. If you give me the chance, Joss, I'll make you smile again."

At that she did smile, her eyes lighting up, transforming her entire face into something so blindingly beautiful that it took his breath away.

"You already make me smile, Dash. You make me feel . . . beautiful. I haven't felt beautiful in a very long time. Thank you for that. For giving me that part of myself back again."

He kissed her belly and then peppered a line down to the apex of her thighs.

"You don't need me to make you feel beautiful, honey. You're so gorgeous it hurts to look at you sometimes. Never doubt that. You don't need any man to make you feel beautiful. You are. That's a fact."

She sighed and rolled her hips as he once more parted her folds and gently blew over her clit. Then he flicked his tongue over the taut bud, delighting in her instant, honest response.

He loved that she held nothing back. No part of herself. She put it out there, making herself vulnerable. He would protect her always. Shield her from any and all hurts. He would encourage her to be herself with him always because he'd always protect her heart and soul. With him, she could be anything at all. He'd never judge her. Never hold her back. He loved her too damn much to ever change her or make her into something she wasn't.

He hoped to hell that he could make her see that. That he wanted her just the way she was.

He licked her again, his fingers digging into her hips as he held her down and open to his mouth. He became more aggressive, growing bolder, encouraged by her response. He sucked and licked, thrusting his tongue inside her to taste her sweet honey.

He ate like a man starved, and he was. For her. He wanted her to come all over his tongue. He wanted to drink deeply of her, not wasting a single drop of her desire.

That all changed with her broken plea.

"Dash, please, I'm so close and I want you inside me. I need you inside me. I want to come with you there. Please, I need it."

Damn if she'd ever beg him for anything. He'd promised her that. No begging. Not for anything he could give her.

And his body agreed with her desperate plea. He wanted inside her every bit as much as she wanted him there. He wanted her body to suck greedily at his cock. Wanted to feel all of that silken heat enveloping him. He wanted to come long and hard deep inside her, filling her with his release.

He broke away, his breaths coming hard, nearly panting with exertion and excitement. His dick was to the point of begging. He was so hard that it was agonizing. He wanted—needed—to be inside her. *Now.*

He propped himself up and over her, sweat dripping from his forehead. One hand went to her forehead, pushing away her hair as he stared down at her. With his other hand, he positioned himself between her legs, lodging the head of his cock at her opening.

At the very first touch of her velvety heat, he nearly lost it on the spot. Teeth clenched, he called on every bit of his strength to hold himself back.

Slowly and reverently he pushed inside her, his eyes rolling back in his head at the exquisite pleasure. She wiggled and arched, trying to draw him deeper.

"Don't," he ground out. "I'm holding on by a very thin thread, Joss. I don't want to hurt you and I don't want to come the minute I get deep inside you. Be very still. Let me do the work. If you move, I'm not going to make it and I want us to come together. I want you with me. Always with me."

Her eyes glowed, her lips curving into a sensual smile. Sultry and provocative. A temptress he had no hope of resisting.

But she acquiesced to his demand. She went still beneath him, giving him complete control.

Her eyes widened, the pupils flaring when he slid all the way inside. God, he'd never felt anything like this. Bliss. Utter bliss.

He'd waited for goddamn ever for this moment. He wanted it to last for fucking ever.

He could spend the rest of his life inside her and die a happy man.

"You feel so damn good, honey. I have a damn good imagination, but fantasy has nothing on the reality."

She smiled, her eyes lighting up at his heated statement.

"I'll be honest. I never fantasized about you," she said. "I don't say that to hurt you, but this is all a shock to me. I'm still reeling from it all. I never imagined this. How it would feel."

He smiled back at her. "I don't fault you for not fantasizing about another man when you were married. But I won't lie. I'd like it very much if you fantasized about me now. It may be selfish but I want you to think of me as often as I think of you. And honey, I think about you constantly."

Delight registered in her eyes, and she reached up to cup his jaw as he went still inside her, deep, surrounded by her heat.

"Who needs fantasy when you can have the real thing?" she whispered.

It was enough to send him right over the edge. He could feel his release boiling up his dick, threatening to erupt.

"I hope you're there," he ground out. "I can't hold back any longer."

Her hand caressed his face, her touch feather light and so sweet. It made his teeth ache.

"I'm there, Dash. Take us both over. Come with me."

He withdrew and slammed forward, rocking her body with the force of his thrust. He pulled back, just an inch, and hammered home again. And again.

She closed her eyes, her face reflecting the strain, the pleasure. How very close she was to reaching completion.

"Open your eyes, honey. Let me see you come."

Her eyelids fluttered open and she stared back at him, drugged, sluggish, like she was zoned out, in another world.

"Tell me what you need, Joss. I want you with me all the way. I'm not coming without you."

Even as he said it he knew that if she wasn't as close as he was, he would leave her behind. He couldn't hold back much longer at all, and he wanted her to orgasm. This was about her and her needs. Her pleasure. Later—another time—it could be about him. Him taking but giving back as much as he took.

She was his now and he wasn't about to let her go. He'd spend every day showing her, proving to her, that she was his first and only priority. The rest could be damned.

"I'm close," she gasped. "Don't stop. I'm there, Dash. Just come. Don't worry. I'll be there with you."

Taking her at her word, he let his urge take over. The urge to master her, possess her, mark her. Branded. There would be harsher ways that he'd put his stamp on her. Later. They had all the time in the world and he planned to make the most of it. The last years of frustration and aching need disappeared with the knowledge that she was finally his for the taking.

He thrust hard and deep, losing himself in her satiny heat.

Their gazes locked. They both tensed for the impending explosion.

No kink. No games. Just two people expressing themselves with their bodies. Him showing her without words the impact she had on him.

He nearly cried out as his orgasm swept him away. His release burst from his cock, an explosive surge that was the perfect mixture of pain and ecstasy. He'd never felt anything to equal this. Never.

His name spilled hoarsely from her lips. Her hands flew to his shoulders, her fingernails digging into his skin, marking him much the same as he marked her. She arched upward, meeting his thrusts as he emptied himself deep inside her.

His orgasm went on and on, each thrust forcing more of his release into her womb.

He'd brought up birth control, his concern of protecting her, but at this moment, he sorely regretted that she was on birth control. There was nothing more enticing than the thought of her swollen with his child.

He knew without a doubt that if she weren't on birth control, they would create a child. Nothing this earth-shattering could possibly result in anything else. A perfect union of heart and mind.

One day. He'd gladly give her the children she wanted so much. As many as she wanted. It would suit him perfectly for her to be barefoot and pregnant in his home. Tied to him irrevocably. Maybe that made him a chauvinistic bastard, but he didn't give a damn.

He wanted to take care of Joss for the rest of her life. Pamper and spoil her endlessly. Surround her with his love and their children. He wanted a family with her, a family he never dreamed would be possible, but was now within reach after Carson's death.

He regretted his best friend's death with all his heart, but he couldn't—wouldn't—give up a dream that was now in his grasp just because the woman he loved had been married to his best friend.

He gathered Joss tightly into his arms, easing his weight down on her, blanketing her with his body as they both trembled with the aftershocks of their lovemaking.

His dick twitched inside her, giving up the last vestiges of his release. She was hot and tight around him, squeezing him gently as her pussy rippled with her orgasm. He could stay this way the entire night. Deeply embedded inside her, a part of her.

She was filled with his seed, a fact that gave him immeasurable satisfaction. He wanted to mark her in other ways. More primitive ways. He wanted to see his semen on her body. Her breasts, her ass, dripping from her mouth.

He closed his eyes, already hardening even after the most gut-wrenching orgasm of his life. She did that to him. He'd never get enough of her.

Reluctantly he withdrew from the warm clasp of her body. Judging by her muttered protest, she didn't like it any better than he did. But he needed to take care of her needs and then he needed to ready her for sleep.

He kissed her swollen lips. "I'll be right back, honey. I have to get a washcloth to clean us both up so we don't mess up the sheets."

"It may be too late for that," she said ruefully. "You came a lot."

He grinned. "I've been waiting a long time for this night. Call it pent-up frustration. You do that to me, Joss. I don't think I've ever come so hard or as much in my life."

He rolled off her, careful not to make a bigger mess. He didn't want her sleeping on sticky sheets. He wanted only the best for her.

Now that she had moved in with him, they'd be using the bed and soiling the linens on a regular basis. He made a mental note to order several more sets of the expensive sheets that adorned his bed. He planned to get a lot of use from them.

FOURTEEN

DASH returned from the bathroom holding a damp washcloth. It was silly to be self-conscious when they'd just made love, but when he gently cleaned between her legs, wiping away the remnants of his release, heat crowded her cheeks and she found herself unable to meet his gaze.

He smiled indulgently, obviously noting her discomfort.

"Get used to it, honey. It's my duty—and privilege—to take care of you. To see to all your needs, even the more intimate ones."

When he was finished, he tossed the cloth aside and climbed into bed next to her. She didn't hesitate when he pulled her to him. She cuddled into his arms and let out a contented sigh as she rested her head on his shoulder.

"That was wonderful, Dash," she whispered. "I had no idea."

She felt his smile, or rather sensed it. She angled her head up to see she was right. His eyes were full of tenderness and . . . joy? He looked enraptured, sated and content. His smile was lazy and a little cocky. Arrogance looked good on him. He certainly wore it well.

"I had a very good idea of how great we'd be together," he said. "God knows I've dreamed about it enough. Thank goodness the reality far surpassed even my most vivid fantasies."

She levered herself upward, pushing against his chest so she could stare down at him. His hand covered hers as though he simply had to touch her. She liked the connection. The intimacy of being held after lovemaking. She'd felt so lonely for such a long time that she savored the fact she wasn't alone any longer.

She had someone to share things with. Her life. She was getting way ahead of herself, but she couldn't help but hope that the best was yet to come and that each day would be better than the last.

"It must have been awful for you," she said, her lips turning downward. "I can't imagine wanting someone for so long and thinking you could never have her."

He stroked her cheeks, palming her jaw as his thumb brushed over her skin.

"You were well worth the wait, honey."

She smiled. "I'm glad you think so. I hope you don't change your mind. I'm . . . liking this—us. I won't lie, I'm still reeling from it all, but it feels right."

He palmed the back of her neck and pulled her down to his mouth. He kissed her hungrily, his tongue delving deep. Hot, wet and exquisitely tender.

"Never going to happen," he said gruffly. "I won't change my mind, Joss, and if I have anything to say about it, neither will you. You're stuck with me now and it will take everything you've got—and more—to ever get rid of me. I'm a persistent son of a bitch and I don't back down from something I want. Ever."

She touched her forehead to his, their breaths mingling. "I'm glad you want me. It makes me feel special and it's been so long since I felt special to someone, Dash. I've been so lonely. At night I lie in my bed and I ache. I hate it."

He pulled her into his arms and stroked his hand through her hair. He dropped kisses on the top of her head while rubbing his other hand down the length of her arm.

"I've been lonely too, honey. But those days are over for both of us. We have each other now."

She nodded against him and then yawned broadly, nearly cracking her jaw with the effort.

Dash leaned over, his hold loosening on her as he reached into the nightstand drawer. She looked at him in question when he pulled out a long, satin sash.

Without a word, he took her wrist and wound the material around it, securing it in a knot. He checked the tightness, inserting his finger between the tie and her skin. Seemingly satisfied, he then secured the other end to his own wrist so that she and Dash were bound together by their wrists.

"Sometimes I'll tie you to the bed," he murmured. "Other times, like tonight, I'll tie you to me."

"What if I have to get up to go to the bathroom?" she blurted.

He smiled. "Then you wake me so I can free you. But under no circumstances, unless it involves your safety, are you to touch the restraints I put in place."

Knowing this was the first true test of her submission, she nodded silently. His eyes flared with approval and he leaned in to kiss her again.

"Get some sleep, honey. I'll make us breakfast in the morning when you wake."

She settled against his chest, the way their wrists were tied forcing her to face him. Unsure of what she was supposed to do with her hand or even if she could move it, she let him take her hand with his and he laid them both between them.

He'd told her to sleep, but even as sated and content as she was, sleep eluded her. She had a sleepy, lethargic heaviness to her limbs, the kind that she hadn't felt since her husband made love to her.

She'd sworn not to bring Carson into her relationship with

Dash. It wasn't fair and it certainly wasn't fair to compare the two men. Not fair to Dash or Carson.

Besides, one wasn't better than the other. They were just . . . different. She found the differences fascinating. Dash was only the second man she'd ever made love with, and yet she'd gotten lucky with both experiences. Two virile, heart-stoppingly gorgeous men. She'd been loved by one, and the other? She wasn't sure if Dash was in love with her. He was certainly infatuated. And he wanted her. He'd been very blunt about that.

Did she want him to love her?

That was the million-dollar question. Her knee-jerk response was no. She didn't want him to love her because she didn't want to love him. It sounded awful, but all she wanted was relief from the overwhelming loneliness she'd endured ever since Carson's death. And who was to say that she wasn't simply a conquest for Dash? Forbidden fruit?

It wasn't out of the realm of possibility that he'd seen her as a challenge. No, he hadn't acted on his attraction. He'd been honorable. He hadn't even pressed her right after Carson's death. He'd waited. But in that time, his fixation could have grown into something that was nothing more than a need to win.

Dash wasn't someone used to not getting his way. He was ruthless in business. Carson had remarked on it many times. He'd admitted that if it weren't for Dash, their business wouldn't be what it was now. Carson fully recognized that he didn't have the heart to be cutthroat. But Dash?

She shivered, realizing that it had been there all along. His dominance. His personality. She just hadn't seen it until now. She'd never really studied him. She'd first seen him as someone who didn't approve of her and later as a friend. But never a dominant, to-die-for alpha male. And never would she have dreamed that she'd be lying in his arms, tied to him after making love.

His free arm was crooked above his head and he lazily ran his fingers through the strands of her hair as he stared down into her eyes. He hadn't turned off the lamp and she could see every part of his expression.

She licked her lips, her thoughts wandering to their earlier conversation about Jensen Tucker. She knew she didn't have the right to ask for what she wanted. Dash owed her nothing when it came to the business he'd owned with Carson.

Yes, Carson had left her a percentage of the business, but she had no say in the running. She was given a portion of the profits, but it had been clear that she was to have no authority. Some women may have been insulted by that dictate, but Joss had no desire—or the knowledge necessary—to assist in the running of her husband's business.

It was in good hands. Dash was the best. She had absolute confidence in his ability to keep them all solvent.

"Can I ask you for something?" she asked quietly.

His brows drew together as if he picked up on her uncertainty.

"You can ask me anything, honey."

"I'd like to meet Jensen. I'm not saying I'm objecting to him taking Carson's place or becoming your new partner. But I'd like to meet him. I'll understand if you say no. I don't even have a solid reason for wanting to meet him before he takes over."

"Of course you can meet him," Dash said gently. "And you don't have to justify your reasons to me. I'll invite him over for drinks, or if you prefer a more public place, we can arrange to have drinks out."

"Whatever you prefer is fine." And then the realization struck that he was giving her the option of not making it public by offering her the chance to meet Jensen outside of Dash's home. Because if they met here, it would be obvious that she and Dash were involved.

Did she care? She didn't even know Jensen. But apparently she would come to know him and see him on a semi-regular basis now that he was partnering with Dash.

It would become public knowledge soon enough. No reason to hide her relationship with Dash. She had nothing to be ashamed of and she'd die before ever making Dash feel as though she were ashamed of *him*.

"We can invite him here," she said, thinking he'd be pleased with the use of "we" instead of saying he could invite Jensen.

And in fact, he did looked pleased with her insinuation, that she'd called his home her own.

"Then I'll call him in the morning and ask him over for drinks tomorrow evening. Will it bother you, Joss? Because I can't pretend that I'm just setting up a tête-à-tête between two acquaintances. I can't pretend that you aren't mine and that you mean nothing more to me than being my best friend's widow. If that bothers you, I need to know now because I have no intention of hiding you—us—from anyone."

"I'm okay with it," she said quietly. "The important people already know. I don't care about anyone else. I won't live my life according to what others think and say."

He kissed her. "That means a lot to me, honey. Though, I'd understand if you needed time to adjust. I know we agreed to jump into things. It's what you wanted and hell, it's certainly what I want. I don't want to wait any longer. But I'd absolutely understand if you want to keep our relationship quiet for a time. At least until you're more settled and sure of yourself."

She sucked in her breath. Did he think she wasn't sure? Had she given him reason to doubt her sincerity? Or was he simply afraid that it was too good to be true?

It was hard for her to believe that she was the source of someone's hopes and dreams. Carson had been happy with her. He'd never let a day pass that he hadn't let her know just what she meant to him. She'd considered herself the luckiest woman alive.

Carson was . . . larger than life. Handsome. Wealthy. Extremely loving and generous. Always affectionate. He wasn't a man who worried about what others thought. If they were together in public, he touched her frequently. Just little shows of affection. He held her hand, put an arm around her or he kissed her, giving others no doubt of his feelings for her.

Any woman would have wanted someone like Carson, and he'd wanted her. Just her. She wasn't in his league. Didn't come from his world, though he'd argue that his current circumstances weren't ones he was born into. His upbringing hadn't been good. He'd fought for every dollar he earned, the lifestyle he'd claimed. For himself and for Kylie.

His devotion to his family, to both Joss and Kylie, forever endeared Carson to Joss. He was one of a kind. How could she hope to ever find that kind of love and devotion again?

Except here was Dash. All of the things Carson was and yet . . . more. He was too perfect for her. The manifestation of every single fantasy she'd ever entertained. She hadn't considered that there was a man in existence who could possibly meet her criteria, and yet he did.

"What will your family think?" she asked.

One of the things she and Carson had in common was that neither had family. Except Kylie. And Joss had come to think of her as her own sister. Not just a sister but her best friend. But her father had divorced her mother when Joss was young, and her mother passed away after an extended illness when Joss was still in college. Her mother was why Joss had pursued a degree in nursing.

The nurses in charge of her mother's care had been wonderful. Compassionate, warm. They'd gone the extra mile to make Joss's mother as comfortable as possible in her final days, and Joss had vowed she would make the same difference in someone's life.

Yet she'd quit her job after marrying Carson. At the time she hadn't minded. She'd been in the throes of a new relationship and utterly confident in their marriage. And the truth was, she'd craved the kind of relationship where she was cared for. Protected. Cherished. Carson had provided all the things she desired. Except dominance.

Perhaps she should consider going back to nursing. She'd kept up her training for that eventuality, but she still hadn't taken steps to go back to work.

"My family will be very happy for me," Dash said. "My brothers thought me a fool for waiting as long as I did. They've known how I felt about you for a long time. My mother worried for me. She thought I was a fool to have a thing for a married woman. And not just any married woman, but a woman married to my best friend and business partner. Talk about a recipe for disaster," he said wryly.

"I hope they like me," Joss whispered.

The idea of meeting his family now made her nervous. Yes, she'd met them in the capacity of Carson's wife, and they had embraced them both. But she'd never known that they knew Dash had feelings for her, and now she'd be meeting them as Dash's . . . lover? Someone they knew was important to him. That changed everything. She just hoped she measured up and they accepted her new role in Dash's life.

Dash smoothed the hair from her brow and pressed a kiss to her forehead. "They'll love you. And they'll be thrilled that we're finally together."

He made it sound so . . . final. A done deal. Inevitable. Though they hadn't talked about anything more serious than a sexual relationship and the fact that she would submit to him, but his actions, the way he spoke, hinted at something far more permanent.

She wasn't certain how she felt about that. What if she was setting herself up for more hurt?

Chessy had asked her if she'd rather have one perfect year with Dash and then lose him or if she'd prefer not to even give them a chance. At the time she'd considered that any time she had with him would be worth it no matter the end result. Much like her time with Carson. She wouldn't go back and change a single thing, even knowing she'd only have him for three years. Three of the best years of her life.

But now? She wondered if she'd been wrong to think that any time with him was preferable to none at all. It had taken her three years to put herself back together after losing Carson. Could she survive losing someone she loved a second time? And for that matter, how did she feel about Dash?

She wasn't in love with him. Not yet. It was too soon. Her feelings confused her. She wasn't sure what to make of the entire situation. It had happened too quickly. So much had changed in such a short period of time and she couldn't afford to let her emotions rule her actions. Not only did she not want to get hurt, but she didn't want to hurt Dash either.

"I know I said I wanted to meet Jensen soon, but if it's all the same to you, I'd prefer to wait on your family awhile."

He smiled tenderly, pressing tiny kisses to her face, eyes and nose.

"We have all the time in the world, Joss. No rush. I like the idea of having you to myself for a while before I have to share you with others."

She yawned and snuggled closer to him, as close as she could manage with their wrists bound together. On impulse, she kissed the side of his neck, inhaling his masculine scent and savoring it.

So many nights she'd spent alone, aching, so very empty. And now she was in bed with Dash, and he was wrapped possessively around her, his leg thrown over hers. She could feel his erection, his quick intake of breath when her teeth grazed his neck. She barely had time to wonder if he planned to deny himself when suddenly she was turned, the hand that was tied to his yanked high over her head.

With none of his earlier patience or tenderness, he roughly spread her legs with his free hand and was inside her, hard and deep, before she could even take a breath.

Pleasure burst over her like an exploding firework. She was too stunned to cry out, to give voice to the overwhelming sensation of him being so hard and thick inside her.

"This time is for me," he growled as he pumped into her. "You make me crazy, Joss. I swore I wouldn't take you again tonight. That I'd take things slow. But your mouth on my neck broke every ounce of my restraint."

She smiled but her vision was hazy. All she could do was feel the power of his movements. His ownership of her body. Her bound hand was pressed firmly into the pillows. He held her down, making movement impossible. And she didn't care. She loved the vulnerability of her position. She loved knowing she was powerless as he slaked his lust. It excited her, bringing her closer to the edge.

No foreplay. No workup. And yet she was already precariously close to coming. All he had to do was touch her, exert his dominance, and she was his to command.

"So damn sweet," he muttered, his face strained as he pounded into her, mindlessly, like a rutting beast in the throes of mating. "I've dreamed of this, Joss. Of you. And me. Together. Finally together. I'll never let you go, honey. I hope to hell you're prepared for that. If you ever try to walk away from me, I'll fight like hell to keep you right where you belong."

She arched upward, wanting, needing more, desperate for release. Her skin itched, like it was alive. Edgy. Bordering on pain.

His impassioned statement spoke to the very heart of her. Soothed every fear. He made her feel cherished and . . . loved. And she hadn't felt loved and adored in so very long.

Even though he'd said that this time was about him, he slid his fingers between them, finding and stroking her clit. She went wet around him, her entire body tightening, clenching with agonizing need.

"Get there," he commanded. "Come for me, Joss. Now."

To her utter surprise, her body obeyed him. She was helpless to do anything *but* obey him. She hadn't thought she was there yet. Almost but not quite. But the moment the forceful command was given, she began coming. Wave after wave washed over her, spreading throughout her body until she felt nothing but the sweetest of pleasures.

He spurted deep inside her, filling her with his liquid heat. For several moments, the only sound that could be heard was the slap of flesh against flesh and their ragged breaths spilling from their mouths.

And then he lowered himself to her body, panting with exertion. He closed his eyes and rested his forehead to hers, his nostrils flaring as he sought to catch his breath.

When he withdrew only an inch, she moaned softly. The sound was part pleasure and part pain. She was deliciously sore in places she hadn't used in a long time. Her entire body tingled in the aftermath of her orgasm. Her clit throbbed, a tiny pulse point between her legs.

"I should clean us up," he murmured. "But I don't want to untie you from me nor do I want to withdraw from your body just yet. I like it here. You connected to me not only by being tied, but me deep inside you for as long as I can remain there."

She wrapped her free arm around him, rubbing her palm over his buttocks and back.

"I like it too," she whispered. "We can always change the sheets in the morning, right?"

He smiled and kissed her lips, the soft smooching sound echoing in the room.

"I'm going to roll us over so you're on top. There's nothing more I'd like than for you to sleep draped across me. I wouldn't normally stay hard enough to stay inside a woman this long, but I swear, honey, you so much as breathe and I get hard and stay that way. I just had the two most earth-shattering orgasms of my life and I'm still hard as a stone."

"I like you inside me," she said shyly.

"It's a damn good thing because I intend to spend a hell of a lot of time inside you from now on."

FIFTEEN

JOSS came awake, violently aroused, her body responding, even in the deep sleep she'd fallen into. Dash was over her, their hands unbound, both of his framing her hips as he plunged deeply inside her.

She gasped, her eyes flying open to see his glittering gaze boring into hers. His expression was intense, his jaw tight as he thrust again and again.

"Good morning," he murmured, leaning down to kiss her.

"Ugh, morning breath," she said, twisting her lips to the side so he wouldn't taste her unbrushed teeth.

He laughed and forced her mouth back to his. "You taste wonderful, Joss. You have nothing to worry about there. Get used to it, because the hell I'm going to wait to have you each morning until you've done all your girly preparation."

He withdrew and she would have protested, but he quickly flipped her over so she was facedown on the mattress. God, he was demanding. So forceful. She loved every second of it.

Reaching beneath her, he lifted her behind just enough that he could plunge back into her from behind. Her fingers curled into the sheets, making tight fists as he rode her roughly, pressing her further into the mattress.

He was deeper, bigger this way. He filled her to capacity,

stretching her, the sensation an exquisite mix of pleasure and edgy pain. She closed her eyes, giving herself over to the sensation, to him. She surrendered completely, allowing him to take his pleasure however he wanted.

His palms cupped her ass, molding the cheeks and caressing as he spread her wider before thrusting again. His thumb brushed over the seam of her ass and she shivered as dark thoughts overtook her.

She and Carson had never tried anal sex. Would it be something Dash wanted? The thought didn't frighten her. If anything, it aroused her even more, and she was already nearly out of her mind with pleasure.

As if reading the unspoken question, Dash leaned down, blanketing her with his body, stilling his movements so he was buried deep inside her. He kissed her shoulder and then nipped a line up the curve of her neck until she shuddered.

"I'll have your ass, Joss. Make no mistake about it. I'll have every part of you and you'll hold nothing back from me. I own you now. You're mine."

The words sent her hurtling straight over the edge. Sex was much more about the mind, at least for women. Desire started in the brain. Her body merely followed suit. And with those words, she was violently aroused. It was too much. Her orgasm flashed, bright and burning hot. She bucked upward, desperate for more. She wanted it hard, deep and fast.

"My darling likes that," Dash murmured even as he powered into her, as fast and as hard as she needed so desperately.

She wilted into the mattress, her strength gone, her mind complete and utter mush. He wasn't finished yet and he took his time, teasing and tormenting her hypersensitive flesh. He dragged his cock through swollen tissues and then plunged forward again until finally he found his own release, straining forward, covering her body with his own.

When he was finished, he lowered his full weight to her body, pressing her down onto the bed. She could feel the sharp rise and fall of his chest as he sought to catch his breath. And he was still pulsing in her pussy.

"Did I hurt you?" he murmured against her neck.

She tried to shake her head but couldn't move.

"No," she whispered. "It was wonderful, Dash."

He remained there a moment longer before finally pushing upward. Then he withdrew, her body still clutching greedily at him as he pulled free.

He pressed a kiss to the small of her back and then got up from the bed. She didn't have time to turn over before he gathered her in his arms and picked her up, carrying her toward the bathroom.

He turned the shower on and after testing the temperature, he pulled her inside with him where he proceeded to wash every inch of her body. It was torment. He paid extra special attention to the still-quivering flesh between her legs. He had her worked up and well on her way to another orgasm by the time he washed and rinsed her hair.

"On your knees," he said gruffly.

She obeyed instantly, lowering herself to the wet floor of the shower. The warm spray cascaded over both of them. His cock was painfully erect, huge and stiff.

"Get me off, Joss," he commanded. "But I want you to get yourself off too. Touch yourself. But don't come until I do. If you do, you'll be punished."

She shivered at the authority in his voice. It was almost worth it to disobey him just to find out what his punishment would entail. Did that make her an idiot? But no. She didn't want to start off by blatantly disobeying him. She didn't want punishment. She wanted pleasure. And he'd already said that he would spank her regardless of whether she disobeyed him or not.

He guided his erection to her lips and she slid her fingers down her belly between her legs to find her clit. Her entire body clenched the moment she touched herself and she knew she'd have to be careful or she would end up coming before he did.

"I've dreamed about this," he breathed. "Your gorgeous mouth wrapped around my dick."

She glanced up, taken by the sight of him naked, wet, water beading and running down his beautiful body. He looked like a god. Utterly perfect. Muscled, lean in all the right places. Not a spare ounce of flesh. He was a man who took excellent care of his body.

She tightened the suction around his cock, enjoying the instant reaction she got. Though he was in command and she was the submissive, she realized how much power she truly had. She liked that feeling. That she held him in the palm of her hand and that she was in control of his pleasure.

Warming to the task at hand, she made love to his cock, savoring the taste and feel of him in her mouth. Hot, so alive, pulsing with strength. He could so easily hurt her, but he was so careful to temper his power. His touch was tender, his movements weighed with her protection in mind.

"I'm close, honey. You need to get there too."

She found her sweet spot, exerting just the right amount of pressure, and then moved in a slow circle, her orgasm rising and swelling deep in her belly. But still she waited. Remembering his directive that she not come until he did.

He palmed her forehead and then reached with his other hand to grasp the base of his cock.

"Take it one more time. Deep, honey. Take it deep. And then I'm going to pull out and come all over your mouth."

The erotic words, the image he inspired, nearly had her coming. Her hand froze, leaving her dangling precariously on the edge. She sucked him deep, taking him all the way to the back of her throat, and she swallowed against the tip, thinking it would bring him pleasure.

His groan told her she wasn't wrong. And then suddenly he ripped himself from her mouth and began pumping his cock with his fist.

"Come, Joss."

His command was guttural, as though he could barely form the words. The first jet of semen hit her cheek. The second splashed over her lips and the third hit her chin. Hot, much hotter than the water. It scalded her skin and she rolled her clit harder and faster, trying to catch up.

As the last jet of semen hit her chin and rolled down her neck, quickly washed away by the spray of the shower, her orgasm rocked her to the core. Her knees gave out and she would have slipped but Dash looped his hands underneath her armpits and held her steady as she quivered and shuddered with her own release.

Gently he pulled her to her feet, supporting her weight until he was certain she was steady. Then he turned her into the spray, rinsing his cum from her body.

The heat of the shower combined with the earth-shattering orgasm she'd experienced left her shaky. He helped her from the stall and then wrapped her in a huge towel. He briskly dried her hair and then made certain he removed the moisture from other parts of her body.

When he was done, he dropped a kiss on her forehead and patted her gently on the behind.

"Dry your hair and comb it out while I go prepare breakfast. Normally, I'll tend to all your needs. It will give me great pleasure to dry and brush your hair for you. But I'm sure you're hungry, as am I. But wear nothing, Joss. We'll eat in the living room with you at my feet."

She hesitated, wondering if her question would anger him.

He glanced curiously at her, cocking his head to the side. Then he cupped her cheek and kissed her lips.

"What is it, honey? I can tell you want to ask. You never have to be afraid to ask me anything. I want you to trust me and be confident in me—us. So ask what it is I can see you're dying to ask."

She smiled ruefully. "I was just . . . nervous. I mean you said you wanted me to wear nothing, but isn't Jensen coming over today? Will you expect me to wear nothing when people are over?"

Color flooded her cheeks and she ducked her head. She wanted this to work. She liked this side of Dash she'd never imagined. The forceful, dominant, utterly alpha male. She'd never felt so . . . free . . . in her life, which sounded absurd given that she'd ceded absolute power and control to another man. She should feel constrained. Confined. But she felt as though she'd finally set free a side of herself that she'd always longed to let loose. Now that she'd tasted Dash's dominance, she had no desire to go back to her stale, sterile existence of the last three years.

Dash's expression became utterly serious. He framed her face in his hands, forcing her to look directly into his eyes.

"I would never do anything that embarrasses or shames you, honey. Never. Yes, when we're alone, I absolutely expect you to wear whatever I tell you. But I would never put you in a position where you weren't comfortable. If we go to The House, yes, you will absolutely heed my instructions in a public setting, and you will be naked in front of others. But not here in my—our—home.

This is your sanctuary and it's the one place above all others where you will feel safe and protected at all times. Nothing touches you here, Joss. Nothing but me."

"Thank you," she said in a shaky voice.

He leaned down and kissed her, slipping his tongue inside to taste her.

"Now, dry your hair and then come into the living room so I can feed my woman."

She smiled, a ridiculous thrill coursing through her veins at his words. *My woman.* Like she belonged to him. And she did even if it was still hard for her to comprehend.

"I want this to work," she said fiercely, surprising herself with the vehemence of her statement.

"It will work," Dash said firmly. "We've overcome the most difficult part. Making the decision to gift me with your submission was the hard part, honey. The rest you just have to leave to me and trust that I'll provide you all the things you want and need. And I'll do that, Joss, or die trying."

She flinched at the statement even though she knew it was just a figure of speech.

Regret simmered in his eyes and his expression softened.

"I'm sorry, honey. That was not well done of me. It won't happen again."

She reached for his hand and slid it around to her lips. She pressed a kiss into his palm and then stared back up at him, smiling. "I know. And I'll try not to be so sensitive. You shouldn't have to watch your every word for fear of hurting me. I'll work on it, Dash. I promise. It's just that the thought of losing you too . . ."

He hugged her to him and she hugged back, savoring the closeness, the intimacy that was still new and shiny.

"You won't lose me, Joss. Believe that."

"Okay," she whispered.

Even as she agreed, she whispered a prayer that things would work out and that nothing ever happened to Dash. She couldn't survive it again. Once had nearly destroyed her. If something ever happened to Dash, she wouldn't survive this time.

SIXTEEN

JOSS reclined onto the sofa, taking the glass of wine Dash offered her. She sipped, her stomach churning with nervousness. It was silly to be so anxious to meet Jensen, her husband's replacement, but she was. She'd likely never come into contact with him after this meeting since she had nothing to do with the day-to-day operations of Dash's business. Kylie would be more affected by Jensen coming on board since she would have to work for him.

She knew Kylie wouldn't take it well. She hoped that by meeting Jensen and offering him her acceptance, it would smooth over whatever objections Kylie had when told of the new partner.

"You're on edge, honey. Why?"

Dash settled down on the couch next to her, reaching for her with his free arm. She went readily, balancing her wineglass in her other hand as she snuggled into Dash's embrace.

"I don't know," she said honestly.

He squeezed her to him and kissed the top of her head. "You'll like him. He's very good at what he does. You must know that I'd never do anything to jeopardize yours or Kylie's futures by choosing the wrong person to bring into the business."

"She's not going to take it well, is she?" Joss asked, turning anxiously to face Dash.

"At first I don't imagine she will, but she doesn't have a choice.

She works for me, not the other way around. She won't have a choice but to accept him. I won't allow her to cause problems. If it comes down to it, she'll have to be let go. It's not what I want and I'd certainly ensure that she's well provided for. I promised Carson that I would always look after the both of you. It's a promise I intend to keep."

She cocked her head to the side, gazing curiously at him. "He asked you to do that? I mean specifically?"

Dash grimaced. "I shouldn't have said anything."

"But you did," she persisted. "Is this something you two discussed?"

Dash sighed. "Yes. We spoke about it a short time before his accident. I've often wondered since then if he didn't know. If he had a feeling that something was going to happen. It's not something we ever discussed and then out of the blue he brought it up. And he was serious about it. It wasn't an off-the-cuff 'just in case' conversation. He was absolutely serious and he wanted my promise that if anything ever happened to him that I'd ensure you and Kylie were taken care of."

Joss weighed his words for a moment, discomfited by the idea that she was merely a method of Dash fulfilling a promise to his best friend. But no, he'd said that he had feelings for her long before then. When she and Carson were first married. A dozen questions bubbled to the surface but she wasn't certain they should be asked.

"I don't like that look, Joss. What are you thinking?"

This time she sighed, casting her gaze downward to his waist. He slid his fingers underneath her chin, forcing her to meet his gaze once more.

"Is that what I am to you? An obligation?"

His frown was immediate. In fact he looked *pissed*. She regret-

ted voicing her brief fear because it was obvious he had no liking
for it.

"Don't answer that. It was a silly question," she murmured.
"But there's another question I wanted to ask you. It's something
I've wondered ever since we began this. Since you told me you
had feelings for me when I was married to Carson."

"You can ask me anything," Dash said. "But be prepared for
an honest answer, honey. If the truth hurts you then be careful
what you ask. Because I won't lie to you. Ever."

She nodded. He'd always been honest. She knew that much.

"When Carson and I first began dating, I felt as though you
didn't approve of me. That you didn't approve of our relationship
or the fact that things moved so quickly. At the time I chalked it
up to you being concerned about your friend. But lately I've wondered . . ."

"What have you been wondering?" Dash asked gently.

She lifted her eyes to his, studying his features.

"You said that you were attracted to me. But you didn't say
when those feelings started. Were you attracted to me from the
very start? Is that why you didn't seem happy about me and Carson being together? Were you . . . jealous?"

Dash was silent for a long moment and then he heaved out his
breath, his shoulders drooping slightly. He turned away from her,
directing his gaze toward the fireplace. His hold loosened on
her and she shifted away, just so she could better see him.

"That was part of it," he admitted. "I was jealous as hell. The
first time I met you. Do you remember? Carson brought you to
the company Christmas party and there you were. So beautiful it
made my teeth ache. You were adorably shy, reserved. And you
clung to Carson's side the entire night. I couldn't look at you without resenting the fact that he'd found you first."

Her eyes widened in surprise. "I had no idea."

"No. It shames me that I treated you so curtly in the beginning. I actually hoped that things wouldn't work out between you and Carson because I wanted you for myself. I had planned to swoop in and claim you the minute things ended between you and Carson. But it became very clear that he had no intention of letting you go. I damned my luck. Here was the woman of my dreams and she was with my best friend. I saw how happy you made him. I fully admit, I looked for faults. I looked for any evidence that you weren't what was best for him. Hell, I hoped that he'd lose interest or you'd do something to put him off. That makes me a total bastard, but that's the truth."

He turned back to her, his eyes dark with regret.

"I wanted you to fail just so I could have you as my own. But I saw how devoted you were to him. I saw how other men made veiled invitations, flirted with you, propositioned you, and you never even looked their way. You were one hundred percent loyal and devoted to Carson. How could I not want that for my best friend? It was hell, Joss. Hell watching him be so damn happy and resenting him with every breath. And worse was the fact that after he found out, he wasn't even pissed. He laughed and said he couldn't blame me for wanting you when he was consumed with that same want. He told me that it was a damn good thing he'd met you first because I would have locked you in my bedroom and never let you out. He wasn't wrong."

She shook her head in bewilderment, unable to process everything he'd said.

"I thought all this time you didn't like me. Not at first. Later, I knew you'd come to accept me, but I always felt like you didn't approve in the beginning. You intimidated me."

He pressed his forehead to hers, stroking her hair with one hand. "I'm sorry for that, honey. You'll never know how much.

But I was in an impossible situation, and having to see you with Carson, seeing the both of you so blindingly happy, was like a fist to my gut every single time. But you have to know, I need you to know, that I never wished him ill. Losing him hurt me, and if I could have him back, I'd let you go in a heartbeat, even if it meant killing myself in the process."

Tears filled Joss's eyes. She blinked furiously, determined not to let them fall.

"Thank you for that," she whispered. "It means a lot to me that you cared so much about him. He loved you, you know. He never had a family. Just Kylie. You and your family meant so much to him."

"I'll regret his death for the rest of my life, but honey, you need to know that at the same time I do not regret having this opportunity with you. I'd give anything to have him back, but I can't bring myself to regret having you in my bed and in my life."

She smiled, a wobbly smile, her lips quivering with the effort. He kissed each corner of her mouth to steady her lips.

"I don't regret it either," she said in a low voice. "I want to see where this takes us, Dash. I'm willing to take the risk."

The doorbell rang, interrupting the intimacy that surrounded them like a fog. He kissed her once more and then smoothed her hair that was slightly mussed. She hastily ran her fingers through her hair as he rose. He touched her cheek.

"You look beautiful, honey. There's not a thing wrong with you. Sit tight and I'll let Jensen in."

She scooted to the edge of the couch as Dash disappeared to answer the door. She sucked in steadying breaths, cursing her sudden bout of nerves. He was just a man. His opinion of her didn't matter. But she wanted this meeting because she was curious about the man who'd fill the vacancy left by Carson.

A moment later, Dash returned, Jensen Tucker close behind.

She sucked in her breath at her first look at the man Dash was taking on as a partner. If she'd thought Dash was intimidating in the beginning, Jensen Tucker scared the hell out of her.

He looked intense, brooding, utterly focused and scary as hell. His skin was tanned, matching his hair and eyes, brown, as though he spent a lot of time in the sun. He had a rugged appearance that screamed military or cop. She wondered what his past was and if she was right in her assessment that he was a warrior.

Kylie would likely dive under her desk the moment she laid eyes on Jensen. Joss felt sorry for her because Kylie feared strong, dominant men, and Jensen Tucker definitely qualified on all counts.

When Dash stopped in front of her, he extended his hand to help her up. She rose gracefully, though her heart was pounding as she stared up at Jensen. Then he smiled at her, a gentle smile that transformed his entire face from brooding to a much softer-looking man. It was as if he knew he intimidated her and was taking pains not to do so.

She swallowed the lump in her throat and extended her hand to his.

"I'm Joss Breckenridge," she said quietly. "Dash has told me a lot about you. I'm very happy to meet you."

Jensen's hand closed over hers, firm, strong, just as he appeared. But he surprised her by lifting her hand to his mouth to press a kiss to the back of it.

He squeezed once before letting her go and Dash reclaimed her hand, pulling her into his side as if to openly declare his possession. Joss found she didn't mind at all. Her heart fluttered over the fact that Dash was publicly putting his stamp on her.

"I'm happy to meet you as well, Joss. Pictures don't do you justice. You're far more beautiful in person."

She blinked in surprise, wondering where he would have seen

pictures of her. She tucked that away to ask Dash later. It relieved her that Jensen made no mention of Carson. No condolences, no dancing around the issue of him replacing her dead husband. He didn't bring it up at all, as Joss had feared he would, and that it would make the entire evening awkward.

Delighted that everything seemed to be off on the right footing, she directed her attention to both men, remembering her duties as hostess. Though it had been several years since she'd entertained, when she and Carson were married, they'd entertained often.

She was naturally shy and it had been hard to overcome her self-consciousness and get used to being open and friendly with strangers. But over time and with Carson's encouragement, she'd managed to become adept at handling social situations.

"What would you two like to drink?" she asked. "And please, sit down and make yourselves comfortable. There are appetizers in the kitchen. I'll bring them out as soon as I've gotten you your drinks."

"You don't have to serve us, honey," Dash murmured, but there was approval in his eyes. "Why don't you get the tray of food and I'll fix mine and Jensen's drinks. Would you like a refill of your wine?"

She smiled. "Yes, thank you. I'll be back in a moment."

Dash watched as she walked away, the heels she wore accentuating her shapely legs. They didn't go unnoticed by Jensen either. The other man glanced up at Dash, a gleam in his eyes.

"I can see why you moved in so quickly," Jensen murmured. "She's a woman a man would do anything to possess."

"Yes," Dash said shortly. "And she's definitely claimed. Remember that."

Jensen chuckled. "No need to get uptight. I prefer very specific qualities in the women I'm with. Not many women are up for what I demand. I doubt Joss would take me very well."

Intrigued, Dash lifted an eyebrow as he studied the other man. They were venturing into personal territory, an area they'd never delved into. Their dealings had been purely business, but he assumed if they were going to be partners that at some point they'd learn more about one another.

"Care to explain that? That's pretty vague," Dash muttered.

Jensen's features were indecipherable. "Submission. I require absolute submission in the women I'm with." He shrugged casually. "Not many women are willing to give a man absolute control."

It didn't surprise Dash in the least. Jensen was a hardass bastard. Dash had figured they had more in common than just business interests, but they'd certainly never discussed their personal lives.

"I think Joss may surprise you in that area," Dash said dryly. "Not that I want you testing her receptiveness. She's mine."

"Apparently we have more in common than I thought," Jensen said. "And if I get what you're saying, then you really are a lucky bastard. Too bad she's taken. If she's not only beautiful and intelligent but submissive as well, then I'm sorry I met her too late."

"Story of my life," Dash murmured. "I was too late the first time. Fate gave me another chance and I don't intend to fuck it up."

Sympathy shone in Jensen's eyes. "So you had a thing for her when she was married. And to your best friend. That had to suck."

"You could say that."

A thoughtful look crossed Jensen's face. "I'm fairly new to the area as you know. When we first met, it was through business trips to Houston. But now that I'm here, I haven't really had time to scope it out. Any clubs here? You know anything about the places in this area?"

"Yeah. There's one good one. Very exclusive. It's called The House. Owned and managed by Damon Roche. Wealthy son of a bitch and he caters to an upscale clientele. He's backed off in recent months. He's married and has a daughter who occupies most of his time, but he still keeps a hand in the operations. I can give you his contact information and put in a word for you. He does an extensive background check on prospective members, but it's a very well-run, safe place. I think you'd like it. There's something for every sexual proclivity there and no shortage of submissive women looking for what a man like yourself provides."

"Thanks. I'll take you up on that."

"Just do me a favor. Since we'll be working together, and not that I expect you to apprise me of your comings and goings, but I intend to take Joss there a few times and I wouldn't want her to be uncomfortable, so I'd appreciate a heads-up if you plan to be there. I'd rather avoid the nights when we'd run into people she knows."

"No problem," Jensen said.

"There is another couple who has a membership there. You'll likely meet them at some point because they are friends of mine and Joss. Chessy and Tate Morgan. They're married and they go, though more infrequently than they used to. I plan to get with Tate to ensure we don't run into them on the nights I take Joss."

"It would appear you're acquainted with many people who share our choice of lifestyle," Jensen said dryly.

"They aren't as uncommon as one might believe," Dash countered. "It's just not something most couples advertise. I never dreamed that Joss would be open to this kind of relationship. Hell, I've waited three long years to make my move and I was damn near too late. She showed up at The House one night when I was there and I hadn't been in a damn long time. It was fortunate I was there or she would have ended up with some other guy who wouldn't treat her as well as I will."

"Lucky indeed," Jensen murmured. "If I had been there, she certainly wouldn't have gone home alone. I'll have to check this place out. You've intrigued me now."

Dash scowled at Jensen's statement until he saw the twinkle in the other man's eyes. Jensen was yanking his chain, the bastard, and Dash had risen to the bait.

"One other thing you need to know, or rather prepare yourself for," Dash said quickly, wanting this part of the conversation over before Joss returned from the kitchen.

Jensen arched an eyebrow.

"You know I told you I wanted to tell Joss and Kylie myself before we announced our partnership. Joss took it very well, but then I expected nothing less from her. Kylie, however, won't take it as well."

"You haven't told her yet?"

Dash shook his head. "I plan to tell her Monday when she comes to work. The thing is, you should know dominant men scare the fuck out of her. I don't know how much you know of her situation. Hers and Carson's. They grew up in hell. Their father was an abusive son of a bitch who ran his household with an iron fist. His brand of dominance was bullshit. No true Dominant would ever abuse his wife or children. But she doesn't know the difference. She fears strong men, and hell, you scared Joss to death when you first walked in. I could see it in her eyes though she covered it well and recovered quickly. But you should know that Kylie is going to be extremely wary around you."

"I'm not going to be a bastard to her," Jensen said, a defensive note to his voice.

"I know that," Dash said. "I just thought you should know where she's coming from. Don't take it personally. It has nothing to do with you and everything to do with her experience with men in general. She doesn't trust anyone. Carson shielded and protected her well into her adult life. I'm not sure he did her any favors even though I understand where he was coming from. I'm just letting you know that things may not be easy at first between the two of you. And I'd appreciate it if you were patient and understanding with her."

Jensen nodded, his expression growing dark. "How bad was it?"

"The worst," Dash said quietly. "His wife tucked tail and ran, leaving the kids at his mercy, and he abused them horribly. Kylie got the worst of it maybe because she reminded him of his wife. Who the hell knows? Carson wasn't always able to protect her, though God knows he tried. Her father raped her and beat her. Repeatedly."

"Son of a bitch," Jensen swore. "No wonder she's so wary around men. Can't say I blame her. I'll be careful with her. I don't want her to fear me. It sickens me that any woman would have reason to fear men as she does."

"In that we agree," Dash said. "Carson couldn't give Joss what she needed. Dominance. And she loved him too much to ask it of him. But he knew. And now that she's taken that step and wants what I can give her, I'll do whatever it takes to make her happy again."

"I wish you luck," Jensen said sincerely. "She's a good woman. You're a lucky son of a bitch."

"I know," Dash said quietly.

They both fell silent when Joss reentered the room carrying the silver tray with the hors d'oeuvres she'd prepared earlier.

She was a dream in the kitchen. When she and Carson had entertained in their home she'd always prepared all the food despite Carson telling her he'd have it catered. She'd always laughed and told him there was no need and that she enjoyed cooking. Dash looked forward to her cooking for him even if he planned to spoil her by cooking for *her*. It was a duty they could share. He liked the idea of being in the kitchen with her. His kitchen. He wanted her to settle in and make herself at home. Put her stamp on his sterile environment. He couldn't wait for her to light up his entire home and make it her own.

"Thank you, Joss. This is delicious," Jensen said appreciatively after downing two of the confections.

"I got caught up in conversation and didn't fix our drinks," Dash said ruefully. "I'll remedy that at once. Hand me your wine-glass, honey. I'll pour yours first."

"Oh, I'll get them," she said hastily. "You two continue your conversation. I can make most drinks. Carson bought me a book one year and it became my mission to be able to make any drink requested when we entertained. Try me. What can I get for you?"

Jensen smiled and sent Dash another look before mouthing, "Lucky bastard." Dash grinned and acknowledged Jensen's silent compliment with a smug nod.

"Surprise me," Dash said. "Fix me whatever you decide. I'll like whatever you make. Promise."

"Same here," Jensen said. "Only thing I don't care for is rum. Anything else goes."

Joss's smile was breathtaking. Her eyes warmed with delight and sudden shyness. Dash could see her worry even as her mind was buzzing with what to fix. She didn't want to disappoint him. Didn't she realize that it wasn't possible to disappoint him? She could fix him rubbing alcohol, and as long as she smiled at him that way, he'd drink it down and never taste it.

"Sit, please, and make yourselves comfortable," Joss said, gesturing toward the chairs. "I'll be back in a moment with your drinks. Dash? Is your minibar stocked or do you store most of your liquor in the kitchen?"

"Everything you need should be there," he replied. "And if it isn't, let me know and I'll get whatever you need."

She sent him another dazzling smile and hurried toward the bar to the far left of the living room. He watched her, unable to tear his gaze away from her. Satisfaction gripped him by the throat, spreading clear to his soul.

"Man, you've got it bad," Jensen murmured. "Can't say I blame you though. She's a jewel."

"Yeah, she is that," Dash said in a low voice as the two men took their seats. "She wanted to meet you. She asked for tonight's meeting. I wonder what she thinks of you and if she's as smitten as you are."

Jensen grinned. "Can't say I'd complain if she was."

"I'll slice your balls off," Dash bit out.

Jensen laughed and Joss looked up from where she was mixing the drinks, a puzzled look on her face.

Dash smiled back at her and waved her off. "Just guy talk, honey. Don't let us interrupt you."

"So this thing with Kylie," Jensen began, turning the subject to a more serious matter. "How much of a problem do you anticipate my presence will be?"

"I can't answer that," Dash said honestly. "I don't think she'd take any new partner well at first. In her mind, you'll be replacing her brother. She's used to working for me and Carson, but more so for Carson. He brought her into the company when she graduated college. A protective measure on his part because he wanted her where he could take care of her. As I said, he likely didn't do her any favors, but I also understand why he wanted to protect her. She's . . . fragile. She still carries the emotional scars of her childhood abuse. Carson was determined to shield her from any hurt in her adult life.

"After he died, she took it hard and it was a while before she could work comfortably with me, even though I'd been there from the start. But she worked in a closer capacity with Carson. I was more of a secondary boss. When I took over, she reported directly to me and acted as my personal assistant. I had one before Carson died, but I dismissed her so Kylie would still have a position.

"I thought she could act as assistant to us both. She is certainly capable of handling the workload and she knows every single thing that comes through the business. She's good. But you may opt to hire your own assistant depending on how she reacts to your presence."

"In other words, she's been babied and coddled by you both," Jensen said.

Dash nodded. "You could say that."

"Please be understanding with her, Jensen," Joss said quietly.

Both men looked up to see Joss standing there, drinks in hand. Her expression was troubled, clear worry reflected in her eyes.

She handed them their drinks and then took a seat next to Dash on the couch. She reached for his hand and he wondered if she even realized that she was reaching out to him for support.

"I have no intention of being a jerk to her," Jensen said gently.

"I didn't mean to insinuate you would," Joss said, her cheeks flushing with embarrassment. "It's just that Kylie is . . . fragile."

Her words echoed Dash's own description of just moments ago.

"She sees things very black-and-white and she's cautious. She's had reason to be," Joss continued. "And you'll frighten her. I don't say that to insult you," she hastily added. "But you're a very intimidating man. I worry about her—for her. When she feels threatened, she lashes out, and I worry that will anger you or perhaps make you want to replace her. She needs this job, Jensen. Not for the money. Carson provided very generously for her and for me. But she needs the stability. The routine. She's very good at what she does. I know most people would look at her and think that she got the job because she was Carson's sister, and that's true to an extent. But she's very intelligent and capable. She graduated with a business degree with honors. She's an asset, as I'm sure Dash can attest."

"Joss, you don't have to defend her to me. Dash has told me of her past, and it's understandable that she'd be wary. I give you my guarantee that I'll do everything in my power to put her at ease. If she does the job and proves herself to be as indispensable as you say she is, then she'll have nothing to worry about."

"Thank you," Joss said earnestly. "She's more than a sister-in-law to me. After Carson d-died, she had no one. Just me and Chessy and of course Dash and Tate."

Dash squeezed her hand, proud of the way she'd managed to speak of Carson's death, only stumbling slightly over the word "died." She was making progress, and it gave him hope that he could come to mean more to her and that Carson wouldn't be a wedge between them even in death.

"You're a very loyal friend to her," Jensen said. "I hope she knows just how lucky she is to have you."

Joss's cheeks colored adorably and she was obviously uncomfortable with Jensen's compliment. Dash wanted to pull her into his arms and hug her. Hell, he wanted Jensen to get the hell out so he could take her to bed and make love to her all damn night.

Already his mind was alive with all the possibilities. Free rein. There were dozens of ways he planned to have Joss at his mercy. He could barely contain himself and couldn't wait to show her all the ways he'd exert his dominance.

"When do you plan to tell Kylie?" Joss asked, directing her question at Dash though she included both men in her question.

"Monday morning," Dash said. "When she comes into work."
Joss frowned but held silent.

"What is it, honey? You obviously want to say something," Dash gently encouraged.

"It's not for me to decide," she began.

"Say what you want to say," he directed.

She drew in a breath. "I just thought that perhaps something like this should be said outside of work. It'll be a shock. And we're friends. I mean, you're more than just her employer. I think you owe it to her to tell her someplace more intimate."

"What did you have in mind?" Dash asked slowly.

She glanced nervously up at him and he wanted to pull her into his arms and reassure her. She had nothing to fear from him. No disapproval. There was nothing she could do that would earn his censure.

"You could invite her here," Joss said. "We could tell her together. It may be easier than at work. It would also give her time to come to terms before she has to go to work. Time to deal with it so she has it together by the time she has to go in on Monday."

"It's not a bad idea," Jensen said. "No one wants her hurt by this and obviously I'm going to be a sore subject with her."

"What if you came too?" Joss said.

Jensen looked surprised and then wary.

"I don't mean right away," Joss said hastily. "But perhaps it would be a good idea for you two to meet in neutral territory. She can see that you aren't an ogre. We could have Kylie over and have a dinner party Sunday night. We could invite Tate and Chessy to come so that Kylie meets Jensen in a group setting. What do you think, Dash?"

Hell, if it meant her coming to terms so quickly with him and her being together, and she didn't mind their friends knowing it?

He'd agree to damn near anything. Kylie be damned. Joss wanting to host a dinner party at Dash's house, as a couple? Hell yes.

Dash glanced over at Jensen. "You up for dinner Sunday night?"

"Say yes," Joss said impulsively, leaning forward to take Jensen's hand. "We're very much family. It's always been that way with Carson and Dash's company. I'd like for you to be a part of that."

Jensen looked befuddled and Dash nearly chuckled. Another victim of Joss's magic. She could soften even the hardest heart and no one could ever refuse her. Not when she asked so prettily. Hell, it would be like kicking a puppy.

"I'd like that," Jensen said, and was rewarded by a blinding smile from Joss.

She latched onto both of Jensen's hands and squeezed, delight shining in her eyes.

"I'll cook a marvelous dinner," she said, excitement evident in her voice. "You'll like Tate and Chessy. You'll like Kylie too when you've had a chance to see what she's really like."

Jensen smiled back at her. Joss's enthusiasm and evident happiness was contagious. Jensen glanced Dash's way, and he didn't even have to mouth the words this time. It was evident in his look. *Lucky bastard*. Yeah, Dash was lucky all right. He didn't know what he'd done to deserve this chance with Joss but he wasn't about to spend any time pondering the whys and wherefores.

He'd grab the opportunity with both hands and hang on for all he was worth.

SEVENTEEN

"MY darling deserves a reward," Dash said in a husky voice.

Joss glanced up as he closed the door after seeing Jensen out. "What did I do?"

He smiled and leaned down to kiss her. "You were, as always, a fantastic hostess. You made Jensen feel welcome and alleviated any potential awkwardness by asking for a meeting before he came on board. Thanks for that, love."

She smiled back and twined her arms around his neck. "I'm glad you approve. Now what's this about a reward?"

His eyes darkened, sending a shiver down her spine. She got the feeling that this reward was not going to be a typical one.

"I'm going to tell you what I have in mind," he murmured. "In exacting detail. And then you have to be honest and tell me if you're up for what I have planned. The hell of it is I don't know who will be more rewarded. You or me."

"Is there any reason we can't both be rewarded?" she asked innocently.

"I hope to hell not," he growled.

"Then tell me what it is you have planned and I'll tell you whether I'm up for it," she said with a grin.

He wrapped his arms around her, keeping her linked to him and her arms in place around his neck. As he walked her backward into the living room, he nibbled and nipped at her neck and up to her ear, sending chill bumps dancing over her skin.

"First you're going to strip down until you're completely naked," he whispered against her ear. "Then I'm going to tie you up so you're completely powerless and subject to my every whim."

"Mmm, sounds good so far," she murmured.

"Then I'm going to insert a plug to prepare you for me. After that I'm going to spank that sweet ass of yours until it's rosy with my marks."

She shivered uncontrollably, her mind exploding with the images he evoked. She let out a small whimper as he sucked the lobe of her ear into his mouth. God, she could come with just his words. She was already aching with need. Her nipples tingled and hardened to painful points. Her clit pulsed and twitched between her legs until she clamped her thighs together to alleviate the burn.

"And then I'm going to fuck your mouth, Joss. But I won't come. Not yet. When I'm close, I'll flog you again until your ass is burning and you're on fire with the need for relief. And then I'm going to fuck that ass. I'm going to take you hard and rough, to the very limits of what you can withstand. I won't be gentle. Not tonight. I'm going to take you as roughly as you can stand. And then I'm going to come all over your ass. I'll mark it with my cum just like I marked you with the crop. And then I'll fuck you some more, filling your ass until it spills down the insides of your gorgeous thighs. Think you can handle that, honey? Are you ready to be completely and utterly dominated? Taken over and used purely for my pleasure?"

The words were silky in her ears, sending her into a dreamlike haze. She could barely form a coherent response, so aroused was she by his statements. It was everything she'd fantasized about, only now it was real and in the here and now and not in her darkest dreams. Was she ready? Was this truly what she wanted or was it merely a fantasy better *left* in the realm of fantasies, never to be brought to life?

"Tell me, Joss," he said roughly, tightening his hold around her. "Give me the words."

As he spoke his demand, his fingers wound around her hair, pulling it tight until her scalp tingled. This was a side of Dash she'd never seen, never dreamed existed. She licked her lips, her mouth dry with desire and need. So much need.

"Yes," she croaked out. "I want it, Dash. I want it all. I want you."

"Your safe word," he said in a guttural voice. "Remember your safe word. If I go too far, use it and I'll stop immediately. Tell me the word so I know you remember."

She scrambled to remember what she'd decided on. She couldn't imagine Dash going beyond her limits when he seemed so in tune with her needs.

"G-ghost," she stammered out.

"Very good," he said softly, sucking at her ear again. "But be sure, Joss. Because when you say that word, it ends and the mood will be broken. There won't be any going back. So be very sure that you truly want me to stop and aren't just overwhelmed by the moment. I'll push your limits. You want a man to push you. You've said as much. So don't chicken out the first time things get intense. Because this will be intense, Joss. You need to understand that. When I say I'm going to mark your ass, it's no game. I will spank you hard. I'll raise welts on that pretty skin of yours. I won't break the skin, but you'll wear the marks the next day and be reminded that I put them there. I want to look at them the next morning and remember that I put them there."

She nodded her agreement but then quickly voiced her acceptance, knowing he'd force her to say the words, to fully acknowledge the step they were taking.

"I won't use it unless I'm absolutely certain I don't want to continue," she said softly. "I trust you, Dash. I know you won't go too far. And I do want it all. The full measure. I don't want you to hold back. I want you to do what it is you want without fear of hurting or frightening me."

"That means a lot to me, honey. Now, if we're finished with talking, I'd rather get on to getting you naked and bound and at my mercy."

"Me too," she whispered.

"Go into the bedroom, undress and kneel at the foot of the bed. I'll be there as soon as I get the necessary items. Remember your position. Thighs spread, palms up and resting on your legs."

"I remember, Dash. You don't have to remind me. I won't disappoint you."

He smiled tenderly at her. "I know you won't, honey. Now go. I'll be there in just a moment."

Joss hurried toward the bedroom, her pulse thudding in her veins. She was so aroused and excited that she was dizzy with it. His words echoed in her mind, vivid and erotic. She was wildly aroused, so excited that she couldn't remain still.

Even when she'd hurriedly undressed and sank to her knees to wait, she fidgeted with impatience. Yes, she'd fantasized about a man having complete control over her body. Of being bound and vulnerable. Of having a man mark her. Inflicting pain that quickly faded to pleasure. But would the reality hold up to her darkest fantasies? Would she enjoy him spanking her and would it be enjoyable or would it be painful with none of the pleasure she imagined?

There was only one way to find out. She'd given herself to Dash to do with as he pleased. She hoped with all her heart that it didn't turn out to be awful. She didn't want to wimp out and use her safe word the very first time he pushed her boundaries.

He'd said she'd never disappoint him, but how could she do anything else if she backed out the minute things got edgy?

The wait seemed interminable, though she was sure only moments had elapsed since she'd left Dash to wait for him in the bedroom. She forced herself to maintain her position and be patient. She'd do nothing to disappoint him. Not when he'd been so patient and understanding with her.

He entered a scant second later carrying rope, a flogger and a plug that looked enormous. Her eyes widened as she imagined taking that into her body. It didn't look possible!

He smiled at her reaction. "Don't worry, darling. I'm not going to just shove it in. I'll work you up and go easy. You'll take it just fine. And then you'll take me. All of me."

She shivered again, her eyes half-lidded as a drugged sensation overtook her. He had yet to touch her and already she had entered another zone altogether. Euphoria heightened her senses. She was painfully aware of his presence. Anticipated that first command, that first touch. She wasn't sure how she'd possibly hold out. She was already so close to the edge and there was so much more to come. He'd very vividly outlined precisely what he planned.

He dropped the instruments on the edge of the bed and then slowly unzipped his pants, pulling his rigid cock free of confinement. Then he positioned himself in front of her, his erection straining upward. He grasped the base and lowered the tip to her lips.

"Maintain your position. Don't move a muscle. Open your mouth and let me in."

Careful to remain perfectly still, she parted her lips as he nudged inward. He didn't take her roughly. In fact, his thrusts were slow and measured, sliding over her tongue, allowing her to taste and feel the thickness of his cock.

She savored the wholly male taste of him. Inhaled his scent. His hands slid into her hair, gripping her harder and holding her firmly in place as he fucked her mouth. A tiny spurt of liquid spilled onto her tongue and she swallowed, sucking greedily for more. He laughed and withdrew, tapping her cheek lightly in reprimand.

He lowered his hand, motioning for her to take it. Then he lifted her to her feet, holding her when she was unsteady, so on edge. Her knees felt like jelly. Thankfully she didn't have far to walk. She felt drunk. High on anticipation, eager to experience all that he'd promised her.

"Get onto the bed. I want you in the middle, on your knees, facing the headboard. I'm going to tie your hands above your head to either post and then I'm going to tie your ankles to the lower bedposts. You'll be helpless, Joss. Completely and utterly at my mercy. And tonight I plan to have no mercy with you. I'm going to push you to the very edge of your limits. We spoke of those limits and that you wouldn't know what they were until you got there. Tonight we'll both find out just what those limits are. Remember your safe word. There is no shame in using it if you're truly past your limits. But give yourself time. Don't back out at the first moment of uncertainty. Trust yourself—and me—to get you where you want to go. Just let go, Joss. I'll be here to catch you. I'll always catch you."

She closed her eyes, his words washing over her like the sweetest of balms. He gave her peace. Reassurance. That she could be who she truly wanted to be with him. That he wouldn't judge her nor would he be disappointed in her if she did back out. His tenderness only made her more determined that she'd take anything he dished out and beg for more.

She crawled onto the bed, her limbs shaking, her entire body quivering with need. Harsh, edgy craving. She wanted him—

what he could give her—more than she'd wanted anything else in her life.

This was the first step in claiming her destiny. Of becoming the woman she'd always wanted to be. Of claiming the man she'd always wanted. Her past melted away. Thoughts of Carson fled. She loved him—would always love him—and this was no betrayal of her marriage.

Peace enveloped her in its tender embrace. Surrounding her, filling her heart. Much as Dash had in only a few short days. How could she have never known?

Because she'd never opened her eyes fully. She'd never looked at him, truly looked. And now that she'd finally seen him, she recognized him as the missing piece of her soul.

"Arms up," Dash ordered.

She arranged her arms over her head, supporting herself on her forearms but holding her hands up for him to coil the rope around her wrists.

He wrapped the soft rope around one wrist and then stretched the rope to the post at the corner. Then he took another piece and repeated the process on the other side so both wrists were bound, the rope pulled tight so there was no give.

When he finished her hands, he went to the bottom of the bed and secured each ankle before stretching the rope to both posts, effectively rendering her motionless. There was no possible way for her to move.

Her thoughts were muddled, scrambled, and she searched for what he'd said was the next step. Then her breath caught. The plug. He'd said he was going to insert the plug and then flog her.

Her pulse accelerated the moment his hand slid over her buttocks, petting and caressing until she was twitching with need. Then he pulled away. She tried to look over her shoulder but it put too much strain on her shoulders so she faced ahead, waiting breathlessly for what came next.

His hand moved back to her behind, parting her cheeks and then she felt the cool shock of lubricant. He traced the seam, pausing at the entrance, smearing the gel over the opening. Then he pushed in with just a fingertip and her breath caught.

Her body protested the barest of penetrations, squeezing and rejecting his finger. But he persisted, exerting firm pressure until it slid inward to his knuckle. She gasped, jolted by the sudden breach.

He leaned down and kissed the plump cheek of her behind and then nipped her flesh with his teeth. Using her distraction, he slid in another finger, more lubricant easing its pathway.

He began to stroke, in and out, lubricating her passageway. After several long moments that drove her insane he withdrew his fingers and then squeezed more of the gel over the seam. Then she felt the blunt head of the plug probing gently at her tight ring. He pushed inward the barest amount before withdrawing it and pushing forward once more.

He slipped his free hand underneath to her belly and then down, through her folds to her tingling clit. He began stroking her, rubbing in a tight circle as he forced the plug deeper into her body.

Her pussy was quivering with need, wet with desire, and she found herself trying to push back against the plug, wanting—needing—more.

"That's it, darling," he murmured. "Almost there. Embrace it. The pain will pass. Reach for it, hold on to it. Allow the pleasure to take over."

His fingers slipped lower, rimming her vaginal opening while he pushed the plug even farther. It was now at its widest point, stretching her impossibly. The burn was intense but his fingers were working magic on her clit and pussy. She was nearly mind-less, restless and edgy, fighting off her impending orgasm be-cause she knew without the intense buildup the plug would only hurt.

Just when she thought she couldn't stand another minute, it was as if her body caved in, completely surrendered and allowed the plug access. His fingers left her clit and she breathed in deep, steadying breaths, sweat beading her forehead as shallow pants burst from her lips.

He kissed her bottom again and then pressed another kiss to the small of her back.

"Give yourself a moment to come down," he said quietly. "I want you so on edge when I finally fuck your ass that you'll be mindless with pleasure. I'm getting the flogger now. I want you to think about how the kiss of leather will feel on your skin. Don't shy away from the pain. Embrace it. Because after the pain comes the pleasure. For many women, pain is the gateway to subspace. Once you reach that level, you'll feel nothing but the sweetest of pleasures. I'll get you there, Joss. Trust me to get us both there."

She nodded, incapable of speech. She wanted his mark on her skin. Wanted to feel the fiery sensation of the leather slapping her skin. Everything she'd heard about, read about, fantasized about was about to happen.

She closed her eyes, listening to the sounds of his movements. And then she heard the sharp smack of leather. Her eyes jerked open. The noise had jarred her from her dreamlike state, but there was no pain. It took her a moment to realize that he hadn't struck her. Not yet.

She flinched when he touched the leather flap to her spine near the base of her skull and slowly slid it down her back to her buttocks where the plug split her cheeks. She held her breath, anticipating, waiting. But nothing happened.

"Breathe, Joss. Don't hold it in. I'll make you wait even longer if you don't relax."

She blew out her breath, sagging as she tried to force herself to comply with his order. And then pain blew over her skin like a blowtorch. She jumped, unable to prevent her reaction to the shock of that first blow. Her eyes widened in surprise. That had hurt!

It was instinctive to immediately say her safe word, to retreat behind the safety that word gave her. But she bit her lip, determined to stick it out.

The second blow didn't take her as unaware as the first. She breathed through the burn until it faded and then, as he'd promised, pleasure replaced the pain, a different kind of burn spreading over her body.

The third didn't hurt as much as the first two even though it was, in fact, harder. By now she knew what to expect and didn't dread them as much as she had the first. Pleasure was faster to replace the discomfort and she reached for it. Embraced it just like he'd told her to.

He peppered blows over each cheek, never hitting the same place two times in a row. He picked up the speed and they came harder now, one after the other, until the world around her fell away. Everything was hazy, a sense of euphoria seeping through her veins, spreading like wildfire over her body.

Was this what he referred to as subspace? She'd read about it. Knew it happened for some women when they entered a different plane and felt no pain, only the sweetest of pleasures.

It was a high she'd never experienced before. She lifted upward, seeking the blows before they fell. She craved them. Wanted more. Harder. Faster.

It took her a moment to realize that he'd stopped. Her flesh hummed and buzzed with heat. She was supersensitive. She flinched when his hand touched her behind, caressing the welts he'd raised.

"So fucking beautiful," he said, his voice thick with desire. "My marks on you. Never seen a more beautiful sight. I know I said I was going to fuck your mouth and then your ass, but honey, I'm dying to get inside that ass. I'll never make it if you wrap those pretty lips around my dick."

She moaned softly, closing her eyes as she imagined Dash fucking her from behind. Taking her where no man had ever been before. And her helpless to do anything but take it. Whatever he wanted to do to her, however he wanted to do it.

He pressed his lips to one cheek and then the other, the reverence in his actions bringing tears to her eyes. She breathed in deep, inhaling the scent of desire in the air. Savoring it, committing to memory this night. All of it. She knew there would be more nights to come, but this was the first. Not the first time they'd made love, but the first time he'd truly demonstrated his dominance—and she, her submission.

It was a beautiful thing. Never would she have imagined the sheer beauty of such an act. Now she understood better why Dash said it was a gift. One to be cherished. But she wasn't the only one offering the gift of herself. Dash was gifting her with his dominance. His absolute care of her. His demonstration of power. It could so easily be abused and yet he walked that fine line between not enough and too much.

He gently began pulling the plug from her behind. Her body clutched at it, not wanting to let it go. He exerted steady pressure and suddenly it was free, her opening caving in after so much pressure. She sagged, feeling deflated once the sense of fullness was gone. She was left achingly empty, bereft of that pleasurable tightness of her stretched around the plug.

How much better would it feel when he was filling her instead of a rubber object? She craved it with every part of herself. Wanted him deeply within her, possessing her, demonstrating his absolute ownership of her.

The bed dipped at her knees as he climbed onto the bed and positioned himself between her spread legs. His hands trailed up the backs of her legs, over the sensitive skin behind her knees and then higher to her ass. He cupped and petted the twin globes, running his fingers over the raised welts before finally spreading her, opening her to his pending invasion.

She immediately tensed, her reaction automatic. He smacked her ass, just enough to jar her, but not enough to hurt her.

"Relax, honey. It'll hurt a hell of a lot more if you tense up like that when I'm trying to get inside you. I used plenty of lubricant. You're ready for me. You can take me. Relax and let me do the work."

She forced herself to do as he commanded. And he waited, maintaining his position behind her, stroking and caressing her body until finally the tension began leaving her and her muscles became loose and limber once more.

It was at that moment that he pushed forward, parting her cheeks and thrusting inward. It wasn't hard or forceful. He only gained about an inch, but she sucked in her breath, her eyes going wide as she felt herself stretch to accommodate him.

If she'd thought the plug was impossible then he was even more so. How on earth could she possibly hope to take him? What choice did she have? Whether she thought she could or couldn't, he wasn't giving her an option. He was going to force his way inside her.

The thought gave her a decadent thrill. A dark and edgy sensation that snaked through her veins, catapulting her right back into the same subspace as before. The whole experience took on a dreamlike quality. She hovered between fantasy and reality as he pushed forward, pressing steadily inward until she stretched even farther to accommodate him.

"Almost there, honey," he soothed, caressing her back with both hands. "Just a bit more and you'll have taken all of me."

"Hurry," she whispered, biting her lip to prevent her from begging for more.

When he pulled away she whimpered her displeasure, but then he was back. With one powerful thrust he was all the way into her. Her cry shattered the quiet and she instinctively tried to lurch forward, away from his invasion, but her bonds kept her from escaping.

His hands curled around her hips, his fingers digging into her flesh, marking her the same way the flogger had. He let out a low growl and yanked her back to meet his thrust. He was buried to the balls. She could feel the heavy sac and the crisp hairs surrounding his cock against her behind.

She was panting, gasping for breath, dizzy and buzzing from a high like she'd never experienced. Then he reached underneath her, stroking lightly over her clit. She let out another sharp cry, her orgasm nearly rocketing through her. Oh God, not yet. She couldn't come yet. It would all be over and that wasn't what she wanted.

"How close are you, honey?" Dash ground out.

"Close," she said in a desperate voice. "Don't touch me. Not yet. Not until you're ready to come. I'm so close, Dash. Too close."

He leaned down and kissed between her shoulder blades, but his fingers stilled at her clit. He twitched and pulsed inside her.

"I'm close too," he said in a guttural tone. "I want it to last. You're so sweet, Joss. So damn sweet. Your ass is as perfect as the rest of you. So tight and hot, sucking me in like a greedy fist."

She closed her eyes, breathing deeply through her nose. He

wasn't touching her and yet she still hovered precariously on edge. It wouldn't take much at all for her to go off like a bomb.

He slid both hands up her body underneath to cup her breasts. He toyed with her nipples as he lay over her, perfectly still inside her. He cupped and toyed with her breasts, caressing and rolling the nipples between his fingertips.

Finally he lifted himself upward again and his hands fell away from her breasts. He grasped her waist and withdrew, hammering forward again, driving deep and hard. For several moments he repeated those motions. Withdrawing until only the tip remained inside her opening and then thrusting savagely.

He'd told her he'd show her no mercy. That he'd fuck her rough and hard. That he'd push her boundaries. But not since that very first blow that had shocked her with the pain and intensity had she even considered calling a halt to it all. She wanted it too much. Craved it with her entire being.

Now that she'd had a taste of his dominance, she was already addicted. Like a druggie desperate for her next fix. She'd never get enough of him. His power. His control. It called to the deepest, darkest parts of her soul. She came alive under his ownership. Like a flower in spring after lying dormant for the winter.

"Going to go hard at you, Joss," he said through clenched teeth. "I'll be rough and I won't stop unless you use your safe word."

She shook uncontrollably. She'd thought he'd been rough and hard already. There was more? Had he been holding back until now?

She soon had her answer when he levered himself higher over her, in a position of greater dominance. He spread her cheeks wide with both hands, holding her open to his invasion. And then he took her with savagery that took her breath away.

Hard. Fast. Deep.

Over and over he rammed into her, overwhelming her with the power of his possession. The room blurred around her. She wasn't cognizant of anything but the power he demonstrated. It hurt. It burned. It was the most intense pleasure she'd ever experienced.

And then he ripped himself from her body and hot jets of semen splattered onto her behind. Some of it slid inside her still-open entrance, distended from his fierce penetration. The rest spilled onto her back and her ass. Then, as he'd promised, he thrust inside her again, still coming, still pumping his release deep into her body.

She felt the hot liquid seep from her opening with every thrust. It ran down the insides of her legs in a hot rush. Then he plunged forward to the hilt, pressing hard against her ass as his body quivered over hers.

He reached around, sliding his fingers over her clit once more. She jerked in response. She was so worked up, so incredibly aroused, that his touch was nearly painful and yet she craved more. Needed more. She needed to come.

"I'm going to stay inside you until you come," he said in a strained voice. "I want to feel you fall apart with me deep in your ass."

His fingers exerted more pressure, rolling her clit in a tight circle. The dual sensation, his cock in her ass, his fingers caressing her clitoris, it was all too much.

Her orgasm crashed over her like a giant wave. She lost all awareness. She was lost in the throes of her release. She was covered in his cum, his cock still deeply embedded in her as she convulsed and squeezed him even tighter.

He groaned. She cried out. And then both fell forward as much as the ropes restraining her would allow.

His chest rose and fell sharply, a match to her own as she struggled to gain her breath.

"You okay?" he asked tenderly as he brushed the hair from her cheek.

"Mmm-hmm," she hummed.

"Give me a minute to get you untied and cleaned up."

"Not going anywhere," she mumbled.

He chuckled at that. "I suppose not since I have you tied securely to my bed. I like it. I like it a hell of a lot. I could get used to having you at my beck and call at all times."

She couldn't even muster a protest to his joking. She was too undone. Tired. Exhausted. But more sated and content than she'd ever been.

Moments later he gently untied her, after cleaning the semen from her skin with a damp cloth. When she was free, he sat her on the edge of the bed and inspected her ankles and wrists for any abrasions. Then he kissed each slightly red spot where the ropes had pressed into her skin and rubbed the feeling back into her feet when she muttered that she couldn't feel them.

For that matter she couldn't feel much of anything. She was too shattered by her experience. She felt numb and out of it, like she'd just come out of a stupor. Perhaps she was still in it.

When he was finished, he pushed up to his knees and pulled her into his arms so her head was pillowed on his shoulder. He stroked his hand up and down her back as he kissed her hair.

"Tell me what you're thinking, Joss," he said quietly.

She attempted a smile as she pulled away, but she was too bone weary to pull it off. Instead she reached out to his face, cupping both her hands over his jaw. She caressed his face, letting her fingers wander over his cheekbones.

"I think that was the most incredible sexual experience of my life. That's what I think," she said honestly.

He smiled, relief evident in his eyes. He leaned forward, resting his forehead against hers. It was an action he often performed. She liked the intimacy of the gesture. Loved that he was openly affectionate. She found it endearing that he liked touching her so often.

"I meant to make it last much longer," he said ruefully. "I'm not normally so quick on the draw. But you make me that way, Joss. You make me crazy. I touch you, kiss you, feel you and I have to have you until I'm nearly blind with lust."

She smiled at him and leaned that inch between their mouths to kiss him. "We have plenty of time to draw it out longer and make it last. We're still learning one another. This is all still new."

"Bet your sweet, sore ass we do," he said with a grin. "Heads-up, because I will put you through the paces and make you last a lot longer than we did tonight."

"My ass *is* sore," she said, wincing as she shifted her weight.

"Then I'll have to kiss it and make it all better," he said in a silky voice.

He reached forward, scooping her effortlessly into his arms, and then settled her onto the bed, pulling back the covers and then arranging them over her. He kissed her again and then walked around to crawl into bed on his side.

She went readily into his arms, enjoying the solid warmth of his body. He didn't tie her tonight. Maybe he'd forgotten or perhaps he was afraid that the rope he'd used earlier had abraded her skin and he was giving her a rest. It didn't matter. She was as close as she could get to him and he was wrapped around her. It was enough.

In the middle of the night, Dash was awakened by Joss stirring restlessly. He started to wake her, thinking she was having a bad dream, but before he could, she murmured, "Carson."

He went still, the single word freezing his heart. She sounded . . . sad. Like she was missing him. Not what he wanted to hear when he'd just made love to her. When she wore the marks of his dominance and possession.

She turned away from him, curling into a ball, never waking. Dash lay there, only inches away but seemingly a world apart.

And while she slept, quiet and peaceful now, Dash lay awake, in brooding silence.

EIGHTEEN

DASH was quiet and almost brooding the next morning. His mood had been off ever since they'd gotten out of bed. She'd hesitantly offered to cook him breakfast, but he'd shrugged off her offer and prepared the meal for them both. But he hadn't fed her as he'd done the last several meals. In fact, they sat across from one another at the small breakfast table situated in the nook off the kitchen.

She tried to initiate conversation several times, but his answers were short and distant, as though he had something on his mind. She replayed the night before over and over in her head, wondering if she'd done something to displease him. But he'd seemed perfectly content with the way things had played out. She hadn't backed down from his challenge. She hadn't used her safe word. She'd seen it out to the very end, regretful when it was over.

But why was he so distant?

She puzzled over it all through breakfast and when they were done eating, she took over, taking their plates into the kitchen without asking him. The truth was she wanted to get away for a few moments to ponder the change in his mood.

She stiffened when he walked into the kitchen behind her, and she turned from the sink where she'd stacked the plates to face him.

"Did I do something wrong?" she asked bluntly.

She hated guessing games. She wasn't someone who could hide her feelings well at all. And Dash would know that something was bothering her, even if it was him that was the problem.

He blinked in surprise and then his features eased and softened, the strain and tension gathered on his forehead relaxed.

"No, honey, why would you think that?"

"Because you haven't said two words to me all morning," she said. "I hate to sound nagging or to intrude if it's none of my business, but it's driving me crazy and I can't think of what I could have done to displease you."

His face softened even further and he closed the distance between them, gathering her in his arms and leaning her back against the sink.

"You did nothing to displease me. I was just pensive this morning. Nothing to do with you. Last night was wonderful, as were you, Joss. I'm sorry if I made you feel that you'd done something wrong. You were and are perfect."

For the oddest reason, she felt like he wasn't telling the truth, or at least the whole truth. She'd caught him watching her periodically through the morning as if he was trying to *discern* her thoughts. He should know by now she was an open book. There was no hiding it when she had something on her mind. It was either there to read in her eyes or she simply came out and addressed it.

It was one of the things Carson had loved most about her. No coy, passive-aggressive games. No pouting endlessly over some imagined slight. If something upset her, he knew about it. He never had to ask because she was too honest and up front, especially with people she cared about.

"Are you sure?" she asked quietly. "I'm still learning all of this and I don't want to mess up, so if I do, you have to tell me, otherwise I'll never know how to correct the mistake."

He kissed her, hugging her tightly against him. "You did nothing wrong, Joss. And if you had, I have every confidence that it would have been done innocently. You're too honest and straightforward about things. It's one of the things I most admire about you. There's no guessing with you because you tend to take the bull by the horns."

She relaxed, some of her worry dissipating. "I'm sorry. I know I sound defensive, but this is very important to me. I need you to understand that. This isn't a game to me. It isn't me seeking out a relationship with just anyone. I chose you. Surely that has to mean something."

"It means everything," he said softly. "More than you can possibly know. What you don't understand is that there are any number of men more than willing to give you the things you want. They'd spoil and pamper you endlessly. They'd lay the world at your feet. But I'm damn glad you chose me to be that man, even if I leaned on you pretty heavily."

She smiled. "No matter how hard you leaned on me, if I didn't want to do this with you, I wouldn't have agreed. Carson taught me a lot about independence and standing on my own two feet. I'll always be grateful to him for that. He taught me that I could be the person I am and I should never be willing to change who I am to please someone else. He was right. And it's something I've tried to do and be in my everyday life."

His features tightened again, his eyes going blank. Did he resent her talking about Carson? Was he defensive about the fact she'd been happily married to another man?

She understood, she supposed. It couldn't be all that wonderful to have her previous lovers, never mind there had been only one, thrown in his face at every turn.

From now on she was going to be more careful about discussing Carson with him. But it was only natural and it would take her time to adjust to the sudden change in their relationship. He'd gone from friend and confidant to her lover in a matter of days. Before, she had no compunction about discussing her relationship with Carson, or even just Carson himself, with a man he'd called best friend. It was nice to be able to talk about Carson with someone who knew him almost as well she knew him. It enabled her to keep his memory alive and talk about the good times they'd always shared together.

"What are we going to do today?" she asked impulsively. "Have you called Tate, Chessy and Kylie to see if they can make dinner tonight? If so I'll need to run into the store and pick up things for the meal I'm planning. City Market has steaks that are simply divine. I thought we could grill steaks and I'll make all the fixings. Baked potatoes, salads, homemade rolls and a really yummy dessert."

He lowered his mouth to her, kissing her with tenderness and care that he hadn't demonstrated this morning until now.

"I think that sounds wonderful. Let me go make the phone call to Tate. Do you want to call Kylie or would you prefer me to call her and issue the invitation?"

"I'll call her," Joss said quietly. "But I'll wait and let you explain when she arrives. I planned to tell her to get here at least thirty minutes from the others so you'd have time to discuss Jensen with her."

"Sounds like a plan. You make your calls. I'll make mine. Then I'll run you to the grocery store to get everything we need."

"I'll need you to take care of the wine," she said ruefully. "Carson despaired of me ever getting it right."

She nearly bit her tongue in frustration. Just moments before she'd sworn that she'd stop bringing up Carson and inserting a wedge between her and Dash. No man would want to be constantly competing with another man, especially a dead man.

Joss waited for the expected surge of pain that always accompanied her speaking of Carson. But it wasn't there this time. There was lingering sadness that she dealt with from time to time but mostly it had subsided. For the first time, she could see the grass on the other side of the fence, and it looked appealing from where she stood.

NINETEEN

THOUGH hosting a dinner party was nothing new for Joss, she had a raging case of nerves because this was her first dinner acting as *Dash's* host. And the attendees were all friends. There was no reason for her to be nervous, but she was. Because though her friends knew of her relationship with Dash, she hadn't openly flaunted it in front of them.

She put the finishing touches on the salad and stuck the bowl in the fridge before popping the potatoes in the oven. The steaks were marinating, and Dash would throw them on the grill closer to the time to eat.

First, they would talk to Kylie, and Dash would tell her that Jensen was partnering with Dash. Joss dreaded the confrontation but knew it was better had here in private, in a place Kylie felt comfortable in, rather than Dash telling her in the office and springing it on her in a place where she couldn't react honestly.

The doorbell rang and she hurried out of the kitchen, calling to Dash that she'd get it. She wanted to be the first to greet Kylie.

When she opened the door, Kylie smiled at her and Joss pulled her into a hug.

"I'd ask how you're doing but your look says it all," Kylie said wryly. "You look . . . happy, Joss. I'm glad."

Joss impulsively squeezed her again. "Thanks. How are you

doing? I know it's only been a couple of days, but I feel like I haven't seen or spoken to you in forever!"

"That's because you wimped out on me and Chessy and e-mailed us," Kylie said in a dry tone.

Joss laughed. "Yes, I did. I figured it would be easier to just e-mail you both and get it out. It would certainly take less time than a phone call because you both would grill me mercilessly."

A grin tugged at the corners of Kylie's mouth as they entered Dash's living room. Kylie glanced around and when she saw no one she turned to Joss, lowering her voice.

"Is he good to you, Joss? You look happy but are you really?"

Joss smiled, letting her happiness show on her face as she looked at her friend. "He's very good to me, Kylie. Things are better than I imagined they could be. I really *am* happy."

Kylie reached out and squeezed her hand. "Then I'm happy for you. I know I didn't seem that way in the beginning, and I'm sorry for that. I was just worried about you. I do want you to be happy, Joss. I hope you know that."

"I do. I love you. Don't ever forget that."

Dash entered the living room and walked over to kiss Kylie's cheek. "Glad you could make it, Kylie. Would you care for a drink? I have something I need to discuss with you before the others arrive."

Kylie sent him an inquisitive look. "Wine will be fine. You choose. I'll like whatever you offer."

Dash poured glasses for both women and returned, holding them out to the two women.

"What did you want to talk to me about?" Kylie asked curiously.

Dash sighed and briefly looked discomfited. But Joss knew he wasn't the type to dance around an issue. He'd come out and say it and then deal with the blowback, whatever it was.

"A new partner is joining our business," Dash said as bluntly as Joss knew he would be.

Kylie's eyes widened and her lips parted but she didn't respond. She simply stared at Dash, seemingly frozen by his statement.

"His name is Jensen Tucker," Dash continued. "Carson and I had considered taking him on a few years ago. When Carson died, I put those plans on hold and focused on keeping the business afloat. But it's time. He's a solid addition and he'll be an asset to the company."

"You're just replacing him?" Kylie said hoarsely. "Why? You're doing a fine job, Dash. Why do you need this guy? What could he possibly have to offer?"

Her voice rose, her tone growing more emotional at the end.

Joss went to Dash and laced her fingers through his, squeezing to signal her support. He squeezed back, shooting her a grateful look.

"You're okay with this?" Kylie asked Joss accusingly.

Joss's face flushed and for a moment she was at a loss for words. No, she hadn't expected Kylie to take it well at first, but she hadn't expected the outright accusation in her tone. That she would direct her anger at Joss. This wasn't her company or her choice. Yes, she owned a part of the business, but she had no power and no say in the decision making. That was all Dash's and now Jensen's. She and Kylie both benefited from the profits. Carson had made certain of that. But neither woman had a say in the running of the business. Carson had trusted that to Dash, and Joss agreed with that choice.

"I can't believe you would support his decision in this," Kylie said in a hoarse voice. "Have you forgotten Carson already? Are you so wrapped up in a new relationship that you'd turn your back on what your husband built?"

"That's enough," Dash bit out, his jaw tight with anger. "You will not direct your ire at Joss. If you have something to say then you damn well say it to me. You will *not* make her feel badly over this. It wasn't her decision, but yes, she supports it and me. Deal with it. You can make this as easy or as difficult as you want, Kylie. That's your choice. Jensen is coming over tonight and you'll meet him then. I expect you to be professional and cordial."

Warmth spread through Joss's chest at Dash's instant defense of her. He was angry and it took a lot to make him so. But he was positively seething over Kylie's outburst and he'd wrapped his arm protectively around Joss, silently and not so silently giving her his absolute support. Just as she'd done for him.

"And if I'm not?" Kylie challenged. "Are you going to fire me if I don't like this person you've brought in to replace Carson?"

"If it comes to that, yes," Dash said in a low voice. "I hope it wouldn't come to that, Kylie. You are very good at what you do. This company needs you. I need you. I would hate to ever have to replace you, but if you make trouble for Jensen, you can and will be replaced."

Kylie paled, her eyes going stark with pain. Her gaze flitted over Joss with the same accusation she'd voiced just moments before. Joss flinched at the look, knowing Kylie saw this as the ultimate betrayal. Not just by Dash but by Joss herself. She'd expected Joss to side with her. To protest Carson's replacement.

It was evident in her every expression, her body language, that she was furious, not only with Dash but with Joss, and perhaps more so with Joss.

"You invite me over, dump this on me like this and then expect me to play nice with a man who is replacing my brother," she said painfully. "How did you *expect* me to react?"

"We invited you over because I would rather tell you in private and give you time to collect yourself before he arrives. The alternative was telling you in the office on Monday, and I thought we meant more to one another than for me to tell you in a business setting. Perhaps I was wrong about that."

Dash's voice was cold, anger radiating from him in waves. Kylie had pushed him too far and her attack on Joss had infuriated him all the more. Joss squeezed his hand again, a silent signal that it was all right.

"It's okay, Dash," Joss said softly, voicing her thoughts so he would know without question. "I understand why she's upset. She doesn't mean it."

"It's not okay," Dash bit out. "She has no right to treat you this way and I won't allow it in our home."

"Our home?" Kylie asked incredulously. "Have things progressed so far then, Joss? Have you already moved on and forgotten the man you were married to for three years? What exactly is going on here? Are we all supposed to just forget that Carson existed? Maybe you can, but I can't. He was my only family and he's not so easily replaced. Not for me."

"If you don't apologize to Joss right this minute, I'll ask you to leave, and furthermore, you will come into the office on Monday only to clear out your desk and tender your resignation," Dash said in a frigid tone. "What is between me and Joss is none of your business. She doesn't require your approval or blessing, though she'd like to have both. She loves you and she'd cut off her arm before ever purposely hurting you. But you're hurting her and that's bullshit. I won't have it and I damn sure won't allow you to come into our home. Yes, *our* home, Kylie. Joss is with me, and you have two choices. Accept it and be happy for her or get out. Which is it going to be?"

Joss felt the color bleed from her own face, a match to Kylie's. She shook uncontrollably and it seemed to anger Dash all the more. His hold tightened around her to the point that she could barely breathe. No, she hadn't expected Kylie to take it well, but neither had she expected Kylie to lash out at her like this.

Was it what Chessy thought too? That she had so easily forgotten Carson and moved on at the first opportunity? Were neither of her friends truly happy for her? Would she lose their friendship because she wanted to be happy again? Why was being happy asking too much? Why couldn't Kylie accept that all Joss wanted was to not be so lonely any longer?

Tears burned her eyelids and Dash saw. His entire body tensed and fury fired through his eyes.

"You've upset Joss and that I won't accept," Dash said tightly. "Apologize or leave, and make it quick. I will not stand by and allow her to be abused in her own home."

Kylie looked shocked and pained at Dash's words. The word *abuse* struck a chord in Kylie and it obviously horrified her that she would be accused of abusing another person.

"I'm sorry, Joss," Kylie said in a near sob. "I didn't mean to hurt or upset you."

"You've done both," Dash said in a curt voice.

"It's okay," Joss said quietly. "I know you didn't mean it, Kylie. Give Jensen a chance. I've met him and he seems like a good man. Carson liked and respected him. That should be enough for you."

Kylie briefly closed her eyes and then she hurried over, throwing her arms around Joss, knocking Dash away.

"I'm sorry. I love you. I do. I'm so sorry, Joss. What I said was awful. There's no excuse. I was just caught off guard. I wasn't expecting it. Please forgive me."

Joss hugged her back, her heart still constricted at the things Kylie had said. She believed Kylie was genuinely sorry but her words still hurt. Like tiny darts finding their target. Was it what everyone would think? That she'd so easily gotten over Carson and could so easily replace him? It had been three years! It wasn't as though she'd hopped into the sack with Dash a week, a month or even a year after Carson died.

Dash looked at Joss over Kylie's shoulder, his expression murderous. He knew Joss was hurt—was still hurting—over Kylie's outburst, and it was obvious he'd do anything to spare her pain.

Joss shook her head at Dash, a signal to drop it. Kylie was emotional. She'd always been so. And she often spoke without thinking. Joss knew Kylie loved her just as she also recognized Kylie's faults. And when you loved someone, you accepted every part of them. Even the not so perfect things.

Dash nodded grimly, accepting Joss's silent plea to let it go. When Kylie pulled away from Joss, she turned her troubled gaze to Dash.

"I'm sorry, Dash. Please forgive me. I'll try to accept him. I won't do anything to embarrass you. And if I still have a position with you, I'll do my best. I'll do the job you've come to expect from me."

Dash's expression softened just a bit and he pulled Kylie into a firm hug.

"I would appreciate that, Kylie. You're damn good at running my—our—office, and I fully expect you'll do the job going forward. But if I hear of you speaking to Joss the way you just spoke to her ever again, I won't be as understanding the next time."

The warning fell over the room. Kylie nodded her acceptance and glanced back at Joss, sorrow and regret brimming in her eyes.

"I forgive you, Kylie," Joss said quietly and sincerely. "Please, let's just forget about it and enjoy the evening. Chessy and Tate will be here soon, as will Jensen. Please give him a chance."

Her tone was pleading but she had always been the peacemaker. She hated dissension or strife of any kind. It was just her nature and Dash was well acquainted with that aspect of her personality. It was why he'd shut Kylie down so quickly and fiercely. She loved that he was so protective of her. She felt safe with him. Not just physically but emotionally, and perhaps emotionally was the most important because she'd already suffered so much in that area. She needed and wanted her feelings protected and cherished. If that made her weak, oh well. It was what she wanted—needed—and Dash seemed determined to provide it for her.

"I'll give him a chance. For you, Joss," Kylie said, making the distinction that she would do so for Joss and not necessarily Dash. Which was odd considering Dash was her boss and it was him she needed to be concerned with pissing off.

But Joss was her friend—her sister—and that bond was solid and unbreakable, or at least Joss hoped it was. She prayed this wouldn't be a strain they wouldn't recover from.

"We appreciate your support," Dash said quietly. "It means a lot that you'll stand behind us, Kylie. You aren't just an employee. You're family."

Kylie's eyes watered and she quickly wiped the betraying moisture away. "We're wasting good wine," she said shakily, a tremulous smile on her lips. She was trying, making the effort, and Joss loved her for that.

"Why don't you come into the kitchen with me while I prepare the hors d'oeuvres," Joss said, extending her hand to her sister-in-law. "We can wait for Chessy to get here and we'll drain a bottle of wine while the guys do their thing over the grill."

Kylie smiled genuinely this time and took Joss's hand, squeezing it in silent apology.

The two women entered the kitchen, awkward silence between them. Joss busied herself preparing the tray of appetizers and she turned the steaks in the marinade. She checked her watch, knowing the others would be arriving shortly. She was impatient for Chessy to get there so she could alleviate the tension between Joss and Kylie.

She breathed a sigh of relief when, a few moments later, Chessy sailed into the kitchen, a cheerful smile on her pretty face.

"Hey, guys," she sang out.

She hugged Kylie and then went over to offer Joss a hug.

"What's up with Kylie?" Chessy whispered against Joss's ear.

"Tell you later," Joss murmured back.

Chessy's eyes narrowed as she pulled away but she quickly pasted her smile back on and went to plop onto the barstool next to Kylie.

Kylie was noticeably subdued even though Chessy chattered on, filling the awkward lapse between Joss and Kylie. But Chessy's sharp gaze didn't miss the discomfort that lay like a blanket over the other two women.

When the doorbell rang, Kylie paled and then immediately excused herself to go to the bathroom. The moment Kylie left, Chessy pounced on Joss, walking around the counter to stand beside Joss while Joss pulled the steaks from the marinade and patted them dry.

"What the hell is going on here?" Chessy demanded. "Kylie bolted like a bat out of hell the minute the doorbell rang."

"Long story," Joss muttered. "Dash is bringing in Jensen Tucker as a partner, and Kylie didn't take the news well at all. That's him at the door. He's coming over to meet everyone. We invited Kylie earlier so Dash could tell her in private, and she freaked. Like really freaked. She said some pretty harsh things. To me."

Chessy's eyes widened. "Really?"

Joss nodded. "Dash was pissed. Extremely pissed. He basically threatened to fire her if she didn't apologize and he told her if she ever came at me like that again he'd fire her on the spot."

"Wow," Chessy breathed. "Not that I don't agree with him protecting you, but wow."

"Yeah. My thoughts exactly."

Chessy grabbed the tray as Kylie reentered the kitchen, as though she'd come over to help.

"Grab the wine, Kylie," Chessy said cheerfully. "We'll go serve up Joss's yum-yums to the menfolk."

Her pretend obliviousness to the entire situation almost fooled even Joss. Kylie looked like a deer in the headlights, but there was no way for her to object without making a scene. She sighed but took the wine bottle from the table and followed Chessy into the living room.

Joss was only a few feet behind and she immediately went to greet Jensen, wanting to make him as comfortable as possible since it was obvious Kylie wasn't going to be as welcoming.

Jensen kissed her on both cheeks and smiled warmly at her.

"Has Dash introduced you to everyone?" Joss asked.

"Everyone but Kylie and Chessy."

She took his hand, pulling him toward where the other two women stood. Jensen looked befuddled while Dash smiled at Joss taking charge.

"Ladies, I want you to meet Jensen Tucker, Dash's new partner. Jensen, these are my two best friends, Chessy and Kylie."

"I'm her sister-in-law," Kylie said pointedly.

"I'm very pleased to meet you both, but especially you, Kylie. I've heard much about you. Dash says you're indispensable at the office. I'm looking forward to working with you."

Kylie flushed at the praise and ducked her head, not meeting Jensen's gaze directly.

"It's nice to meet you too," she said stiffly.

Chessy extended her hand to shake Jensen's and he pulled it up as he'd done with Joss the night before and brushed a kiss over the back. Then he pointedly extended his hand to Kylie and when she reluctantly took it, he pulled hers up as well, but he was much slower to lower it once he'd kissed hers.

Kylie snatched her hand away as though she'd been burned and tucked it protectively behind her back. If Jensen noticed her reaction he didn't show it. His smile was bland and he didn't so much as blink.

"How long have you known Dash?" Chessy asked curiously.

Trust Chessy never to miss a beat. She was an absolute charmer, and it looked as though Jensen was enchanted with her. Who wouldn't be? Was it any wonder Tate was so forbiddingly possessive of her? But Dash had said he shared Chessy with other men. Joss still couldn't wrap her brain around it. Even now Tate was watching intently, taking in Jensen's reaction to his wife. Though he was across the room, his gaze never left Chessy, and he'd frowned when Jensen had kissed her hand. He was broodingly watching the interaction between Jensen and all the women. Though Dash was conversing with Tate, Tate's focus wasn't on Dash. It was squarely on Chessy.

Chessy was a born flirt. Vivacious. Beautiful. She never met a stranger, and her laughter was infectious. Joss had always been envious of Chessy's confidence and her outgoing personality. Joss was quieter and more reserved than Chessy. But Carson had never minded. He'd adored Joss's shyness. Had been delighted that he was her first lover. He'd told her how much it meant to him that she'd waited. For him.

Joss shook her thoughts from Carson. She hadn't thought of him all day. Not until Kylie had thrown her dead husband in her face. And now he dominated her thoughts and it was the last thing she wanted. Not when she was in Dash's home acting as his hostess. Something she'd done for Carson any number of times.

But these people were her friends. Yes, she'd only just met

Jensen, but she'd warmed instantly to him. He was quiet and brooding. He'd intimidated her at first glance, but he'd quickly made her feel at ease, and he'd been understanding of Kylie's feelings. Even now he didn't seem to take her reaction to him personally. He stood there conversing politely, seemingly oblivious to Kylie's obvious discomfort.

"Excuse me," Joss said.

She walked over to where Dash stood with Tate, and Tate smiled warmly at her, pulling her into a quick hug and pressing an affectionate kiss to her cheek.

"Hey, darlin'. Long time no see."

She smiled back at him. "You need to stop being such a stranger, Tate. Work keeping you busy these days? I swear it's been forever since I've seen you."

His eyes twinkled. "I'd hardly think you'd notice my absence. It appears Dash has been keeping you pretty occupied lately."

She blushed to the roots of her hair as both men laughed. Tate reached for her hand and squeezed it warmly.

"I'm happy for you, sweetheart. You deserve happiness, and Dash is just the man to make it happen for you. I wish you both the best."

Her face still flaming, she glanced shyly at Dash before returning her attention to Tate. What had Dash told Tate about her? Or maybe Chessy had been the one to share the details of her relationship with Dash.

"Thank you," she said sincerely. "Dash makes me happy."

Dash's face softened at her words and Tate smiled gently.

"You deserve to be happy, darlin'. And you won't find a better man than Dash."

"I know," she said quietly.

Then remembering why she'd come over, she glanced back up at Dash. "The steaks are ready to go on the grill. Everything else is ready. Potatoes are in the oven, and they'll be ready by the time you take the steaks up. You guys can head back to the grill. I'll make drinks or there's beer and wine. Whatever y'all want."

Dash leaned down to kiss her forehead and then cupped her face in a gentle caress. "Thanks, honey. I'll round up Tate and Jensen, and we'll go do our manly duty. Everything going okay with Kylie?"

His gaze searched hers intently, looking for any signs of upset.

Joss nodded. "She's not very comfortable around Jensen, but we expected that. He can be very . . . intimidating. Just the type of man who'd put Kylie on edge."

Tate grimaced. "This is going to be hard for her. I hate it but she has to put her past behind her at some point. She can't continue to let it rule her present and future. I'm glad you stuck to your guns, Dash. She needs that."

Dash nodded his agreement as his expression darkened. He glanced in Kylie's direction, his frown deepening. "She was out of line for lashing out at Joss the way she did. That I won't allow. She can say whatever she wants to me, but I'll be damned if she pulls that shit with Joss."

Joss's heart warmed all over again. She pressed into Dash's side and tipped her head up to kiss him on the mouth. He seemed surprised and then delighted at her spontaneous show of affection.

"Thank you," she whispered. "It means a lot that you'd stick up for me the way you did."

He put a finger underneath her chin, tipping it upward to meet his steady gaze. "Always, honey. I'll never allow anyone to hurt you. Count on that."

She smiled and then shooed him toward the kitchen.

"If y'all don't get the meat on, we'll never eat. We're hungry!"

Laughing, Dash headed in Jensen's direction, Tate following

behind. After a moment the three men disappeared into the kitchen, and Joss heard the door to the patio open and then shut as they went out to tend the grill.

Noticing Kylie's and Chessy's wineglasses were nearly empty, she went to fetch a bottle and refilled theirs as well as hers.

She motioned for them to sit and get comfortable, knowing they had half an hour before the steaks were ready.

It was just like old times, only Carson wasn't there. He was the only missing component, and now there was Jensen, filling that void. It would never be the same, and for the first time Joss felt optimistic about that fact. No, nothing would ever be the same, but it was certainly possible that it would be *better*.

TWENTY

AS if knowing how trying the evening had been for Joss and how emotionally fragile she was, Dash made love to her so tenderly that she was overcome. Afterward, he pulled her to him, binding their wrists as he'd done previously and then cradled her in his arms, her head pillowed on his shoulder.

She loved the intimacy of the act. Of being bound to him. It was more than just a physical binding. She felt connected to him on a much deeper level. One she welcomed and savored with her entire heart.

She fell into a deep sleep, contented and sated, and yet when her dreams came, they were disturbing. Carson was there, smiling at her, holding out his hand. Dash was on the other side, standing with his heart in his eyes. The voice inside her head told her to choose. That if she had the choice of having Carson back or remaining with Dash, which would she pick?

She frowned even in sleep, her forehead creasing in pain. How could she make such a choice? She'd always said she'd do anything to have Carson back. Anything at all. But now it wasn't so simple. Now she had Dash.

She was caught in the middle of two men she cared about, each pulling her in a different direction. The dream didn't make sense. She couldn't have Carson back, so why was she being tormented with the choice?

And yet each man was demanding she decide. Carson's smile faltered and sadness entered his eyes. His hand dropped, his shoulders sagging in defeat. But Dash didn't look triumphant. He looked tortured, as though he'd do anything in the world to spare Joss the pain she faced.

Dash turned away from her, making her decision for her, but that wasn't what she wanted. Still, she didn't reach for Carson. She remained standing, frozen with the impossibility of the task before her.

How could she choose? Her past or her present? Her future? Carson was dead. She couldn't—wouldn't—betray Dash's faith in her. Even in her dreams, she wouldn't allow such a thing to happen.

Her heart in pieces, she watched helplessly as Carson turned, slowly fading away, becoming transparent, the look on his face slashing her open, leaving her bleeding on the inside.

"I'm sorry, Carson. I'm so sorry," she whispered.

Tears slipped down her cheeks, warm against the coolness of her skin.

Dash watched her in the darkness, helplessness gripping him. She was fighting her demons even in sleep and he was powerless to do anything about it. Worse, she was crying for her dead husband, apologizing to him. For what? For cheating on him? For betraying his memory as Kylie had accused her of? Did Dash ever have a hope of winning her heart or would a dead man forever own it?

He silently untied the sash binding their wrists together and this time it was he who turned away, putting his back to Joss. And again, sleep eluded him. He lay there, fighting his own demons while Joss battled hers, just inches away and a world apart all at the same time.

TWENTY-ONE

JOSS awakened the next morning feeling emotionally wrung out from her troubled, upsetting dreams. She automatically reached for Dash, needing the comfort he offered, a shelter from the emotional turmoil of her dreams.

To her surprise not only was her wrist no longer bound to his, but he wasn't in bed. She struggled to sit up, brushing back her hair so she could see. Across the room Dash stood in front of the dresser buttoning the sleeves to his dress shirt. His expression was solemn, as if he were deep in thought.

"Dash?"

His name came out shaky and soft, but he heard her and turned immediately, his expression indecipherable.

"I have to be in early this morning," he said in a neutral tone. "There's a lot to do before Jensen's partnership is announced. I'm not sure how late I'll be but I'll call to let you know when I'm on my way home."

Her brow furrowed. His mood was the same as it had been the previous morning when she hadn't been able to discern what was bothering him. And it was evident that something was. She may be an open book when it came to her emotions, but Dash was similar in that she only had to look into his eyes to know if something was off. And for the second morning, he wasn't his usual, loving self.

He didn't even come to the bed to kiss her, and she felt too self-conscious to get out of bed to go to him. She was too afraid he'd reject her and so she remained where she was, studying him from underneath her lashes.

"Be careful," she said quietly. "I'll look forward to you coming home. Shall I cook dinner for us tonight?"

"Whatever you like," he said indifferently. "We can eat out if you prefer."

"I'll cook," she said firmly, wanting to do something to please him.

He nodded and then turned back, collecting his watch and wallet and car keys.

She waited for him to kiss her. For him to offer a sweet word. For him to tell her he'd miss her. Anything. Something. But he simply collected his belongings and strode toward the door, leaving her in bed, her lips parted in surprise.

She flopped back onto the pillow, staring up at the ceiling. What the hell was going on? What was with his Jekyll and Hyde act? It was exhausting trying to keep up with his mood swings. She'd been nothing but honest and open with him at every turn, and yet he was holding back from her.

Supposedly women were the moody, emotional creatures. According to men. But men were far more guilty of being volatile. Up and down. One minute he was sweet, tender and absolutely adoring. The next? Silent and brooding over God only knew what.

Maybe he just wasn't a morning person. Admittedly, until recently, she had zero experience with him in the mornings. She'd never had cause to see him or interact with him in the early hours of the day. Her exposure to him had been limited to afternoons and evenings, and he'd been nothing but charming on those occasions.

Oh well, she'd have to have enough morning cheer for both of them apparently. She's always been an early riser and what she considered a morning person. Carson had teased her about being disgustingly cheerful the moment she rose from bed.

Thoughts of Carson brought back the disturbing dreams from the night before. Her lips turned down into an unhappy frown. What did they mean? Dreams were inexplicable, a manifestation of the subconscious. Who the hell knew what they really meant? Maybe they meant nothing at all. Maybe it was just a battle between her past and present, colliding at night when her thoughts were unguarded.

At any rate, she wished they'd go away. Carson was gone. He wasn't coming back. Last night's dream had bothered her immensely. The heaviness followed her into the waking hours, weighing on her as she remembered the impossible choice she'd faced in the dream.

It was silly because she'd never face that choice. It was pointless to even dwell on it and think about which way she'd go because it was never going to happen. The choice had been made for her.

Would she choose Carson if she could have him back? Would she turn her back on Dash and everything he offered? She shook her head, refusing to go there. It would only lead to guilty feelings on her part because in her dream she hadn't chosen him.

"Stop thinking about it, Joss. You're only upsetting yourself and feeling unnecessary guilt. Carson would want you to be happy. He wouldn't want you to mourn him forever. Get over it and move on."

She briefly wondered if she should see a doctor. Not a shrink. God, anything but that. But perhaps her doctor could give her something to make her sleep more soundly so she wasn't tormented by dreams of her husband and her current lover.

Filing that away and making a mental note to place a call to her physician, she forced herself out of bed, wondering what she'd do the entire day while Dash was at work.

What had she done before she'd moved into his house?

More and more she considered going back to work as a nurse. She needed a purpose. Something to occupy her time so she wasn't doing nothing day in, day out. Her CEUs were current. She had her license. She could go back to work at any time.

What would Dash think? He'd made it clear that he wanted her time to be his own, but he had to work. He couldn't just drop everything to be with her twenty-four-seven, and she wouldn't expect him to.

She didn't necessarily want to go back to shift work, and it wasn't probable that she'd score a day shift job, coming in as low man on the totem pole. Yes, the swing and night shift made more per hour, but she didn't need the money. She was financially secure thanks to Carson. What she needed was something to occupy her time.

Maybe she could seek employment at a doctor's office. At least then her hours would be normal and she'd have weekends off.

And there was the fact that she'd planned to go back to school to become a nurse practitioner. She had classes and credits toward that goal, but she'd quit when she'd quit her job. She only lacked a year and she could have her license and go to work under a doctor in private practice.

It was something she was going to give serious thought to. She was tired of being at loose ends and it was time for her to take charge of her life once more. She was young. She'd already taken charge of her sexuality and taken the plunge with Dash. All that remained was for her to decide on going back to work.

She would discuss it with Dash and get his thoughts when he was in a better mood. Not that she needed his approval. She was perfectly capable of making her own decisions. Yes, she'd given him her submission, had wanted him to have absolute control over her. But she still retained the option of making the important decisions that affected her happiness. And if Dash truly cared for her, he wouldn't stand in the way of her happiness.

Feeling marginally better about her future, she went through the motions of the day. She spent half an hour on the Internet looking up recipes. She wanted to make Dash something special. Finding a yummy-looking chicken and cheese casserole dish that would be simple to prepare, she then took stock of Dash's pantry and fridge and realized she'd have to go out to pick up the necessary ingredients.

For that matter his pantry was pretty empty and his fridge wasn't much better. Happy to have something to do, she made a list and planned a series of meals, making sure she wrote down the necessary ingredients for all the recipes. When her list was completed, she then took stock of the bathroom and toiletries.

She hadn't brought all of her girly stuff, though she'd gotten most of it from home. She'd run by her house and pack more of her things to bring over to Dash's since it appeared he had no intention of her spending the night anywhere but in his home.

By the time she was on her way, her mood had lightened and some of the heaviness had lifted away. She was nearly to the grocery store when she realized she hadn't let Dash know where she'd be. She wasn't used to having to answer to anyone, but it was common courtesy now that she was living with Dash to at least let him know her whereabouts.

She sent him a quick text letting him know what she was doing and that she was cooking a special dinner for him, adding a smiley face and a heart at the end of the text.

She cringed, wondering if he'd find the emoticons annoying. Carson had found them endearing and cute. They were "so her," as Carson had put it. She sighed, catching herself in mental comparison yet again. She had to quit it. Carson was gone, as she reminded herself on a daily basis now. The endless thinking back to what he liked and didn't like was getting old. And it would most certainly get old with Dash. Thank God she hadn't voiced her thoughts aloud to him and only went through them mentally.

Her phone went off and she smiled at Dash's response. And to think she'd worried that he'd find her text annoying.

Thanks, honey. Looking forward to it. xoxo

It had been a long time since she'd cooked for someone else. Oh, she'd fixed lunch and dinner a few times for the girls, but she hadn't prepared an intimate meal for a lover since . . . No, she wasn't going there, damn it.

She enjoyed her trip to the grocery store and realized halfway through that she should have stopped by her house first because she'd have perishable items waiting in her car and the temps were well into the upper eighties today.

Oh well, she'd just have to make her stopover at her house quick.

She cranked up the radio on the way to her house, singing along as she rolled up in her driveway. With a smile, she hopped out and hurried inside to collect the things she needed.

Five minutes later she shoved an extra suitcase into the minuscule backseat—if it even classified as a real backseat since a person certainly couldn't fit—because her tiny trunk was filled to bursting with the groceries she'd purchased, and she headed back in the direction of Dash's house. Her home now.

It would take time for her to consider it hers. She still very much considered it Dash's house. But if things worked out long term . . .

She stopped, realizing this was the first time she was thinking long term. She'd been hesitant to put her hopes into it becoming more. Permanent. But things were off to a very solid start if she didn't count his morning moodiness. But she could deal with that. She could be cheerful enough for them both.

It took her five trips into the house to get all the bags out of her trunk and one last one to collect her bulging suitcase. Dash would laugh at all the stuff she considered essential.

After putting away all the groceries, she laid out the ingredients for tonight's dinner and wondered if she should start it now or wait until he got home.

Her forehead wrinkled as she pondered her options. Dash had been clear on how he wanted her to be waiting when he got home each day, but she hadn't heard from him on when he would arrive. She glanced at her watch. It was only four thirty. A typical day was five o'clock, and he'd said he might be later today.

She'd decided to go ahead and get a start on supper when her phone rang. Glancing at the screen, she saw Dash's name and smiled, reaching eagerly for the phone.

"Hello?"

"Hey, honey. I'm on my way home."

A light shiver worked over her shoulders. "I'll be waiting," she said huskily.

"I'm looking forward to it," he said in a low voice that matched hers.

"See you soon."

"Bye, honey."

She punched the button to end the call and then hurriedly put away the stuff for supper. It wouldn't take much time to prepare at all and she could do it after he got home. For now she wanted to focus on being exactly as he wanted her. On her knees, naked, waiting in the living room so she was the first thing he saw when he walked through the door.

TWENTY-TWO

DASH pulled into his driveway and saw Joss's car parked there in the space next to his. He sat for a moment, hands clenched tight around the steering wheel. He had no idea what to expect when he walked into his house. He'd been a jerk this morning. He knew that. But he hadn't been able to summon his usual tenderness when his mind was eaten alive by Joss crying over Carson after making love to Dash.

He hadn't slept, and the result had been him acting like a grumpy bear with a sore paw.

With a sigh he kicked open his car door and got out, determined to see this through.

He opened his front door and walked inside, moving automatically to the living room.

The sight that awaited him took his breath away. Joss was kneeling on the rug in front of the fireplace, naked, her beautiful hair streaming over her shoulders, her nipples playing an erotic game of peekaboo through the tendrils.

He was being the worst sort of ass and yet she waited, just as she'd agreed, naked and kneeling. For him.

She was making the effort. No matter what was going on in her head, she was trying. She was trying to make this work between them. How could he do anything less?

Forgotten was the previous night as he absorbed the image of her, transfixed by the sight of her kneeling in submission.

"Ah honey," he whispered as he crossed the room to her.

All thoughts of dominance fled. He only wanted to hold her, to apologize for the way he'd treated her this morning. He wanted her in his arms, soft and precious. He looped his hands underneath her armpits and lifted, her startled gaze fixed on his face as he hauled her up and into his arms.

He wrapped himself around her, kissing her until they were both breathless, their chests heaving for air. He delved his hands into her hair, wrapping the silken mass around his fingers only wanting to touch her. To surround himself with her.

Again, he kissed her, devouring her lips, tasting and licking. His body surged to life, hard and aching against her belly. He had to have her now. Right now.

He walked her back to the couch and settled her on the cushions before hurriedly freeing himself from his pants. His dick jutted forward, straining, so hard his balls hurt.

When she leaned forward to take him in her mouth, he took a step back and placed his hands on her shoulders.

"No, honey. You aren't pleasuring me right now. I was an ass this morning and I have a lot to make up for. Let me pleasure you. Let me make you feel good."

Her eyes warmed, instant forgiveness in her gaze. But that was Joss. Never one to hold a grudge. He felt infinitely unworthy of her in this moment. Unconditional and unwavering. This was the woman he loved and adored, and he was doing his best to fuck up everything before they even had a shot.

He stood back and stripped his clothing off, barely able to control his urge to take her hard and deep. But he'd promised her the ultimate pleasure and he'd do it even if the waiting killed him.

"Spread your legs and lean back against the back of the couch," he said in a husky voice.

Desire made her eyelids heavy and she looked up at him with drugged, intoxicated eyes. He knelt in front of her, running his fingers lightly down the insides of her thighs.

Her pussy was open and bared to him, perfect pink folds, delicate and feminine just like her. He traced a line over the hood, brushing her clit and continuing down to circle her opening before pushing in the barest of inches.

She moaned softly and went wet around his finger. So responsive and receptive. Her body clutched at his finger as he withdrew as if it didn't want to let go. Then he lowered his head, his tongue lapping at her sweet moisture.

"Dash!"

His name came out, explosive in the silence. His name. Not Carson's. That fact gratified him immensely. Her husband may occupy her dreams, but Dash had her in the present. For now he'd take that and hold on for all he was worth. Sooner or later he'd have her dreams as well as her in the waking.

He nibbled lightly and then sucked, rolling his tongue over her clit, exerting just enough pressure to make her wild beneath him. Her fingers thrust into his short-cut hair and then dug into his scalp, encouraging him, holding him in place.

She was in control, and he found he didn't mind at all. For this moment, she was calling the shots and he'd allow it. Whatever she wanted. He was hers to command.

A soft hum blew from her lips. Satisfaction and desire all rolled into one. She arched upward, moving him to the places that brought her greater pleasure. He was an apt student, taking in her body's response when he hit a particularly sweet spot.

He was a quick study and soon she didn't have to direct him.

He learned her body, absorbing the knowledge of what made her crazy with want.

He placed an openmouthed kiss to her pussy entrance and then thrust his tongue as deep as he could get into her liquid warmth.

He wanted her to come in his mouth, an instant hot rush of release. He maneuvered his fingers, two of them below his mouth, and plunged them inside, caressing the silken walls of her vagina.

He probed gently, seeking the spot where the texture was more plush and different, slightly rougher. He pressed upward, eliciting an instant cry from her. She grew wetter and panted, the sounds an aphrodisiac to his ears.

His cock was flat against his belly, so hard and pulsing that he was nearly out of his mind with the need to claim her. But he'd deny himself that ultimate satisfaction. For her. This was all about her. Only for her. His silent apology for being a bastard and taking out his black mood on her.

He didn't like feeling jealous. Especially of a dead man. A man who'd been his best friend. But there it was. He was insanely jealous of Carson's hold on her even from the grave.

"Are you close, honey?"

"Yes! Please don't stop, Dash. I need you."

The heartfelt plea seized his very soul, warming him from the inside out. Liquid sunshine. He basked in her radiance, her pleasure and need.

He thrust with his fingers, exerting firmer pressure on her pleasure spot as his tongue circled her clit and sucked gently. She quivered uncontrollably underneath him, her thighs shaking, her knees knocking against his sides.

"Give it to me," he rasped. "Give it to me now, Joss. Everything. Let go."

She arched upward, her cry endless and pained. He quickly covered the mouth of her pussy with his own and sucked hard as she pulsed and vibrated in her orgasm. Her honey coated his tongue, spurring his need even higher.

His thumb moved up to her clit to replace his tongue and he rubbed gently, coaxing wave after wave of release from her.

Finally she sagged onto the couch, her body going limp. He glanced up to see her half-lidded eyes lazily surveying him, glowing with contentment. She reminded him of a satisfied cat and she was all but purring.

When he would have stood to replace his clothing, she quickly sat forward, her hands going to his hips to stop him. Then without a word, she grasped his cock and guided it toward her mouth, slipping the head between her lips.

"Don't deny me the same chance to pleasure you," she said, her voice laced with the husky remnants of her orgasm. She sounded hoarse and needy, as though she still had a ways to go to complete her pleasure.

"Just stand there, Dash. Let me love you."

He closed his eyes, a wave of contentment rolling over him with the power to bring him to his knees. God yes, he'd allow her to love him. It was everything he'd ever wanted.

His hands tangled in her hair, lifting it and pulling it away so he could see her face, could see her lips wrapped around his dick. She sucked him deep, holding him at the back of her throat and then swallowing around it, milking him.

"I won't last long, honey."

Her lips curved into a smile around his cock.

"I know."

And then she began to pump her fist around his dick, sucking him hard and deep. It was a pace destined to drive him over the edge within seconds. And it did. Before she'd sucked him deep the fourth time, he was already coming, jetting and pulsing deep into her throat.

She swallowed greedily, sucking, demanding more. Not a single drop spilled from her lips. Her fingers gently lowered to his balls, caressing and rolling them in her palm. He was up on tiptoe, straining forward, his body so tight that he felt he was coming apart at the seams.

The last of his semen erupted and still she sucked and licked gently, bringing him down until he was simply too sensitive to bear her tender ministrations any longer.

He caught her hand, forcing her to still her motions, and then he carefully withdrew from her mouth, her tongue running along the back of the length as he pulled away.

He pulled her to stand in front of him and caught her in his arms, hugging her tightly to him. He buried his face in her hair and pressed gentle kisses to her head.

"I didn't deserve that," he said hoarsely. "But I won't turn it down. Ever. Thank you, honey. Thank you for forgiving me."

She pulled away, a gentle smile curving her lips. "There's nothing to forgive, Dash."

His feeling of unworthiness skyrocketed. God, but she was perfect. And he was an asshole taking out his frustration on her two mornings in a row, and yet she forgave him as sweetly as a woman ever forgave a man.

"If you'd like, I'll fix you a drink and you can come sit in the kitchen and keep me company while I prepare dinner," she said.

"I'd like that. I'd like that a lot."

The idea of them being so domestic. Of him sitting and watching as she cooked for him. The image was powerful and brought him immeasurable joy.

He quickly dressed and then she held out her hand to his.

"Come on then. I'll fix your drink and then if you don't mind,

I'll get dressed. I don't want to be near a hot stove or oven naked," she said ruefully.

"Use my robe," he said gruffly.

There was nothing he'd like more than to see her wrapped in his robe while she puttered around the kitchen.

"All right," she said softly. "I'll get your robe just as soon as I've fixed your drink."

TWENTY-THREE

THE last two weeks had been a dream. Dash couldn't be happier. Joss glowed with contentment. She'd fallen into her role as a submissive, submissive to him, as though she'd been born to it. And maybe she had.

Maybe it was what she had always craved—needed—and Dash was supremely arrogant and pleased that he was the man who'd provided it for her. There had been no reoccurrence of her saying Carson's name in her sleep. No upsetting dreams. She was, he was beginning to have confidence, his. Completely and utterly his.

He drove faster than normal, eager to get home. Tonight he'd broach the subject of taking Joss to The House for the first time as a couple. He hadn't wanted to rush into it, especially after Joss's first experience at The House. He hadn't wanted to take her there until things were perfect between them. Until that first encounter was wiped firmly from her mind and no embarrassment or shame lingered.

She was ready. He was certainly ready. Ready to take things to the next level. He wanted to publicly claim Joss, but he also wanted to give her what she'd been looking for that very first night.

He was confident that she'd agree, that she'd even be eager to experiment with all of the pleasures The House provided.

Before he'd decided on the night, he'd made damn certain that neither Tate nor Jensen would be there. He wouldn't cause Joss even a moment's discomfort. Jensen had joined and gone through the vetting process and had received his membership just days before.

According to Tate, he and Chessy hadn't been in a long while. Dash had frowned over that fact, remembering his conversation with Joss about Chessy and Tate and her concerns over Chessy's happiness. Tate had seemed awfully preoccupied with work lately. His company was growing by leaps and bounds and the demands on his time had increased.

But he hadn't broached the subject with his friend because it wasn't his business. And he had no way of knowing if the couple was having problems anyway. No need to plant the seed of doubt in Tate's mind if there was no cause for concern. Tate adored Chessy. Dash knew that much. And it would likely make Tate crazy if he even suspected Chessy wasn't happy.

The couple would work it out in their own time. Dash was confident of that. Tate was over the moon in love with his wife. He'd give her the world—had always given her the world. He treasured Chessy's gift of submission. He was damn lucky.

But no, Dash was every bit as fortunate now. He had Joss. Perfect, submissive, loving Joss. She'd gone to great lengths to please him, worrying endlessly that she'd disappoint him. As if.

Dash now knew that even if Joss weren't able to give him what he needed—desired—by being submissive, Dash would forgo that aspect of his personality for her. There was no sacrifice too great to make in order to have his heart's desire.

Joss was enough. She would always be enough.

He pulled into his drive, parking beside Joss's car, and he idly wondered if he should buy her a new car. Something that was from him. A clean break from her past. She'd already moved out of her house, though she hadn't yet put it on the market. They hadn't even discussed it. But it was a subject he'd bring up soon. He wanted Joss here, permanently. He didn't want her to have her own home to go back to. A house she shared with Carson. A home purchased by Carson just as the car she drove had been purchased by her husband.

She could sell the house and bank the money for her own use. She'd never want for anything Dash could provide. He wanted no penny of the money given to her by her husband. It and the income generated by her part of the business would be hers alone. And any children they had in the future.

A goofy grin spread across his face as he got out and headed for the door. The idea of giving Joss the children she so wanted—his children—filled him with absolute happiness. Little girls that looked just like their mother. Boys with his arrogance and her gentle spirit.

Damn, but life was good. And it would only get better.

He knew there were two things Joss dearly wanted that Carson had been unable to provide. One, Dash had already provided. Dominance. The other? Children. Carson had been reluctant to have children, but Dash had no such reservations.

As soon as he convinced her to make their relationship permanent and legal, as soon as he got his ring on her finger, they'd discuss her becoming pregnant. There was no need to wait. Joss had already waited long enough. He wanted nothing more than to make all her dreams come true.

He walked inside and as he'd come to expect, Joss was waiting, on her knees, naked, her eyes welcoming as he strode into the living room.

He went to her instantly, picking her up and cradling her in his arms. He kissed her lovingly, allowing all the love he felt for her to show. He hadn't given her the words, but his actions told her on a daily basis. Surely she knew. And soon he'd give her those words. When he felt the time was right.

"Hi," she said breathlessly, her lips swollen from his passionate kiss. "Good day I take it?"

He grinned. "Not until now, no. But coming home to you is the very best part of my day. Every day."

She smiled and cupped his jaw with her hand, lightly caressing. He savored her touch, craved it with everything he had inside him. He hadn't lied. He looked forward to the end of every day, merely going through the motions at work. He hadn't been late a single day because it would mean missing out on this time with her.

The evening was now theirs. No interruptions. No outside world to interfere. Only their world behind the closed doors of their home. Their home.

"It's my favorite part of the day too," she said in an adorably shy voice. "When you call me and I come into the living room to wait, it seems interminable."

"Sorry, honey. Is it uncomfortable for you to kneel that long?"

He wanted her to suffer no discomfort. Not on his account. Yes, he wanted her waiting, kneeling, naked and utterly submissive. But not if it caused her an ounce of discomfort.

She smiled and shook her head. "No, darling. I love the moment you walk into the living room and I love how your eyes light up when you see me. I wouldn't trade that moment for anything."

He was absolutely and absurdly delighted over the endearment she used. She'd never used one, never called him anything but Dash. He was a grown man and nearly taken to his knees over the sweetness of her calling him darling.

"What is it, Dash?" she asked, worry furrowing her brow. "Did I say something wrong?"

He kissed the lines away from her brow. "Not at all, honey. You said something very right. You called me darling. I like it."

She blushed and ducked her gaze, but he forced her back, cupping her chin so he could kiss her again.

"I like it, Joss," he reiterated. "I like it a damn lot. It makes me feel special. Like I'm special to you."

"You *are* special, Dash," she whispered. "I hope I've shown you that in our time together."

"You have, but it's still nice to hear it."

She reached up and kissed him, wrapping her arms around his neck as he stood holding her, cradling her in his arms. He never wanted to let her go.

He walked to the sofa and eased down, still holding her firmly in his arms.

"I have something I wanted to mention to you. I wanted it to be a surprise, but I thought it might be better if you're prepared for it. And if it's not something you want to do, then just say so. I won't be angry. I don't want to do anything you aren't comfortable with."

There was confusion in her eyes, but she remained silent, waiting for him to continue. He loved that about her. That she didn't immediately panic or protest. She trusted him and he savored that trust.

"I thought we could go to The House tomorrow. As a couple. It's a place you were interested in, and I can make the experience special for you, Joss. Trust me to know what will please you."

To her credit, no doubt marred her expression. Just trust, shining in her eyes as she stared up at him. She didn't even appear to be nervous or apprehensive.

"I do trust you, Dash. If you want to go, then I'll be happy to go with you. Just tell me what I should wear. I don't want to disappoint or shame you."

"You will never shame me," he said gruffly. "There is nothing you could ever do that would bring me shame. It's not possible."

She smiled back at him, her eyes warm and full of . . . love? Dare he hope for that so soon? He pulled back from that thought, not wanting to set himself up for disappointment, no matter that he'd just told her he could never be disappointed in her. That was the one thing that could shatter him. Her not returning or being able to return his love.

"What time would you like to go? And what shall I wear?" she asked.

There was excitement and anticipation in her eyes. She was looking forward to their excursion. Already his mind was alive with the possibilities. He would be very exacting in his plans for her. He wanted this to be perfect.

"Something sexy," he murmured. "A short cocktail dress that shows off your gorgeous legs. And heels. Definitely heels. I want to fuck you in them in front of everyone."

Her eyes went cloudy with answering lust. She shivered delicately in his embrace as if the image appealed to her every bit as much as it did him. He hoped to hell it did.

"But it doesn't really matter," he added. "Because shortly after we arrive, I'll have you naked and bound."

She sucked in her breath and he studied her closely, searching for any sign that she wouldn't be up for what he had planned. But there was no resistance that he could see. Just intrigue and arousal.

"What time?" she whispered. "What time will I need to be ready?"

"We'll have dinner out. Be ready when I get home. We'll eat and take our time and arrive at The House around nine. Things don't really kick off there until later in the evening. And I want the whole damn world to see what is mine. I want every man there eaten alive with jealousy over what is mine and will never be theirs. They can look but they damn well can't touch."

She smiled, pleasure shining in her eyes. "I like that you're so possessive of me, Dash. It makes me feel . . . safe. And so very cherished."

"I'm glad," he said gruffly. "Because you are."

Her eyes suddenly widened and panic flared in their depths. "Oh my God, dinner! I completely forgot dinner, Dash. I got sidetracked when you came in. Damn it, I hope it's not burned!"

As she spoke, she scrambled out of his lap, and laughing, he let her go, watching as she fled toward the kitchen.

He followed behind and his heart clenched when she turned from the open oven, her look utterly crestfallen.

"It's ruined. I'm so sorry, Dash. I had planned a special dinner for us and timed it so when you got home we'd eat immediately."

She looked so adorable that he could only cross the room and pull her into his arms, shutting the oven with one hand and reaching up to turn it off.

"Let it burn," he murmured. "Get dressed and I'll take you out to eat. I don't give a damn what I eat as long as I get to be with you."

TWENTY-FOUR

JOSS was nervous, excited and extremely aroused, all rolled into a bundle of nerves. She knew, without arrogance, that she looked her best. She'd been very careful with her appearance, no matter that Dash had told her she'd be naked in short order.

But she wanted to look good, not only for her own confidence, but for Dash. She wanted him to be proud of her. To be proud to have her at his side and on his arm when they walked into The House.

Dash helped her from his car and tucked her arm underneath his as they walked toward the entrance.

How different this trip was compared with her last, when she'd been terrified and so nervous her stomach had been one gigantic ball of nausea. At least this time she didn't have to go through the motions of the social rooms downstairs where people gathered to hook up for the night. No worry over picking the wrong man or someone who would hurt her.

Dash was with her, his possession evident in his every expression and movement. There would be no choosing another man tonight. Her choice was made. Dash and only Dash would take her through the paces of whatever he planned.

Not knowing exactly what it was he planned for her added an element of intrigue and only heightened her arousal. Her nipples were taut and aching. Her pussy was clenched tight and she knew she was wet already.

Dash escorted her through the social rooms where he got her a glass of wine. But she knew that the biggest reason he made an appearance here was because he wanted to show her off and that gave her ego a huge, much-needed boost.

He was proud of her. It was evident in his gaze. It never left her, scorching a path over her skin every time it raked over her. He barely left her side even to get the wine. He was always within touching distance, his hand on her, his arm wrapped around her.

But when Craig, the man Joss had been with that first night, entered the room, his gaze sweeping over the women with a predatory gleam, Dash immediately stiffened and drew Joss farther into his side.

His hold on her screamed possessiveness and he met Craig's mocking gaze with a frigid look of his own.

"Corbin," Craig said curtly, nodding in Dash's direction. Then his gaze swept appreciatively over Joss. "You're looking beautiful, Mrs. Breckenridge."

Dash stiffened at the manner of address, and Joss's hand went to his arm, squeezing lightly.

"Thank you," Joss said politely. "Now if you'll excuse us, we'll be moving on."

But Dash didn't immediately move away. He pushed into Craig's space so they were nose to nose. Well, almost nose to nose since Dash had a good three inches in height over Craig.

"I don't want to see you in the common room," Dash bit out. "I'll throw you out myself. You don't so much as look at Joss. Got me?"

Craig chuckled. "You don't control my comings and goings, Corbin. I have a right to be here, same as you. So go fuck yourself. I'll look all I like."

"You don't come up those stairs," Dash said menacingly. "I will take you apart and I don't give a shit if I get barred from the premises from now on. It would be worth it to take you down a few notches. Try me. I dare you."

Craig paled and backed down, fear evident in his eyes. Dash had been coldly serious. Joss absolutely believed that he'd rearrange Craig's face and it was evident that Craig held that same belief.

Without a word, Craig backed away and turned to leave the room, casting a disgusted look in Dash's direction.

Dash curled his arm around Joss and guided her out of the room and toward the stairs.

"Come on, honey. I won't let him ruin our night."

"He wouldn't have ruined it anyway," she said gently. "I don't care if he was here. I'm here with you, Dash. Only you. It doesn't matter to me who sees me because I belong to you."

He paused at the bottom of the stairs and pulled her into a breathtaking kiss.

"Thanks for that, honey. I just don't like the guy and I like it less that he's had his hands on you once. That he touched what I consider mine and have considered mine since before we ever got together."

She smiled and wiped the lipstick off his lips. "You've messed up my makeup."

He growled, the sound rumbling from his throat. "It's going to get a lot more messed up before I'm finished. Your hair's beautiful, sweetheart, but I'm afraid that delicate updo is just going to end up destroyed."

She shivered and smiled in delight. "I can't wait."

"Then let's get to it," he murmured, pushing her up the stairs.

When they entered the common room it was alive with activity. There was recognition on Dash's face as his gaze swept the occupants. Damon Roche saw them in the doorway and headed in their direction, a welcoming smile on his face.

A gorgeous dark-haired woman was glued to his side and she guessed that this must be his wife, Serena.

For a woman who'd had a baby not so long ago, her figure was perfect, showing no signs of pregnancy.

"Dash, Joss, it's good to see you both," Damon said warmly.

It seemed the height of awkwardness to be exchanging pleasantries while everyone around them was indulging in hedonistic pleasures. Naked, moaning, fucking, sucking. The smack of a flogger against flesh. Cries and moans of pain and pleasure. The scent of sex and arousal was thick in the air. It brought a prickle of chill bumps to Joss's skin.

How could she casually undress in front of these people?

As if sensing her unease, Dash's arm tightened around her as they conversed with Damon and Serena.

A moment later, two men on either side of a striking Asian woman walked up to where she and Dash stood with Serena and Damon.

Dash's face lit up in recognition and genuine pleasure.

"Lucas, Cole, Ren," he acknowledged. "It's damn good to see the three of you. It's been a while."

The men extended their hands to Dash, and Dash leaned in to kiss Ren on either cheek. It quickly became obvious to Joss that Ren was with both men. Her mind came alive with curiosity, imagining what it would be like to have two such strong, dominant men at the same time. Was it permanent or were they just seeking a night of pleasure in a haven that catered to every sexual whim?

"We've been in Vegas quite a bit over the last few months," Lucas said. "Introduce us to your lady friend, Dash. I don't think I've ever seen her here before."

Dash pulled her forward, squeezing her hand.

"Honey, this is Lucas Holt, Cole Madison and Ren Holt-Madison. Guys, this is Joss. She is mine."

The simple introduction sent warmth all the way to her toes. His matter-of-fact way of saying she was his. He was saying publicly that she belonged to him. That he was her Dominant and she his submissive. If she thought she would ever be embarrassed to be introduced this way, she now knew she was wrong.

She loved it.

"It's very nice to meet you, Joss," Cole said gently, brushing a kiss over her hand.

Lucas took her hand next, his dark gaze penetrating her until she felt bare. There was something about both men that made her feel . . . vulnerable. She glanced at Ren, who looked extremely content to be between them, and wondered at the strength the smaller woman must possess to be able to take on both of these obviously dominant men.

Cole pulled Ren closer into his side while Lucas kept hold of her hand, their fingers laced tightly together. They obviously had no reservations whatsoever about the world knowing of their unusual relationship. Dash had introduced Ren using both of the men's last names. Was she married to both? Bound to them both?

The situation intrigued and fascinated her. She'd have to remember to ask Dash about them later.

"We'll let you get to tonight's entertainment," Damon said politely as he gathered his wife to his side. "Is there anything you need? You've only to ask one of my men and they'll get whatever it is you require."

"Is the bench unoccupied?" Dash asked, a gleam entering his eye.

Both Serena and Ren glanced at Joss, and she could swear envy entered their gazes. Whatever the bench was, it must be

pleasurable because both women looked as though they wanted
to be in Joss's position.

"It is. I'll have it reserved for you for the night if you like,"
Damon said graciously.

"I appreciate that. I'll need restraints and a flogger."

Damon nodded and then Dash said their farewells, Joss echoing them as well as expressing her happiness over having met
them. Dash led her away from the group of people and farther
into the room.

"They're your friends?" Joss asked.

Dash nodded. "I met them here."

"Cole, Ren and Lucas. They're together? The three of them?"

Dash smiled. "Yes. A not so unusual situation for here. Though
theirs is a permanent arrangement and not confined to nights of
fun at The House. She belongs to them both, and they both adore
the ground she walks on."

"She's lucky," Joss said wistfully.

Dash's eyes narrowed. "Is that your fantasy, Joss? To have two
men making love to you? Cherishing you?"

She shook her head quickly. "One is quite enough for me," she
said with a laugh. "All I need is you, Dash. You're all I can handle!"

He looked smug. "Glad to hear it, honey, because I have no
intention of sharing you with any other man, at least not on a
permanent basis."

"I think that's obvious after the way you threatened Craig,"
she said dryly.

He guided her toward a padded bench that looked like a huge
saddle. It was curved in the middle and had V legs extending out
from the bottom. In front there were two posts and she wondered
what they could possibly be used for.

"I'm going to undress you, Joss. Here and now in front of
everyone. I don't want you to focus on anyone but me. Only me.

Forget about everyone else. There is only me and you in this room and what we do together."

She nodded, swallowing back her nervousness.

He was slow and reverent as he gently divested her of her clothing. Each piece was carefully stripped away. He took his time as if savoring the process. Exposing her skin inch by inch.

When she was naked, he stood to his full height, inhaling deeply as he stared over her nude body.

She felt . . . beautiful. Worthy. And proud.

Dash was a gorgeous, alpha dominant male and he wanted her.

Never had she felt so feminine and powerful. Yes, Dash held all the power. He had control over her. And yet she felt powerful in her own right. As though she held his pleasure and satisfaction in the palm of her hand.

"I want you to bend over the bench, belly down on the padding. Make sure you're comfortable and tell me if you're not. Extend your arms outward toward the posts. I'm going to secure your hands to those posts and then I'm going to tie your ankles to the legs so you're incapable of movement."

Her heart fluttered and her breaths sped up, puffing erratically over her lips. Now it became clear just what those posts were for. She would be spread and bound securely so he had access to every part of her body.

When she was positioned to his satisfaction, he began winding the satin-covered rope around her wrists. When they were firmly secured, he turned his attention to her ankles, tying them tightly to the legs of the bench.

Then he caressed her bottom, spreading and petting the globes. Would he fuck her ass? Her pussy? Both? Her mind was alive with the possibilities. Desire buzzed in her veins like a potent drug. She was sluggish and high, already well on her way into the dreamlike plane she entered every time Dash dominated her.

But then she remembered him asking for a flogger. She sucked in her breath, realizing that he intended to spank her. And she was in the perfect position, her ass, her back and the backs of her legs vulnerable to his strikes.

He walked around in front of her, ducking underneath one outstretched arm that was tied to the post, and then unzipped his slacks, pulling his erection from his underwear. It bobbed in front of her lips and then he palmed the top of her head, forcing it upward so her mouth was open to his advance.

He slid in roughly, plunging deep on the very first thrust. It was clear that he was as aroused as she was and that he wouldn't be gentle tonight. She didn't want him to be. She wanted his dominance. His strength. His absolute power over her. She liked how vulnerable she felt with him. Gloried in the fact that he could— and would—use her mercilessly. Rough. Hard. She wanted it all.

For several long moments he fucked her mouth with ruthless, exacting precision. Precum leaked into her mouth and dribbled onto the floor before she could swallow it all. Then he pulled away, stiff and distended, and caressed her cheek in approval.

"Very good, darling. You please me very much. Now I'll take you further. I'm going to flog you, Joss. And I'm not going to be easy. Remember your safe word. I won't gag you because I want you to be able to say that word if necessary."

She nodded her understanding but she'd already resolved that she wouldn't use the word no matter what. She'd pass out before allowing her safe word to cross her lips. She wouldn't disappoint Dash or herself that way.

He picked up the crop and trailed it down her back, caressing the length of her spine with the leather tip. Then he smacked the fleshy part of her bottom, eliciting a gasp. She tightened her lips, determined that no further sound would escape. She would bear stoically everything he dished out.

Another blow fell and she bit into her lip to stanch the cry that threatened to burst free. He hadn't lied. He wasn't being the least bit gentle. His blows were harder than they'd been before. Sharper, with a burn that faded and was replaced by glowing pleasure.

By the sixth lash, she'd entered a dreamy state, sluggishly reacting to every strike. She tried to arch upward, seeking the sweet heat caused by the repeated blows.

He struck harder, as if sensing she'd already slipped into drugged unawareness. The eighth broke through her reverie, bringing her sharply back into focus. He peppered her back, her behind, even the backs of her thighs until she was certain her entire body was ablaze with color, rosy from his marks.

She was gasping now, her breath hitching as he showed her no mercy. Up to her shoulders, the sensitive skin on fire as he covered her entire back. There wasn't a part of her body that wasn't tingling. She twitched, unable to keep still, trying anything to alleviate the exquisite burn.

Her head drooped lower, sagging when she could no longer hold herself up. But his hand twisted ruthlessly in her hair, yanking her head back up to slide his cock into her mouth.

He fucked her for several long moments, the sucking sounds she made the only noise she could hear. She had no awareness of what went on around her. Had no idea if others were watching, observing Dash's mastery over her body. She didn't care. For her there was only him and her. And this moment.

He slid in, pressing his groin to her chin, and remained there until she struggled for breath. But she forced herself not to panic. She trusted Dash. He knew her limits. He wouldn't go too far.

Then he eased out, pulling the rest of the way from her mouth, and the fire of the lash returned as his blows grew more intense. She was barely conscious, not because she was overcome with pain but because the world had ceased to exist around her. There was a heavy fog of pleasure surrounding her, invading her veins. She craved more. Begged for more. She could hear herself as though she were a distant voice through the heavy haze.

And then his body came down over her back, blanketing her with his warmth and strength. He whispered close to her eyes.

"Darling Joss. So very beautiful and submissive. You have no idea how precious you are to me, how beautiful you look with my marks raised on your skin. I'm going to fuck you now and I'm going to fuck you hard. Your pussy first and then that sweet ass. And I'm going to have another man flog you while I fuck you."

Her eyes flew open as her body came to life. She was violently aroused at the image he invoked. That she would be flogged by another man while Dash possessed her, claimed her, fucked her.

How would she survive it? She was already so far gone that she could barely remember her own name. And now Dash was upping the ante and pushing her further than she'd ever imagined.

He grasped her hips roughly, pushing into her with a brutality that took her breath away. He was deep, wedging himself as far into her pussy as he could go. She was ready, more than ready for him, and yet she was so tight around him. He was huge within her. So aroused that he was thicker, longer, broader than ever.

He hammered into her, rocking her against the bench and stretching the restraints to the point of pain. And she took it all. Craved more. Wanted more. And more.

And then the lash fell as Dash pulled back. The two men worked in perfect rhythm. The flogger fell as Dash retreated and raised when he slammed back into her.

She was sobbing helplessly, so far gone in her pleasure that she wasn't even sure whether she'd orgasmed yet or not. If she had, she was well on her way to another, her need building to a frightening intensity.

And then he pulled out, spread her ass cheeks and quickly smeared a generous amount of lubricant over the seam. He positioned himself at her tiny opening and hammered forward, giving her no time to adjust to his invasion.

She cried out despite her vow not to. She couldn't help it. His name was a litany on her lips as she sobbed it over and over, begging him for more, for mercy, though she wanted none.

Her safe word never even threatened to burst forth. It was the furthest thing from her mind. She couldn't even remember it, didn't want to remember it because she didn't want this to end.

Over and over he fucked her ass and then the blows began to fall, peppering her back and ass when Dash pulled back each time.

"I want you to come," Dash ordered. "With me, Joss. I want you with me. Tell me what you need to get there so I can make it happen."

Her brain was utterly scrambled. She didn't know what she needed when her entire body was on fire and aching with unfulfilled need.

A strange hand gently parted her folds underneath where Dash fucked her hard and furious. It wasn't Dash's touch. She knew it intimately. This was the man who'd flogged her. He was gently caressing her clit, trying to bring her fulfillment.

She trembled, turned on by the idea of two men touching her. Dash had said another man would never have her, and indeed, it was Dash possessing her, filling her while the other man merely touched, aided Dash.

Her legs began to shake. Her entire body trembled as her orgasm swelled to greater heights. The fingers became more forceful, circling and rubbing her clit and then down to her entrance, the fingers plunging inside as Dash fucked her ass with all his strength.

She went off like a bomb, her cry loud in her ears. She screamed Dash's name, bucking wildly against him, nearly unseating him though her movements were confined by the ropes binding her hand and foot.

She felt the hot jets of semen spurting onto her skin, lashing her buttocks and then filling her opening. Dash pushed into her again, still spilling inside her, thrusting and jetting until cum ran down her legs, dripping to the floor.

Then he blanketed her body, whispering soothing words close to her ear. But she couldn't make out what he said because of the roar still thudding in her veins. She was panting, her strength completely gone, wrung out from the most explosive experience of her life.

This was what she'd been missing for so long. She didn't spare any guilt or self-consciousness over the fact that she'd craved what others would find depraved. She was in a public setting where anyone at all could see her and Dash in the most intimate of acts. And yet even though it was indeed public, the intimacy was not broken because those other people didn't exist for her. Only Dash and the pleasure he gave her.

He kissed her shoulder and as he lifted himself off her, he trailed a line of kisses down her spine before finally easing himself from her still-quivering body. Then he and the other man carefully untied her and Dash pulled her into his arms, supporting her so her knees didn't give way.

The other man flashed in her vision for a brief moment before she fixed her unsteady stare on Dash. He looked at her so tenderly, his gaze filled with so much love, that if he hadn't held her so firmly she would have fallen down.

He kissed her, whispering his approval, pride and satisfaction. She soaked up those words like a rain-parched desert. She leaned into him, wanting and needing that closeness now that she was so vulnerable after her earth-shattering orgasm.

"Turn around and thank the man who assisted me," Dash said gently. "Give him your thanks and then return to me."

"What do I do?" she whispered. "I mean what is expected of me? Am I supposed to p-pleasure him?"

"No, honey. Not at all. He was more than satisfied to take part in seeing you come apart and react so beautifully under the kiss of leather. I've said no man will have you but me, and that means your pleasure as well. He shared in yours, yes. But you will thank him and nothing else."

She turned, still wobbly as Dash supported her. She glanced up at the man, taking in his features. He was older than Dash, perhaps ten years or so. There was just a hint of silver at his temples but he was very handsome. He smiled gently at her as she murmured her thank-you. He took her hand, lifting it to his lips to press a tender kiss to her skin.

"Dash is a very lucky man," he said solemnly. "You're a beautiful sight, Joss. There wasn't a man in this room who wasn't envying Dash with his every breath just now."

She smiled. "Thank you. Thank you for your generosity. You brought me pleasure. You and Dash both. For that you have my thanks."

"It's I who owe you my thanks for allowing me to have a small part in something so beautiful," he said gravely.

He nodded his head at Dash and then turned away, melting into the crowd that Joss had just noticed gathered around her and Dash.

Her cheeks warmed as she took in the fact that she and Dash had been the focus of the entire room. Everyone had stopped what they were doing to watch her and Dash. His mastery of her. Women stared, jealousy evident in their gazes that drifted meaningfully over Dash. They wanted him. They made no effort to disguise it. And the men. She sucked in her breath, surprised by the naked desire she saw reflected in their stares.

She glanced up at Dash, baffled by their reactions.

He smiled tenderly down at her, pulling her into his arms. "You're beautiful, perfectly submissive and you react to the whip like a dream. What man wouldn't look at you with lust in his eyes?"

"I only want you to look at me that way," she whispered. "Take me home, Dash. I want to go home with you."

He kissed her forehead and then reached for her discarded clothing. He helped her dress after wiping the remnants of his release from her skin. The clothing was uncomfortable against her still-burning flesh and she flinched when Dash zipped up her dress.

He kissed her shoulder and grazed his teeth up her neck.

"When we get home, I'll take you out of your clothing and draw you a bath so you can have a nice long soak. And tomorrow you'll wear nothing the entire day. I don't want to cause you any discomfort."

TWENTY-FIVE

JOSS was at a booth at the Lux Café waiting for Chessy and Kylie to arrive. For once, she was the first to arrive, but she was anxious to see her friends. She'd shamelessly neglected them over the last few weeks and she felt guilty for not making the effort to see them more. Especially Kylie.

She'd heard reports from Dash about how Kylie was taking Jensen's position in the company, and he'd said things were noticeably strained at the office but that Kylie was handling it. Whatever that meant. He'd only said that she was quiet but did her job without complaint.

Other than a few phone calls and exchanged e-mails or texts, she hadn't seen her friends alone at all since their lunch in this same place the day she'd told them of her decision to go to The House.

How much had changed since then! She'd been so utterly wrapped up in her budding relationship with Dash that every-thing else had faded into the background.

She looked up when Chessy and Kylie came in together and she rose, hugging them both in turn before they sat down.

"I'm so glad to see you both," Joss said sincerely. "I've missed you."

Chessy's eyes sparkled. "Uh-huh. You expect us to believe that when you've been wrapped up in that hunk of man of yours?"

Joss laughed but she studied Kylie carefully. It was obvious that she was indeed under an enormous amount of strain. There were dark smudges underneath Kylie's eyes, which told Joss that her dreams were tormenting her again. Still.

Joss sighed, worried over her friend. She reached out to squeeze Kylie's hand.

"How has work been? How is Jensen working out?"

Kylie made a face. "He bugs me."

"How come?" Chessy asked curiously. "That man is divine to look at. So dark and brooding. He makes me shiver, and I have my own very possessive dominant man to go home to."

Joss laughed again but sobered at Kylie's haunted look.

"That's just it. He's so quiet and intense. He just looks at me. Stares. Like he's trying to see into my mind or whatever. It bothers me, and what am I supposed to say? I can't very well tell him to stop looking at me. He and Dash both would think I was crazy. Maybe I am," she added with a shrug.

"You'll be fine," Joss said, still holding on to her hand. "He seems very nice and I'm sure you'll warm up to him."

Kylie didn't look convinced. Instead she directed the conversation back at Joss.

"So how are things with you and Dash? I have to say, I've never seen the man so happy. He's in a disgustingly good mood every day at work. And he all but races out the door every day between four thirty and five. I don't think a complete meltdown in the business would force him to stay after hours."

Chessy giggled. "He's in looooove. It's obvious. The man is a complete goner. 'Stick a fork in him' done."

Joss's cheeks colored as heat rose in her face.

"The question is, are you?" Chessy asked pointedly.

Joss sighed and then rubbed her face with her hands. "Yes. No. I don't know," she admitted. "It's bothered me because I think of Carson less and less. I used to think about him all the time, and now? I'll go days without even bringing him to mind. Does that make me a terrible person?"

Chessy's face wrinkled in sympathy. Even Kylie's expression softened. Both women reached for one of Joss's hands.

"No, honey, it doesn't," Chessy said gently. "You loved Carson and he loved you. But he's gone. He's been gone for three years. That's more than enough time for you to grieve. It's time to let go and move on with your life. With Dash if he's who you choose. You have no reason to suffer guilt over not thinking about Carson as much now. It's normal. You have a new love. Embrace it. Don't hold back. You can't live in the past forever."

"I know I said some horrible things to you, Joss, and I hope you'll forgive me. I want you to be happy. Truly, I do. As Chessy said, Carson is gone."

Kylie's voice broke and she visibly had to collect herself before she continued.

"Dash is a good man. The best. And it's so obvious he cares deeply for you. If he is who makes you happy, then go for it. Don't let what I or anyone else thinks hold you back."

Tears burned Joss's eyelids as she stared back at the sincerity in her friends' gazes.

"Thank you," she choked out. "It's been weighing on me so heavily. I had dreams a few weeks ago. When things with Dash were just heating up. Right after I moved in with him. And in those dreams, I had the choice of whether to have Carson back or hold on to Dash. And I couldn't decide," she said, agony in her voice. "I felt terrible because I'd always dreamed of having Carson back. I would have done anything to make that happen. And yet in my dream, I didn't take that chance. I hesitated because Dash was there and I didn't want to lose him."

"Fuck your dreams," Chessy said crudely. "They fuck with

your mind, and here's the thing, Joss. You can't have Carson back, so it was a stupid dream and just your guilt manifesting itself in that dream. Carson is gone. So whether you would choose to have him back is a moot point. You can't have him back. You'll never get him back. So what you have to decide is if you're going to spend the rest of your life grieving for him or if you're going to take control of your future and not let a man who adores you go."

"Trust Chessy to open up the can of whoop-ass," Kylie said in amusement. "But I agree with her here. Carson loved you, Joss. He adored you. There was never any question of that. And I don't believe for one minute that he'd like what you're doing to yourself. He'd want you to be happy. I want you to be happy. But you have to want it for yourself."

Joss nodded. "I love you guys. I'm so glad to see y'all both. I swear I won't be so absent from now on. You're too important to me."

"Bet your ass you won't," Chessy muttered. "I'll come to Dash's house and haul you out by the hair. I was close to doing just that when you called to invite us to lunch, so consider yourself warned, girlfriend. I won't be as patient in the future."

Joss and Kylie both burst into laughter. Joss's heart lightened as she stared at the women she loved so much. She'd needed this. This time with them and their advice and support. She hadn't realized just how much the whole situation with Carson and Dash had weighed on her until she'd voiced her issues.

They seemed silly now and maybe she'd needed her friends' approval even as she cringed over the idea that she couldn't simply own her choices and move forward. It wasn't fair to Dash or herself.

"So when are you going to tell him you love him?" Chessy asked curiously.

The question startled Joss because she hadn't fully admitted the depth of her feelings to herself, much less anyone else. But as she pondered Chessy's question, she realized that she did. It was there. Maybe it had been there from the start.

"It just seems so soon," Joss murmured.

Kylie snorted. "Like you didn't fall for my brother just as quickly? Hell, Joss, you both fell head over heels. I think Carson was a goner before you were. And look how well that turned out. If you're concerned that falling in love so quickly is a bad thing, consider that you and Carson would still be together and in love if he hadn't died. Falling fast doesn't make it any less strong. If it's there, it's there."

"A timeline doesn't make love any less real or true," Chessy said gently. "Kylie's right. You and Carson both fell hard and fast, and it didn't make your love any less solid, just like it won't make your feelings for Dash any less strong just because you fell so quickly. Look at me and Tate. We were together, what, two weeks before he proposed?"

"And are you still happy?" Joss asked challengingly.

She and Kylie exchanged quick glances. It was obvious Kylie was as worried about Chessy's marriage as Joss was herself. It was equally evident, though Joss hadn't spent much time with Chessy over the last weeks, that something was off between her and Tate.

Chessy's smile faltered but she quickly recovered. "It's fine. We're fine," she amended. "Just different now. But relationships are like that. We can't stay in the honeymoon stage forever. Our needs are different now. He's juggling a very difficult business and he's often called away with clients or has to travel. But we'll be okay. I still love him as much as I ever have and I know he loves me."

Somewhat reassured by her friend's fervent response, Joss nodded. Kylie still had a look of doubt on her face, but that was Kylie. Fiercely loyal and protective of her friends, even if her mouth got away from her at times. But Joss knew that Kylie had her's and Chessy's best interests at heart, and that her heart was as big as the state of Texas.

"So let's order. I'm starving," Chessy said, swiftly changing the topic.

Joss allowed her to redirect the focus from her and Tate's relationship, and Joss motioned for the waiter hovering nearby. The women ordered and then spent the rest of lunch laughing and catching up.

But Joss's thoughts drifted time and time again to Dash. And when she'd fully cement their relationship by offering him the words. *I love you.* Such simple words, and yet they terrified her because it signaled a whole different level of vulnerability for her.

She thought Dash cared for her very deeply. Perhaps he had for a long time, judging by his past comments. But he hadn't told her he loved her. Perhaps he was merely waiting for her to say it first. He'd already risked so much, and she could understand why he wouldn't want to put himself out there before knowing exactly where she stood.

If he could do so much for her and be so patient while she got her head together, the least she could do was take the first step and put everything on the line.

But what if he didn't believe her? What if it was too soon and too fast? Would he think she was so caught up in the moment that her emotions ruled all else?

Her brow furrowed in concentration. Chessy and Kylie both looked curiously at her but neither spoke, though question was obvious in their eyes.

"I'll tell him when we aren't making love," Joss declared and then promptly blushed to the roots of her hair as she realized how far her outburst had carried.

Chessy and Kylie laughed and then Joss joined in, not caring who heard her.

"Good idea," Chessy drawled. "Wouldn't do for him to miss your declaration because he was too caught up in the moment when his dick is ruling his brain."

"Oh for God's sake, Chessy," Kylie muttered.

Chessy shrugged. "Not saying it's a bad thing. Sometimes men are better off when they let their dicks do their thinking for them. You get better results that way."

"I'm going to tell him tonight," Joss said impulsively, suddenly eager to share her feelings with Dash.

She sobered momentarily as she silently regarded her two best friends. "I never thought I'd find love again. I thought I'd used my only shot at finding my soul mate with Carson. But Dash . . . I love him. Is it possible to find perfection twice in a lifetime?"

Chessy and Kylie both smiled softly at her.

"You just answered your own question, girlfriend," Chessy said. "You love him. So I guess you did find your second soul mate."

TWENTY-SIX

JOSS flew around the kitchen, making sure dinner was prepared at just the right moment. Dash had called a mere five minutes ago and he would be home in ten. Which meant she only had a few minutes to set the table, plate the steaks and sides, before hurrying into the living room to wait for him naked and kneeling.

His welcome would be brief or dinner would be kept waiting and end up cold. But she had plans for tonight. She wanted it to be special even if they veered momentarily from him controlling all aspects of their relationship.

Tonight she wanted to be granted the opportunity to do for him. She wanted to direct the events. An intimate dinner. And then she wanted to tell him she loved him. Before they made love. She wanted him to be sure of her. To know she wasn't caught up in the moment and overcome and wouldn't be blurting out words she didn't mean.

How would he react? It was the question that had burned in her mind ever since lunch with Chessy and Kylie. And would he return the words? She knew in her heart that he loved her. Had likely loved her a long time. She hoped he'd greet her declaration with joy and relief and they could move forward in a more solid, permanent relationship.

It befuddled her that just weeks earlier she'd greeted the anniversary of her husband's death with sadness and resignation that she was doomed to a loveless existence and that she could only hope to fill the aching void with sex and dominance. But she hadn't expected . . . love.

And she certainly hadn't expected a longtime friend, her husband's best friend, to be the one whom she fell in love with.

A wide, goofy grin split her lips and she took the sizzling steaks off the stovetop grill and plated both. Next, she took out the potatoes and plated them while laying out all the condiments.

Checking her watch, she realized she had barely two minutes, perhaps less if there had been no traffic. She flew to the bedroom and quickly disrobed, taking a moment to straighten her hair. Then she went back into the living room and not a moment too soon because she heard Dash pull into the drive.

She sank to her knees, her entire body trembling. Her nerves were coiled tight and she was jittery with anticipation. This could be the best—or worst—night of her life. She was praying for the best.

The door opened and there he was, filling the living room with his larger-than-life presence. His smile was immediate when his gaze fell on her, and he strode toward her but then he stopped just in front of her and sniffed the air appreciatively.

Then he leaned down and pulled her up and into his arms. He kissed her long and leisurely, his voice husky.

"What's cooking, honey? It smells wonderful. I swear, every day coming home to you is better than the last. I don't know how you keep topping the day before, but somehow you manage it."

She smiled broadly, wrapping her arms around his neck to pull him down for another kiss.

"Steaks and baked potatoes. I have something special planned for this evening. Do you mind?"

His eyebrows rose. "Do I get any hints?"

She grinned. "Nope. You'll just have to play along."

He smiled back at her. "In that case, lead on. I'm yours to command."

She took his hand, lacing their fingers together in a familiar gesture. They often touched, even in not so intimate ways. She had gotten used to having him close at all times. His open affection. She loved it—and him.

She led him into the dining room, where the places were set. Candles were lit and she left the overhead lights off, with just the light from the next room casting an intimate glow over the table.

It was so natural for her to be wearing nothing now that she gave it no thought as she slid into the chair catty-corner to his at the head of the table. She was naked and waiting every day that he came home, and more often than not, they had dinner together with her wearing nothing.

"Let me," he murmured as she began to cut into her steak. "There's nothing more I'd like than to feed you tonight."

She stopped, allowing him to cut her steak into bite-size portions. He dressed her potato just like she liked it and then fed her the first bite of the tender meat.

He alternated feeding her a bite and taking one of his own. They didn't converse. Heavy silence had fallen over the couple, but they never once broke their gazes, never looked away. Dash seemed to sense the importance of tonight. There was an air of expectation, and he seemed eager to get through dinner and onto whatever it was she had planned.

She smiled to herself. She wouldn't make him wait long. Normally they'd watch television or a movie in the living room, she curled against him while he stroked her body or hair. He said he loved simply touching her, just being with her and sharing her company.

Other nights they'd sit on his back porch with a bottle of wine and talk about his day. How Jensen was working out and Kylie was grudgingly accepting her new boss.

But tonight she planned an early bedtime. She wanted to be in his arms when she told him she loved him and then she wanted to make love to him. She wanted to be the bold one. She wanted to show him the depth of her feelings for him. She only hoped he allowed it.

"Just leave the dishes," she said huskily when they'd finished. "I'll clear them away later. Right now I want us to go into the bedroom."

Dash lifted one eyebrow, his eyes going dark and smoky with desire.

"Never let it be said I denied my darling anything."

She smiled, allowing her love to shine in her eyes. He may wonder, but tonight she'd remove all doubt. It was time. Past time to take the next step. Hold her breath and take the leap.

She held out her hand, mimicking his actions of the past when he always held out his hand for her, usually to obey one of his commands. Tonight she was issuing the demands, however shyly done.

His hands roamed over her body as they walked side by side to the bedroom. It was as if he couldn't keep himself from touching her. Like he was as addicted to her as she was to him.

When they entered the bedroom, she led him to the bed and pushed him down until he was perched on the edge. He stared at her with blatant curiosity but remained silent, allowing her free rein.

Then she sank to her knees between his open thighs and gathered his hands in hers.

"There's something I want to tell you, Dash. Something important. And I wanted it to be at the perfect moment. When we weren't making love. When we weren't so caught up in the moment because I wanted you to know how much I mean these words."

The hope and fear in his eyes was nearly her undoing. He looked as though he was torn between the two emotions and afraid to put his faith in the outcome.

She lifted his hands to her mouth, pressing a kiss to those gentle hands.

"I love you, Dash," she whispered. "I love you so much."

The instant joy that flooded his eyes was all the response she needed. His shoulders sagged and he closed his eyes as if savoring the moment. When they opened, there was a sheen of moisture, shocking her with the intensity of his reaction, his emotions.

"God, Joss," he choked out. "If you only knew how long I've dreamed of this moment."

He gathered her into his arms, lifting until she was in his lap, cradled against his chest. He held her tightly as if fearing she would slip away. He pressed kisses to her head, her temple, and then turned her face to kiss her eyes, her nose, her cheeks, every inch of her skin he could cover.

"I love you too, darling. God, I love you. I love you so much I ache with it. It's been killing me not knowing, hoping that you felt the same for me as I feel for you. Have felt for you for so very long. Are you certain, Joss? Are you ready for this?"

Anxiety crept into his gaze as he awaited her response. She smiled, allowing the full force of her own joy and relief to bleed into her expression.

"Oh yes," she breathed. "Do you really love me, Dash? Truly?"

"Honey, if I loved you any more, I'd die with it. You have no idea how very long I've loved you, ached for you, wanted you with my every breath."

"Then neither of us has to hurt any longer," she said softly. "I'm yours, Dash. Completely and utterly yours. I always will be, if you'll have me."

"Have you?" he asked hoarsely, incredulously. "Honey, I'll take you any damn way I can get you. But I want you to be sure that this is what you want. Not just me, but our relationship. My dominance. Your submission. Because if it's not what you want long term, then it doesn't have to be that way. There is no sacrifice too great to make for you."

Her smile widened and tears glittered in her own eyes. "I wouldn't change a single thing about you—us. I want you just the way you are. I want us just the way we are right now. I want this, darling. I want us. I need your dominance. I want it with my every breath. It's a part of me now, the best part. Never change, Dash. Never feel that you have to change for me. Because I want you just the way you are."

He crushed her to him, his breaths coming raggedly, blowing over her hair. He trembled against her as if overcome with emotion. And then he kissed her again and again, like he was starved for her love. As though he needed it as desperately as she needed his love.

"Make love to me," she whispered. "For the first time, truly make *love* to me."

"*That* you never have to ask me for," he whispered back. "But honey, it's always been lovemaking from my point of view. No matter what we've done and will do, it's always been with love. Always. That will never change."

He rolled with her, tumbling her to the bed even as he fumbled with his clothing, pulling and tearing at them impatiently as she lay on the bed waiting. His naked body covered hers, their legs twining, his erection cradled in the apex of her thighs.

The words made a difference. She hadn't considered how much, but it made all the difference. Now that the words had been spoken, there was an urgency—and tenderness—that hadn't been there before. Not that Dash had ever been anything but wonderful with her, but now there was so much more.

He kissed her passionately, taking her breath away and then returning it as their breaths mingled. He murmured his love between each kiss, and she savored the exquisite sensation of feeling that all-consuming love again. She'd never believed she could find it again, and she'd been so very wrong.

Dash was all she could hope for. She'd never want for anything else in her life. As long as she could have him. God forbid she ever lost him. She'd never survive losing the love of her life twice.

And their love was still new, shiny, still so much more to grow and learn. Just as she and Carson had done in the beginning. Their love had happened quickly but it had grown stronger with time, not weaker. She believed with everything in her heart that it would be the same for her and Dash.

"I've waited so long for you, Joss," he whispered against her breasts. He lavished attention on each nipple, coaxing them to rigid peaks. "I never imagined having this. You. Your love. It's more than I can take in. Swear to me you'll never leave me. That you'll be with me forever."

"I'll never leave," she vowed. "You'll always have me and my love, Dash."

He crushed her to him again, nudging impatiently between her thighs as he slid, warm and deep, into her welcoming body. His body arched over hers, driving deep. He raised her arms over her head, connecting their hands and holding hers down as he undulated over her again and again.

"I'll never forget the way you look tonight," he said in a tender voice. "The way you looked the first time you said you loved me. I'll remember this to my dying day."

"As long as you don't die anytime soon," Joss said, pain filling her at the very thought.

His face was an instant wreath of regret. "That was thoughtless of me, honey. I didn't mean it that way. I'll never leave you willingly. Believe that."

She smiled. "I know, Dash. I'll try not to be so sensitive."

"You can be any damn way you want to be. I wouldn't change a thing about you, my love."

He closed his eyes as he drove deeper still. But his movements were so very gentle and loving. He filled her, withdrew and then slowly and leisurely pressed forward again. Her orgasm, not as sharp as in the past, rose, mellow and smooth, spreading to the depths of her soul. It was a different kind of release. Emotional release and not just physical.

It was . . . love. And it made all the difference in the world.

"Come with me, Joss. Be with me. Always."

"I'm with you," she whispered. "Don't hold back, Dash. Take us both over."

He lowered his forehead to hers, a gesture she loved. He lightly kissed her even as his body shuddered above her and her own release fluttered like the sweetest rain. He let go of her hands and she wrapped both arms around him, holding him close, and they fell over together, consumed by the fires of their love.

Though it was early, she had no desire to get up. To even move. She was content to remain right here, in his arms, replete. Confident in his love. The future had never looked so bright. She felt as though she could take on the world and that Dash had given her wings back so she could fly.

"Stay with me," she whispered as his body covered hers. "Just like this. Stay inside me. Let me feel you."

He kissed her again and settled his weight more fully on top of her. She stroked her hands up and down his back as they both drifted off into sweet sleep.

TWENTY-SEVEN

THE dream was even more vivid than before. In her sleep, Joss moaned quietly as she faced Carson and Dash standing side by side. Both men looked expectantly at her, each demanding she make her choice.

"You can have me back, baby," Carson said in the gentle, caring voice he always used with her. She couldn't remember a time he'd ever raised his voice to her, even in anger.

They'd had arguments. What married couple didn't? But he'd never once lost his temper. He hadn't trusted himself not to lash out physically, as his father had done time and time again.

"We can be together again. Just like before. You just have to choose."

Dash stood silently to the side looking as though he'd already lost. There was resignation in his eyes, and he began to turn away, much as Carson had done in her previous dream.

"No!" she cried. "Don't go, Dash. I want . . . you."

Carson's look of shock ripped her heart in two. She could scarcely believe she'd chosen Dash over her beloved husband. Then sadness gripped his features and he glanced over at Dash.

"Take care of her," he said in a low voice. "Love her as much as I do."

"I will. I do," Dash said.

Then he reached for Joss and she took a hesitant step forward. Then another and another until she was in his arms. When she glanced in Carson's direction, he was gone, fading until it was as if he had never been there.

"Carson," she whispered brokenly. "I'm sorry. I'm so sorry." Then she glanced up at Dash, offering him reassurance. That she'd chosen him. "I love you," she whispered. "*You.*"

TWENTY-EIGHT

DASH slowly came awake, the memory of the previous night fresh and vivid in his mind. He smiled, reaching for Joss, fully intending to make love to her all over again. But when he turned to her, he froze because she had a fretful look on her face and she was shaking her head, a low moan escaping her lips.

Her next words paralyzed him. Cut him to the core, slicing open his heart and draining away all the optimism he'd awakened with.

"Carson," she whispered in a tortured voice. "I'm sorry. I'm so sorry." There was a short pause and then, "I love you. *You.*"

Irrational anger seized him. Hurt and betrayal pounded through his veins. *Goddamn it.* Would Carson forever be between them? Would she never be able to let him go?

Her eyelids fluttered open and she looked up at him in sleepy confusion. Then her brow furrowed as she saw the evidence of his fury.

"Dash?"

"I'm glad you realize who's in bed with you," he said in an icy tone.

Her mouth dropped open. *"What?* What are you talking about?" She pushed up to her elbow, her hair falling like a curtain over her shoulders. "Dash, why are you so angry?"

The hurt confusion in her voice just pissed him off even more.

"You can't let him go," Dash said harshly. "Within hours of telling me you love me, you're dreaming of him. Telling him you love him in your dream and *apologizing*, for fuck's sake. For what? Cheating on him? Being disloyal to a dead man? Here's a piece of information for you, Joss. Carson is dead. He's not coming back. He left you and he's not coming back. Get over it and deal with it."

She went utterly pale, staring at him in disbelief.

"I'll never measure up," he continued brutally, driven to make her hurt every bit as much as he was hurting. "I don't appreciate being a poor substitute for the man you lost, the man you can't have. I'll be *damned* if I do it any longer. I've been patient. I've been understanding. I've given you everything you've asked for."

"You were never a substitute," she said hoarsely.

"I refuse to have a third person in our bed, Joss. A dead man at that. It's occurred to me that any man would have done for you. You don't *want* to move on. You just want someone to fuck you and play master to your submissive. Hell, it *would* have been just any man, or don't you remember that night at The House? It's obvious you weren't particular and any dick would have done."

"You're wrong," she choked out, tears clouding her eyes and knotting her throat. "And I'm not going to lie here while you say things to purposely hurt me."

"Good," he said savagely. "It's about time you hurt a tenth as much as I've hurt over the last years. I'm tired of trying to live up to a dead man's memory. When are you going to accept that he's gone? Jesus, Joss, even your safe word is a reminder of him. As if you need him to protect you from *me*. He's constantly between us because you put him there and I can't continue this lie any longer."

"Are you saying we're over?" she asked, her voice cracking,

much like his own heart was shattering. "After I told you I loved you?"

"I can't go on like this any longer, Joss. I've wasted far too much time waiting for something that will evidently never happen. I can't continue putting my life on hold for a woman who will never truly be mine. I deserve better. You deserve better. And until you can put the past behind you for good and let go and move on, we don't have a chance."

He ran his hand roughly through his hair, frustrated, heartbroken and pissed.

Joss pushed herself up and hugged her knees together protectively, and it killed him that she thought she needed protection against him. But then hadn't he just ripped her into the same shreds she'd ripped him into?

"I can't believe you would be so callous," she said, tears slipping down her cheeks. "You demanded my trust, expected it and would accept no less, but it's obvious you haven't given me that same trust you've demanded. I can't be with a man who demands everything from me but gives nothing of himself in return. And certainly not his trust."

"I guess that's that then," he said savagely, furious that she was making him feel guilt that he shouldn't. He wasn't the one holding back. He wasn't the one refusing to let go of the past.

"Get out," she said in a low voice. "Just get out. Go to work. Do whatever it is you do. But leave me the hell alone."

"This is *my* house, goddamn it."

She went even paler and then rolled from the bed, scrambling for clothing. "You're right, Dash. This is your house. Your home. Not mine. It's never been mine. I haven't been allowed in. It's you putting barriers between us, not me."

"Bullshit," he bit out. "Don't kill yourself getting your stuff.

I'm out of here. You'll have the day to do whatever the hell it is you want to do."

With that he strode to the closet, yanking out pants and a shirt, not bothering with a shower. He needed to get out before he said or did worse. Before he did something really stupid like get on his knees and beg her forgiveness. Like telling her it didn't matter if he could never have all of her, that he'd take whatever she had to give. He'd once thought that he could be satisfied with any part of her. Any part at all. He'd thought that something was better than nothing.

He was wrong.

He couldn't—wouldn't—settle for anything less than one hundred percent of her.

Joss maintained her composure only until Dash slammed out of the house and then she fell to her knees, burying her face in her hands as sobs tore from her throat.

How could he love her and say all the horrible things he'd said? She'd been so careful not to put Carson between them. Since they'd gotten together she'd stopped mentioning Carson at all. When before they talked easily about a man they both loved. Now? It was as if Carson never existed because they *never* brought him up.

Dash didn't trust her. She'd been right. For all he demanded of her, he hadn't given her the same in return. It wasn't fair. She'd given him everything. Her trust. Her love. Her submission. And he'd vowed to cherish that gift. To protect her. And yet he'd torn her apart with bitter, careless words.

There was no going back. No undoing what had been said. His words rang in her ears, would always ring in her ears. No amount of wishing would make their memory go away.

She had to get out. Couldn't stay here a minute longer. She

frantically began stuffing her belongings in her suitcases and went about systematically ridding the entire house of her presence.

But the things Dash had bought her, gifts, jewelry, clothing? She left it all neatly piled on his bed so he would see it when he returned and know she didn't take a damn thing with her. She didn't want it. She couldn't be bought. Not when she'd been willing to give him everything freely and without conditions.

She fumbled with her cell phone, punching Chessy's number in with shaking fingers. She needed a shoulder to cry on. Needed someone who would understand the turmoil she was going through.

"Hey, girlfriend. How's it going? Did you tell Dash the big news?"

A low sob welled from her throat.

"Joss? What the hell is wrong? Are you *crying*? What's happened? Where are you? Are you all right?" Chessy demanded.

"I need you," Joss choked out. "Are you home? Can I come over?"

"Of course, honey. I'm here. But you sound so upset. Where are you? I'll come get you."

"No," Joss said in a low voice. "I'll come to you. I'll explain everything when I get there. Give me half an hour, okay?"

"I'll be here," Chessy said firmly. "Be careful, Joss. And when you get here I want to know exactly what happened, and you don't leave a word out."

Joss agreed and then ended the call. She made another sweep of the house, making sure she hadn't overlooked anything. And then she made three trips, hauling her luggage out to her car.

When the last suitcase was stuffed into the passenger seat, she turned and stared back at Dash's house one last time. A house she'd considered her home for a brief, beautiful period of time. Now? It represented hell.

She pulled out of Dash's neighborhood driving much too fast. She eased off the accelerator, not wanting to be reckless and take unnecessary risks. She pounded the wheel in frustration when an accident ahead backed traffic up. She turned onto another street, intending to cut over and drive around the park. It was longer, but with the slowdown in traffic, it would take her the same amount of time, and she wouldn't be stuck in stop-and-go traffic.

She just wanted to be at Chessy's, where she could pour out her grief to someone who loved her. It felt as if the rug had been yanked from underneath her and she supposed it had. After a night when the future had seemed so utterly perfect, it was now a gaping, yawning black hole stretching as far as the eye could see.

She didn't see the child dart into the street chasing a ball until it was too late. Horrified that she could hurt or kill the little girl, she yanked the steering wheel as hard as she could, not even having time to slam on the brakes.

She hit the curb hard enough to blow out her front tire, and as she looked up, she saw the sprawling oak tree dead ahead. There was nothing she could do. Her tiny convertible hit the tree with a sickening crunch of metal and the sharp sound of shattering glass. Her head slammed forward as the air bags exploded in her face. Pain registered and as she blinked, blood slid down her forehead, clouding her vision.

She wondered if she'd live just as she blacked out and floated away in a sea of nothingness.

TWENTY-NINE

DASH stared broodingly out his office window and replayed the morning's events over and over. Had he overreacted? Part of him said yeah. The other part, the practical, unemotional part, said no, that he'd been right to be angry. And certainly he had no right to lash out at her like that, to hurt her so badly.

But damn it, enough was *enough*. What should have been the best night of his entire life, the culmination of an impossible dream, had ended in his worst nightmare. Maybe it had always been an impossibility. Perhaps Joss wasn't ready—would never be ready—to let go.

So where did that leave him? A week ago he would have vowed that he would be satisfied with any part of her. That he would wait, be patient for her to come around and hope that eventually she would be in a place where she could give him back in full measure what he was willing to give her.

But when she'd told him she loved him, and then wept for her husband the morning after, he'd been seized by a fatalistic sensation that she would never truly be his. His hopes had been crushed in that one instant, and he'd reacted much like a wounded animal. Hell, he *was* wounded. The kind of wound one never recovered from.

His office door burst open and he turned, irritated over the interruption. To his surprise Tate strode inside, his expression angry.

"What the hell did you do to Joss?" Tate demanded.

Dash sighed. "That didn't take long."

"What the fuck is that supposed to mean? Chessy is worried out of her mind. Where is Joss? What happened between the two of you?"

Dash's brow furrowed in confusion. "What are you talking about? Why are you asking me where she is?"

"Because apparently you were the last person who saw her," Tate said through gritted teeth. "She called Chessy in hysterics over two hours ago. She was upset and crying but she wouldn't tell Chessy what was wrong. She asked Chessy if she could come over, that she needed her, and that she would be there in half an hour. She didn't show and Chessy can't get an answer on her cell number, her home number or your home number for that matter. She sent me to drag your ass out of your cave since you aren't answering your cell either."

Dash paled, dread gripping his insides. "I don't know where she is. She was at my house . . . in my bed when I left." He winced, closing his eyes. "Or at least she was in my bed, but she would have left."

"And *why* would she have left?" Tate growled.

"That's none of your fucking business," Dash said icily.

"The hell it's not! Chessy is home worried sick about her. Hell, the only way I could get her to stay her ass at home and not run out to look for her is by promising to find her myself. Joss is not the hysterical or irresponsible type, so if she was that upset and she's missing, then something is damn well wrong."

The knot grew larger in Dash's throat. Panic slid down his spine, momentarily paralyzing him.

"I said some pretty terrible things to her," Dash murmured. "Jesus. When I left, she was crying."

"You left her that upset?" Tate asked in a disgusted voice.

Dash closed his eyes. "I was pretty pissed."

"I'm not even going to ask because the only thing I give a fuck about is my wife worrying herself sick over Joss and whether Joss herself is all right. I take it *you* haven't heard from her."

Dash shook his head. "She pretty much told me to go to hell. But I'm already there. I have been for years."

Tate's phone rang and he snatched it up. "Chessy?" he said. "Is she okay? Did you hear from her?"

There was a long pause and then Tate paled. Dash rushed to where Tate stood, trying to hear Chessy's voice, but Tate held it too close to his ear for Dash to tell anything.

"Goddamn it. No, you aren't going anywhere. No, Chessy! I'll be right over. Don't you dare leave the house. One accident is enough. I don't want you driving when you're this upset."

Dash's knees buckled and he had to grab his desk to keep from hitting the floor.

Tate hung up and then fixed Dash with a cold stare.

"The hospital just called Chessy. Apparently they saw she was the last call on Joss's cell and they called her. Joss has been in a car accident. It appears to be serious. They wouldn't comment on her condition over the phone, but they asked that Chessy or her closest family member get to the hospital as quickly as possible."

"I'm going," Dash bit out. "What hospital? I can be there before you go home and get Chessy."

Tate looked at him, anger brewing in his eyes. Then he blew out his breath. "Hermann Memorial. The ER."

Dash didn't wait for anything more. He grabbed his keys and ran out the door to the bank of elevators. Kylie called out as he passed her office, but he didn't stop. He didn't have time to explain, even if Kylie should know. Chessy would call her later. For now, his only purpose was to get to Joss and pray he wasn't too late.

THIRTY

WHEN Dash strode into the emergency room, he immediately demanded to know Joss's condition and if he could see her. A police officer was standing close to the reception desk, and when he heard Dash say Joss's name, he motioned for Dash.

Frustrated by the delay, he stepped aside with the cop.

"Do you know how she is?" Dash asked bluntly. "Did you work the scene? What the hell happened?"

The police officer sighed. "Can I ask the nature of your relationship to Mrs. Breckenridge?"

"I'm her fiancé," he lied. "She lives with me." Another lie. "I saw her just this morning, not long before this apparently happened. I left for work and now this." At least that much was the truth.

"Was she upset about anything? Under duress? Stressed?" He paused a moment. "Do you have any reason to believe that she's suicidal?"

"*What?*" Dash asked incredulously. "What the fuck are you getting at?"

The cop looked uncomfortable. "There were no signs of tire marks to indicate she braked. She hit a tree dead-on. Going at least forty-five miles per hour in a residential zone."

"And you think she tried to kill herself?"

"I'm examining all possible leads. Until I speak to Mrs. Breckenridge myself, there's no way to determine the cause of the accident. But you could help by letting me know her emotional state when you last saw her. I understand she's widowed. Could she be depressed over the loss of her husband?"

Dash was at a loss for words. Her emotional state? She was upset. Extremely so. Hell, he'd all but kicked her out of his house. And then she'd wrecked. Good God. Could she have done it purposely? How the hell else would she hit a tree dead-on going that fast and no signs of braking?

"I have no idea," Dash said numbly. He'd like to be able to defend Joss, but who the hell knew what was going on in her head?

Guilt clutched him like a fist. He should have never left her this morning. He'd been angry, absolutely. But he should have calmed down, and they should have discussed it like two rational adults. Only he *hadn't* been rational. Whether or not she'd tried to take her own life, the entire thing was *Dash's* fault.

But he couldn't contain his fury that she would have given up. Have been so weak. That wasn't the Joss he knew. Or thought he knew.

He turned from the police officer and strode back to the desk, planting his hands down on the surface.

"I want to see Joss Breckenridge. *Now.*"

"I'm sorry, sir, the doctors are working on her now. If you'll wait in the waiting area, I'll call you back the minute you're allowed to see her."

"What do you mean 'working on her'?" Dash demanded. "What's wrong with her? How badly is she injured? Is she going to live?"

The clerk's face shone with sympathy. "I know it's hard waiting and not knowing, but I assure you, our physicians are doing their absolute best, and as I said, the moment I know anything I'll inform you at once."

Dash threw up his hands and paced back into the waiting area, but he couldn't sit. How could he? It was déjà vu all over again. Another day. Three years ago. Same hospital. Same horrible wait only for the worst news. Carson dead. They'd been unable to save him. His injuries had been too extensive.

Only his wreck had been an accident. There'd been nothing he could have done to avoid it. Could Joss say the same? Had she been so upset and distraught that she'd driven her car into a tree hoping for death?

He couldn't wrap his mind around it. Couldn't fathom it. But it was what the police suspected. Why else would they want to know if she was suicidal? What if Dash had pushed her to it?

He finally sat and buried his face in his hands. What seemed an eternity later, a nurse poked her head out the door and called for Joss Breckenridge's family. As he was the only one there at the moment, he hurried forward.

"How is she?" he demanded.

The nurse smiled. "She'll be fine. She's pretty banged up, but you can see her. She's a little woozy from the pain medication we gave her, but we couldn't medicate her until all the X-rays and CT scan results came back."

He didn't give a fuck what condition she was in as long as she was alive.

The nurse led him back to one of the exam rooms and then opened the door, allowing him entrance. He sucked in his breath when he saw Joss lying on the stretcher, pale and bruised. There was dried blood at her hairline and at the corner of her mouth.

She looked so damn fragile that he was afraid to touch her.

He went to her bedside and fury gripped him all over again. She blinked drowsily and then focused her gaze on him. Instant hurt crowded the silky depths and she turned away. It only pissed him off all the more.

"You little fool," he hissed. "Did you *try* to kill yourself, Joss? Was life without Carson so unbearable that you tried to join him?"

Her gaze yanked back to him, fury replacing the hurt of just moments ago.

"Get *out*," she said through clenched teeth. "I don't want you here. I don't want you anywhere *near* me. Go to hell, Dash. That's apparently where you're most comfortable. God knows, I've only kept you there and nothing I do changes that."

"Not until I have a damn answer," he seethed. "You scared ten years off my life, Joss. What the fuck did you think you were doing?"

"What I was doing was avoiding a child," she said in a frigid tone. "She ran into the street, and I knew I'd hit her if I didn't swerve. I never saw the tree. Didn't care about the tree. All I cared about was missing her. I could have never lived with myself if I'd chosen my life over hers. I was upset and wasn't paying attention. I should have seen her earlier. I didn't. But I'll be damned if she was going to pay for my mistake with *her* life."

All the breath left him in a rush. He sagged precariously and gripped the bed rail for support.

"I'm sorry," he whispered.

"I don't want to hear your apology," she said stiffly. "I want you out. I don't want to see you again, Dash. You said all you needed to say this morning. And you know what? It was all bullshit. But you wouldn't even give me a chance to explain."

"Explain what, honey?"

"Don't call me that," she spat. "Don't call me anything at all. I've been feeling so guilty because I've all but *forgotten* Carson. A man who meant *everything* to me. A man I loved with all my heart and who loved me every bit as much. I was *married* to him, Dash, and you resent that. You've *always* resented that. You accuse me of continually putting him between us, but I never have. You did. *You*. Not me. You, damn it. You couldn't let go because of your *own* insecurities.

"Two weeks ago I had a dream. One that upset me greatly. Because in that dream, I had a choice. I could have Carson back or I could stay with you. And I couldn't choose. God, I felt so guilty because I'd always said I'd do anything at all for just one more day with Carson. If I could have him back, I'd never ask for anything more. But I *didn't* choose him. I hesitated. And he disappeared."

Dash felt like throwing up. He gripped the bed rail even tighter as he listened to the words that would damn him forever. He'd jumped to conclusions. Horrible conclusions. And Joss had paid a heavy price. Hell, he'd paid the heaviest price of all because he'd lost her when he'd *finally* had her. And he'd thrown it all away in a moment's time when he could have simply asked her what she'd been thinking, dreaming.

"And then last night, I had the same dream. Carson spoke to me. He said we could be together. But I chose this time," she choked out. "And I didn't choose him. I chose *you*."

Dash closed his eyes, tears burning the lids. What could he possibly say to any of that? How could he ever make up for the terrible things he'd said to her? The things he'd *accused* her of.

"I gave you *everything*, Dash," she said painfully. "My love. My submission. My trust. What did you give me? You may have given me sex, but you didn't give me love or trust. Because you can't love someone you don't trust. Not truly. And you haven't trusted me from the start. You've continually put Carson between us. Do you know that I wouldn't even bring him up in conversation? Before we were together I never thought twice about it. He was my husband and your *best friend*. It's only natural that you were the one person I could speak with about him. But you took even that away because I knew you didn't like it. So you tell me, Dash. What the hell did you sacrifice for me? Because the way I see it, I'm the one who made all the compromises and sacrifices."

She shuddered, flinching in pain that the movement caused.

"We won't even get into the horrid accusation you just launched at me. You obviously don't think much of me at all or you would have never thought, even for a moment, that I'd purposely crash my car. Especially when that's how Carson died. Even if I were that bent on self-destruction, I'd *never* cause my loved ones the kind of pain I went through when I lost Carson."

Each word was a tiny dart that directly hit his heart. She was right. Every word the absolute truth. It shamed him to realize just how wrong he'd been. From the very start. She was right. He *hadn't* trusted her. He'd been so insecure, so worried that he could never have her that when she'd given herself to him he hadn't trusted in that gift because he'd been too afraid of losing it. Of losing her. He'd been so damn wrapped up in his fears that he hadn't recognized the beautiful gift he'd been given until it was too late. God, it couldn't be too late. He wouldn't allow it to be. Whatever he had to do to make it right, he'd do.

He opened his mouth to apologize. To get down on his knees if necessary. Anything to gain her forgiveness and another chance at her love. But the door burst open and Chessy and Tate hurried in.

Tate took one look at Joss's face and turned his black scowl on Dash.

"What the hell is going on here?" Tate demanded.

Chessy rushed to Joss's bedside and Tate pushed in front of Dash, effectively barring him from Joss's sight. Chessy grabbed

Joss's hand, the one that wasn't bandaged. Dash only now noticed the cast on her left arm and his insides froze. He hadn't even asked her condition. How seriously she was injured. He was just so goddamn relieved that she was alive that nothing else had mattered.

Tate bent over, pulling her into a gentle hug. Joss buried her face in Tate's neck and gripped Chessy's hand for dear life.

"Please," Joss choked out, her voice aching with tears. "Just make him go. I don't want to see him now. Just make him leave. *Please*. I can't bear it any longer."

The fact she was begging, something Dash had sworn she'd *never* have to do, flayed him open until he was bleeding on the inside.

Tate carefully let her go and then rounded on Dash, fury glinting in his eyes.

"Get the fuck away from her. You're only hurting her more. I swear to God, Dash. I don't know what the fuck your problem is or why you insist on kicking her when she's down, but that shit is going to stop now."

"I'm not leaving her," Dash said emphatically. "If she doesn't want me in her room, fine. But I'm not leaving this hospital until I know exactly what's wrong with her and how long it'll take for her to recover."

"She'll recover a hell of a lot quicker without you upsetting her," Chessy said in a furious voice. "Get out or I swear I'll make Tate throw you out."

"Him and what goddamn army?" Dash said frigidly.

"I'll call security if I have to," Tate said in a low voice. "You aren't helping, Dash. Look at her. Take a good look at what you've done. She's in tears and she's hurting. Stop being such a selfish bastard and for *once* do the right thing and leave."

Joss's face was turned away as though she didn't want Dash to see her tears. But how could he miss them? Trailing down her cheeks in silent, silver trails. His gut clenched and grief overwhelmed him. Not even Carson's death had devastated him as much as Joss lying there, hurt, grieving. Because of him.

He'd sworn never to be a source of pain or anguish to her. And yet he'd done just that. He was the reason she was lying in a hospital bed, bloody, with broken bones and bruises. And he didn't know if he'd ever get over that.

"I'll go," he said, barely able to keep his own tears at bay. "But I'm not giving up, Joss. You may have thought I did, but I didn't. I was an ass. I was a complete bastard to you, but I swear if you'll give me the chance, I'll make it up to you. I'll make it right between us, honey."

She didn't move, didn't acknowledge his heartfelt declaration. She kept her eyes tightly shut as Chessy hugged and soothed her.

"I'll call Kylie," Dash murmured. "She'll want to be here. She loves you. *I* love you, Joss."

At that, Joss turned, fire in her eyes. "Never say that again," she said hoarsely. "It's not like you to lie, Dash. You've always been honest. Painfully so. So don't change now."

Dash pushed past a protesting Tate and leaned in so he could look Joss in the eye.

"I have never lied to you, darling. And I don't intend to start now. I said and did some horrible things. I hurt you and I'll never forgive myself for that. But I love you. I've loved you for fucking *ever*. That will *never* change. I'll go because it's what you want. And I'll give you time to recover. But goddamn it, Joss, I'm not giving up on us. And I won't let you either."

"You never gave *us* a chance," she said in an achingly sad, forlorn voice.

It cut him to the quick and left him without a response. He

stepped back from her bed and slowly, painfully turned to walk out the door.

She was wrong. She was right and she was wrong. He may not have given them a chance before, but he wasn't giving up. He'd move heaven and earth and go to hell and back if that's what it took to make her his forever.

THIRTY-ONE

JOSS stared sightlessly from the window of the guest bedroom where she was staying—and recovering—at Chessy's house. Kylie was by every day after work, worried about her. Both her friends were concerned, as was Tate. Not about her injuries. They were minor and would mend with time. Her heart was another matter.

The pain was back, throbbing in the background, but she lacked the energy to get up to down one of the painkillers the doctor had prescribed. She'd fractured two ribs and her left arm. Her arm had only suffered a hairline fracture, not a complete break. She'd be out of the cast in four weeks.

Her head had struck something—she still wasn't sure what—and she had several stitches for a laceration on her scalp. She had facial bruising, and the rest of her body was sore from the impact. Her neck was stiff, a mild case of whiplash, but the doctor had cheerfully informed her she was a very lucky woman.

So why didn't she feel lucky? Why hadn't Carson been as fortunate as she? Why was fate such a fickle bitch as Dash had once described it? Why was she alive and Carson dead?

It wasn't as though she'd wanted to die. No matter what Dash may have originally thought. Yes, it was certainly her fault, and she thanked God on a daily basis that her carelessness hadn't cost a child her life. But she hadn't intentionally driven into that tree.

She should have let Chessy come and get her like she'd offered. She should have never been behind the wheel of a car in the emotional state she'd been in. Live and learn. At least she *had* lived to learn that particular lesson.

"Joss?"

Chessy's soft voice came from behind her but Joss couldn't turn. She still hurt too much so she waited for Chessy to enter.

Her friend's concerned face appeared a moment later and she saw that Chessy was holding a glass of water and the bottle of painkillers. It shamed her that she was relieved she didn't have to get up to get them.

"Are you hurting?" Chessy asked in concern.

Joss nodded. "I couldn't muster the energy to get up and get them. Thank you."

Chessy frowned and shook out two of the pills, dropping them into Joss's right hand. After giving her the glass of water to swallow them, she sat down on the ottoman at Joss's feet.

"I'm worried about you, sweetie. Tate and I both are. Hell, so is Kylie. She's on her way over, by the way. I thought I'd warn you. She sounds . . . determined. I wouldn't be surprised if she doesn't plan to kick your ass."

Joss smiled. "I love you both. Tate too. You've been so good to me. I'm being a complete baby. There's no reason I can't go back to my own house, but I appreciate you letting me stay here. I just haven't wanted to be . . . alone."

"Oh, honey, I understand." Sympathy shone brightly in Chessy's eyes. "And you can stay here as long as you like. Tate's been so busy with work that he hasn't been home much in the last weeks. Is it horrible of me that I've been happy that since your accident he's been around more? Oh God, don't answer that. It is horrible of me to think, much less say."

Joss laughed. "No, not at all. I know you've been missing him.

Is that the reason you've been so unhappy, Chessy? Is it work that's been keeping him so preoccupied?"

"I *hope* it's only work," Chessy said in a low voice.

She looked as though she regretted the words the moment she spoke them. She looked away, as if avoiding the inevitable question in Joss's eyes.

"You think he's cheating?" Joss whispered. "Talk to me, Chessy. You know you'd never let me get away with not telling you something so important. Hell, you pulled every last detail about what happened between me and Dash from me."

Chessy's smile was rueful. "No. Yes. I don't know. And it's the not knowing that's eating me alive."

"Have you talked to him about it?"

Chessy slowly shook her head. "What if he's not? Do you know how hurt he'd be if I questioned him? If I displayed a lack of faith in him?"

"Okay, let's start with why you think he'd be cheating," Joss said, glad to have something other than her own failed relationship to discuss. And if she could help her friend, then at least one of them would be happy.

"I don't have any solid evidence that says he is," Chessy admitted. "It's just that he's been so . . . distant. You know we have a Dominant/submissive relationship, but lately I'm lucky if we manage to have vanilla sex, much less delve into the normal course of our relationship."

"Is it possible that he's just under a lot of stress at work? Ever since he struck out on his own and quit working for Manning-Brown Financial, he's been crazy busy. Even I can see that."

"It's more than that," Chessy muttered. "The guy he partnered with, the one he left Manning-Brown to form a partnership with, decided to retire. This was only a few months after he and Tate started working together."

Joss's mouth fell open. "Why didn't I know about this? When did this happen?"

Chessy squeezed Joss's uninjured hand. "You were busy with your own stuff. You and Dash. Besides it wasn't anything worth burdening you over. Nothing has changed really. Tate had always done the bulk of the work anyway, but Mark had brought a lot of affluent clients over to the partnership when they both broke off from their respective firms. So Tate's been scrambling to keep them all happy because he doesn't want to lose any of them. So far, only one has left, and he wants to keep it that way. Which means him being at their beck and call all hours of the day, seven days a week."

Joss's nose wrinkled. "I wouldn't have thought a financial planner would be so . . . busy. I mean I know he does a lot, but what could there possibly be for him to do during nonbusiness hours? It's not as though banks or the stock market are open after hours during the week or on weekends."

"You'd be surprised," Chessy said. "They call him at all times of the day, sometimes with legitimate concerns, sometimes with the absurd. But it's Tate's job to pacify them and reassure them or arrange their finances. He has to walk a very fine line because as I said, he doesn't want to lose the clients he's worked so hard to gain."

"Is he going to take on another partner to lighten his load?"

Chessy shrugged. "That I don't know. He doesn't discuss it much with me. He doesn't want to worry me. I used to love that about him. How he always sheltered me from anything he thought would hurt or worry me. Now? I'd take any form of communication because I feel this gap opening and widening between us and I hate it. I *hate* it, Joss," she said, anguish filling her voice.

"I know I'm probably being silly and I'm overreacting, but I hate this uncertainty. I hate feeling like I don't matter any longer. And I know that's not true. I know he loves me. But he doesn't *show* me like he used to. I've known from the day we met that I was his priority, and it makes me sound self-centered but I love being first and foremost in his mind. I loved that he always made me feel . . . special."

"And you don't feel special now," Joss murmured.

Chessy slowly shook her head. "I'm not unhappy but I'm not happy either. And it's eating me up on the inside. I keep wondering if this is as good as it gets and if I should be grateful he's still with me. I don't like how selfish I feel for wanting more."

Joss leaned forward, ignoring the discomfort in her ribs. "You aren't selfish," she said fiercely. "Sweetie, you are the most unselfish, loving, giving person I know. Why don't you talk to him about it? Lay it out just like you laid it out to me. I can't imagine that he wouldn't listen. That it wouldn't horrify him to know you feel this way. He loves you so much. I can see it in the way he looks at you."

"I wish I saw the same as you saw," Chessy said wistfully. "I just want to go back to the way it was when we first met, and maybe that's not possible. Maybe when you're with someone as long as we've been together, when the newness wears off, you settle into tolerance."

Joss shook her head adamantly. "I don't believe that for a minute. I know Carson and I were only married for three years, but we were as in love at the three-year mark as we were the first year, and you and Tate have only been married a little less than five years."

"Maybe you're right," Chessy said with a sigh. "Maybe I should just talk to him. But I freeze every time I think I'm going to ask. The words just stay locked in my throat because I know it will hurt him if I ask him if there's someone else. And the thing is, if nothing *is* wrong except that he's occupied with work, my doubt *will* cause a rift in our relationship that I'm not sure will ever mend."

Joss grimaced, knowing Chessy could very well be right. Tate would be horrified if he knew Chessy thought he was having an affair. He might not forgive her doubting him even for a moment. Tate was rigid that way. He was an extremely honorable man and he was utterly protective of Chessy. If someone else was hurting her, Tate would do whatever was necessary to make it end. But what if he was the one hurting her? What then?

"Maybe you should just give it a while. Be patient and understanding. Love him. Show him your love and support and perhaps when things die down a bit at work and he's more confident that he has everything under control, things will get better," Joss quietly advised.

Chessy squeezed her hand again. "Thank you. I came up here to check on you and to cheer you up. Not to dump all my woes on you."

Joss smiled. "I love you and I'd kick your ass if you ever didn't come to me with whatever is bothering you. You and Kylie are my best friends. That won't ever change."

"Speaking of Kylie, there she is," Chessy said brightly, looking beyond Joss to the doorway. Then she cast Joss a quick pleading look not to bring up the subject in front of Kylie.

Kylie was more of a direct, confrontational person, and if she even *thought* Tate was cheating on Chessy, she'd go straight to the source and kick his ass.

Joss squeezed Chessy's hand back, a silent promise to keep their conversation secret.

"Hey, Joss," Kylie said, coming over to hug her, though she was careful not to hug too tight. "How are you feeling today?"

"Better now that my personal nurse brought me the pain medication I was too lazy to get up and get for myself," Joss said dryly.

Kylie smiled and plopped down on the ottoman beside
Chessy. Her gaze swept over Joss as if judging for herself how her
sister-in-law fared.

"How's work?" Joss asked brightly, and then fearing it would
be an invitation for Kylie to talk about Dash, she quickly amended
her statement. "How are things with Jensen? Are you two getting
along okay now?"

Kylie made a face. "He's an overbearing, rigid ass."

Chessy laughed. "Sweetie, you just described half the male
population, Tate and Dash included."

Joss flinched but refused to show any outward emotion over
the mention of Dash's name.

"Dash is a walking corpse," Kylie said bluntly. "The man
hasn't slept since your accident. I don't even know why he bothers
coming in and going through the motions. Jensen's had to pick
up all the slack, as have I, because he's worthless."

Joss closed her eyes, pain swamping through her that even the
strongest medication couldn't ease. He'd called her a dozen times
a day and each time she'd let it go to voice mail. It made her a
coward, but she wasn't prepared to deal with him now. Maybe
ever.

He texted her, e-mailed her and he came to Chessy's at least
once a day, asking to see her. Each time either Tate or Chessy had
told him that she was in her room sleeping. A lie. One he'd easily
see through but she didn't want to see him. Maybe ever.

He was absolutely relentless but then she knew that about him.
But he'd gotten what he'd said he most wanted. She'd given
him everything. She hadn't asked him to change who and what
he was because he was what she wanted. She'd wanted his

dominance, his control, but more than that, she wanted his love and his *trust*.

Maybe she hadn't wanted that in the beginning. She hadn't believed she could ever find a love to match what she'd had with Carson. But Dash had fulfilled her in a way she'd never been fulfilled with Carson, and that hurt to admit. It hurt even more that she'd lost that.

She'd found perfection twice in a lifetime, and both times she'd lost it all. How was she supposed to recover from that again?

"I don't know what to do," she whispered, pain evident in her voice. "He doesn't trust me. How can he say he loves me when he doesn't trust me? Do you know what he accused me of?"

Both women shook their heads. Joss hadn't told them what Dash had said to her in the hospital. The pain from that accusation had yet to fade in the four days she'd been at Chessy's house. Hiding.

"He accused me of trying to kill myself. He asked if I'd *purposely* driven my car into that tree hoping to die."

Chessy and Kylie both sucked in their breaths but thankfully neither held question in their eyes. They didn't believe it. Thank God. She couldn't bear it if her dearest friends also harbored doubts as to her mental stability.

"He thought that life without Carson was so unbearable that I chose to join him in death."

"Oh, sweetie," Chessy said, her voice aching with sympathy and pain. "I'm sure he didn't mean it. You scared him. And after your argument he likely felt horribly guilty. He felt responsible for your accident because he upset you so badly."

"He lashed out at you because the alternative was accepting the blame for what happened," Kylie said quietly.

"I have a lot of thinking to do," Joss murmured. "About my future. And whether or not it will involve Dash. He says . . . He says he loves me and he wants another chance. He's called, texted, e-mailed, come by here every single day. He swears he's not giving up. But I don't know if I can give him another chance. Without his trust, what do we have? A one-sided relationship, where I give all and he gives nothing in return, is not what I want. Yes, I wanted a dominant man. I wanted to give up power and control. But in return for that, I want his love and his trust. And you can't have one without the other."

"I agree with you there," Chessy said carefully. "But the question you have to ask yourself is if you can forgive him his mistake. It was an emotional situation all around. You told me what happened that morning, and, sweetie, I am not taking his side, but I can understand why he would have reacted to what he thought you were feeling when you murmured Carson's name and seemed so heartbroken the morning after you told Dash you loved him."

Joss glanced at Kylie, gauging her reaction to Chessy's statement.

Kylie sighed. "I admit I had reservations at the start. About all of it. What you wanted, what you said you needed. But I felt a hell of a lot better about it when you ended up with Dash, someone I knew would treat you well and I didn't have to worry about a total stranger abusing you. But you're good together, Joss. I never imagined you with anyone other than Carson. You two just fit. But you and Dash are . . . perfect. When he's not being a total dickhead, that is."

Chessy laughed and Joss smiled, some of the horrible darkness lifting away from her soul.

"I just wish I knew what to do," Joss said, rubbing at her aching temples. "I've gone over it in my head until I'm dizzy with it. I'm so scared of handing complete control back to him and him hurting me again. I'm tired of hurting. I just want to be . . . happy."

"As I once told you, life is about risk," Chessy said gently. "You just have to decide which risks are worth it. You're miserable now. So what's the difference if you go back to Dash and things don't work out and you end up miserable then? Either way you're miserable. But if things work out? You have a shot at bliss."

"She certainly has a point," Kylie pointed out. "You're as much a corpse as Dash is, only he's walking and you aren't. How long has it been since you were out of this room, Joss? Have you gotten up even once except to go to the bathroom? You can't continue like this. Neither of you can. Either make a clean break and end it so you both can move on, or take a chance and put it on the line. You'll never know until you give him a chance."

Joss grimaced. "You're right. You're both right." Then she sighed. "I can't go anywhere right now. I just took those damn pain pills."

"I can drive you," Chessy offered. "Just tell me where you want to go and I'll make it happen."

Joss sucked in a deep breath. Never had she faced such an important decision. It was simple and yet so very complicated. But her friends were right. She was miserable *now*. She had a shot at happiness. All she had to do was reach out and take it. Risk it all. Prove to Dash that she *had* let go of the past. That he was the one who couldn't let go of it.

Resolve settled over her, removing the blanket of despair that had clung so stubbornly for the last several days. She was not a coward and she wasn't weak. She'd faced utter devastation twice and she'd survived. She'd survive this, whatever this turned out to be.

"Let me get dressed and then take me to Dash's," Joss said, finally making her decision.

It scared the holy hell out of her, but she had to try.

THIRTY-TWO

"YOU don't have to do this, darlin'," Tate said, glancing into his rearview mirror at Joss, who sat in the backseat as he and Chessy drove her to Dash's.

"Yes, I do," Joss said quietly. "This has to be resolved, Tate. I have to know if we have a chance. If Dash can trust me. If he loves me."

"Well, I can't speak on the trust issue but I know the bastard loves you," Tate said grimly. "I've never seen a man so wasted over a woman. If I wasn't so pissed at him for hurting you the way he did, I could almost pity the man."

Joss smiled faintly.

As they neared Dash's house, Chessy turned in her seat and fixed her stare on Joss. "I'm not going to leave you there with no way home. I don't want you to have to depend on Dash. I'll have my phone on me. You call me the minute you're ready to leave. If I don't hear from you in an hour, I'm coming back. An hour is long enough to hear him grovel."

Joss laughed. "You seem so certain he's going to grovel."

"Oh, he'll grovel," Tate muttered. "A man as desperate as he is will do anything to get back in your good graces. And that's the way it should be. When a man fucks up as badly as he has, he *needs* to humble himself."

Chessy glanced sideways at her husband, a look Joss didn't miss. There was pain in her eyes and it hurt Joss to see her friend hurting. She shook away thoughts of Chessy and Tate. They'd work things out. Tate seemed oblivious to there even being a problem. Once Chessy got the courage to confront him and work it out, all would be well. Joss was confident of that. She didn't believe for a minute that Tate was having an affair. Why would he when he had Chessy?

Chessy was beautiful, smart. She had a smile that would light up an entire city block. And she was utterly submissive, entrusting her entire well-being to her husband's hands. He'd be a fool to ever risk that for a piece of ass on the side.

"Okay, we're here," Chessy said. "Are you sure this is what you want, Joss? It's not too late to change your mind. We can take you back right now. Just say the word."

Joss sucked in a deep breath. "No. I'm ready. One way or another, I need this to be over. Either we'll have a new beginning or I'll have closure, but either way, it ends tonight."

DASH paced the floor of his living room, agitation gripping him by the balls. Four days. Four goddamn days Joss had been out of the hospital and he hadn't so much as laid eyes on her. He'd gone to the hospital on the day she was going to be released, only to find she'd already been discharged into Tate and Chessy's care. He'd been fully prepared to sweep in, take over and not back down. He had every intention of taking her back to *their* home, where he'd take absolute care of her until she was fully recovered. But Chessy and Tate had taken her to their house, an impenetrable fucking fortress for all the luck Dash had had getting in.

His calls, texts and e-mails had gotten no response from Joss.

Silence lay as heavy as concrete between them and with each passing day, with each failed attempt to reach her, he'd felt her slipping further and further away.

What the hell was he supposed to do? How could he lay his heart at her feet if he couldn't get to her in order to do it? He reached for his phone, wanting to call her again, but he knew she wouldn't answer. Just as she hadn't answered the dozen other times he'd called her today.

Despair was his constant companion and he cursed his wayward tongue. If only he hadn't let his anger—and paralyzing fear—control his thoughts and words that fateful morning. He was to blame. Not Joss. Him. He'd done this to her. To them. And to any chance he had of having forever with her.

He bowed his head, regret burning a hole in his gut.

He was so absorbed in his grief that he didn't hear the car in the drive. Never knew anyone was there until a soft knock sounded at his door.

His head jerked in the direction of the sound, in no mood to deal with whoever had encroached on his private hell. When a knock sounded again, firmer and louder than before, he swore and strode angrily to answer, fully intending to bite off the head of the unfortunate idiot disturbing his self-recrimination.

But when he yanked open the door, his heart stopped because it was Joss standing there, looking pale and fragile, the bruises from her accident still vivid against her skin. Her broken arm was in a sling, hugged protectively against her chest. And there was resolve in her eyes that gutted him.

Her lips were pressed into a thin line and he wanted to yell *no*! His heart told him that she was here to tell him to go to hell. To stop calling, texting, e-mailing and coming by Chessy and Tate's house every day. It was no more than he deserved, but he couldn't bear to hear those words from her lips.

But she was here! Not locked behind the walls of Tate's house with Tate and Chessy acting as her personal guard dogs. She was in front of him, and here was his chance to humble himself before her and beg her forgiveness.

"Can I come in?" she asked softly when he continued to stand there, stunned, his mind an utter mess of all the things he wanted to say but couldn't summon.

She looked suddenly vulnerable and doubt crept into those beautiful eyes. Fear. That he'd reject her? That he wouldn't allow her to come inside her home?

He threw open the door and very nearly swept her into his arms. Only the memory of how fragile she was, how injured she still was and how much pain she still had to be in stopped him. And yet she was here. When she should be in bed. Resting. Getting better.

"Joss," he croaked out. "God yes, honey. Please. Come in. Let me help you. You shouldn't be up. You should be in bed. Are you hurting?"

Her lips twisted into a wry smile as she walked into his house. He slammed the door quickly behind her, afraid she'd change her mind, or that she was a manifestation of all his dreams and that she'd disappear as soon as he awakened.

"I took pain medicine half an hour ago," she said quietly. "It's why Tate drove me. I didn't want to risk another accident, and I'm not supposed to drive for a few weeks anyway."

Guilt slammed into him all over again. He touched her uninjured arm, savoring that brief moment of contact. He wanted to do so much more. He wanted to hold her, comfort her, just be with her, close enough to smell, to touch.

"Come into the living room," he said quietly. "The couch should be comfortable. I can get the ottoman or you can sit and lean back against the side so you can put your feet up. Are your ribs okay? Is the pain medicine working?"

He was a babbling idiot, but the flood of questions simply wouldn't stop. He'd never felt so unsure of himself in his life and he hated that she was so quiet.

He took her hand, rejoicing when she didn't yank it away. He led her to the couch and eased her down, hovering, looking for any sign she was in pain.

She let out a sigh, briefly closing her eyes as she leaned back against the sofa.

"Damn it, you *are* hurting," he swore. "Did you bring your pain medicine with you? Should you take another dose?"

"Some hurts can't be eased with medicine," she said softly. "I needed to talk to you, Dash. I need this to be . . . resolved. I can't go on like this. It's killing me."

He sank to his knees, gutted by the sadness in her eyes. Gathering her free hand in his, remaining in a position of vulnerability, he stared intently at her.

"Please don't tell me we're over, honey. Anything but that. Curse at me. Yell at me. Call me names. You have every right. But please, I'm begging you. Don't give up on me—us. I love you, Joss. I love you so damn much I can't sleep at night. I can't eat. I can't function. I can't work. There's a gaping hole in my heart only you can fill."

The corner of her mouth quirked up in a half smile. "Kylie says you're useless at work. She doesn't even know why you go in because nothing gets done."

"She's right," he said hoarsely. "I need you, Joss. You're my other half. I'm only whole when I'm with you."

"I love you too, Dash."

Relief made him weak. He was so wobbly he could barely

maintain his position on his knees. And he'd stay on his knees, begging her forgiveness for as long as it took. He was the Dominant and she was the submissive but right now she held all the power and he held none. Because without her, his strength meant nothing. Without her precious gift of submission, his dominance didn't mean a damn thing. His life had no meaning.

But something in her gaze stopped him from saying anything in response.

"But that isn't enough," she added softly. "You *say* you love me, but you don't trust me. And without trust, love isn't enough. Without trust, we have *nothing* but lust and sex between us."

He bowed his head, his eyes and nose burning. The knot in his throat was so huge he could barely breathe around it. He glanced up again to see answering sadness in her eyes. Eyes that screamed defeat. She was giving up. On him. On *them*.

"*You* are the one who keeps putting Carson between us," she said gently. "Not me. I moved on, Dash. I let him go. I did that when I went to his grave so many weeks ago. I knew it bothered you for me to talk about him once we entered a relationship even though you appeared to be fine with it before. I even understood *why* you wouldn't want to be reminded of a man I once loved when I was in your bed. But your own insecurities are what kept him between us. I was honest with you. The entire time I was nothing but honest. And I gave you everything you asked—demanded—of me, and yet you didn't offer me those things in return. Not your respect. Not your trust. You say you loved me, but I don't believe love can exist without trust and respect."

"Please. Don't say another word," Dash begged. "Let me apologize. Let me beg your forgiveness, Joss."

She sent him another sad look that flayed his heart open. There was so much resignation in her gaze. As if she had no hope for their future. He'd have to have hope enough for them both.

He brought her hand to his mouth and tenderly pressed kisses to her open palm. "My darling Joss. How I love you. I love you so much it's killing me. Being without you is killing me. I can't survive without your love. I don't want to live without it. Please give me—us—another chance. I'm on my knees before you, honey, and I'll stay on them the rest of my life if that's what it takes. Just stay and give me a chance to make it up to you."

He took in another deep breath, plunging recklessly ahead before she could respond. So she listened to everything he had to say.

"You're right. I was deeply insecure. You caught me unaware that night in The House. I hadn't planned to make my move so soon and maybe it was me who wasn't ready yet. I was forced to act or risk losing you, and that wasn't an option for me. I was . . . afraid. So afraid of losing you. Of not being what you needed. Of not being able to compete with Carson's memory. I overreacted. I admit that. It was the worst mistake of my life and I almost lost you because of my stupidity and irrational jealousy. It won't happen again, Joss. You are my life. I trust you. You say I don't, but I do. It wasn't you I didn't trust. It was *me*. I didn't trust that I would ever be enough for you. Didn't trust that I could make you happy. That you'd be as happy as you were with Carson, and that ate at me, chipping away at my confidence until all that was left was an angry shell of the man I needed to be for you. You did everything right and I did everything *wrong*."

Her gaze softened and her eyes glittered brightly with unshed tears. She lifted her hand from his grasp and gently stroked his cheek. He was shocked by the moisture on her fingers when she pulled away.

"I love you," he said hoarsely. "The morning of your car accident was the worst day of my life. I was so scared I'd lost you and, worse, that I had caused it. I lashed out at you, accused you of terrible things, because I was so fucking scared that I had done this to you. I knew I had done it and yet I made that terrible accusation. I implied that you were weak, Joss, and God, you're anything *but*. You're the strongest woman I know. I hope you can be strong enough for both of us, because it's *me* who is weak. Not you. *Never* you."

"It's all right, darling," she whispered. "It's all right. It will be okay. I love you."

Her love echoed in each of the words, a soothing balm to the ache in his soul. Tears ran freely down his cheeks and then she leaned forward, wrapping her arm around him, holding him against her breasts.

"No, don't, Joss," he protested. "You're hurt. I don't want to cause you further pain."

And still, she hung on, refusing to let him pry her gently away from his body.

"The only way you'll cause me more pain is if you refuse me," she said tenderly.

He lifted his head and rested his forehead against hers, their breaths mingling, as did their tears.

"Never that, honey. I'll never refuse you anything. I'll give you the world on a silver platter. Whatever you want, you'll have."

"All I want is you," she said simply. "*You*. Your love. Your trust. And your dominance."

"You'll have all of me," he vowed. "But, Joss, do you trust me with your submission? Your heart? After all I've done to hurt you? You must know I'd never force you into a lifestyle you don't want. I'll make any sacrifice to have you. There is nothing more important to me than you. Just you. In my arms, in my bed, in my heart. Every day. No matter how I have you. It's enough. It'll always be enough."

She smiled, her breath hitching over a low sob. She closed her eyes as more tears squeezed from the corners.

"I want you as you are, Dash. Warts and all. I suppose it won't always be easy, but if you'll give me your love and your trust, I'll never ask for more. I swear it."

"You have them. Always, Joss. I'll never give you reason to doubt my trust in you again."

She emitted a sigh, one that sounded painful, and he immediately picked up on it.

"Are you hurting?" he demanded. "Damn it, Joss. You should be in bed resting. Not sitting here holding me in a position you can't be comfortable in."

She smiled, radiant and beautiful, lighting up his entire heart. "There's no place I'd rather be than here with you. Pain be damned. For the first time in a week, I don't hurt. Not the way I did. The rest is just physical pain, and it will pass. But a broken heart can only be mended with love. And you've given me that. I'll be all right, Dash. I can take anything as long as I have you."

He cupped her beautiful face in his hands, framing it as he leaned in to kiss her reverently on the lips.

"I love you."

"I love you too," she whispered back. "But I need to call Chessy and let her know she doesn't have to pick me up. She didn't want me to be stranded here without a way to leave, so she said if she hadn't heard from me in an hour, she was coming over to get me."

He straightened and reached for his phone and then handed it to her after punching in Chessy's number.

"Let her know that I'll be over to get your things as well as your pain medication," Dash directed. "As soon as you're off the phone with her, I'm putting you to bed. *Our* bed. And then I'm going to take care of you until you're completely recovered."

She smiled and then spoke a few words to Chessy, assuring her that everything was okay and that Dash would be over to collect her belongings. When she hung up, Dash stood up and then eased onto the couch next to her, careful not to jar her.

He wrapped his arms around her, hugging her against his side, his face buried in her sweet-smelling hair.

"I missed you, honey. If there was ever a doubt that I needed you, there's not one now. I haven't been worth killing the last week. It's been the longest week of my life and one I never want to experience again."

"For me too," she murmured. "Let's put it behind us, Dash. We have so much to look forward to. The past only hurts us. It's time to let go and move on."

"I couldn't have said it any better myself," he said, tipping her chin up so he could claim her mouth. "But one thing I'll never let go of, Joss, is you. I love you."

She smiled, warming him from the inside out. "I love you too."

And then he gently pushed her upward and once more slid to his knees in front of her. She looked puzzled when he took her hand and then reached into his pocket. He pulled out the ring he'd bought a mere day after she'd moved in with him. A ring that had waited for just the right time to be presented. Dash could think of no better moment than now.

"Will you marry me, Joss? Grow old with me and love me? Have the children we both want so badly?"

Her intake of breath was swift, the sound sharp in the ensuring silence.

"Would you want them right away?" she whispered, her tone so hopeful that it nearly undid him.

He slid the ring onto her bare finger, a finger that had been bare since she'd moved in with him. He'd noticed the day she'd taken Carson's ring off her finger. It was a significant moment and one that should have told him that she was ready to move on. But he'd been stupid and insecure.

"I'll give you all the babies you want just as soon as you want them," he said tenderly. "In fact, I propose that the minute you recover sufficiently, we get in lots and lots of practice."

Her smile would have brought him to his knees if he wasn't already on them.

"Then perhaps we should think about getting married soon," she said teasingly. "I'd hate to be an out-of-wedlock mother."

"As soon as you're able to travel, we'll fly out to Vegas and get married immediately," he declared. "I don't want you to have any time to change your mind, so the sooner the better. And if you hold out on me, I'll just be sure to knock you up so you *have* to marry me."

She laughed and the sound filled the last remaining hole in his heart. He was a lucky son of a bitch. The woman he loved—had loved forever—was giving him another chance to prove his love to her. He'd never give her another reason to doubt him, and he'd love her and the children they had until the day he died.

EPILOGUE

DASH stood at Carson's grave site. The first time he'd come alone since the day he'd been buried. All his other trips had always been with Joss. But he hadn't wanted her to come. For one, she'd promised herself that she wouldn't come back, that this wasn't the way she wanted to remember her husband.

And this would be the last time he came here himself. But he needed closure. Joss wasn't the only one who'd needed to let go. So now he stood at his best friend's grave, prepared to confess everything and assure Carson that Joss was loved and would always be taken care of.

"I fucked up, man," Dash said bluntly. "You already know that. You're likely up there wanting to kick my ass for all the pain I've put Joss through. The pain I've caused her. I deserve it. I've certainly kicked my own ass over it all."

He drew in a steadying breath, caught unaware by the emotion that overwhelmed him, tightening his chest as long-held grief came rushing out.

"I made you a promise and it was a promise I didn't keep. I'm sorry for that. You gave me an extraordinary gift and I'll always be grateful for that gift. For understanding and never judging me."

He paused another long moment, getting his emotions under control.

"She's happy now. We're happy. I made things right. We're married now. I know you know that. But I just had to come and tell you. To reaffirm the promise I gave you before you died. I love her, man. With all my heart. Thank God, she didn't give up on me, that she gave me another chance.

"I won't let her down again. I won't let you down. I'll love her and protect her always. With my life. There is nothing I wouldn't do to make her happy, just like you always did whatever was necessary to make her happy.

"I hope you're at peace now, Carson. Joss and I both loved you. Will always love you. But she has a huge heart and an endless capacity to love. She loves me now, but she'll always love you too, and I'm okay with that because I realize there's room in her heart for both of us. Loving you doesn't take away from her love for me, and I can accept that now. I didn't before."

He drifted off, watching a cloud blow by, beaming sunshine down on the grave. He was instantly filled with a warmth so beautiful that it could only be Carson's presence. Loving and forgiving, just as he'd been in life.

"I came to say good-bye, just like Joss said her good-byes all those weeks ago. I won't be back. It's a choice Joss and I have both made because this isn't the way we want to remember you. We have too many other good memories and those are the ones we want to cherish.

"Thanks, man. You'll never know how grateful I am for you trusting her to me. We're happy. She makes me so damn happy that I can't even look at her at times without going to my knees. I know you're familiar with that feeling. It's how you reacted around her too. She's a very special woman and we're both lucky bastards to have won her love. Her warmth and generous spirit.

"We're planning to have children. Right away if I have any say in it. It's what she's always wanted and I understand why you couldn't give them to her, even though Joss and I both know you would have loved them, protected them and never ever hurt them.

"We've decided to name our first son for you. It's fitting since you brought us together. Your memory will live on through him, and Joss and I will keep your memory alive between us. No pushing it away. You were important to us both, an essential part of our past. But now we're looking ahead and we're both ready to let go and move forward with our lives."

Dash briefly ran his hand over the headstone and then straightened to his full height.

"Thank you for loving Joss. And me," Dash whispered. "You don't ever have to worry anymore. She's in good hands, and I'll die before ever hurting her again. You have my word. Good-bye, my friend. May you rest with the angels until we all meet again."

His heart lighter, a great weight lifted from his shoulders, he turned and hurried back to the car, where his wife waited for him. As he neared his car, she opened the door and stepped out, her smile beautiful and breathtaking. So warm that even the sun couldn't compete with her radiance.

Her eyes softened and she extended her hand to him as he approached. She said nothing, simply squeezed, offering her silent support. Never once did she look back at Carson's grave as he ushered her back inside the car before walking around to the driver's side.

When he slid in, he didn't immediately start the ignition. Instead he turned sideways so he could see his wife. His beautiful, loving, generous wife.

"I love you," he said, his throat still knotted with emotion.

She leaned over the seat and palmed his cheek as she kissed him.

"I love you too, darling. Now let's go home and start practicing making those babies you promised me."

He grinned, suddenly feeling he could take on the world. Get her pregnant? Hell yeah. She'd been off birth control an entire month, and the timing in her cycle was right. If he had his way, they'd spend the next two days in bed, and he'd do everything in his power to start the family they both so desperately wanted.

But more important was the fact that Joss was his. His wife. His lover. His best friend. His cherished submissive. What she didn't know, however, was that while he was the Dominant, he was absolutely at her feet, humbled by her unconditional love.

She may have submitted to him, but he would forever be *her* slave.

"Let's go start making those babies," he said huskily. "I can't wait to see you swollen with my child. As beautiful as you are to me right now, I can only imagine you'll grow even more beautiful when you're heavy with our baby."

Surrender to the powerful sensuality and
erotic romance of

Maya Banks

in her sensational new trilogy

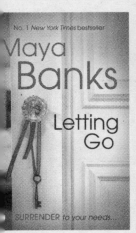
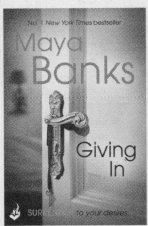
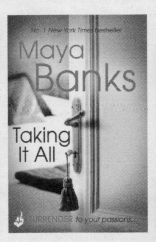

'Powerful, emotional, and steamy hot' *Fresh Fiction*

headline
ETERNAL

Giving In

Kylie sees the dark promise, and that rough edge of dominance she knows he possesses, in the way that Jensen looks at her. But dominance is the one thing that frightens her. She barely survived a childhood steeped in violence and abuse and she could never give up total control and submit to a man. Could she?

Jensen sees the shadows in Kylie's eyes and knows he has to tread carefully or risk losing any chance he has with her. All he wants is the opportunity to show her that dominance doesn't equal pain, and that emotionally surrendering and giving in to him will fill the aching void in her heart in a way nothing else ever will.

'That's what I want from you . . . Your emotional surrender. Your trust. Your heart. Your soul.'

headline
ETERNAL

Surrender to your passions . . .

Taking
It All

In the beginning, Chessy and Tate's passionate marriage
was everything she wanted. She offered her submission
freely and Tate made her feel safe and loved. But as the
years have passed, and Tate's business built, their
marriage has taken a back seat and Chessy knows that
something has to give or they stand to lose it all.

Tate loves his wife and providing for her has always
been his first priority. Worried that she is unhappy,
he arranges for a night together to reignite the fire that
once burned like an inferno between them. But a business
call at the wrong time threatens everything he holds dear.
To win back his beloved wife's love, Tate determines to
show her that nothing is more important than her –
and that he will do and give whatever it takes to get
back the passion and trust they once had.

'You're it. And I want it all, but I want it with you.'

headline
ETERNAL

headline
ETERNAL

FIND YOUR HEART'S DESIRE...